# FIRE ACROSS THE VELDT

*by*

John Wilcox

**Magna Large Print Books**
Long Preston, North Yorkshire,
BD23 4ND, England.

British Library Cataloguing in Publication Data.

Wilcox, John
    Fire across the veldt.

        A catalogue record of this book is
        available from the British Library

        ISBN    978-0-7505-3793-3

First published in Great Britain by Allison & Busby in 2013

Published in Large Print 2013 by arrangement with
Allison & Busby Ltd.

Magna Large Print is an imprint of Library Magna Books Ltd.

Printed and bound in Great Britain by
T.J. (International) Ltd., Cornwall, PL28 8RW

# FIRE ACROSS THE VELDT

Simon Fonthill, along with his wife Alice, old friend Jenkins, and tracker Mzingeli, is travelling across the continent to Pretoria to meet with General Kitchener. When their train is derailed the quartet are forced to continue their journey on horseback, but are quickly surrounded by Boer commando leader General de Wet and his soldiers. Former captain and army scout Simon Fonthill must rejoin the British military and prove his ability as a commander, as he leads the battle to capture the elusive Boer leaders. With information that the next Boer move will be to attack the Cape Colony, Fonthill must race to locate and defeat the enemy forces in time.

*To the memory of Nigel Cole, lover of history, follower of the adventures of Simon Fonthill and great old friend, this book is fondly dedicated.*

# CHAPTER ONE

*On the veldt in the Orange Free State,*
*South Africa.*
*September, 1900*

'Damn,' Simon Fonthill swore softly and wrinkled his eyes against the glare from the veldt. 'Damn again. I think they're Boers. Hand me the field glasses.'

The British army-issue binoculars were thrust into his hand and he focused them on the kopje that stood out from the plain, perhaps a mile away – except that, as he knew well, distances were deceptive on the veldt and it was more likely to be some three or four miles distant. He focused the glasses and stood erect in the stirrups, the better to see.

Yes. Boers all right. They sprang into view as though moving just a few hundred yards away. Bearded men wearing loose civilian clothing, wide, broken-brimmed hats and bandoliers across their chests, mounted on small Basuto ponies, streaming down from the chiselled rocks of the kopje, spreading out across the undulating grass and moving towards them. Fast.

'Do we fight 'em, bach sir?' asked Jenkins, easing his Lee Enfield rifle from its saddle holster.

Fonthill, still squinting through the binoculars, shook his head. 'No. There are about twenty-five of 'em. Far too many. We have no cover. These chaps are the best marksmen in the world and they'd pick us off easily from a mile away before we could get a shot off.' He lowered the glasses. 'We'd stand no chance. They will be after our horses and our rifles.'

He looked ruefully across at his wife, sitting less than comfortably in the small Cape cart that carried their provisions and tent. 'Sorry, darling,' he said. 'Thank you for not saying I told you so.'

Alice Fonthill inclined her head. 'Ah, how nice – and how unusual – to be acknowledged as having been in the right for once. So what do we do, then?'

'We try and talk our way out of it. But I don't want to lose the horses or the rifles and revolvers.' He turned to their two companions. Jenkins, his former batman and fellow survivor of dozens of hostile encounters in Queen Victoria's 'little wars' in the British Empire over two decades, sat, like him, on horseback alongside the cart. Mzingeli, once their black tracker in Matabeleland and now the manager of their farm there, sat quietly holding the mule reins on the driving seat of the cart, his rifle by his side.

'Tuck the rifles under the tent in the cart.' Fonthill spoke quickly now, the glasses at his eyes once more. 'Try and do it unobtrusively. They will have glasses on us too. Put your revolvers into Alice's bag, right at the bottom. Now, when they get here, let me do the talking.'

'Umph.' Jenkins's snort was quite audible. But he said nothing more and his eyes were cold as he carefully buttoned up Alice's bag and looked out

10

towards the approaching horsemen, easing in its scabbard the long knife that hung from his belt.

Fonthill had, indeed, ignored his wife's warning – and that of several British officers – in downloading their cart, mules and horses from the armoured train that had carried them all from the Cape Colony when it had been derailed some ten miles to the south. The Boers had made a thorough job of tearing up the rail track. 'They're getting good at it,' confessed the sapper officer accompanying them. 'We spend more time repairing these blasted lines than we do chasing their commandos.'

He had advised them to wait while camp was made for the night and work was begun on the bent and twisted tracks. Alice, too, had suggested that the Boers who had torn up the line might still be in the vicinity and it seemed unwise to put themselves in harm's way when they were in no great rush to reach Pretoria, the headquarters of Field Marshal Roberts and General Kitchener. Fonthill, however, had insisted that they save time by riding on some forty miles to the north where a branch line joined the main one and another train was expected along it early the next morning. 'The Boers won't be interested in us,' he said. 'After all, we're just civilians.'

Yet now, he reflected, as he looked around him, they were civilians carrying British rifles, an army-issue tent, binoculars and rations. The explanation would have to be good. Unless, of course, the approaching party was made up of simple burghers with no one of seniority in command. If that were so, they stood a chance.

11

The Boers were upon them quickly and they fanned out to surround the little party. They did, indeed, look like Dutch burghers – farmers, however, who had been living out on the veldt in all weathers with their sheep and cattle and who had not seen their homes for many a day. Their clothes were torn and threadbare and some had forsaken boots for native sandals. Their long beards were unkempt and spread out across their chests, making them look like biblical prophets. Only their oiled cartridge bandoliers and their long Mauser rifles, the stocks of which now rested on their thighs, hinted at their fame as fighting men who had at first humiliated and then taunted the British army for well over a year.

Fonthill knew of their reputation. The war was supposed to have been over months ago when, after the Boer successes at Colenso, Modder River and Spion Kop, the British army had been re-inforced and, laboriously but surely, had marched north and crushed the Boer army in the field at Paardeberg, relieved Ladysmith and Mafeking and then occupied the Boer capitals of Bloemfon-tein and Pretoria. But that had been the easy part. The Boer army – this force of amateur mounted infantry – had melted away to re-form out in the veldt, behind the British lines, as fast-moving commandos, striking at the imperial lines of com-munications and making a laughing stock of Field Marshal Roberts's claim that 'the war was as good as over'. It was to help the army in fighting this new-style, elusive, guerrilla warfare that Simon had answered the call from General Kitchener, Roberts's chief of staff, to come to South Africa.

12

Now Simon ran his eye along the stern ranks of the horsemen with interest. Would they have a leader of some sophistication? A man who would see the soldier behind Fonthill's civilian garb and wife-companion?

His answer came as one man pushed forward to address him. He seemed to be just below medium height – maybe five foot seven inches – and he was dressed like the rest in a homespun and now well-worn suit, with dirty, wide-brimmed hat. But he wore long riding boots and a Prince Albert gold chain was looped across his waistcoat and, lugubriously, a battered briefcase was tied to his saddle pommel, his only sign of rank. His beard was neatly trimmed and his dark eyes were set well apart above high cheekbones in a face that seemed hard and unforgiving. He looked directly at Fonthill.

'You are English?' he asked, with the nasal intonation of an Afrikaner.

'Yes. My name is Simon Fonthill.' Fonthill turned courteously and indicated the others. 'This is my wife Alice, my friend Mr Jenkins and my farm manager Mr Mzingeli.'

The horseman frowned at the appellation 'Mister' given to Mzingeli.

'We don't call Kaffirs "mister",' he said.

'I know you don't. But I do. And he is not a Kaffir.'

Mzingeli did not move but sat quite still, his black eyes staring far away at the horizon, his tightly curled white hair peeping out from under his wide-brimmed hat.

The Boer did not rise to the reply but paused

for a moment before asking. 'Where have you come from and what is your destination?'

'We were travelling up from the Cape Colony on board the train which was derailed about ten miles or so south of here. I was anxious to get on to Pretoria and so chose to download our horses and Cape cart and proceed that way in the hope that we could pick up another train tomorrow.' He risked a smile. 'We were warned that there were Boers in the area but, as we are civilians, I felt that we would come to no harm.'

The smile was not returned. 'Nor shall you, but you must hand over the rifles,' he nodded to the cart, 'that you have hidden under that tent there and I will also take your horses. You may retain your cart, tent and mules.' The Boer turned and gave a brief order. Immediately, the tent was thrown onto the ground and the rifles seized. One was handed to the leader.

He examined it with interest. 'Hmm. A point 303 Lee Enfield. British army issue.' He looked up. 'What is a civilian doing with the most modern British army rifle?'

Fonthill shrugged his shoulders. 'We had to have rifles. We had a long way to travel and war or no war the African veldt can be a dangerous place. The only rifles one can buy in Cape Town these days are old British issue. You will see that these are not exactly the latest thing. They are Lee Enfields Mark I. I believe the army now have either Lee Metfords or later Enfields. From what I hear of your shooting, I think I'd rather have Mausers, anyway.'

This time the Boer allowed himself a half smile.

14

'Very well.' Then he frowned. 'Ah, but you have three rifles. One presumably for each man. That means that you have armed your Kaffir.' A low murmur rose from the ring of horsemen. 'It is against the rule of warfare for your people to arm the blacks and coloureds. This is a white man's war. We shoot all Kaffirs we find who carry arms.'

Fonthill sighed. 'Well,' he said slowly, 'if you shoot Mzingeli – *Mister* Mzingeli – then you must shoot all of us, because we shall all attack you. To repeat, Mr Mzingeli is not a Kaffir. He is not a servant. He is the son of a Matabele chieftain and he partly owns and manages my farm in Rhodesia. I asked him to travel here so that we could discuss farm matters. You will not, I repeat, *not*, shoot him.'

A silence fell on the little gathering. Mzingeli remained looking steadily ahead. Jenkins's hand drifted slowly towards his knife.

The impasse was broken by Alice. She stepped down from the cart and moved towards the Boer leader. 'Excuse me, sir,' she said, 'but if we are all going to die I would be so grateful to know your name.' And she looked upwards into the man's face with a sweet and ingratiating smile.

'What? Oh. Ah. My name is Christiaan de Wet.'

'Ah!' Alice seemed jubilant and from somewhere had already produced a notebook and pencil. 'I thought so. More like *General* de Wet I believe. How do you do.' She held up her hand and grasped that handed reluctantly to her. 'Perhaps you do not know it, sir, but you have earned widespread fame back in England as the most intrepid of the Boer commando leaders.

15

Perhaps I should explain. I am Simon Fonthill's wife but I am also known as Alice Griffith, my maiden name, and I have been a war correspondent for the London *Morning Post* for the last ... ahem ... nearly twenty years. In fact, we are on our way to Pretoria so that I can be registered with General Kitchener as part of the corps of correspondents assigned to his headquarters. Oh, I am so glad I have met you, General. Now, please, before you shoot us all would you be so kind as to answer just a few questions?'

'What? Ach, madam. I am not going to shoot you all. But I cannot stay here to be interviewed.' He looked around him. 'It is getting dark and...'

'Oh, just a couple of questions while we have you.' Alice stood poised, pencil over notebook. 'Surely, you cannot hope to win this war by conducting guerrilla operations, can you? Swooping down from out of the veldt like brigands and then riding off again. Now what is your objective, exactly?'

De Wet stiffened in the saddle. 'We fight, madam, to free our country. We are an independent state and we fight to stay that way.'

'But how long can you continue?' She gestured with her pencil. 'If I may say so, your command here looks a little,' she smiled again, 'shall we say lacklustre? Your troops look as though they could do with a good meal and a bath.'

Fonthill drew in his breath with a hiss, but his wife was continuing.

'And, of course, you are severely outnumbered by the British. This is just a small band. To repeat, how long can you continue fighting in this way?'

De Wet scowled down at her. 'We fight until the end, madam. We are Boers. We live in the saddle and we shall harry and attack the Khakis until they leave our country. And there are many of us fighting in the veldt across the Free State, in the Transvaal, and soon, in the Cape Colony.' He swung his arm behind him. 'This is not all of my commando. The rest of it is there behind that–'

He halted in mid flow, realising that he was talking far too much. 'Enough of this.' He turned back to Fonthill. 'Dismount now and,' he nodded to Jenkins, 'you too. We take this horse also.' And he untied the reins that linked Mzingeli's mount to the cart. He issued an order and the rifles were swept up and the horses were taken in tow.

De Wet turned to go. 'I am not sure,' he said, addressing Fonthill, 'that you really are a civilian. But we cannot take prisoners so you are free to continue your journey to Pretoria in your cart and we leave you your tent and provisions. But the next time we meet your Kaffir with a gun, we shoot him.'

He wheeled his horse round. Then a small smile returned to his face and he doffed his hat to Alice, bowing low in the saddle. 'I did not wish to be interviewed, madam,' he said, 'but tell your readers in England that we fight on until the end. This will be the war that will not end. Mrs Fonthill, I wish you good–'

Once again he broke off. Then he looked back at Simon with a keen eye. 'Fonthill,' he murmured. 'Fonthill.' He urged his horse close to Fonthill and looked down on him. 'It is an unusual name. There was an Englishman at Majuba

17

nineteen years ago when we thrashed the Khakis for the first time in the Transvaal war. I think he was a Fonthill.'

Simon inclined his head. 'Yes,' he said. 'I was there.'

De Wet removed his hat again and leaning down in the saddle extended his hand. 'So was I. I remember. We were both much younger. You, in particular, fought well. To the end.' He shook Fonthill's hand and replaced his hat. 'I think you are here to fight again.' He grinned. 'So Kitchener must be desperate. Go now, but I think we will meet again.'

Then with a shouted order he wheeled his mount around and the party of Boers cantered away in the lowering twilight, back towards the kopje, moving fast on their light ponies.

Simon's little party was left standing by the cart exchanging glances. Jenkins broke the silence, his voice rising in Welsh indignation. 'Bugger me,' he said. 'I was on that bloody Majuba 'ill fighting all them years ago just as 'ard as you, look you. Why didn't 'e remember me?'

Fonthill grinned and looked at Jenkins, standing only five foot four inches tall but, menacingly, almost as broad as he was tall. 'Because, my little giant,' he said, 'you're so easily overlooked, look you.' He turned to his wife. 'Alice, if I may say so, you were bloody marvellous. I think you saved the day, there.'

Without looking up from where she was scribbling, Alice nodded. 'Yes, you may indeed say so.' She tossed her head. 'Barbaric toad, threatening to kill Mzingeli. He wasn't even holding the bloody

18

rifle. I had forgotten how bad these Afrikaners are with natives.' She looked across at Mzingeli, who stood listening to the exchange with a faint smile lingering on his very black, seamed face. 'Sorry, Mzingeli,' she said. 'I hope all of that didn't upset you.'

The tracker shook his head. 'Ah no, Nkosana. Reminded me of the old days, when I was in the Transvaal. Not good, though. Not good.'

'Certainly, not good.' Then Alice looked across at Simon and gestured to her notes. 'But I've got the first interview ever with this famous commando leader. Darling, it's what you've always called a shovel and the Americans call a scoop. It's an exclusive. He's told me of their determination to go on until the bitter end and, what's more,' she waved her pencil in the air in triumph, 'he revealed that they're going to invade the Cape Colony and raise the rebels there. He didn't mean to, but he did.'

Simon Fonthill gazed at his wife with affection. The sun was now setting quickly, peeping through a purple cloud and sending beams of light low across the plain. Alice stood smiling, her face illuminated, emphasising her high cheekbones and the bronzed skin – not for her the pale aversion to sunshine of the Indian memsahib. Her grey eyes were alight with delight at her achievement and Simon revelled once more at his good fortune in marrying such a blithe, unquenchable, free spirit. She stood there now, dressed in a white blouse, riding breeches, with an old green scarf tied around her fair hair, her legs thrust apart in a masculine fashion and yet

19

looking delightfully, intriguingly feminine. Alice was now forty-five – his age – but only the rather intrusive squareness of her jaw prevented her from being classically beautiful. Their relationship had not been without its vicissitudes. She had married unhappily for the first time and, newly widowed, had rushed into his arms only to see their child stillborn, with no hope of a second pregnancy. Since then, fifteen years ago, they had farmed together and fought together, with Jenkins, in a series of adventures, she reporting for the *Morning Post*, he and the Welshman following their sporadic careers as freelance army scouts. Now they had landed once again in South Africa, where they had first served together in the Zulu War, she as a young, untried war correspondent and he as an equally young subaltern, with Jenkins as his servant.

Fonthill returned her smile. They made a handsome couple in their young, healthy, middle age. At five foot nine inches he was broad-shouldered, with only an incipient trace of corpulence now just beginning to break the slimness of a body hardened by years of farming and campaigning. His fair hair was still full, his cheeks as tanned as those of his wife and his brown eyes retained a slightly withdrawn gentleness unusual in a man of good birth who had spent so much time in remote corners of the British Empire. The only obvious evidence he carried of past hardship, however, lay with the nose which, years before, had been broken by a Pathan musket and had been left slightly hooked, giving him a predatory air, that of a hunter, slightly uncertain, perhaps, but one still

20

seeking his prey.

Opposite the pair Jenkins stood loosely at ease, as befitted an ex-soldier of Her Majesty's 24th Regiment of Foot. Lugubrious, perhaps, was the term that best described him. Known usually only as '352', the last three figures of his army number to distinguish him from the other Jenkinses in this most Welsh of regiments, he had met Fonthill at the regimental hospital at Brecon and had become the young subaltern's servant-batman, mentor and friend, crossing the divisions of class in this most hierarchical of periods in Britain's cultural history. He was four years older than Simon but no grey strands had had the audacity to push through the thicket of black hair that stood up vertically on his head, nor in the great moustache that swept from ear to ear across his face. Five inches shorter than Fonthill, he was hugely broad, exuding great strength, a fighting machine at home in barrack room, bar and battlefield anywhere in the world.

The quartet was completed by Mzingeli, who now selected a blanket from the tangled tent on the ground and draped it round the shoulders of Alice, who was beginning to shiver as the sun slipped away. Of indeterminate age – although the white hair tightly curled to the scalp showed him to be by far the oldest of the four – he was also the tallest. Slim as a flagstaff, his name meant 'The Hunter' and he looked the part. He was dressed in old corduroy trousers, boots that had seen better days and a loose flannel shirt. His face, under its wide-brimmed Boer hat, was not without nobility, for his lips were thin and his nose long, with flared nostrils. Of the Malakala tribe, his black eyes seemed to carry all the sadness of his race. He had met the other three when they had hired him to track for them as they hunted in the far north of the Transvaal in the 1880s, then sharing in their adventures as they crossed into Matabeleland with Cecil G. Rhodes's invading force, before agreeing to manage the Fonthills' farm in the newly created colony of Rhodesia. Summoned by Simon's telegraph, he had met the others after they had landed in Cape Town, for Fonthill knew that he would be needed in the tasks that lay ahead of them all.

Mzingeli's draping of the blanket stung Jenkins into life. 'Right, then,' he said, rubbing his hands, 'better get this bleedin' tent up, then – ah, sorry Miss Alice. Language again. Sorry.'

Alice tugged the blanket tighter in frustration. '352, if you apologise for your disgraceful language again, I shall scream. How many more times have I to remind you that I am a brigadier's daughter. As a reporter, I have covered the British army's campaigns in Zululand, Afghanistan, East Africa, Egypt, the Sudan, the Transvaal and China, so I am well acquainted with army terminology. So do stop bleedin' apologising. D'you hear?'

Jenkins had the grace to look crestfallen. 'Ah, yes, miss – missus. Sorry. I'll put the ordinary tent up, then.'

'No, don't do that.' Fonthill extricated his compass and took a bearing on the horsemen who were fast disappearing in the twilight towards the kopje.

'Blimey, bach sir.' Jenkins looked woebegone. 'It's September, look you, which means the rainy season's just round the corner. If we don't freeze 'ere out in this veldt place, we'll drown in one of them sudden storms. You remember 'em?'

'Yes, of course, I do. And you have a point. But we're not going to camp.'

'What we goin' to do, then?'

The others were now looking at Fonthill in some consternation. The wind that had made Alice shiver was not unusual in this early spring, for the veldt of the Orange Free State stood some five to six thousand feet above sea level.

Alice pulled the blanket tightly round her. 'Yes, Simon,' she repeated. 'What are we going to do, then?'

'We're going to get our horses back – and our rifles, too, if we can.'

'What?' Jenkins's jaw dropped for a moment and then his face gradually segued into a wide grin. 'Of course we are,' he said. 'Of course we are. I should 'ave known.'

'Don't be ridiculous, Simon.' Alice stamped her foot. 'There are probably two hundred horsemen camping behind that kopje. There is no way you can drive this stupid mule cart up there and demand our horses back. This time we *will* all be shot.'

'I'm not going to ask for them back. I'm going to take them. Now...' He gazed around him. The sun had slipped down behind the purple cloud and the horizon that it hid and a soft, velvet light had fallen across the plain, deepening as he looked. Only a few other kopjes – black, flat-

23

topped rocky hills that rose vertically – gave features to the plain and they were now slipping out of sight as the darkness grew. They were now quite alone again on this endless veldt.

His tone sharpened. '352, get the revolvers from Alice's bag. Good thing we hid them. Mzingeli.'

'Nkosi?'

'I've got a compass bearing on the kopje so we can find it in the dark. But do you think you can track the horsemen and find where the commando is camped? They won't be riding on in the dark.'

'Better when moon comes up. But I find them, I think.'

'Good man. But I hope the moon's not too bright. We will wait until it is properly dark, then we'll move across to the kopje.'

'Simon!' Alice looked like some chastising governess as she stood frowning, the blanket wrapped tightly around her. 'Let us camp for the night and then get in the cart early in the morning and make for that hoped-for train and then get on to Pretoria where I can file my story. For God's sake, you can't take on a whole Boer commando with three men, three handguns and a feeble woman.'

He grinned at her. 'I can't see a *feeble* woman anywhere. And I don't intend to take them on. We shall steal the horses. Now, put the tent back on the cart and let's make for the kopje. Then Mzingeli will have to take over. Move now.'

Mzingeli urged the mules into life and the two men walked alongside Alice as she sat in the cart. There Simon outlined his plan such as it was.

24

'The Boers,' he said as they trudged along, 'are magnificent horsemen, probably the best shots in the world and good soldiers, up to a point. What they lack, however, is discipline – the discipline of a trained soldier. They fight like tigers but I remember from the Transvaal War that on the simple bread-and-butter things of soldiering they fall down. And why shouldn't they? They're farmers who fight, that's all. So I am gambling that they will not have set proper guards on the horses. They will have tethered or hobbled them so that they can't stray but, hopefully, will have set only one or, at the most, two sentries. After all, they believe that we will be no threat to them and they know that the nearest British force is ten miles at least to the south, trying to fix the broken rails with the armoured train.'

'So...?' asked Jenkins.

'So we leave Alice at the foot of the kopje with the cart and we three steal up on them, put the guard or guards out of action – although no shooting, mind – and lead the horses quietly away.'

'Humph!' The snort came from Alice. 'Even if this works, they will find the horses gone, and come after us. And, slowed down by this damned cart, they will easily overtake us before we get to the railway line.'

Simon shook his head. 'We won't go north, towards Pretoria, because they will expect us to go that way. And we will leave the cart and set the mules free. We will go – on horseback, because we can make better time that way – to the south and rejoin the train. I hear that commandos rarely take black trackers with them so I am gambling that they won't pick up our spoor until it is too late.'

Jenkins nodded. 'Very good, bach sir. That sounds a good plan.'

'Now that's just fine,' said Alice. 'There are four of us and three horses. Tell me, pray. Do I walk?'

'Only if you want to, darling. No, you share a horse with me. Uncomfortable, but we only have about ten miles to go.'

'With respect, bach sir,' said Jenkins, 'I think Miss Alice should ride with me. That way she won't fall off.'

'When you say "with respect", 352, you damn well don't mean it. I'm a much better horseman than I used to be.'

'Ummph! But she should still ride with me.'

'Oh, very well.'

They proceeded in silence until eventually a wan moon rose, bringing the kopje suddenly into focus before them. It stood like a black, squat thumb rising from the plain but, as they neared, they could see that a track of sorts wound upwards between the fissured rocks. Mzingeli looked at it and at the ground and shook his head.

'Not that way,' he said. He led them around the base of the kopje until its verticality gave way to a more gentle incline and a much wider track threading its way upwards. 'Here,' he said. 'Boers like to camp high so that they have view of plain. We keep very quiet now.'

'Right,' whispered Simon. He turned to his wife. 'Stay here with the cart and take this.' He gave her one of the Webley revolvers. 'It is fully loaded. But I recommend you don't fire at the

26

Boers with it. It might annoy them. If we are not back by daylight, make your way back along the railway track the way we came until you meet the train.'

'I'd rather come with you.'

'No.' He grinned. 'Can't have a feeble woman with us. If we are caught, then I doubt if the Boers will shoot us. They don't like to be bogged down with prisoners, so they will probably slap our wrists and turn us loose again. In which case we shall be back where we started. But I intend to get those horses. Be careful, darling.' He kissed her quickly and turned away. 'Lead on, Mzingeli.'

Treading carefully in the semi-darkness, the three men began their climb. It was not arduous, for it seemed as though the Boers had not dismounted, although, in truth, Simon could see little sign of the party having come this way, for there was no soil or sand lining the track, only shreds of coarse grass struggling through the rocks. It betrayed no indentations. Mzingeli, however, showed no hesitation and continued to stride upwards.

After fifteen minutes, he held up his hand and waited for the others to join him. 'Horses up just ahead,' he whispered. 'I smell them. I go alone now. Come back and tell you.' And he was gone.

Jenkins crouched down next to Fonthill, his knife gleaming in his hand. 'What's the plan, then, bach sir?'

'Put the knife away, 352. I don't want any killing unless we absolutely have to. It depends how many guards there are. If there is only one, I want you to creep up behind him, put a revolver at his

27

head and tell him to be quiet. Here's a gag and some tent cord. We will bind him and take the horses – but quietly, oh so quietly.'

'An' if there's more than one guard?'

'I'll have to think again.'

Mzingeli was back, it seemed, almost as soon as he had gone. He slipped down between the two. 'Camp is on a plateau over the back,' he whispered, gesturing with his hand. 'Away from horses, which are nearer.'

'Now there's a stroke of luck,' beamed Jenkins. 'How many guards?'

'Only one I see. He up on right there, on top of path. We must get round him. But I think he sleeps.'

'Ah.' Fonthill's teeth flashed in the moonlight. 'As I said. Bad soldiering. Good. Now, 352, crawl away to the right and get behind the guard. We will go to just below the top and wait until you've dealt with the Boer – I know you can do it. Very quietly. Now. Off you go.'

Jenkins wriggled away like an eel between the rocks and Fonthill followed Mzingeli as the tracker crawled upwards, placing hands and feet with care. As the hunched figure of the guard came into sight, silhouetted against a now star-strewn sky, they froze onto the grass. They kept their eyes fixed on the man, who remained im-mobile, crouched like some ancient shepherd guarding his flock. Then, as they watched, a figure suddenly rose behind him, putting one arm under his throat and presenting the stumpy barrel of the revolver to his ear. The man attempted to rise and shout but Jenkins clasped a hand to his mouth

28

and whispered to him. Immediately, the guard froze, immobile.

Simon and Mzingeli were upon him in a flash. Fonthill forced open the man's mouth and thrust a rolled handkerchief into it, tying it into place with a bandana knotted at the back of his neck. Then they rolled him over and bound his hands behind his back before tying his legs together. The Boer lay looking up at them, eyes bulging.

'Can't see any more guards, bach sir,' whispered Jenkins. 'The camp's over there,' he nodded with his head, 'beyond the 'orses. They've 'obbled all the 'orses by binding one foreleg back. I call that bloody cruel. An' them supposed to be marvellous 'orsemen, look you.'

Fonthill nodded. Jenkins had been brought up on a farm in the north of Wales and was a superb horseman. He was also a lover of horseflesh.

'Mzingeli,' he whispered. 'You and Jenkins see if you can find our horses and bring them over here quietly. The Boers will have got back here in the darkness so there's just a possibility that they've not unsaddled them. Go now. I'll watch over this fellow.'

Within minutes the two were back, leading three horses, all fully saddled and bridled. 'Look,' said Jenkins, his face expressing disgust. 'They've even put our rifles back in the saddle holsters, see. Lazy bastards. They know nothin' about 'orses, absolutely.'

'Splendid. Right. Let's go. Quietly, now.'

They had retreated some five minutes down the path when Jenkins gave the reins of the horses he was leading to Mzingeli. 'I'll just be 'alf a mo', bach sir,' he said.

'No,' hissed Fonthill. 'Where are you going? Come back. Now.'

But the little Welshman had disappeared back up the hill into the night.

Cursing, Simon indicated to the tracker that they should continue the descent but they had reached the bottom and were met by a relieved Alice before Jenkins rejoined them.

'Where the hell did you go?' demanded Fonthill.

'I couldn't let them beasts stay up there with one leg tied up,' he said. 'So I cut as many free as I could. Too many, o'course, to do 'em all. But enough to let 'em wander about a bit and stray, like. That'll give them Boer buggers a bit to think about first thing in the mornin', see. Oh.' He held up his knife, the point of which was blood-stained. 'I just poked this into the leg of that guard, see. Not far. Just a bit of a scratch. That'll teach 'im to sleep on guard and serve 'im right for treatin' 'orses that way, so it will.'

Fonthill blew out his cheeks. 'For God's sake get on your horse. Alice, you get in the saddle, 352 can ride behind you. Leave the cart and the mules. We must ride hard through the night so that we don't have a horde of bloodthirsty Boers breathing down our necks. Right. Now ride!'

Heads down, with Jenkins clinging to Alice for dear life, they rode through the darkness as fast as the horses and the terrain would allow. Just before dawn they reached the armoured train. It was getting steam up, for the sappers had worked through the night to repair the rails. They were

30

just in time to wolf down hot tea and bacon sandwiches before the train snorted into motion, on its journey to Pretoria, the newly captured capital of the Transvaal, carrying them aboard.

## CHAPTER TWO

On the journey, which proved uneventful, Fonthill looked again at the cable that he had received only last month in the half-ruined British consulate in Peking, after the siege of the capital had been raised. He, Alice and Jenkins had been visiting his wife's uncle, a missionary in China, when the Boxer Rebellion had burst around their ears. The three of them had played a role in the defence and final relief of the besieged consulates in the heart of the city – a role that had been well reported in the world's press. As a result, General Kitchener, Roberts's chief of staff in South Africa, had cabled him:

WE NEVER MET IN SUDAN BUT WARMEST CONGRATS ON YOUR WORK CHINA STOP WAR WITH BOERS HERE FAR FROM OVER STOP DESPERATELY NEED YOU HERE FOR URGENT TASK STOP CAN YOU SHIP TO CAPE TOWN SOONEST STOP LETTER FOLLOWS STOP

Kitchener had been only a major of intelligence when Fonthill and Jenkins had infiltrated the

31

Dervish lines around Khartoum to reach the besieged General Gordon years before. But Simon knew, of course, of the meteoric nature of the man's rise to become Sirdar of the Egyptian army and the eventual conqueror of the Mahdi's forces at the Battle of Omdurman two years before. He was now Lord Kitchener of Khartoum – 'K of K' – and rumoured soon to take over from the elderly Roberts as commander-in-chief in South Africa.

Fonthill, having rather surprisingly received Alice's approval, had cabled his acceptance but Kitchener's explanatory letter had revealed little more when it had arrived just before they took ship for the Cape. It merely referred to a need to find 'a new way of fighting the Boers', for which Fonthill's wide experience and 'unconventional military methods' would eminently suit him. Simon remembered ruefully that that very un-conventionality had brought him into conflict several times years before with General Roberts in the second Anglo-Afghan war and that Kitchener would surely have conferred with his chief before sending the cable. So Roberts had approved of the choice. There could be no more validation of the need for 'something new needed'. He was undeniably intrigued. Of one thing, however, he was certain – he would never return to the regular army.

They arrived in the pretty little Transvaal town of Pretoria, final destination of the Boer *voetrek-kers* so long ago, and Fonthill booked them all into a small hotel in the centre – not without a disputatious argument before Mzingeli was accepted as a guest. Then he sent a message to Kitchener's headquarters, announcing his arrival and requesting an interview. A reply came flatteringly quickly, asking Simon to call at four p.m. that day.

The army HQ was Melrose House, a two-storey, wooden dwelling near the centre of the town, fringed by a conventional African veranda or *stoep* and whose only clue to its militaristic role was the presence of a flagpole bearing a Union Jack, and the constant toing and froing of uniformed men at its entrance. Fonthill presented his card and was asked to wait in an anteroom.

The wait was short and Simon was ushered into a much larger room. He absorbed a quick impression of map-covered walls and tables holding what seemed to be *objets d'art* of an eclectic variety and he recalled reading somewhere that the soldier was a collector of such things. Then he was confronted by Kitchener himself, who strode towards him, hand extended, seeming to fill the room.

Fonthill regarded him intently. In a very short time, Kitchener had come to represent the imperial age in a manner that had even eluded such eminent military leaders as Wolseley and Roberts. Perhaps it was the great moustache, which thrust across the man's upper up, oiled, clipped yet luxurious and slightly tilted upwards at the end so confidently. He was tall but surprisingly narrow-shouldered, and quite slim. The face behind the moustache was bronzed with purple, heavy jowls and hair slicked back either side of a central parting. It was the eyes, however, which drew the gaze. They were set far

33

apart and there was a curious cast in the right eye. And they were china blue, exuding a kind of intensity that was compelling.

'Good of you to come so quickly, Fonthill,' said the general. He grasped Simon's hand in a firm grip. 'Do sit down.' Kitchener strode back to his chair but remained standing, holding his visitor's card in his hand. He indicated it. 'C.B. eh? Order of the Bath. That was for Khartoum, I seem to remember?'

'Yes, General. Came up with the rations.'

'I'm sure it didn't. Getting through the Mahdi's lines, being captured and then escaping was quite a feat. Didn't your man get a DSM?'

'Yes. Jenkins, the Distinguished Service Medal. That certainly didn't come up with the rations. Couldn't have done a thing without him.'

'And is he still with you?'

'Yes, he's here now. We've been together, one way or another, for more than twenty years.'

'Splendid. We can use him, too. Now then. You must be wondering what I have in mind, eh? Don't suppose my letter helped much?' Fonthill noted that Kitchener never seemed to smile. His face remained set, despite the modulations of his voice. It was as though it was that of an icon.

'No, sir. But I am anxious to help.'

'Good. The C-in-C assured me you would.'

Fonthill marvelled at this. The last time he had met the famous "Bobs", the general had distinctly taken umbrage at Simon's refusal to rejoin the army. He kept silent now. It was up to Kitchener to do the talking.

'Yes. Quite. You must have been quite a bit out

of touch in China with things here in South Africa? Yes?'

'Very much so.'

'Very well. A bit of background is necessary. Come over here.'

The two men approached the biggest of the maps, which almost covered one wall of the room. It was a large-scale ordnance of the whole of South Africa. It was studded with pins, red and blue.

'Disregard the flags,' said Kitchener. 'Look here. This is where the war really started, here on the Natal border.' He indicated the right-hand side of the Southern African continent. 'This is where the Boers made their first thrust, while we were outnumbered and before Buller arrived with reinforcements. That bloody fool Sir George White...' He looked up sharply. 'Fonthill, I am treating you as a senior officer and speaking freely to you. I presume I can rely on your discretion?'

'Absolutely, General.'

'Good. Well, White got himself cooped up here in Ladysmith with a goodly portion of his Natal command and remained stuck there. Same thing happened to a smaller degree at Kimberley where your old friend Rhodes stayed with his mines, squealing to be rescued, and to an even smaller degree here in the north-west at Mafeking. Now, when General Buller arrived with his army he felt that his main priority had to be to relieve Ladysmith – not least because White had got a large unit of our cavalry stuck there doing nothing; and cavalry, I don't need to tell you, Fonthill, is worth its weight in gold in this country.'

Simon nodded.

'Trouble is that Buller got himself into an awful hole here on the Tugela and was savagely mauled by the Boers, firing from entrenched positions under the Boer general, Botha, at Colenso. Same thing had happened to the west on the Modder, where Methuen tried to get through to Kimberley and was soundly defeated. Shortly afterwards, Buller caught it again at Spion Kop, another bloodbath. It was a terrible time and that's when it was realised back home that we were fighting a savagely determined foe, equipped with the latest weapons.'

Kitchener regarded Fonthill with his icy stare. 'Not Afghans with muskets nor Dervishes with spears. But marksmen, with Mauser rifles that could outrange us and extremely modern Creusot and Krupps artillery from Europe. This had become a war where the range of the modern rifle had spread the battlefield over five or ten miles. Conventional scouting was made impossible over the flat ground of the veldt, where the best scouts in the world could be picked off by the enemy more than a mile away.

'What's more,' Kitchener went on, speaking quietly, 'our artillery turned out to be useless, as I expected. All our field guns were originally twelve-pounders, they were then bored out to make them fifteen-pounders, with the result that they could be used only with reduced charges.' The general smoothed upwards the edges of his moustache and his voice took on a confidential air, as though breathing confidences to a friend. 'Do yer know, Fonthill, we had become virtually the laughing stock of Europe. We had sent overseas the biggest British army in history to overcome one of the world's smallest nations – although to be fair, most of the army had not yet arrived. Even so, we were ridiculed, with Germany leading the laughter. The Boers were saying that our command was so incompetent that they would court-martial any of their men who killed a British general.'

A silence hung in the air for a moment and then the general continued. 'So Roberts was sent out to take command, with me as his chief of staff and with a vast number of reinforcements. You will remember, of course, from Afghanistan that the field marshal knows what he is doing and his grasp of the situation and the increased size of the army soon produced results. He outflanked the enemy and relieved Kimberley and then we cornered a large section of the Boer army here,' he tapped the map, 'at Paardeberg and Cronje was forced to surrender with some five thousand men.'

Simon nodded. 'The turning point?'

'In terms of conventional warfare, yes. I was able to throw out the Boer commandos who were trying to foment rebellion in the Cape Colony and in the north there were further successes when we beat Botha at Diamond Hill, here, near Pretoria, and even better when we were able to relieve Mafeking and then take Johannesburg, with its important mines, and the Transvaal capital here. Importantly, Buller – a falsely maligned general, in my view – was able, at last, to break through to relieve Ladysmith and the Boers were unrolled all across the map, with President Kruger fleeing through Mozambique in the east here to take ship to Holland.'

For the first time, a faint smile crept across Kitchener's broad face. 'War over, then, eh?'

Fonthill returned the smile. 'Except that it wasn't.'

'Quite so, except that the chief, Field Marshal Roberts, is more or less convinced that it is. You may have heard that Wolseley is retiring as head of the army at the Horse Guards?'

'Ah, no. I had not.' A faint pang of regret shot through Fonthill at the news. He and Jenkins had served under the field marshal – guyed by W.S. Gilbert as 'the very model of a modern major general' on the London stage – in campaigns on the Mozambique border, in the conquest of Egypt and then in the abortive attempt to relieve Gordon, and he had great respect for the little man.

'Yes. Bobs will return to England very shortly to take up the post and I will take over here. I think the chief believes that he will be leaving me with just a bit of clearing up to do. But I knew it wouldn't be as easy as that and that is why I sent for you. Now, come and sit down and I will explain.'

The two strode back and Fonthill looked across at the tall soldier now with a growing regard. No one had greater respect for the Boers than Simon. He had seen, in the Transvaal War, how competent they had been in outmanoeuvring a conventional army in the field and then defeating it in a pitched battle at Majuba. But to hear a British general give an 'amateur army' credit was new to him. From Isandlwana ('let the Zulus come – we'll give them a bloody nose') to the Sudan ('the Dervishes are not disciplined, they will never break a British square') he had heard British officers pour scorn on their opponents. The change was refreshing. He sat on the edge of his chair listening carefully to the tall man opposite.

Kitchener leant forward. 'We were told that the Boers would run away. Well, they ran away very often, but they always came back again. We were told that they would never hold together in any cohesive formation but I fully believe that there is no one more self-confident of his own individual opinions than the Boer. They have subordinated themselves to their leaders and have worked together with discipline. We have seen them courageous in attack and in retreat. They have always shown an ability to give lessons to us all.'

Fonthill opened his mouth to speak but the general held up his hand. 'There is another characteristic they have displayed which, if we are true descendants of our forefathers, we ought to be most capable of fully appreciating. I refer to that wonderful tenacity of purpose, that "don't know when you are beaten" quality which they are prominently displaying in this war. There may be individuals among them whose characteristics and methods we do not like but, judged as a whole, I maintain that they are a virile race.

'Now, this was underlined about six months ago, when we were rolling 'em back all along what we then thought was the front in the north, and the Boer leaders held a meeting – they call it a *krijgsraad* or council of war – about a hundred and thirty miles north of Bloemfontein just a few days after the fall of the Free State capital. They seemed to have lost the war. It was Christiian de Wet, the new commandant of the Free State army, who had a different idea. Guerilla warfare. Take to the veldt.'

The general was now almost animated and made a slashing motion with his arm. 'Cut out the cumbersome wagon trains so beloved of the Boers from the Great Trek and which trapped Cronje. No more fighting "at the front". Instead, adopt a raiding strategy behind the British lines, attacking our lines of communications, which, Fonthill, are damned long and vulnerable, swooping down on our flanks, hitting and riding off again, hitting us where it hurts. Riding swiftly and carrying little provisions–'

Fonthill interrupted. 'Just a bag of flour, a parcel of tea and a few strips of biltong on the saddle bow.'

Kitchener frowned. 'What? How do you know that?'

'I saw it.' And he explained his party's brush with de Wet on the Free State veldt.

The general blew out his cheeks and leant back in his chair. 'Well bless my soul, Fonthill. You're not in this damned country five minutes and you meet one of the enemy's leading generals, raid his camp and steal back your horses from him.' The glare softened into a grin that seemed to sit ill at ease beneath the great moustache. 'Well done, my dear fellow. And you say he betrayed his intention to invade the Cape Colony?'

'So he let slip to my wife. She is here to write for the *Morning Post*, you know. She seized her opportunity to interview him.'

'Ah yes. The formidable Miss Griffith.' A brief look of embarrassment flashed across Kitchener's face. 'Yes, excuse me, Fonthill. Fact is, I don't have much time for the Fleet Street scribblers who are out here. Neither does Roberts. He ... ah ... of course remembers your wife from the second Afghan War, you know.'

Fonthill stifled a smile. Alice had infuriated Roberts by reporting on and attacking in print his policy of destroying Afghan villages. To say that they had clashed would be an understatement.

Then that unfamiliar smile crept back across the general's fierce countenance. 'Still,' he said, 'if she's writing for the *Morning Post* that should get that arrogant young pup Winston Churchill off my back. He can't make up his mind whether he's is out here as a politician, a serving officer or a journalist. Perhaps your wife will knock him off his perch.'

'Perhaps so, sir. But you were saying...?'

'Yes. The Cape Colony. I would be grateful if your wife could come in here as soon as possible and tell me exactly what de Wet said. If they are going south again, I need to be prepared. Milner – he's the high commissioner in the Cape, don't yer know – is in a constant funk about rebellion there.'

'Of course, sir.'

'Right. Now back to you. Apart from our long and vulnerable lines of communication, the army's problem out here is that it is slow and ponderous. We are even worse than the Boers with their wagon trains and women and children.

41

We can't stray more than eight miles from the railway lines before we get into trouble. Enteric fever is growing and we are burdened with the need to look after this huge army and feed it. We can fight all right, but we can't pin down these Boer commandos to oppose us. Very selfish of them. It's not just de Wet in the Free Province. Botha has reorganised his fighting men to do the same thing in the Transvaal and there's de la Rey there, too, another good man. Hit and run. It has only just started but it will get worse.'

Fonthill frowned. He thought he could see which way Kitchener's mind was working. 'So,' he said, 'fight them at their own game...?'

'Exactly.' The general had tilted his chair backwards but now it came thudding down to give emphasis to his words. 'Two things.' He held up one surprisingly slim finger and slammed it into his other palm. 'Firstly, I aim to cut off these commandos' source of supply. So destroy the farms that supply them...'

Simon had a momentary memory of Afghan villages burning high up in the Hindu Kush and his wife's tears and fury at the sight. Here, he thought, trouble could lie.

But Kitchener was continuing. The second finger crashed into the palm. 'Secondly, as you perceptively say, fight 'em at their own game.' He leant back in his chair again. 'The key to doing that, of course, is cavalry and horses. And both have been in short supply in this war. But now we are getting horses from all over the Empire and I am beginning to form flying columns that can move like the Boers do – live out on the veldt on

42

horseback without a supply train, picking up information, tracking down the enemy and leading our men to them. Pinning them down before they can take flight again. I want you, Fonthill, to lead one of those columns. Not one of the heavier groups that will confront the Boers but an irregular unit – a scouting force with a bit of depth – that will catch 'em, perhaps pin 'em down until the larger column comes up. What do you say?'

Fonthill frowned. 'What do you mean, General? Back in the army, formally, after all these years?'

'Yes. Rank of colonel, a special service officer. Your man as senior warrant officer. At home, all sorts of chaps are rallying round to the colours and shipping out here. Which is fine. But, my dear fellow, I particularly need you. Someone who can think outside the framework of conventional soldiering. Someone not – what shall I say – bogged down by years of regimental command. I hear that it was you who laid out Wolseley's plan of attack on the bPedi camp on the Mozambique border back in the eighties. Brilliant piece of thinking. Roberts warns me that you will never rejoin the regular ranks. But I think he is wrong. The point is, Fonthill, your country needs you.'

The china-blue eyes penetrated his own.

Fonthill shifted in his seat. 'As I say,' he said eventually, 'I am anxious to help, but I do not wish to take up a commission again. I am – what shall I say – uneasy at the thought of conforming–'

But Kitchener interrupted. 'That's the whole point. You won't conform. You will be out on your own, with your men, breaking the damned rules if you have to. Only reporting to John French,

43

who commands my cavalry, when you have to, and getting provisions and that sort of thing. Very much your own command, Fonthill, after all these years.'

Simon seized on the point. 'Ah, cavalry, General.' His mind recalled stiff-backed Hussars and Lancers with their pennanted spears, the gallant *arme blanche* of the army, charging with raised swords to a bugle call and led by brave and quite stupid officers – all that was wrong with the regular army. 'What you describe would not be a task for the cavalry,' he said. 'It must be mounted infantry. Good horsemen but no sabre rubbish. They must be excellent shots but able to dismount and deploy in a second and–'

He was interrupted again by what sounded like a chuckle from the general – except that his face hardly seemed to move. 'Absolutely, my dear fellow. Couldn't have described it better myself. So you will accept?'

Fonthill thought quickly. 'How many men do you see in this command?'

Kitchener leant forward. 'Not many. Not a conventional battalion or anything like that. Perhaps about a hundred men, maybe a few more. Suck it and see. Find out how many you need in practice. Not so many that you are strewn out across the veldt but enough to frighten a commando when you surprise them. I will get you some of the best horses newly arrived from home.'

'No.' Fonthill spoke quickly. 'No cavalry mounts. They would be too big for this job – too difficult to feed and too large a target for the Mausers. We would need local mounts happy out on the veldt, used to feeding on what pasture there is, even in winter. Basuto ponies would be best. They are what the Boers use. What about men?'

'You recruit them yourself. We have lists of chaps wanting to do their bit. Johannesburg is the best place. It's full of uitlanders – they're the locals, but adventurers and originally from all parts of the Empire, some of them miners, disenfranchised by the Boers and the cause of all this trouble in the first place and anxious to have a go at them. You will need a handful of good NCOs and, say, three commissioned squadron commanders to work with you, and we can supply these from our mounted infantry units – and I'll get you the ponies you want. We've captured enough Boers to supply these.' The wintry half smile reappeared. 'Our cavalry chaps wouldn't dream of using 'em. But you can have 'em. So...' His voice tailed away for a moment and then came back strongly. 'You are in, then, Fonthill, eh?'

Outside a wagon creaked and a distant voice barked a command. Simon sighed. 'Very well, General. Very well. I shall take the Queen's shilling again – words I never thought I would say.'

'Good. Never doubted it, although the chief will be surprised. Now, you will need to be commissioned again, of course, and your man given warrant officer rank. Come back here tomorrow and see my ADC. He will set you up with the bureaucracy of the thing and also introduce you to the people you will need for provisioning, setting up your recruiting office and so on.'

The general stood up and held out his hand. 'Delighted to have you back, Colonel. You should

start your planning now. You will get your marching orders from French, when you are ready.'

Fonthill gripped the outstretched hand. 'Thank
you, sir. Ah. One more thing.'

'Yes?'

'If I'm to be hunting Boers out on the plain and
up in the hills, I will need the best intelligence I
can get.'

'Indeed you will. I will make sure that our
people help you all they can.'

'Thank you for that, sir. But I had rather different thoughts.'

Kitchener lifted a bushy eyebrow. 'What do you
mean?'

'In my experience, in all these damned colonial
wars in which I have been involved over the last
twenty years, it's natives who know what's *really*
going on. It's their country, after all. I have
brought with me my farm manager from Rhodesia. He's originally a black Malakala, the son of
a chieftain, but he has hunted in the Transvaal for
years. He has no love for the Boers and he is the
best tracker I have ever seen. Good thinker and
fighter, too. I would want him to recruit a small
gang of trackers who would work with us out on
the veldt and liaise with local natives to bring us
news of the movements of the commandos.'

'Hmm.' Kitchener's face was impassive as usual
but it was clear that, perhaps, this could be an
unconventional step too far. 'We have our own
intelligence sources, you know.'

'Yes, but they don't seem to have worked too
well. I guarantee this would work better.'

'Very well. But you must not arm them. To do

so would be against the rules of warfare out here. There is a kind of unofficial agreement with the Boers about this and I would not wish to give them further propaganda opportunities on this score.'

'I agree to that.' But, Fonthill added to himself, with the exception of Mzingeli.

Kitchener held up his hand. 'One last thing. I should warn you that this won't be easy. This country is vast and you can hide an army on the veldt and in the valleys. These fellers know what they are about. Botha, of course, beat us at Colenso and Spion Kop and de Wet is as slippery as an eel.'

One eyebrow in the bronzed face came down in a frown and the other went up, as though in consternation. 'We thought we had de Wet fair and square back in July this year. He was penned in and more or less surrounded in the Brandwater Basin, in mountainous country in the middle of the Free State. Somehow, during the night, he moved two thousand six hundred horsemen, five guns, four hundred wagons – a column stretching three miles – over a pass, within a mile of the British camp. He got clean away, taking the Free State president and government with him. Now he's running riot in the great plains either side of the Vaal River. He's a tough customer, Fonthill. Nab him and the war is half won.'

'I'll do my best, sir.'

Fonthill stepped down from the *stoep* of the house into the warming sunshine of a typical Transvaal spring day. The purple jacaranda blossom lining the street reminded him of

47

Bloemfontein years before, and birds were singing. Then a platoon of British infantry, dressed in anonymous khaki and wearing wound puttees around their calves and cloth-covered pith helmets on their heads, marched by and smartly saluted a major astride a beautifully groomed stallion. The officer raised his riding crop to the rim of his hat in languid reply.

Simon lifted his eyes to the heavens. He was back in that world! What would Jenkins – not to mention Alice – say? A world of saluting, of obeying orders blindly without equivocation. A world of conforming to army regulations. A world dominated by senior officers whom not only the enemy but their peers in Europe (and almost certainly the United States of America) now looked upon with derision, given their performance so far in this war against armed farmers.

He shrugged his shoulders. Well, he must carve out his own destiny within the parameters outlined by Kitchener, a man who surely was of a competence well above that of the men who had led the British soldiers to their deaths at Colenso, the Modder and Spion Kop. And yet Kitchener's own experience had been confined to fighting aboriginal warriors, armed only with muskets and spears. He himself had yet to be truly tested in this new sort of warfare. Who would win out there on the unforgiving veldt?

Fonthill strode away back to his hotel, his brain buzzing.

# CHAPTER THREE

On hearing the news, Alice was surprisingly unperturbed. 'Well, my love,' she said, looking up from the cablegram she was composing, 'I didn't think we'd come all this way just for you to serve tea to the troops. If you are going a-soldiering again, then better and safer that you are within the formal structure of the army. Apart from which,' she slanted a quick grin at him, 'it will be quite nice to be a colonel's wife again.' Her first husband had been Simon's first commanding officer in the 24th Regiment of Foot.

Jenkins, on the other hand, revealed his displeasure predictably. 'I'd sworn I'd never go back into the bleedin' army again, bach sir, you know that,' he fulminated. 'I'd be back on a charge again as soon as I'd swallowed my first pint o' beer. That's not the life we've lived this past twenty years, look you. We've bin out on our own, like, fearin' no man and not 'avin' to salute anyone. Free as the air we was, see. Now what are we goin' to be doin?'

'Fighting the Boers, that's what. And you won't be on a charge, you will be issuing them. You will be my RSM.'

The frown gradually faded and was replaced by a faint smile. 'What? Regimental sergeant major. Me? Now, that's a thought. It's quite intrug ... intrigo...'

'Intriguing?'

'That's what I said. But out there, tryin' to catch the Boers. Livin' in the saddle, day in an' day out. With respect, bach sir, you'd better get some ridin' lessons in. I'll show you.'

'You've been trying to show me for more than twenty years. I can ride perfectly well, now, thank you very much and, anyway, there won't be time for that. But I will need you to vet these recruits' horsemanship. We will need only the best and I shall want you to assess them all. We will only take the best marksmen, too. So we will need to get them down to the butts and I shall want you to oversee that. Lots of work to do, Sarn't Major, starting tomorrow. We go to Johannesburg to start recruiting, so avoid bars and the beer, and that's an order. Now I must see Mzingeli.'

The tracker sat and listened to what Fonthill had to say with his usual, imperturbable courtesy. When asked if he would join in fighting the Boers, he nodded.

'Yes, Nkosi,' he said. 'I do not mind that. They whip me often. The farm is looked after so I can stay. But you want me to find others?'

'Yes. Perhaps about a dozen. Good trackers, like you, and native people – ideally from both the Transvaal and the Free State – who know the veldt and who will be able to talk to the *Kaffirs* on the farms. The Afrikaners on the homesteads are unlikely to give us information but their black boys will, if approached in the right way. We need to know where the commandos ride and how many they are. Do you think you can arrange that? We can guarantee a pony for each man and good wages.'

'Oh yes. I will put out word. There could be many who will come.'

'Splendid. Start recruiting at once but take only the best. They will not be uniformed so they must bring their own work clothes. I want them able to ride with us by the end of the month.'

The next day, as Alice prepared to keep her appointment with Lord Kitchener, determined to trade information about de Wet in exchange for whatever he could tell her for the *Morning Post* on his plans for fighting this new guerrilla war, Simon and Jenkins were kitted out in new uniforms and Fonthill briefed a transport major and then an armourer on the needs of his new unit. It was decided that it should be called 'Fonthill's Horse' and Simon fought off the armourer's suggestion that each man should carry a sabre and only a short-barrelled Metford carbine as a firearm.

'Those bloody things are only popguns and will be outranged easily by the Boers' Mausers,' he said. 'And we won't be making death-or-glory charges, waving our toothpicks. I want the latest .303 Lee Enfield rifles, so cut a hole in the bottom of the regulation saddle buckets so that they can carry them.'

And, to the supply captain: 'No. We don't want regulation helmets. We shall need wide-brimmed hats, with one side of the brim pinned up, in colonial style. We are going to be irregular troops, so give us plain khaki tunics but with painted, not brass buttons. And can you put a strip of native beadwork around the base of the hat crowns? Good man. Give us a bit of style.'

On the matter of his officers, Fonthill had no choice. Two captains from mounted infantry units were seconded to him. The first, a survivor of the bloodbath that was Colenso, John Wills, was a thirty-year-old Hampshire man with a clipped moustache and quiet manner. He was diffidently enthusiastic about the task allocated to the new unit. 'We need a new approach, sir,' he murmured. 'I like the sound of it.'

The second, a twenty-seven-year-old, clean-shaven and far more boyish captain from the Warwicks, named Cecil Cartwright, had only just arrived in South Africa but he had come with the reputation of being a fine horseman who had been with Kitchener at Omdurman. 'Couldn't think of a better posting, Colonel,' he grinned, wringing Fonthill's hand.

The third of the squadron commanders was also to serve as Simon's second in command. Major Philip Hammond had been seconded – on the insistence, Simon was told, of Lieutenant General John French, Kitchener's cavalry commander – from the Hussars and had been in the van when French had stormed into Kimberley, the home of Cecil Rhodes, after he had taken his cavalry on its famous ride outflanking the Boer army. Tall, with a cavalryman's wide moustache, he seemed older than his thirty-five years and regarded Fonthill with deep-set blue eyes that reminded Simon of Kitchener's.

'Do sit down,' gestured Fonthill, in the small hut on a mine site in Johannesburg that had been allocated to him for interviewing. 'I shall be relying heavily on you, Philip, for this is my first command in the field and, although, of course, I am very familiar with action, I shall regard us as a team, if I may. So please let us start off with you calling me Simon.'

'Ah, very kind, Colonel,' said Hammond in what Fonthill immediately recognised as a cavalryman's drawl, 'but I'd rather not, if you don't mind. Would ... ah ... feel just a touch uncomfortable doing so. And perhaps not a good example to the junior officers, if you don't mind me saying so.'

Fonthill shrugged his shoulders. 'I don't mind you saying so, at all. In fact, you have leave to say anything you like to me, now or in the future. But I should tell you that I intend to command the column as a very irregular force, operating on the edge, so to speak, of the main army. I believe that this is the only way we are going to be able to match and catch the Boers out on the veldt and in the hills, where I intend to pursue them. And we shall be mounted infantry, not cavalry.'

Hammond flicked up the edges of his moustache. 'So I understand, Colonel. May I ask, though, if General French appreciates your ... ah ... views and so on?'

'French?'

'Yes. Lieutenant General John French. He commands the cavalry. I understand that you will be reporting to him.'

'I see. I have no idea because I haven't met French yet. But I have taken my orders from Lord Kitchener, who approves of the way I intend to operate. And, to repeat, we will *not* be part of the cavalry.'

'Quite so. My ... ah ... slight apprehensions

were purely based on the need for discipline in any unit of the army, particularly one operating far from base, so to speak.'

'Discipline will be maintained, Major, I assure you, although we shall not be polishing buttons out on the veldt nor having kit inspections every other day.'

'Of course not, sir. Didn't wish to give the wrong impression, don't you know. But may I raise just one other point?'

'Of course. As I say, as my second in command you are free to raise anything with me you wish.'

'Good of you, Colonel. Good of you. Yerse... It was the question of your senior warrant officer, Sergeant Major Jenkins.'

'What about him?'

'I understand that, like you, he has not served in the army for more than twenty years?'

'That is true.'

'Quite. And that he had only held the rank of lance corporal in the 24th before, in fact, being reduced to the ranks and serving time in detention.'

'That is also true.'

'Yerse... Just wondered, d'you see, if he's quite the chap to be leading the NCOs and the men. A regimental sergeant major usually has years and years of service – and good conduct, of course.'

Fonthill sighed. This is what he had feared, but he made an attempt to be ameliorative. 'I understand your question, Philip,' he said. 'But speaking of service, Jenkins was awarded the Distinguished Service Medal back in the eighties when, with me, we slipped through the Mahdi's lines surrounding

54

Khartoum to take Wolseley's message to General Gordon. And, like me, he was lashed by the Mahdi when we were captured. He has also served with me – *in a most irregular manner*,' he stressed the words, 'in the Zulu war, in Wolseley's fight with the bPedi tribe, at the battle of El Kebir in Egypt, when we invaded Matabeleland with Rhodes's force, and in China, from which we have just returned and where we got caught up in the Boxer Rebellion.'

Hammond opened his mouth to speak, but Fonthill held up his hand. 'I have seen Jenkins,' he continued, 'fight unarmed and beat a Zulu armed with assegai and shield, take on a Thug in India and kill him with his bare hands, and been grateful to him for rescuing me from a Pathan camp high in the Hindu Kush. He has saved my life countless times and if I have to go into battle here against the Boers again – as we did on Majuba Hill nineteen years ago – there is no man I would rather have with me. If our NCOs and men listen to what Jenkins has to say and follow him, then they will perform well.'

Nearby, a mining drill bumping into life broke the brief silence that ensued. Hammond cleared his throat. 'Quite so, Colonel. Quite so. I was, of course, not aware of all that. I shall look forward to meeting the ... ah ... sergeant major in due course. Look forward to it, very much.'

'Good. Now if you have no more questions, I would be most grateful if you would give Jenkins a hand when the time comes to vet our recruits in terms of riding abilities. I want only good horsemen. Jenkins is one himself and, as a

55

cavalryman, your eye will be invaluable. We hope to start doing this in a couple of days' time.'

Fonthill stood and extended his hand. The major took it, gave a slight bow and strode out of the room, spurs clanking. Simon sat down again on his camp chair, tilted it back and stared at the ceiling. This was not a good start. The army, of course, at its bloody worst!

Ah well! He and Jenkins would just have to learn to put up with it.

That afternoon, Fonthill, together with Hammond and Jenkins, interviewed the six sergeants and eight corporals who had been seconded to the new unit. They were all regular soldiers and, Simon was glad to see, not one had been put forward from a cavalry regiment. Perhaps French did not wish to spare any of his horsemen for this untried, very irregular, flying column. Fonthill didn't know and he didn't care, but he was pleased that all of them were of a certain seniority, all had been in action in the war so far and all had come from mounted infantry.

Hammond was strangely quiet during the interviewing process, merely going through their records – particularly checking to see if any had ever been demoted (they had not) – but Simon was pleased to see how easily Jenkins fitted into his new role. He asked pertinent questions such as how each man regarded the accuracy of the Lee Enfields, whether they habitually fired high or low and how and when they used the new safety catches fitted for the first time to a British army issue rifle. He also demanded to know how each man would take charge of a company about to advance on an entrenched enemy if the officer commanding was wounded or killed. Would they advance in open order or close order and, if so, what would be the distance set between each man? It was clear from the answers that these men had both suffered and learnt from the perils in attacking in close order in the early campaigns. It was also clear from Jenkins's questions that he retained enough memories of his army training – and from the many actions he had shared with Simon – to understand what was needed in modern warfare. Fonthill was proud of his man and secretly hoped that he had impressed Hammond also. Of this, there was no sign. For the major hardly addressed a word to Jenkins, after the first introduction.

For his part, Simon contented himself with hearing about each NCO's experience of the encounters they had gone through with the enemy. Here, he was learning as much about how the Boers had comported themselves in the set-piece battles as how these NCOs and the men under them had reacted. From this, it was clear to him that, even in victory – and particularly during the 'Black Week' of last spring, when the Boers had been victorious three times within seven days against forces that greatly outnumbered them – they were anxious to mount up and ride off again after their success. Even if they were part of a large army in the field, they seemed involuntarily inclined to fight on the retreat. They also did not occupy high ground, which, in theory, would give them advantages in directing their artillery and even rifle fire. Instead they dug in at the foot of the kopjes and on riverbanks, in soft soil, where the lyddite high-explosive shells from the huge British naval guns did little damage and where their own long-range Mauser rifles could fire devastatingly horizontally. Fonthill made a mental note.

The next day, Jenkins and Hammond were due to assess the riding skills of all those recruits who had passed their medical tests and Fonthill resolved not to get directly involved, but rather to observe where he could not be seen. He wished to gain some personal impression of the men's riding skills without interfering with Jenkins's and Hammond's judgement. However, he also wished to see, unobserved, how the two men got on.

Hammond's questions about Jenkins had made him face the fact that he and his old comrade now could not continue their long-standing free-and-easy relationship. He was concerned about this, for his ties with the Welshman were close and ran deep, cutting across the divide of class in a manner that a man like the major could never understand. He would raise the matter with Jenkins as delicately as he could and it would have to be delicate because he certainly would not wish to upset his comrade. Jenkins's reaction when first hearing that they were both to rejoin the army showed that he, at least, had immediately foreseen the problems. For, however irregular the unit, the relationship between a commanding officer and his regimental sergeant major must not be capable of being misconstrued. Simon realised that he should have considered this more carefully before allowing himself to be bullied into acceptance by Kitchener. However, the die was cast now and throwing Hammond and Jenkins together without a word to the volatile Welshman first could be like putting a flame to dry tinder. But how to do it?

The officers and Jenkins had been given small bell tents each to themselves at the mine site in Johannesburg while they were recruiting, with slightly larger, communal tents being allocated separately to the sergeants and the corporals. That evening, Fonthill sent a message asking Jenkins to visit him at his tent after the evening meal.

Simon had uncorked a bottle of Scotch when he heard a familiar cough outside the tent flap. 'Come in, old chap,' he shouted.

'Evenin', sir,' said Jenkins deferentially. 'Difficult to knock on a canvas flap, ain't it?'

'Pull up that camp chair. And, when we are alone, I would prefer "bach sir" to "sir", any day. Now that I'm loftier than God as a colonel and commanding officer, however, when others are present I'm afraid it will have to be just "sir". I do hope you understand, 352 ... er, sorry, S'aren't Major, sir.'

'O'course I understand, bach sir. Good Lord, does that 'appen to be a bottle of whisky in the Colonel bach's 'and, by any chance?'

'Yes it does. I don't suppose you'd care for a dram?'

'Well, only a taste – to see if it's all right for you, like.'

Fonthill poured out two heavy measures and raised his glass to Jenkins. 'To Fonthill's Horse and all who ride with them.'

The Welshman reciprocated: 'To Fonthill's

Horse and particularly to their commanding officer and regimental sergeant major.' The two raised and clinked their glasses. Jenkins downed his in one gulp.

'Which reminds me,' said Simon refilling his glass. 'For God and my sake do *not* get drunk on this posting, 352. Particularly with Major Hammond about. In fact, I need to tell you about him...' And he related his conversation with his second in command.

'Ah, yes.' The Welshman wiped the fringe of his moustache and nodded his head. I 'ad a bit of a feelin' about 'im. Probably a bit of a discipline ... disciplinity ... discap...'

'Disciplinarian?'

'That's what I said.'

'Yes, I think he probably is. I can handle him all right and everything depends upon how he behaves once we are in action. But he is undoubtedly a conventional cavalry officer and they can be the worse reactionaries, you know.'

'I think I know what that means, but I'm not sure.'

'Dyed in the wool. Of the old school.'

'Ah yes. That's what I thought.'

'But there is something else. Lieutenant General Sir John French is in charge of the cavalry arm under Lord Kitchener and I am to report to him, which doesn't exactly delight me, because I am insisting that Fonthill's Horse are not cavalry. I haven't met French yet and he certainly sounds like a fighting soldier. The general obviously thinks so and the man has added to his reputation considerably by dancing round the main Boer army and capturing Kimberley behind their backs, so to speak.'

'So...?'

'So I have a feeling that French might just have placed Hammond with us to keep an eye on me, so to speak. If that is right, I don't like the sound of it at all and I shan't tolerate it. But I don't want to look for trouble with the man, for Hammond could be very useful to me as a second i/c, given his experience. But – and here's the point – stay on the right side of him, 352, because he might use you to get at me, if you know what I mean. Don't stray out of line. And we must observe the niceties in public, you and I, so please remember that too.'

Jenkins nodded slowly. 'Very good, bach sir. I know you was goin' to offer me another drink but, given the ah ... niceties ... I shall refuse it, see.' He rose to his feet. 'So goodnight, Colonel bach. And good luck in this blasted war. I shall be looking out for you, as always, look you.'

'Good luck to you, my dear old 352 – and I shall be looking out for you, too, be assured of that.' The two comrades shook hands and Jenkins ducked his head and left the tent.

With more than a hundred men to assess, the horse trials began shortly after dawn the next day. A temporary ring had been cleared on the outskirts of the mine and twenty or so of the tough little Basuto ponies, captured from the Boers, had been gathered together and saddled. Already waiting and under the care of two of the sergeants were a line of recruits. Arriving equally early, Fonthill walked down the line, engaging

61

every third man or so in a brief conversation. A little later, keeping out of sight, he noted the arrival of first Jenkins and then Hammond, whom Simon was glad to see that 352 saluted smartly. Then the two men began talking earnestly, obviously planning the equestrian tasks to be set. Fonthill breathed a sigh of relief. At least the day seemed to have begun equably.

The men to whom he talked were a strange mixture. Mostly they were incomers to South Africa: British, Canadians, Australians and a smattering of New Zealanders, mainly of farming stock but who had come to earn better money in the gold mines of the rand – typical uitlanders, in fact. All claimed to have grown up on horseback and with hunting rifles in their hands and with a strongly acquired dislike of the Boer burghers of the Transvaal who had denied them a vote in their new home. They welcomed a chance at last to fight them. The newest arrivals, however, were the most interesting. They had sailed at their own expense from Britain to Cape Town and travelled north to army headquarters to enlist. Some were ex-officers and wished to enlist as 'gentlemen rankers' and, as they said, to 'fight for the Empire'. Fonthill made a mental note of them.

Then he took up his position behind a tree and watched as Hammond, Jenkins and the sergeant put the men through basic exercises to test their horsemanship. Fonthill had agreed that the tests should be fairly elementary for there was much to do in just a couple of days. The men were asked to mount and dismount, walk, trot and then gallop their mounts around the ring and then take a couple of low hurdles. It soon became clear that most of the would-be recruits' claims to be horsemen were honest and only a few were weeded out. Fonthill was satisfied with what he saw and hoped that the shooting trials would be equally rewarding. He had insisted that the foot drill and other conventional army training should be kept to a minimum. He wanted his men to be in the field as soon as possible and he desired them to prove to be an elite force, specialised in what they were asked to do: track down the Boer commandos and then corner them. He had communicated this to his officers, which had met with immediate approval from his captains and a glassy stare and brief nod from Hammond.

That afternoon he travelled back to Pretoria to consult the quartermaster about supplies and also to see Alice. She had been accredited to the group of journalists who were attached to army headquarters and he met her back at the hotel at the end of the day.

'They're a hard lot,' she said, flopping on the bed. 'Not a woman among them, of course, but I'm used to that. Battersby has been here for the *Morning Post* since the start but I've yet to see him. God knows where Churchill is. I think he's a bit of a free spirit, coming and going as he likes. I don't think he's much liked by the others. They say that his mother – *his mother* – has arrived in Cape Town, would you believe it! There's Steevens of the *Mail* and Bennet Burleigh of the *Telegraph* – them I have met before and I respect. Melton Prior is here, drawing for the *Illustrated London News* and then there's Henry Nevinson, of the *Daily Chronicle*.'

'And how do they regard you?'

'Well, the older ones know my name from the early campaigns, of course, and they've all read what I wrote from China, so I think there's a grudging respect, but,' she pulled a face, 'there's a touch of "what the hell is a woman doing out here?" about them, despite all that. Mind you,' she grinned, 'when they read that I've already met and interviewed de Wet and had a good session with Kitchener they will have to stick their prejudices down their riding boots.'

'Quite. How *did* you get on with the general?'

Alice sat up and swung her feet over the edge of the bed. 'Haven't seen him yet but it sounds as though he's a stuff box, of course – very correct and he clearly hates the press, just as Wolseley used to. I don't think I can tell him much about de Wet, because we didn't have much time with the man, but I would think he is going to send French back down to the Crown Colony, in case there is another attempt at invasion there.'

'Sounds plausible. I suppose that could involve my column.'

'Indeed. Have you had orders yet?'

'No. I am waiting to meet French, who is somewhere down in the south.'

'So you don't know when you will take to the field?'

'No. We are not ready yet, in any case. We have only just begun recruiting and training. But we will not have time for the luxury of polishing and honing the men. Kitchener wants us out and riding soon, probably within less than a month.

There is much to do.'

Alice nodded sympathetically. Then she frowned. 'Simon, you will be careful, won't you?'

'Careful? Well, of course I will. What do you mean, exactly?'

She looked at the ground for a moment and then directed her level gaze back at him. 'My darling, I cannot think of anyone more brave or capable than you, but riding as a two-man army – just you and Jenkins – way out on your own, acting on your own initiative, is one thing. Commanding a regular army unit in the field is another. It will demand skills and attributes which will make new demands on you, my love. So be cautious, I beseech you.'

Fonthill stiffened slightly. 'I am aware of the problems, Alice, thank you. I shall act with ... ah ... care, I assure you.'

'Of course you will.' She smiled. 'And you will end up as one of the most unlikely field marshals the British army has ever seen. Now.' She leant forward. 'What of your regimental sergeant major? How is dear old 352 shaping up?'

'Remarkably well, I think. But there could be a problem or two there.' And he related his first brush with Major Hammond.

Alice listened carefully and nodded when he had finished. 'Tread warily, my love. It won't help you if I upset Kitchener, so I will step carefully in that direction myself. I suppose the days of our old freedom are over. We shall just have to buckle down, won't we?'

The next three weeks passed in a blur of activity for Fonthill, preparing his command. One hundred and twenty men were selected from the volunteers who had presented themselves and they were divided into three squadrons, each consisting of two troops. Simon soon realised that his three officers were insufficient for the needs of the unit and he immediately commissioned all of his sergeants to be subalterns and commanders of the six troops, under the squadron leaders. Hammond immediately protested against this but he was overruled by Fonthill, who repeated that he wanted battle-hardened men for this role, whatever their backgrounds, and explained that there was no time, anyway, to transfer men from elsewhere.

The column moved out onto the veldt, camping out in the rain, sleeping without tents and living on basic rations of bully beef, biltong, biscuits and only the water that each man could carry in his bottle. The ponies proved to be sturdy, good-tempered and able to move quickly over the bad ground. They existed on eight pounds of fodder a day – oaties, mealies or compressed grain – compared to the twenty pounds that the larger, less equable British cavalry mounts demanded.

Given that the men were all virtually new recruits, Fonthill was happy with the way they performed during the exercises. But he was particularly delighted when, on their return to Pretoria, Mzingeli produced his native scouts. There were twelve of them, mainly from the Transvaal but four from the Free State. Mzingeli said that, between them, they covered an area almost as big as the two states and were familiar with the terrain. Most were in their thirties, tall and stringy, like Mzingeli himself, with a handful in their early twenties. Each one, however, spoke good English, as well as Afrikaans and his own dialect, and all were eager, happy to have their own pony and to be free to ride with the unit and, of course, to receive pay far higher than what they could earn on farms and on the mines.

'They can all track, too, Nkosi, I have tested them. When do we ride?'

'In a week's time. General French is arriving here in a few days' time and will probably want to inspect us all. So I am taking the command out onto the veldt for one last exercise to sharpen them up before he gets here. I shall want you and your boys to ride with us.'

The black man inclined his head. 'Very well, Nkosi. We will be ready.'


## CHAPTER FOUR

For the exercise, Fonthill set a course to the south-east of Pretoria, well past the urban sprawl of Johannesburg and out onto the high veldt, away from the roads and railway tracks. They left just before dawn and, despite the early hour, Alice came to wish them well, fluttering her handkerchief in response to the salute from each squadron as it rode by.

In the van of the column rode Fonthill, Jenkins and Mzingeli, the latter with a blanket casually thrown over the butt of the rifle protruding from its saddle bucket. Behind, Hammond, Wills and Cartwright led their squadrons within which the subalterns rode ahead of their individual troops. The black guides brought up the rear, except for three of their number whom Simon had sent ranging far ahead to ensure that the veldt was clear. This was not merely for training purposes, for he knew that he was riding into the territory of General Louis Botha, and he had no wish to fall in with a Boer commando before his command was fully trained.

They had been riding for nearly two hours when, at last, the sun peeped out from between two violet banks of storm clouds and immediately revealed the great circle of the horizon and turned orange the coarse grass that covered the plain. This was still early in the rainy season and there was little green to be seen. As they rode south now, several of the isolated kopjes were revealed, however, pointing upwards like stumpy dumplings, the tough taibosch shrub on their flanks giving a blue tinge to the sandstone. The sun had roused a couple of turquoise-headed bustards from their nests and they sailed regally by high above while, at the feet of the horses, a score of kittiwitties, tame tiny birds, sported about in the sand. The sun's rays bestowed welcome warmth on the riders and Fonthill turned in the saddle to look back at his men.

They were riding in column of four abreast and although there were no cavalry-type pennants to be seen – Fonthill had declined their use – they presented a fine sight, keeping a tight formation and the early sun lighting up their sunburnt faces.

Despite all his apprehensions – was he the man to be leading a hundred and twenty men into a war? He respected the Boers, why was he fighting them? How to reconcile a tight-arsed cavalry officer with a free spirit like Jenkins? – he tingled with the glow of the now fine morning and the pride at leading such a good-looking body of men. Being back in the regular army had its compensations after all. He felt an unaccustomed deep sense of satisfaction, of sublimation to all that surrounded him: the rolling miles of plain, the jagged kopjes, the glimpses of exotic wildlife.

'Look!' A cry from Jenkins made him turn. To their right, two springbucks, the lightest and fastest of the deer and antelope that dotted the veldt, were running with long, springy leaps. Sighting the column, they turned and bounded away, showing the pear-shaped patches of white that tapered down from the middle of their backs to their tails, the annulated horns that crowned their heads nodding as though to give them greater speed.

'Permission to hunt for the pot, sir?' asked the Welshman.

'Very well. Keep the column in sight as best you can. Mzingeli, you go with him.' And then in a low voice, 'Make sure he doesn't get lost.' Jenkins, bravest of soldiers, with the firm seat of a jockey and the accuracy of a marksman, notoriously couldn't find his way from A to B if the trail stretched before him like a railway track.

The two men gave their reins the lightest of tweaks – the Basuto ponies were remarkably sen-

69

sitive – and, to the cheers of the men, Jenkins and Mzingeli were off in the hottest of pursuits. The troopers were not merely cheering the hunt. They knew that, if the two were successful, there would be fresh meat instead of bully beef at camp that evening.

In no time, the two were out of sight and Simon called to Major Hammond. 'Philip. I know it's early, but I think we'll take a tea break to give those two a chance of getting back to us without trouble. The men may smoke.'

The major opened his mouth to speak but merely frowned and nodded. 'Very good, sir.'

After fifteen minutes, there was still no sign of Jenkins and Mzingeli and Fonthill could catch no glimpse of them through his field glasses. He cursed inwardly but reassured himself that even 352 could not get lost on the veldt with Mzingeli with him. So he gave orders for the column to mount again and continue its journey.

Hammond pulled alongside him. 'I hope you don't mind mentioning it, Colonel,' he said, 'but don't you think it would have been wise to have put vedettes out to front and sides as a precaution against being taken by surprise?'

Fonthill nodded. 'Normally, yes. But I have posted the natives out; one to the front and one either side of us. In addition, we can see for miles out here and we should be able to sight any body of men long before they come upon us.'

'Quite so, sir. It's just that these damned Boers can materialise in a flash – from a depression in the ground or from behind a kopje. And I wonder whether the Kaffirs will be as reliable as our own men as vedettes, don't you know?'

'I appreciate your point, but I think we can rely on these black scouts well enough. Ask the officers, though, to keep a keen watch, will you?'

'Very good, sir.' But Hammond rode back with a disapproving frown on his face.

The column continued its ride out into the veldt, with the sun climbing higher. Eventually, Fonthill held up his hand to halt it and called for his officers to come forward.

'Now, gentlemen,' he said, nodding to a small kopje that lay in their path, about half a mile away. 'The RSM has not returned yet, but never mind. I want to conduct an exercise. We will attack that kopje as though it is an enemy camp, well entrenched. We will gallop towards it and then, on my command, we will halt, dismount and disperse by squadron, with each squadron in open order to right and left of me and then taking the best cover available. A Squadron will disperse to my right, B and C Squadrons to my left. Every fourth man, as usual, to take the horses to the rear. I want the whole action to take place within five minutes, from mounting, the charge, the halt and dispersal. I shall be timing it. Understood?'

'Sir.'

'Good. Take your posts with your men.'

Simon watched the officers resume their positions with their squadrons and troops and then shouted, 'Column will dismount. Dis ... mount. Stand by your mounts. Prepare to mount. Mount. To the front, walk march.' Then after a few paces, 'To the front, gallop,' and then, 'CHARGE!'

This was the first time that he had given such a

71

heroic order and Fonthill felt slightly ridiculous, as, gripping tightly with his knees, he led the charge, hoping to God that his nimble little pony could pick its way safely between the potholes that pitted the surface. He had enough to do steering his mount between the red, conical houses of the ants, some of which stood four feet high and, made of compacted mud and grass, posed a frightening obstacle to a galloping horse. So he was relieved, then, when he was able to hold up his hand, stopping the charge some four hundred yards from the kopje.

'HALT!' he shouted. 'Dismount and disperse in open order. Horses to the rear.'

He took out his watch and began timing the exercise, watching the men run to right and left of him and fling themselves behind whatever cover they could find. He frowned, for the operation was going by no means smoothly, with B Squadron at first mistakenly scurrying to his right before Captain Wills screamed at them to turn around and run to his left, which forced them to scramble around C Squadron, which was already spreading out to take up firing positions.

Fonthill looked up and shouted, 'Not good en–' And stopped. Streaming around the kopje was a stream of Boer horsemen galloping in pairs and fanning out to surround the tangled column before them. Sucking in his breath, Simon did a rough estimate: a hundred and fifty, at least. No – more, for they kept coming. His column, dispersed out front in a single line, was outnumbered and shortly to be taken from both flanks and in the rear.

At the top of his voice, he bellowed a stream of orders. 'B Squadron, double to the rear and link to the others to form a circle. AT THE DOUBLE, QUICKLY NOW! End men in A and B Squadrons bend round to complete the circle. Horse handlers, double back and get your mounts to lie down in the middle. Trackers go and help them. A Squadron at the enemy at front, OPEN FIRE! FIRE AT WILL!'

Were they in time? He watched, heart in mouth as the horse handlers ran, pulling their horses behind them, and with the trackers slapping the flanks, into the centre of the rough circle formed by the rest of the troopers, who were half running, half scrambling to close the ring. Then, blessedly, the men of A Squadron, who had been the first to their positions, opened fire on the rapidly closing enemy.

Simon blessed his luck that the Boers had appeared from round the furthest point of the kopje, so that in splitting to encircle the column, a line of the horsemen had to ride parallel to where A Squadron were lying. The range was comparatively short and the fire from the prone men immediately brought down a dozen or more of the Boers. Even so, enough of the horsemen thundered by to rein in, leap from their saddles just where the defensive ring was being linked together and to open up a devastating fire on the men of B Squadron.

The other file of horsemen were firing as they galloped round to complete the encirclement and bullets hissed by Fonthill's head as he stood desperately trying to direct the movement of his men. But, fine marksmen as they were, even Boers could not accurately fire from the backs of galloping horses and he remained unscathed, standing long enough to be sure that the defensive ring had been completed, albeit with gaps on the farthest side of the ring, where B Squadron were lying.

Hammond appeared at Simon's side. 'Get the men to take cover behind the anthills,' Fonthill shouted to him. 'Bites are better than bullets and the Boers will pick 'em off if they are lying in the open. Did each of the men ride out with fifty rounds?'

'I believe so, sir.'

'Well, I bloody well hope so. That was the order. The Boers are not going to rush us now that we are in some sort of defensive position. They will try and outshoot us, creeping nearer all the time. Tell Wills and Cartwright to tell their men to husband their ammunition and keep their heads down. Fire only when they see a target. The enemy will try to make us expend our ammunition.'

'Very good, Colonel.'

The major doubled away, crouching. The horse handlers had done a good job and only a handful had been cut off by the Boers. Amazingly, in the middle of the shooting, the horses were lying still, their handlers lying among them, soothing them. Fonthill knew that the Boers would take care to avoid hitting the ponies, for they would be anxious to take them as prizes.

Head down, rifle in hand – Fonthill was grateful that he had decided not to carry the Webley revolver that was the officer's formal side arm –

he hurried to where Wills, the commander of B Squadron, was crouching.

'How many men have you lost, John?' he asked, trying to adopt a matter-of-fact tone. He had no idea of how these men would react to what was clearly a tight situation and it was important to set a good example.

'About ten, so far, sir. I think five of them fatally, as best I can see.' Wills replied in an equally sanguine tone. Simon looked at him sharply, then remembered that the man had spent a whole day lying on the veldt in the hot sun at Colenso, where the Boers from their trenches had shot any man who lifted his head or arm more than six inches. 'It's the wounded that's the problem, though, Colonel. The Boers are keeping up...' he ducked his head as a bullet thudded into the anthill behind which he lay '...a pretty heavy fire as you can see. We just can't get to the hurt chaps.'

'Damn! Well it can't be helped. The Boers won't rush us while we have ammunition, so conserve it. They won't enjoy lying out here in the sun any more than we will.'

He nodded and crawled on, dodging between whatever cover he could find, until he came up to Cartwright. 'Casualties, Cecil?' he asked.

'Not too bad, sir, so far. One man killed and another two wounded, although only lightly.' The young man grinned. 'I thought the Boers would be better shots than that.'

Fonthill nodded. 'Don't underestimate them, my boy. See that your men return the fire but take no risks. It will probably be hard pounding for the rest of the day, but I think they'll ride off

75

when they find that we are not easy pickings.'

Simon continued his circuit of the ring, exchanging words with each man he passed and stopping to talk a little longer and encourage the subalterns. They, all ex-sergeants and survivors of several actions, were cool and composed, he was glad to see.

Eventually, he was back to A Squadron and crawling up to its commander, Major Hammond. 'Casualties, Philip?' he enquired.

'Two men dead and four wounded, one of them badly, I fear.' The drawl was still languid, although perspiration was slipping down the major's forehead as he lay, his revolver poking round the side of an anthill. 'Pity we've lost our regimental sergeant major, though, Colonel, don't you think?'

Fonthill nodded his head. He recognised the comment for what it was, an implied rebuke. But he did not rise to the criticism. 'Jenkins will be back,' he said, 'and hopefully bringing fresh meat for dinner when we've sent this lot riding back from where they came. But it will be hard work until then. The point is that although I estimate that we are facing a whole commando out there and we are outnumbered, the Boers cannot afford to take heavy casualties. So far in this war they have avoided this whenever they could. So once they see we are determined and have plenty of ammunition, I believe they will ride off.'

'Well, I hope you are right, sir. But we are not exactly in a good position, I fear. Not too much cover, don't you know. They can pick us off.'

Fonthill glanced around. 'Hmm. Can't see a

better position that we can move to, under this fire. And I don't see anyone riding to our aid. So we will just have to stick it out. My feeling is that the Boers might try just once to rush us – they're not exactly bayonet men, remember – and then ride off when they fail. So we must try and preserve our ammunition until then. We won't be here all day.'

In fact, Simon was far less sanguine than he sounded. With eight men dead and eleven wounded, his force had already been severely reduced. To be pinned down on the open veldt behind inadequate cover and under fire from the finest marksmen in the world was not exactly the best way to exercise his untested men. The longer this situation lasted the more his force would be eroded by the enemy fire. He did a quick estimation. Perhaps they could hold out for a couple of hours more, but it all depended upon how long the ammunition lasted. He had ordered that each man should ride with at least fifty rounds, but Hammond did not sound at all sure that this order had been carried out. And where the hell were Jenkins and Mzingeli? He grabbed his field glasses and raised his head to risk a quick scan of the kopje and surrounding veldt. Nothing. Had they been taken by the Boers? His heart sank at the thought. Then he shook his head. Not Jenkins. He was indestructible.

A second thought struck him. He had not given a thought to the native trackers he had sent out as scouts. They would surely have encountered the commando, or at least seen evidence of their presence on the veldt. It would be difficult to hide the tracks of two hundred men or more. He was thankful that he had resisted the impulse to arm the trackers, for, if they were taken, the Boers would surely shoot them. But would the enemy recognise their ponies as being Boer mounts originally? That could well be the signal for executions. Well, he had other things to worry about for the moment.

Fonthill crawled back to where the depleted B Squadron were lying, reasoning that this was the weakest section in the ring. He found a declivity in the ground, nestled his rifle stock to his cheek and sighted along the barrel. The Boers, of course, were using smokeless ammunition, as they had done since virtually the beginning of the war. As a result, it was incredibly difficult to pick them out, so good were they at maximising whatever cover the veldt could offer. Then he saw a small black object move about a hundred and fifty yards ahead. He fired but had no idea if the shot had found a target, for he had to duck his head quickly as several answering bullets hissed over his hat.

Would the Boers try and rush them? That's what British troops would do. But then the soldiers of the Queen were trained to use the bayonet...

As if on cue, he heard a guttural command in Afrikaans and then the Boers rose from their positions and began to half stumble, half run towards the British positions. They were alarmingly close, far closer than Simon imagined they could have reached, given the fire that B Squadron had been able to mount. Obviously, however, it had not been severe enough and he

78

cursed the order he had given for ammunition to be preserved.

He screamed: 'Select your target. Rapid fire!'

Having deserted their cover, however, this time the Boers presented easy targets at such short range. The rapid fire of the troopers decimated the front rank as it picked its way between the potholes and, without hesitation, the men behind turned and ran for their lives.

'Keep firing, dammit!' shouted Fonthill, as his men raised a feeble cheer.

He turned towards where Captain John Wills was lying. 'Good shooting, John,' he cried. 'I don't think they'll try that again.' But Wills did not respond. His head had fallen to one side and a neat black hole had appeared in the centre of his forehead, from which a thin trickle of blood was oozing.

'Oh, hell!' He crawled to the man's side, but Wills, the seasoned survivor of the massacre at Colenso, was quite dead. Fonthill looked round. 'Lieutenant Forbes,' he called. One of the newly promoted ex-sergeants, lying further away in the ring, raised his head.

'Sir.'

'Captain Wills has been killed. Take command of B Squadron. Please check casualties and let me know how many men you have left and the state of your ammunition. Keep your voice down. I don't wish the enemy to hear–'

Then he was interrupted by a voice from the Boer lines. 'English,' it cried. 'A truce for half an hour while we bring in the wounded. Yah? What do you say?'

Fonthill looked up. About one hundred and fifty yards ahead of him – still infuriatingly close – a rather portly man was standing with a white handkerchief tied to his rifle. He looked at first glance remarkably like one of Simon's men in that, unlike the majority of the Boer burghers who dressed like farmers, he wore a smart, high-buttoned khaki tunic, riding boots and a wide-brimmed hat, turned up to the crown at the side. His beard, again unlike that of most Boer soldiers who seemed to emulate biblical figures, was neatly trimmed into a European-style Van Dyke cut.

Simon rose. 'Very well,' he called. He pulled out his watch. 'We will resume hostilities at 11.15 a.m.' Then he turned to his men. 'Squadron commanders. Nominate six men from each troop to tend the wounded. Leave the dead where they are for the moment.'

He had heard, however, that the Boer guerrilla commandos had begun to trick the British troops by donning captured British uniforms and even firing under cover of white flags. He added, therefore: 'Do not send the men out, however, until the Boers begin to retrieve their own wounded. The rest of your squadrons should watch their front at all times.'

There seemed no subterfuge at play here, however, for the Boer lines immediately came to life with burly, tweed-suited men advancing to where their wounded were lying, many of them now beginning to cry pitifully. The British wounded, of course, had not left their lines but the cruel enemy fire had prevented anyone reaching them where they lay behind anthills and rocks and now it was possible to give them first aid.

Fonthill made a mental note that his command, designed to move fast and be self-contained, possessed no medics – no one trained in even elementary first aid, let alone more sophisticated medical treatments. He kicked himself. His lack of experience as a field commander in the regular forces was beginning to show!

He called to his officers to gather round him. They stood, a silent group in the middle of the ring, where the horses were now beginning to become restive, rearing their heads, neighing and shaking off the administrations of their handlers. Looking at them, Fonthill was glad to see that, despite the heavy shooting, not one of the animals seemed to have been hit – another testimony to the Boers' accuracy.

'Any further casualties?' he demanded. Since the last count, two more men had been hit, in addition to Wills, although not seriously.

'Good,' he responded. 'I had expected more.' He looked closely at his officers. He had led them into what could well have been a trap and he felt his inadequacy keenly. No one, however, seemed to regard him critically, although Hammond, as usual, did not catch his eye but was staring away into the distance. 'What is the state of the men's ammunition?'

All reported that an average of some fifteen to twenty rounds per man had been expended, leaving each with thirty to thirty-five cartridges.

He nodded. 'We don't want to be caught in this way again. It will have to be seventy rounds per man the next time we ride out. However, gentle-

81

men, my estimation is that we have given as good, if not better, than we have received and that the Boers have taken a bit of a hiding. They certainly will not try to rush us again. I believe that, once the wounded have been gathered in, they will keep up a more desultory fire and slowly withdraw until they mount up and ride away. What do you think, Hammond?'

'That sounds reasonable, Colonel. Will you ride after them?'

Fonthill shook his head. 'No. They still probably outnumber us and I doubt if we've got sufficient ammunition to fight a pitched battle. Also, of course, our men are still fairly new to this kind of thing. Although I think they've done remarkably well, I wouldn't want to expose them again just yet. For one thing, we lack medical support and that must be remedied.'

There was a murmur of agreement, then Captain Cartwright spoke. 'That Boer chappie who asked for the truce and who seems to be their leader.'

'What about him?'

'Well, sir, I have a feeling that he's General Botha, the chap that gave us such a hiding at Colenso and Spion Kop. I saw a photograph of him in the *Illustrated London News* before I came out and he looks remarkably like him. Quite a distinctive figure, don't you think, among that bunch of farm labourers, what?'

Fonthill's interest was immediately roused. 'Yes, indeed. Well, let me investigate. I may be able to learn something.'

'Careful, sir.' For the first time Hammond

showed some concern. 'These Boers can be a tricky lot. Here, take my revolver.'

'Thank you, Philip.' Simon tucked the Webley into his belt, then looked at his watch. 'Eight minutes to go. If they shoot me, then make bloody sure that we fire back, eh? And make sure our wounded are being treated.' He smiled and strolled out behind the fringe of the circle towards where the Boers were kneeling, tending their wounded.

Immediately, the Boer leader strode towards him.

Fonthill held out his hand. 'Fonthill,' he said. 'Colonel.'

'I am Louis Botha,' the Boer said, more formally. 'How do you do?'

'Ah, General Botha. I have heard so much about you and I am delighted to meet you, although I could have wished for more sociable circumstances.'

Botha smiled faintly. His English was perfect. 'And you, I believe, are the Fonthill who was on Majuba Hill all those years ago. I heard that you had arrived in South Africa. So Lord Kitchener has set you to catch us, yah?'

Simon marvelled at the speed at which news spread in the Boer ranks. He made a mental note that, although the commandos in the field acted individually, they obviously had an efficient system of inter-unit communication. He grinned. 'Well, it seems that I have succeeded, although,' he looked around, 'I am not sure who has caught whom, exactly.'

'Quite so.' They stood in silence for a moment

83

and Fonthill had the impression that the Boer general was a man of few words. He drew out his watch. 'Forgive me if I leave you soon, General,' he said. 'The truce will be over in a moment, so I should return.' He looked quizzically at the rather well-rounded figure before him. 'How long do you think this stupid war will continue?' he asked.

'Until, Colonel, you leave our country. We shall continue to fight as long as you deny us our freedom.' He stood looking at Fonthill with a level gaze.

Simon nodded. 'But your main army has been defeated,' he said, 'and the capitals of both states have been occupied. You are completely outnumbered in the field. Don't you think that it is an unnecessary waste of life,' he gestured at the bodies around them, 'to continue with this guerrilla warfare?'

'No, sir, I do not. While there are British troops in our country we shall continue to harass you. You don't seem to understand. Your professional soldiers occupying our states here live to fight. We fight to live.' He gave a half smile. 'Colonel, you are outnumbered and surrounded. I suggest it is you who should think now of saving life and surrendering to us. That would be no discredit to you.'

Fonthill shook his head. 'We have plenty of ammunition, General, and I must tell you that your shooting today has not lived up to its reputation.' He had a sudden thought. 'And I should add that, before you appeared from behind that kopje, I had sent off my regimental sergeant major and our

84

chief tracker scout back to Johannesburg to suggest to General French that he should reinforce us, as we had heard that you may be in the vicinity. So I am content to stay here until relief comes.'

This was a ploy. If Botha had captured Jenkins and Mzingeli, they would have taken their horses and their rifles and turned them loose on the veldt, for the commandos rarely took prisoners. If this had happened, then Botha would surely tell him that his messengers had been taken and that relief, therefore, was not to be coming. But the Boer merely smiled and shook his head.

'We will stay too,' he said. 'Now, good day to you, sir. Please rejoin your men.'

They exchanged courtly half bows and, with one look around to assess the Boers' strength, Fonthill strode back to his circle.

'What have we been able to do for the wounded, Philip?' he asked of Hammond.

'Just applying field dressings, that's all, I fear. But there are surprisingly few, after all. The Boers shoot to kill, so although we've picked up nine dead, including poor Wills, the ratio of wounded to fatalities is surprisingly low.'

'Very well. I estimate that we have inflicted more casualties on the enemy than they on us, but we are still outnumbered. Their commander is, indeed, Botha, so they are well led. They will probably hang on for a while, trying to further reduce our numbers and/or make us run out of ammunition. So we must be prepared.'

As though to underline his words, a shot rang out from the Boer positions, hissing past Fonthill's head. He and Hammond immediately fell to the ground and Simon crawled to where Forbes was lying, with B Squadron.

'Are you all right, Forbes?' he asked.

'Right as rain, sir. If we keep our heads down, I reckon we should be all right.' He paused for a moment, then: 'Pity we've lost the RSM. I hear he was a rare fighter.'

Simon felt his stomach move again. 'Oh, I don't think we've lost him.' His words sounded hollow to him but he pressed on. 'Something must have happened, or he would have been with us. Perhaps he lost a horse on this rough terrain.' He pulled clear his field glasses and tried to focus on the veldt, in the direction from which Jenkins had ridden out. He could see nothing and risked exposing himself for a second to scan the kopje ahead of them. Was it his imagination, or did he catch a glimpse of movement in the taibosch shrub, about a third of the way up the rock? It was difficult to see and certainly not possible to stay focusing more sharply, for the Boers had resumed firing.

The thought of losing Jenkins and Mzingeli now closed in on him, as he lay fumbling in his bandolier for more cartridges. Perhaps Botha had, indeed, come upon the Welshman and the tracker and the two had put up a fight, ending in their deaths. This would be typical of Jenkins. The Boer might well have chosen not to admit this – particularly if Mzingeli had survived and they had executed him for being armed. Simon shook his head, slipped the rounds into his magazine and tried to sight his rifle.

Then a cry from further along the line made

86

him turn his head. A trooper was pointing at the kopje. 'Firin' from up there, sir,' he said. 'I'm pretty sure of it. It looks as though the Boers 'ave climbed up to get a better shot at us.'

'No, sir.' The trooper's neighbour shook his head. 'Whoever's up there is fightin' at the bleedin' Boers. Look.'

Fonthill rolled over onto his back and attempted to focus his binoculars up the rock. Then he saw it. Two gun flashes. Then, two more from positions a little way to the right. He counted ten seconds and then two more shots were fired from different positions. He scanned the Boer lines. He saw the barrels of two rifles elevated upwards from behind an anthill. The Boers were indeed firing back at whoever was attacking them from up the kopje. And yet *six* men seemed to be firing down. Who could they be?

Hammond's voice called across to him. 'Colonel, I think they are leaving. Look.'

Fonthill rose to his knees. In the mid distance he saw horses being brought up and Boers mounting them. As he watched, one of the horsemen fell from his mount as a gun flashed from the kopje up above. He now saw the backs of the enemy as the Boers scrambled back; they were slipping away as silently now as when they had crept up to encircle the troopers.

'They are retreating,' Simon shouted. 'Fire as you see them. Take out those horsemen at the back. Don't let them get away unscathed.'

Once again a scattered cheer came from the British lines and it seemed to be echoed faintly from a little way up the rocky flanks of the kopje.

Some of the men in the ring were now standing the better to aim and others were waving their hats in triumph.

A moment of doubt flashed through Fonthill's mind. Were the Boers mounting to gallop to the base of the kopje, to climb it and dislodge the men firing down on them? But no. They were now streaming away to the east, in the direction from which they had first appeared. And they were riding fast, heads down, whipping their ponies. In minutes they had disappeared, not circling away round the base of the kopje but stretching away, across the veldt.

Simon nodded his head. Botha had believed his story about sending for reinforcements and must have thought that the little party up on the kopje were the advance guard for French's approaching force. But who were the marksmen up on the rock? Too many to be Jenkins and Mzingeli. He must find out. He called for his horse.

Disregarding cries of warning from Hammond and any thought of Boers still remaining to act as a rearguard for the main body, he galloped towards the kopje. At its base, he reined up and looked up.

'Who are you?' he called.

A familiar voice answered. 'We're fifteen battalions of the old 24th Regiment of Foot and we're all dyin' for a beer, look you.'

'Jenkins! Where the bloody hell have you been? And who else is with you up there?'

''Ang on, bach sir. We'll come down and all will be revealed in a minute, see.'

A feeling of huge relief surged through Fonthill

88

as he sat in the saddle, grinning like a clown and trying to catch a glimpse of the figures above him. Eventually, just as Hammond joined him, he saw first Jenkins and then Mzingeli emerge from the belt of scrub and scramble and slide down the remainder of the rock. They presented a sorry sight, for their clothing was torn and their hats seemingly lost. Perspiration poured down their faces but they each still carried their rifles.

Fonthill dismounted and, with Hammond present, resisted the temptation to embrace them both. Instead, he shook their hands. 'Where are the others?' he asked.

'What others?'

'There were at least six men firing. I saw the shots.'

A great smile split Jenkins's face. 'Ah bless you, ba ... er ... sir. I remembered one of your old tricks. So old Jelly an' me fired an' moved, fired an' moved, to give the impression that we was more than just two, look you. It affected our shootin' a bit, 'cos we only downed about four of the bastards, but we 'ad to be quick, see.'

Fonthill exchanged looks with Hammond, whose normally solemn face was now carrying the trace of a smile. 'Well, you fooled me and the Boers. They must have thought you were a relieving force. So what happened to you out on the veldt?'

'Ah yes.' Jenkins's jowls seemed to sag for a moment. 'Sorry to be late back reportin' like, sir. My 'orse broke 'is fetlock when 'is foot caught in one them rat 'oles or whatever they are and I 'ad to shoot 'im. We also 'ad to give up our chase of

89

them springbuck animals. Jelly's pony 'ad to carry the two of us and we was on our way back when we 'eard shootin' in the distance. We 'id the 'orse round the back there and climbed a bit of a way up the koppey thing to 'ave a look and saw that you were in a bit of a mess. So I made old Jelly 'ere an 'onery member of the 24th Regiment and we decided to attack. So to speak. But, before you say anythin', sir, I would like to point out that we didn't get lost.'

'No,' said Fonthill dryly. 'You had Mzingeli with you. Come on, let's get your horse and rejoin the column. We have wounded to get back to our base.' He nodded to the tracker. 'Well done, Mzingeli. We seem to have lost the three scouts I sent out. Any idea where they might be?'

'No, Nkosi. I hope Boers do not meet them.'

'So do I. Come along. We must move.'

In recovering Mzingeli's mount they discovered a small pool surrounded by a few stunted trees, so Fonthill ordered the horses to be watered there. The Boers had ridden off without their dead and, as usual, their wounded, for they knew that the British would look after them. A burial party was mustered to bury the enemy dead, after their bodies had been searched and their identity noted so that their relatives could be informed, but the British were wrapped in capes and slung across horses to be taken back to Johannesburg for interment. The lightly wounded were ordered to ride back but those who could not were carried on makeshift stretchers, made from wood from the trees near the poolside and slung between two horses.

This mournful task completed, the column turned back for the base that had been established for it at the mine outside Johannesburg, but this time Fonthill took care to set scouts riding far to the front, on each flank and the rear. They had been on the move for an hour before the first of their black trackers rode in and, in quick sequence, the second and then the third. The third, who had been riding point, far ahead of the column, on the march out, reported that a Boer commando had been seen riding fast to the east.

'Humph!' snorted Hammond. 'Now he tells us.'

They eventually reached their base just before dusk. The wounded were taken into care and the men were dismissed. Fonthill scribbled a quick note to Alice, in Pretoria, and then settled to write his report, not without some anxiety. He had seemed, after all, to have ridden into a trap and had not set out conventional vedettes to safeguard his column against just such an attack. As a result, nine of his men had been killed, including a squadron commander, and thirteen wounded, some eighteen per cent of his command. In addition, he had lost five horses, taken by the Boers before the handlers could regain the ring when first attacked.

However, he made the best of it. The Boer dead totalled eighteen, with a further seven left wounded. The enemy had, indeed, had slightly the worst of the engagement and had left the field first – an important factor in judging in military terms the success or otherwise of an encounter. He commended Jenkins and Mzingeli for their initiative and his men for their coolness

91

under fire. At least there had been no panic.

He completed his report by candlelight in his tent, late that night, adding a request that a doctor plus two medical orderlies should be added to his column, put it in an envelope and sealed it. But to whom should it be addressed? Lieutenant General John French was his immediate superior officer but he had no idea where he was located. He sighed, scribbled French's name on the envelope and was about to retire when he heard a familiar cough outside his tent flap.

'Come in Sergeant Major,' he called.

'Saw your light on, bach sir,' said Jenkins, ducking through the narrow opening, 'and thought I'd just come and wish you goodnight, see.'

'Pull up that canvas stool. The bottle is underneath it. I think we've both earned a dram. Here are two glasses.'

'Ah well, if you insist.' Jenkins uncorked the bottle and poured two generous measures. 'What's next then, for us?'

'We await the pleasure of General French. But I have no orders and don't know where he is.'

'Ah well, bach sir. I can tell you that. I 'ear that 'e is due to arrive on the train tomorrow midday. I expect 'e will want to thank you personally for putting the wind up that Botha bloke.'

Fonthill sighed. 'I doubt it. But I suppose I shall have to report myself to him. You know, 352, I'm not sure I like being back in the bloody army, after all.'

They sat in silence for perhaps a minute and then Jenkins drained his glass and wiped his moustache with the back of his hand. 'Ah well. If you remember, like, I did express a mild doubt about it myself.'

'So you did. So you did. But time to turn in now. I am probably going to be carpeted by a British general tomorrow for the first time for ... what? Oh, nearly twenty years. It will seem like old times. Goodnight, old chap.'

'Goodnight, bach sir.'

# CHAPTER FIVE

Alice had decided that she would prefer not to join the rest of the foreign correspondents under canvas in the cantonment that had been reserved for them in Pretoria, near the chief of staff's headquarters, and she had retained the hotel room she shared with Simon in the heart of the little town. She was not daunted by discomfort and it was, of course, more expensive, but she wanted to preserve her independence and have somewhere for Simon to stay when he was not riding out with his column. Luckily, money was no concern because the *Morning Post* had agreed very acceptable terms with her and, anyway, she and Simon had been left well endowed following the deaths of their respective parents some two years before.

She had cabled her first story, describing the brush with General de Wet and painting a word picture of the Boer commando: their bucolic rusticity clashing with the militancy of their rifles and bandoliers; the paucity of their provisions lashed to their saddles; the incongruity of de Wet's Prince Albert's watch chain linked across his tunic and the civilian briefcase tied to his saddle pommel. She had led her story, of course, with his hint that the Boers would be looking to infiltrate the porous border with the Cape Colony. To her surprise, the official censor – a rather pompous little major – had let it through without demur. She made a mental note that he would probably be in hot water for that but she tossed her head at the thought. That was his problem. She had received a congratulatory cable back from her editor, welcoming her and demanding more.

More to the point, Alice now sat sucking her pencil to report on her meeting with Lord Kitchener. Predictably, he had played his cards close to his chest but his decision to 'clear the veldt' of the farms supporting the commandos had become common knowledge and she questioned him closely on this.

'Where, pray, will you put the people you take from the farms?' she asked.

Kitchener had crossed one highly polished, booted leg over the other and had glared at her with those intimidating blue eyes. 'They will be well looked after, madam, I assure you.'

'Yes, General, looked after, but where and how? Clearly, women and children cannot be left on their own on the veldt to scratch a living from the land amidst the charred ruins of their farmsteads?'

'Camps, madam. Camps. We are intending to concentrate them in camps, mostly near the rail-

94

way lines, so that we can supply them easily.'

Alice scribbled away. 'Concentration camps, you say. Will they be allowed to move freely, coming and going, so to speak?'

Kitchener cleared his throat. 'Ah ... not exactly. That would detract from the point of detaining them. They will be retained within wired compounds, in huts that we shall erect. But, I assure you, they will be well looked after.'

Alice frowned and looked up. 'What? You will put women and young children behind wire on the open veldt, with the rainy season coming on? Won't this seem to be an overreaction? The great military fist, so to speak, crushing the Afrikaner civilian population?'

The general's countenance betrayed not a flicker of emotion. 'Not at all. These people have been giving succour to their menfolk in the commandos who are raiding our lines of communications and our camps. The only way these Boers have been able to continue the fight out there on the plains is with the support of their families, giving them food, water and other comforts. We could not allow this to continue. It may be rough justice but it remains justice. People back home will understand that.'

Alice sat forward. 'Now let me get this clear. You intend to clear the veldt of these farms – a huge task, I would have thought, on its own. But surely this will free the men of the raiding commandos from any worry about their womenfolk and families back home. They will know that they are being fed and watered and this leaves them with even greater freedom to ride across this vast

95

country, continuing the war that we were assured was now virtually over?'

Kitchener remained unperturbed. 'That may be so, but this will give us a counterbalancing freedom to hunt down these commandos, for they will be denied food, relief mounts and so on. They will have nowhere to go for such essential succour. We shall be on their tails, night and day, following them, outnumbering them and harassing them, until, eventually, each one will be cornered and either made to surrender or to stand and fight. We shall starve them out.'

Alice shook her head slowly. 'Cruel, General. Cruel. After all, they are only defending their country.'

'You may put it like that, madam. Others would say that they are an arrogant, reactionary minority who have shown no leanings towards democracy in their governing and have, indeed, evidenced brutality to their black peoples. If it is cruel, then, I fear that war is always cruel. The majority of the Boers have already surrendered honourably and agreed terms with us. These raiders are now virtually stubborn outcasts who have only themselves to blame for the hardships they are imposing on their kith and kin.'

Alice had left the general with a feeling that she had perhaps gone too far in criticising his strategy and even revealing that she was pro-Boer. A mistake, for journalists were supposed to be strictly objective – although most of them out here with the army, she had observed, were jingoistically supportive of the British Government and its policies in the field. Sitting now, sucking her pencil, she frowned at the thought that she might have compromised Simon's position. After all, he was no longer an independent freelance only loosely attached to the army. He was now a serving officer, sworn to serve the Queen and obey the orders of his superiors. Damn! She really should have curbed her tongue.

She applied herself once more to her story, going back over what she had written and making subtle alterations, painting Kitchener in a less doctrinaire light, making him seem more aware of the potential problems of housing the Boer families. Then, with a curse, she tore up the pages and rewrote again, quoting Kitchener directly and using her scribbled notes (oh, how she wished she had learnt shorthand!) to transcribe his exact words as best she could. She read what she had written with satisfaction. If this was going to get the general into trouble back home, then so be it. She must report what she had heard. On Kitchener's head be it.

She finished her story and then re-read it, to ensure that she had presented it in efficient cablese, for the *Morning Post* was careful with its money. Then she tucked it into her hand valise and walked out into the late evening sunshine.

Almost immediately, she was accosted by a tall, casually dressed youngish man – perhaps in his early thirties – who doffed his wide-brimmed hat and half bowed. 'Miss Griffith, is it not?' he enquired.

Alice inclined her head. 'Yes?'

'May I introduce myself. My name is James Fulton. I am a colleague. Like you, I have just

97

arrived. I shall be covering for the *Daily Mail*.'

Immediately, Alice regarded him with interest. The *Mail* had been launched only four years before by the Harmsworth brothers and had become an immediate, indeed sensational, success. Costing only a halfpenny, compared with the one penny charged by most other London dailies, it was now the first British newspaper to be printed simultaneously in both Manchester and London and its sales were now rumoured to have reached well over half a million copies. Lord Salisbury, the Tory prime minister, had condemned it as 'a newspaper produced by office boys for office boys' and it was unashamedly populist in tone, aiming for a readership of the newly literate lower middle-class market resulting from mass education, and setting out its stall with human interest stories, serials, features and competitions. But Alice cordially disliked it for its patriotic line on the Boer war, slavishly supporting the government's policy. It was thunderously jingoistic. She held out her hand, then, to Fulton, with a degree of reserve.

He took it and held it rather too long. 'Delighted to meet you, Miss Griffith,' he said. 'I have been an admirer of yours for so long.' His moustache was trimmed unfashionably to a thin line and his good teeth flashed as he smiled, looking up at her through his lashes as he bowed over her hand.

'How kind,' responded Alice distantly. The man was tall, with a handsome figure, accentuated by the white shirt opened sufficiently to show a suntanned chest and the beginnings of tightly curled hairs. His breeches were perhaps a little

98

too tight and his hair, bleached by the sun, fell in waves to meet the side whiskers. He was, she concluded, far too handsome for his own good. Nevertheless, she felt a faint stirring of ... what? Attraction? Certainly a feeling she had not experienced for many, many years. She shook her head in a tiny movement of self-disgust.

'But you have Steevens reporting here, surely?' She knew him to be one of the most experienced of the war correspondents.

'Ah, you have not heard. He died, I'm afraid, during the siege of Ladysmith. That's why I am here.'

'Oh, I am so sorry. I had not heard. I don't hunt with the pack, you see. I wondered why I had not met him. I respected him.' Alice cleared her throat and withdrew her hand from his. 'Tell me, Mr Fulton, have you ... er ... covered many other campaigns with the army?'

'No, ma'am.' He flashed his teeth again. 'I am very much a new boy at this game, don't you know. Until now, I have been trying to keep up with the *Daily Mail*'s passion for domestic crime, the strange doings of country clergymen and all that sort of thing.' He clutched his hat to his heart as though to emphasise his veracity. 'I am going to need all the help I can get out here, my dear Miss Griffith, so I do hope we can be friends.' His eyes were of the softest brown, reminding her of Simon's, although his eyelashes were longer. Much longer.

'Of course, I like to be friends with all my colleagues. But we are all competitors, too, you know. You will find, Mr Fulton, that this is a very

competitive ... er ... game. Yes, very competitive.'
She forced a smile. 'But these days I am no threat
to anyone. As you can see, I am now very much
the eldest of the correspondents out here. Nothing more, really, than a middle-aged housewife.'

Immediately, she cursed herself inwardly for
sounding arch. Fulton pounced instantly on her
false modesty.

He reached out again for her hand, but she kept
it to her side. 'Well, ma'am,' he said, 'if I have to
have a ruthless competitor, then I could only
wish for one so charming and, may I say, beautiful – as well, of course, as skilful at the ... er ...
game we play.'

Alice blushed. 'No, Mr Fulton,' she said firmly,
'no. You may not say that. Too many compliments,
I fear. They are out of place here,' she gestured at
a platoon of infantry who marched by, rifles
resting on their shoulders, 'where we are reporting on death and misery. I wish you good day, sir.'

She gave him a bobbed half curtsey and cursed
herself again for accompanying it with a smile in
return for his. He called after her, 'Good day,
Miss Griffith. I look forward to us meeting again
soon.'

'At the game we play...' She mused on his words
as she strode towards the censor's office. He was
clearly skilled at verbal dexterity and double
entendre, particularly with the opposite sex. Oh
dear! She shook her head as she walked. She did
not wish to have an admirer on this campaign, it
would all be too complicated, just too much
damned trouble...!

Alice Fonthill had never, of course, been unfaithful to her husband in thought or deed since their marriage. Nevertheless, she had always been aware that she retained her attractiveness to the opposite sex and, as a journalist, working in a strongly dominated male field, she had never shrunk from using her looks to extract information and to nail her story. But gratuitous flirting was not for her. She tossed her head. Particularly at her age – and with someone what, fifteen years younger? And yet Fulton was attractive, there was no doubt about that. Damned attractive. She found herself humming a little tune as she stepped forward to meet the pompous major.

Some twenty miles away, on the southern fringe of Johannesburg, Simon was visiting his wounded troops in the field hospital when a message was handed to him. It stated that Lieutenant General French would like to see him immediately. He enquired of the orderly when the general had arrived and was informed that he had just disembarked from the train from Pretoria, having visited General Kitchener there on his arrival from the Cape Colony earlier in the day.

Fonthill nodded and buttoned up his tunic, loosened at the collar to give some respite from the heat. French moved fast! As, indeed, was his reputation. Simon knew that the cavalryman was considered to be the up-and-coming man of the top command in South Africa. He and his bright young chief of staff, Major Douglas Haig, had been the last soldiers to escape from Ladysmith before the besieging cordon closed in. At forty-seven, just two years older than Fonthill, he now commanded a full division and had led five thousand horsemen, including mounted infantry, on that mad dash to take Kimberley – answering the ultimatum, it was whispered, of Cecil Rhodes, who had threatened to surrender the town to the surrounding Boers unless the freeing of his diamond mines were given top priority in the British army's surge north.

It was, then, with keen curiosity that Simon regarded the man sitting writing at a trestle table in a bell tent erected very near to the horse lines. It seemed that the cavalryman liked to be near his horses.

French stood and beckoned him forward. He looked every inch a horseman. At just under medium height, he was thickset, with large jowls and a bull neck. His legs were bowed, almost in cartoon caricature of a cavalry general. He held out his hand to his visitor but his eyes did not smile.

'Do sit, Fonthill.' He gestured to a stool opposite the table. 'I've read your report. Quite a skirmish you had out there.'

'Yes, General.' Simon deliberately refrained from offering a 'sir' at this stage in the conversation. He was anxious not to dilute his independence by appearing too submissive. 'I wish I could have reported a more positive result, but I am happy to say that we just about had the better of it.'

'Hmmm.' French looked down at what was obviously Fonthill's report. 'Why did you allow yourself to be taken by surprise? You knew, I presume, that you were in Botha's territory?'

'Yes, that is why I posted vedettes out in front and on the flanks of the column. But Botha somehow slipped through or around them to attack.'

French fixed him with a unblinking gaze, his pepper-and-salt moustache set in a grim line. 'But you did not post proper vedettes. You sent out native scouts, when the situation surely demanded posting trained cavalrymen who knew what they were about. You cannot expect Kaffirs to do that sort of work.'

Fonthill made a mental note. His report had only stated that he had posted scouts in the van and on the flanks. He had not mentioned the nationality of the vedettes. Someone must have informed French of the ethnicity of the men. Hammond...?

'I must point out, General,' he said, 'that none of my men are fully trained yet. The purpose of the exercise was to train them. Under the circumstances I do feel that they comported themselves well. As for the natives, my experience both in the Transvaal War and when invading Matabeleland with Jamieson was that good native scouts were unparalleled in this sort of work. I have to confess that I do not know how they did not pick up Botha's tracks on this occasion and I am currently investigating why this was so. But I do take your point, and my vedettes will be troopers in future.'

'Very well.' French's features remained set in a faint scowl. He looked down again at the report and then back at Fonthill. 'I see you allowed your warrant officer and chief scout to pursue game. Wasn't this ill-advised, given, once again, that you were in Botha's backyard, so to speak?'

'In hindsight, possibly yes. But I have driven the men hard in training – we have been given very little time to get up to operational level – and this has involved living on hard tack when out on the veldt. I felt that fresh meat would be a well-deserved treat for them. If Sergeant Major Jenkins's horse had not become injured and had to be put down, he would have only been away for less than ten minutes.'

A silence fell on the two men as French's gaze returned to the report and Fonthill studied the canvas roofing of the tent. Eventually, the general put down the paper and pushed it to one side.

'I'm afraid that I have to say that you have not exactly made a good start, Fonthill,' he said, his face remaining firmly set. 'I do not regard the loss of nearly twenty per cent of your command as a fair price to pay for the damage you inflicted on the enemy.'

Simon felt his temper rise and fought to remain in control. He was, after all, back in the bloody army...!

'I am sorry that you feel that way, General. Forgive me if I don't agree with you. My command was – and still is – fresh to battle and our training was not complete when we met up with a Boer commander who the world knows has already humiliated British forces considerably larger than his own. Nevertheless, we did, in fact, inflict greater damage on him than we sustained and he fled from the field. Knowing how few the Boer commandos are in number compared with the forces now pursuing them, I would suggest that their losses will have far more impact on them than mine will have on our numbers overall. I would like to add that I was proud of the way the men fought and have every confidence in them for the future.'

Once again silence fell on the tent. But French's expression softened a little. 'Hmmm. How are your wounded coming along?'

'Very well, thank you, sir.' He conceded the title of respect as a concession to the general's slight relaxation in attitude. 'The surgeon reports that none of them is in danger. Would you care to visit them? I know the men would appreciate it.'

'Ah ... er ... yes. I will make the rounds this evening. Shall we say 6 p.m.?'

'Very good, sir.'

'Fonthill...'

'Sir?'

An expression of something approaching embarrassment slipped for a moment over the general's features, then was replaced by his set-piece frown. 'I am familiar, of course, with your record and reputation, both of which, ah, does you credit, of course.'

'Thank you.'

'But ... ah ... you have not had experience, of course, of regimental command, since, indeed, you were a subaltern all those years ago – and then you would only have commanded at platoon level, no doubt.'

'That is quite true.'

'This war, as you know, is not at all over yet. We shall have much hard riding and hard fighting to do before we have cleared the country of these commandos, deploying as they do these guerrilla tactics and their knowledge of this vast and very unforgiving country. Do you ... ah ... consider yourself suited to command a column in the field, fighting in this very unconventional way? Eh, what?'

Fonthill clenched his fists and drew in a deep breath. 'It is quite true, General,' he said, keeping his voice level, 'that I lack experience of command in the field. But I do have considerable experience of warfare and of fighting quite unconventionally in many parts of the Empire over the last two decades. In fact, as I understand it, this was the very reason that General Kitchener invited me to come to South Africa to help in this new type of warfare.' French opened his mouth to speak but Simon pressed on. 'In fact, he led me to believe that I had more to offer than most line officers who, he felt, had already shown themselves to be rather constrained by tradition and ... what shall I say ... a *regimented* approach to fighting. "Playing the Boers at their own game", I think was the phrase he used. If, however, you feel that, even at this early stage, I am not what *you* want in this campaign, then, of course, I must offer my resignation. Except that, of course, I must insist on submitting it to General Kitchener himself, since he commissioned me.'

French held up a conciliatory hand. 'No, no, Fonthill. I fear you misunderstood me. It has certainly not come to that.' The general looked uncomfortable and shifted in his chair. 'Ah, no. I merely wished to ensure that you have the confidence to continue. Which ... er ... clearly you have. And this is most important, of course, because I

106

have work for you. Ah, yes, indeed.'

Fonthill forced a smile. 'I am glad to hear it, sir.'

French nodded and leant forward, speaking now with more ease. 'You will know of the situation, I believe. The Boers are seeing the way in which General Kitchener is going – the burning of the farms and the placing in detention camps of Boer civilians, so that they can no longer provide support to the commandos.'

Simon nodded.

'It is quite clear, therefore, that the enemy must try a new tack. It can't continue to use the high veldt up here in the north as its playground – raiding our columns and camps, blowing up the rail lines and so on and then disappearing back to their farms for supplies before swooping down again. It won't win the war.'

'Quite so.'

Now French became almost agitated, pushing back his chair and gesturing with his pen. 'There is, then, only one way it can go, effectively.'

'To the south?'

'Exactly. To the Cape Colony.'

Fonthill nodded. 'Of course. When I met de Wet he virtually said as much.'

French's frown returned. 'You have met de Wet?'

'Yes. I had a slight brush with him.' He described the circumstances.

'I see. Hmmm. You regained your horses, you say. Well, I congratulate you on getting the better of him. He seems a most resourceful chap, although I don't like his methods. Now, back to the Cape. As a British colony, of course, the

107

support for the Boers there is far less strong and so there can be no question of us burning the farms. However the Dutchmen in the country, outside the cities, have sympathy with these rebels and, indeed, our minister there, Milner, is very worried about a possible uprising. We must therefore make every effort to see that none of these commandos gets through to the Colony in force to rouse that support. D'yer follow?'

'Yes, sir.'

'Now, the Boers have tried to do this before – Hertzog, Kritzinger and de Wet himself have had a go but we have managed to drive them all back north of the Orange. Their aim was and remains to unify and reorganise the surviving, scattered Free States bands holed up in the tangled mountains of the Eastern Cape, then cut through to the Western Cape and set the Cape alight, so to speak, maybe even preparing the way for a full-scale invasion of the Colony. Do you get the picture?'

'Yes, indeed.'

'Right. How quickly can you ride out again?'

'Well, give me a day to replenish our supplies – oh, and find a doctor and a couple of medical orderlies. I trust that will be in order?'

'Yes. Talk to Kitchener's staff about this. Say I said so. A new medical corps has just been formed and they have new medics up there in Pretoria. So ... when could you saddle up again?'

'Two days' time. There won't be time to replace the dead and wounded but we will still be a viable force.' Fonthill felt a quick moment of apprehension. 'Will we ride out with you, General?'

'No. I must stay here for a day or two.'

Relief flooded through Simon and he made a strong attempt to keep it from his expression. Riding under French's close supervision would have been abhorrent to him. 'What are my orders, then?'

What was almost a smile twitched French's moustache. 'I hope that they will be welcome to you, Fonthill. I want you to chase your old friend de Wet. He has linked up with Steyn, the president of the Orange Free State. We did believe that, with Smuts, they would attack the mines at Johannesburg but our intelligence tells us that that is out of the question now. Our forces are far too well entrenched there for them to try that. We understand that de Wet and Steyn have recrossed the Vaal here,' he unrolled a map on his desk and stabbed a finger on it, 'and are making for Bothaville on the Vaal, where the majority of the Orange River Commando are waiting for them. Then, they will make for the Cape Colony border.'

'How many men will there be in the commando?'

'About eight hundred, we believe. It will be a formidable force. We understand that they have four Krupps field guns, a pom-pom, plus artillery that the Boers captured from us – a fifteen-pounder and a twelve-pounder.'

'Hmmm.' Fonthill gave a rueful smile. 'Bit of a mouthful for my lot to digest, I fear.'

'Oh dammit, Fonthill.' French's irritability returned. 'I am not expecting you to take on this commando with your little column. No. Your job is to find 'em and lead our men to them. We have Major General Charles Knox with a large force roughly in the area. But his column, I know, will move too slowly to catch de Wet unless we can lead him by the nose to him. That's your job.'

He gestured to the map again. 'We believe that the commando will be somewhere around here. But, of course, we can't be sure. Get down here as soon as you can, Fonthill. Get your native scouts out and track this bloody man down. On no account must you attack the commando yourself but make contact with Knox and lead him to our quarry. It's difficult country so it won't be easy but it's vital that we nail de Wet. He's beginning to make a fool of us. Can you do it?'

'I believe I can, sir.'

'Good.' French stood and held out his hand. 'Good luck to you, Fonthill. Now, I must ask you to excuse me because I have some orders to give. I will see you at six tonight.'

Back at his tent, Simon immediately summoned Mzingeli.

'Have you had a chance yet of examining the men we put out as vedettes and finding out why they missed the Boers?'

The tracker's face betrayed no expression. 'Yes, Nkosi. They say they saw no tracks, except when Boers were riding away.'

Fonthill frowned. 'I can't believe that. They were split out wide on either side and then to the front. The Boers were too many to leave no tracks and they came at us from the front. Do you believe the men?'

'No, Nkosi. I think that when they out of sight of column they bunched together to talk and laugh, probably on left of column.'

'What makes you say that?'

'Man on left of column funny man. People like to be with him. Others join him, I think.'

'Are you sure?'

'Yes, Nkosi. Others tell me that.'

'Ah. Very well. Dismiss all three.'

Mzingeli's eyebrows shot up. 'You want to get rid of them? No give another chance, after warning?' It was clear that the black man, so used to generosity from his employer, was shocked at the severity of the sentence.

Fonthill sighed. 'Those days are over, Mzingeli. You saw that we were fighting for our lives against the Boers out there. We cannot afford any slipshod work from the trackers. This will be a warning to the rest. Do what I say.'

'Very well, Nkosi.'

On the fourth day after the column's return, it set out again, this time heading due south. Four white troopers were set out as vedettes, to the front, left, right and behind the jingling horsemen. At the head, Fonthill rode, his face set and hardly exchanging a word with Major Hammond, who rode behind him.

## CHAPTER SIX

Fonthill's first aim was to find Major General Knox who, with his division, was stationed somewhere to the north-west of the little town of Kroonstad in the middle of the Free State. Knox had doggedly pursued de Wet for more than three months now, without pinning down the Boer leader to a fight. The point now, however, was to stop de Wet and his commando from crossing the Orange into the mountains of the northern part of the Cape Colony.

As he rode, more taciturn now but keeping his eyes ranging over the plain, Simon pondered the gossip he had picked up in Johannesburg about the state of affairs in the Cape, the oldest and most prosperous of the South African colonies. The British powers in Cape Town were terrified of a possible wholesale rebellion by the considerable number of Boers living and working in the Colony. An invasion by well-equipped and well-led commandos could ignite such a revolt, give new hope to the Transvaal and invigorate and unite the scattered Boer units operating in the Orange Free State. If de Wet was planning to springboard his invasion by gathering his forces together on the banks of the Vaal, he had to be hit hard before he could consolidate.

But where the hell exactly was de Wet? It was big country down there, fringed by mountains, and a man who could slip two and a half thousand men, plus wagons and cattle, unseen between large forces of waiting British troops, could be comparatively invisible now, given the geography. Fonthill frowned. His black trackers were going to have to prove their worth now, there was no doubt about that.

The need to move fast was strong, but Fonthill decided that he would not force the pace unduly, for he was anxious not to tire the horses. Hard

112

riding could be demanded of them once they caught up with the fast-moving Boers. It was three and a half days, then, before his outriders reported that General Knox's camp was within sight.

Knox proved to be a bluff, conventional senior officer, completely in the mould of Queen Victoria's army. Red-faced, with a fiercely waxed moustache, he welcomed Fonthill, however, with genuine warmth.

'Can't find the little bugger anywhere, my dear feller,' he confided. 'We've been in touch with his rearguard regularly enough further north, with one or two scraps, but they've always held us off long enough for his main laager to move off before I could come up with the main body. Then, they all slip away. Very frustratin', yer see. Feller never stands and fights and he moves very fast.'

'I presume you have scouts out now, General?' Riding through, Simon had detected a certain permanence about the division's camp, with cooking pots bubbling over open fires between the lines and men lounging in their cotton long johns. He wondered how quickly the men could break camp and follow a lead.

'Of course. Combin' the countryside.'

'Are they troopers or black chaps?'

'Oh, troopers, of course. Can't trust the Kaffirs to bring us information.'

'And are they calling on farms?'

'Of course.'

'Forgive me for pushing this, sir, but the Boer farmers, even if they're not fighting, are unlikely to betray the commandos, wouldn't you think?'

'Eh, what? Well, you might be right but we're

113

offering a reward, so I would think that they would give us a lead, don't you know.'

'Well, I'll off-saddle my men now, sir, but I shall push out patrols from dawn tomorrow and explore all along the Vaal. De Wet should need the river for water if he's got eight hundred men. And I'll have my black trackers go off ahead. They might pick up something from the Kaffirs working on the farms, who might not have much time for their employers, from what I hear.'

'Do what you wish, Fonthill. I will give you a free hand, but stay in close touch with me here.'

'Very good, sir.'

Well before dawn, Simon sent off his trackers individually to scour the area. Giving them provisions, he instructed them to ride far, sleeping on the veldt and not to return for three days, unless they picked up a lead. Then he split his command into troops, sending three troops to cross the Vaal and explore along the far bank, while the other three ranged along the north-west bank.

For three days they found nothing. Simon then realised that a commander as astute as de Wet would be unlikely to camp on the riverbank, where his options for a quick retreat would be limited. He would be more likely to concentrate his men around an isolated farm, away from the river, perhaps in a fold in the hills. He instructed his troops and trackers accordingly, riding out himself on the fourth day with Jenkins and the newly promoted Captain Colin Forbes and his B troop.

It was November now and the miseries of the rainy season were fading, with the promise of summer showing. The veldt was turning a verdant green before the sun burnt it brown and offering good pasture for oxen and horses. Good, thought Simon. Perhaps de Wet would stay feeding his men and his laager that little bit longer, before committing himself to the inhospitable territory of the Cape border.

He was on the point of ordering the troop to return to base when a black horseman appeared from the north, riding fast. He reined in, his horse lathered with sweat, and spoke urgently in Bantu to Mzingeli.

'He say,' reported Mzingeli, 'he think Boers are camped on a farm, near a ruined village called Bothaville near Valsch River, not Vaal. Lots of them. He could not find Kaffir to confirm but he saw enough Boers to think it a big commando. They have wagons and big guns.'

'How far away?'

'About twelve miles. He can lead us there but needs a fresh horse.'

'Get him one, Sergeant Major. Forbes, get me six of your men who can ride fast.'

Simon looked to the west and saw that the sun was beginning to dip in the sky. They had about an hour and a half before darkness.

He made a quick calculation. There was no hope of summoning Knox in time for an attack that day and he would be lucky to find his other troops in time for them to gallop back to him before the light went completely. If the tracker had seen artillery, then this must be de Wet's main commando, so he would need every man he could summon if he was to consider an attack able to stop the commando slipping away again.

That would have to be just before dawn, he reasoned, when perhaps the commando was still sleeping or at least drowsy – if, that is, de Wet had not inspanned his oxen already and moved after the tracker had left – perhaps even because he had been seen and the alarm given.

Simon gave his orders quickly when the six troopers cantered to him. Five were to find the other troops – he knew roughly where they would be – and order them to move quickly back to him at a point some five miles ahead. The sixth was to ride like hell back to Major General Knox and ask him to move forward quickly to Bothaville. He would attempt to detain de Wet long enough for the main column to come up.

Then he paused for a second. What was it French had said? 'I am not expecting you to take on de Wet with your little column...' He shook his head. Needs must. The fact that Knox had never pinned de Wet down was probably because he moved too slowly. Well, that wiry Boer with his briefcase, farmer yet most efficient fighter, would not get away this time. Fonthill would attack at dawn.

The troopers galloped away and Simon looked back at his little command: just fourteen men. There was not much he could do with that number but when the other troops came up, perhaps they had a chance – if, that is, the Boers were taken by surprise. He motioned for the troop to move forward at a canter, following the tracker on his fresh horse.

Fonthill was aware that Jenkins had edged his

116

pony to be alongside him. 'What's the plan, bach sir?' he asked quietly.

'It looks like it's the main commando, 352. If it is – and whether it is or not – if they're still there I intend to deploy around them, as best we can in the dark, and then attack just before dawn.'

'What, with fourteen men?'

'Don't be silly. The others will be with us soon. Then we'll send the tracker on ahead, with Mzingeli, to reconnoitre the position. I reckon we've just about got enough men to hold them down, for a time, at least.'

'Blimey. How many men in that commander thing?'

'About eight hundred.'

Jenkins nodded solemnly. 'Ah. Pretty good odds, o'course. Should be easy.'

Simon grinned. 'Oh, quite easy. The point is, we'll take em by surprise, probably when most of the Boers are still sleeping and they will not know how many we are.'

'But they will 'ave guards out, for sure.'

'Maybe. But remember what happened the last time we met this fellow. The guard was asleep. The Boers are good fighters, but as farmers they are not disciplined in the way of a regular army. We'll gamble on that. But if they do have guards out, we'll just ride through 'em.'

'Very well, Colonel. But just remember to grip the bloody 'orse with yer knees if we charge. And don't let go of the reins.'

'Thank you, Sarn't Major. What splendid and original advice.'

Jenkins sniffed. 'Well, I promised Miss Alice

that I would look after you an' shoot you in the leg if you did anythin' stupid and brave. Sounds to me as though this attack comes under that 'eadin', look you.'

'No. Shoot the bloody Boers, not me. And you know I can ride as well as the next man now.'

'That maybe so, if the next man's not very good, see.'

'Get on with you, or I'll have you shot for insubordination, look you.'

It was just before dusk when the first of Fonthill's troops came riding in, led by Major Hammond. Then the others followed quickly. Simon looked around. He had about a hundred and twenty men (they had managed to take in some half-trained replacements for the wounded before leaving Johannesburg). He immediately called a council of war with the officers and explained the position.

'Surprise is the essence, here,' he said. 'So, once the trackers report back, we shall dismount and deploy in the dark. Once we are *in situ*, we will remount and charge the camp.'

'With respect, Colonel.' Hammond's voice was characteristically languid. 'We can't really do a proper cavalry charge without sabres or lances, don't you think?'

Fonthill's mind immediately recorded the fact, once again, that French's man was in his camp and would be reporting to his chief. Things had better go right this time!

'We are not cavalry, Major,' he replied evenly. 'We are mounted infantry. We shall fire from the saddle and then, once we are into the camp, we

118

will off-saddle and take whatever cover we can. The aim will be to stop the commando riding off with all its trappings. There will be a rearguard, of course, but I hope we can strike terror into them all before that rearguard is able to rally.'

'Very good, sir.'

'Right. More when we know the disposition of the enemy. Now let us ride on.'

The horses walked on in the semi-darkness. Fonthill reasoned that there was no point now in wasting valuable energy and strength by trotting or cantering and also risking being unsaddled or injuring the horses on the uneven ground. He looked around him and was glad that he had instructed all horse brasses and accoutrements to be smeared with mud before leaving Knox's camp to avoid reflections from sunlight and, as now, a jingling that would carry far across the night air of the veldt.

They had been riding for some two hours in the darkness, carefully picking their way, when an outrider from the rear came galloping up. 'British troops coming up in the rear,' he reported.

Fonthill turned away and, with Hammond and Jenkins, rode to meet them. It was difficult by obscured starlight to define the size or the origin of the force but an officer carrying the insignia of a lieutenant colonel rode forward and touched his helmet.

'Are you Colonel Fonthill?'

'I am indeed. Awfully glad to see you.'

'Le Gallais,' responded the officer. 'You're not as glad to see me, Colonel, as I am glad to have found you in this light. We are General Knox's advance guard, the 5th and 9th Mounted Infantry. He got your message and sent us off immediately. He is coming on. We have been riding like hell. Where is the enemy?'

Fonthill gestured ahead. 'I think they're about a mile and a half away. They are encamped by the Vaalsch – that's a tributary of the Vaal, where, like a fool, I have been looking for him for the last four days. We've been fishing up the wrong river. It seems to be de Wet's main commando, which means that he must have President Steyn with him. He's got artillery and supply wagons with him too, and, by the sound of it, some eight hundred men. How many do you have?'

'About six hundred. And we have twelve-pounder guns.'

'Splendid. We can't wait for Knox to come up. I was going to attack at dawn. Do you agree?'

'Absolutely. We might have the blighter at last. But, with respect, I don't think you would have got far with your hundred chaps. What was your plan?'

'Don't wait to surround them because de Wet has a reputation of always keeping a strong rear-guard, and I don't want to alert them and lose the advantage of surprise. Once we are deployed, I suggest we go in strong, firing as we go, and take advantage of surprise. I understand they've got the guns in a kraal near the homestead, so we should cut them out.'

'Quite so. Well, you're senior to me, Colonel, and it's your show. You found him. We will do as you say. Let me get my fellows up and we will walk on with you. I presume you have scouts out in front?'

'Just the tracker who found them and the chief tracker. They are leading us in.'

'Very well. We will follow.'

'Can you send someone reliable back to the general and ask him to hurry here? He should be able to heliograph once he's near the camp. We could have quite a fight on our hands, knowing the Boers.'

'Of course.' Gallais touched the brim of his helmet and turned his horse.

Jenkins urged his mount alongside Fonthill's. 'Nice to 'ave a bit of company, now, isn't it? I didn't fancy attacking the whole bloody Boer army on my own, look you.'

Simon nodded. 'Yes, well you've probably lost the chance of a VC. Ride on, Sar'nt Major, and see if you can find Mzingeli and bring him back. I want to know how near we are to the Boers – and particularly, of course, if they are still there.'

'Very good, sir.'

Very soon Jenkins returned, accompanied by Mzingeli. 'Boers still there, Nkosi,' the tall man said. 'We about three hundred paces from camp. Guards seem to be asleep. My man still watching them. Everything very quiet.'

Lieutenant Colonel Gallais rode up. 'We're with you now, Colonel.' He spoke in a low voice. 'Was it your intention that we should go in on horseback?'

'Yes, to create a bit of terror and cut off the retreat.'

'Understand the thinking. But I would advise against it. My chaps, at least, are not trained

121

cavalry and I'm not sure how easy it would be to regroup them once we've charged through the camp, particularly under fire. With respect, I suggest we go in on foot, firing as we go. The surprise should still be as great, if we're lucky.'

Fonthill thought for a moment. Despite his dislike of the cavalry and his distrust of its methods, he had nurtured a vision of creating havoc as his men thundered through the camp, firing from the saddle. With a larger force, however, the result could well be chaos. He nodded to Gallais.

'Very well, Colonel. Dismount your men and summon your officers so that we can brief them here. Make sure voices are kept low and there is no noise from the harnesses. We are little more than three hundred yards away now.'

The group of officers gathered around Fonthill and Mzingeli as the tracker described the enemy layout, as best he could. The Boers, he said, were spread in a large circle around an old stone farmhouse and its outbuildings, with what appeared to be seven pieces of artillery, including two large Krupps guns, stationed within a low stone kraal. The men of the guard outpost appeared to be fast asleep – ah, that indiscipline again! – as were the rest of the burghers, coiled up under blankets on the ground.

'Now,' said Fonthill when the black man had finished. 'Colonel, please allocate a hundred and fifty men to make for the kraal to seize those guns and, as soon as you are able, bring your own guns up to fire on the buildings, because they are bound to harbour men. The rest of us will deploy as best we can around the rear of the camp and, when you hear my whistle, we will all go in firing. Tell your men to have no compunction about firing on sleeping men. As soon as they are awake, they will be a handful, for the Boers sleep with their rifles. If they get to their horses, shoot the horses. We want to reduce the number of men who get away as much as possible. Understood?'

Thirty heads nodded.

'Right. Good luck to you all.'

Silently, just as the dark sky began to lighten in the east, the British began their advance. There was little to be seen ahead in the darkness, but the smell of woodsmoke showed that a large host of men was camping ahead of them.

Simon's little band led the way, following the dim figure of Mzingeli in the van, Fonthill at his side. The officers were walking with their squadrons and troops, but Jenkins paced two steps closely behind Fonthill, his darkened bayonet fixed and his rifle carried at the trail.

Instinctively, Simon turned and grinned at his old comrade, who nodded back, his face set grimly. The grin, however, was not an honest reflection of how Fonthill felt. In fact, his mouth was dry and his stomach muscles seemed as contracted as the ridges of a washboard. It had been a long time – a very long time – since he had led men into an attack and his mind raced. Could this be the end, at last? He knew only too well how fiercely the Boers fought and, despite Le Gallais's arrival, they were still outnumbered. Was now the time for his luck to run out? His nostrils seemed to draw in the sour smell of cordite. Then he thought of Alice and his heart seemed to miss a beat. He shook his head. Enough of that! He was too old to be frightened and, of course, Jenkins, dear old 352, his friend and survivor from dozens of man-to-man conflicts, was only an arm's length away. He trudged on.

At last, Mzingeli held up his hand. Immediately, Fonthill spread his arms out wide to either side, the signal for his men to deploy. He stood still, fingered his whistle and looked behind him. After what seemed like an hour but which must surely only have been a few minutes, he saw the tall figure of Hammond nod his head. Ah, all in position! He looked to the east. The sun was just beginning to split the dark sky with golden shards of light. Time to go! He blew the whistle, waved his free arm and trotted forward, thrusting his rifle and its bayonet forward. Immediately, a great cheer arose from the men behind him and Fonthill felt his fear disappear, to be replaced by the great and familiarly exalting sensation of battle.

Hoarse shouts arose from ahead of him and he saw figures, half awake, rise from the ground and turn and run. Others, but only a few, picked up their rifles and tried to fire but were immediately shot down. So much for the posted guard! He crested a low ridge and saw that the great camp ahead of him was in a state of alarm. As far as he could see, men – some of them still half draped in their blankets – were running, seemingly in different directions. It was as though a termite's nest had been disturbed. Many had made it to where the horses were picketed. There, some just cut the halters and flung themselves onto the backs of their mounts, without attempting to saddle up, and rode away, bareback and bare-headed. Others just turned and ran.

Not all fled, however. Some, like the night guard, had rolled out of their blankets, picked up their rifles and were kneeling and firing, their extra distance from the attackers giving them time to do so. Away to his right, across a cart track, Fonthill glimpsed a low stone wall with some white buildings beyond. From this enclave a more determined fire was beginning to ensue, with the bright flashes of the rifles lighting up the top of the kraal. To the left, only some two hundred yards away, a red farmhouse, also built of stone, was being occupied by Le Gallais's men, who took shelter in it from the fire from the kraal.

'Watch out, bach!' Jenkins's cry made Simon whirl round, just in time to see a huge burgher, clad only in breeches and dirty grey vest, running towards him, attempting to work the bolt on his rifle as he ran. Fonthill fired from the hip, predictably missing, but Jenkins's bullet took the big man in the chest and he fell without a word.

'Thanks, 352,' gasped Simon. 'Keep moving forward. We've got to find de Wet before he gets away.'

Jenkins, perspiration running down his cheeks, stood still and pointed. 'Who's that, then?'

In the middle of the chaos, by the horse lines, a familiar, stocky figure was whirling his mount to and fro, screaming at the men streaming past him. As the two watched, he produced a sjambok – the Boer farmer's hide cattle whip – and laid about him, attempting to make the fleeing men stand and fight. Then the man, seemingly oblivious to the bullets hissing past his head, pulled his horse round and pursued the horsemen, whirling his whip in a vain attempt to halt the rout.

'It's de Wet, all right,' shouted Fonthill. 'Can you get a bead on him?'

'Too late, bach sir. 'E's 'opped it, see, with the rest of 'em.'

'Blast. He's got away again.'

But not all of the Boers had fled. Some were lying strewn around the campsite, either inert, or moaning from their wounds. More, however, were now standing dismally, their hands above their heads in surrender, being grouped together by Le Gallais's men. Fonthill looked around him and saw Hammond leading his squadron forward.

'Hammond,' he cried. 'Get your horses and lead your squadron after those fleeing men. De Wet's with them and probably President Steyn too. They're riding to the east. Take a tracker with you. Do what you can to catch 'em up and bring 'em back. I'm going to make sure we take their guns.'

'Very good, sir.'

The fire being exchanged between the burghers huddled behind the low stone walls which fringed a garden, its attached white building and the kraal beyond, and from Le Gallais's men in the red farmhouse, was now severe. The Boer shooting was accurate and was sweeping across the site of the camp, making it difficult for any realistic pursuit of de Wet and his fleeing men to be set up.

'It's de Wet's famous rearguard,' muttered Fonthill. 'They're doing their job and protecting their general again.'

Jenkins removed his helmet and wiped his brow

with a dirty handkerchief. 'More than that, bach sir,' he said. 'They're tryin' to stop us getting at their guns, see.' He pointed to where men could just be seen manhandling artillery into position beyond the kraal's stone wall.

'You're right. Listen. Go and find Colonel Le Gallais and get him to bring his twelve-pounders up and direct fire onto where the Boers are firing. Tell him to avoid the white farmhouse – there might be the farmer's family inside. And, of course, avoid the guns.'

'Very good, bach sir. Er ... and where would the colonel be, then, d'yer think?'

Fonthill grimaced. He remembered that 352 Jenkins, now a much respected sergeant major in Fonthill's Horse, harboured among his few failings as a soldier the fact that he had no sense of direction. 'Just find an officer and ask him to take you to Le Gallais, there's a good fellow.'

'Ah yes. Now what are you goin' to do, then?'

'I'm going to direct the fire onto the kraal. Off you go.'

'Very good, sir. Take care now.'

Fonthill had to crawl on his belly, taking a circuitous route, before he was able to reach the questionable haven of the red farmhouse. The Boers had posted snipers outside the kraal, somewhere near an old pigsty, and they, together with the men behind the wall and inside the kraal, were now shooting with accuracy and intensity. This was making the red house a place of slaughter, which it was impossible to relieve, for bullets were hissing across the open ground all around it. The doorway was open – in fact, there was no door – and as Fonthill crawled inside, he realised that it was going to be virtually impossible to get out again, for bullets thudded into the stonework on either side of him, sending out showers of splinters. It was as if small-calibre artillery shells were being fired.

Inside, he found Le Gallais himself sprawled on the earthen floor, a young lieutenant attempting to stem the bleeding from a ghastly wound in his body. The colonel lifted his head. 'Bit of a bloody mess, I'm afraid, Fonthill,' he whispered. 'Can't get at that rearguard, I'm afraid. They've pinned us down.'

'Don't talk, old chap,' said Fonthill. 'I've ordered up your guns. We should be able to dislodge them with your twelve-pounders. Now, lie still.'

Fonthill looked around. The farmhouse was a typical Boer dwelling: one huge living-sleeping room, with galleried sleeping quarters above it. From open windows and loopholes bayoneted out of the stonework, men of Le Gallais's Mounted Infantry were attempting to direct fire onto the Boers, who were crouching behind their stone walls only some hundred and fifty yards away. Le Gallais was not the only casualty. Seven other men were harbouring wounds, some of them serious. Lt Col Wally Ross, the CO of the 8th MI, was crouching with the lower part of his jaw shot away and Major Williams, Ross's staff officer, was lying, barely alive, with six bullets in his body.

'Good God,' muttered Fonthill. 'This is like a charnel house.'

The young lieutenant looked over his shoulder from where he was attempting to fix a dressing

128

on Le Gallais's chest. 'The Boers are using soft-nosed bullets, sir,' he said. 'They're exploding like bombs on the stonework. They're bastards. It's contrary to the Hague Convention.'

'I'm not sure the Boers have signed that, my boy. Keep your head down. I've sent for reinforcements. We'll soon clear them out of there.'

But it was not to be that easy. The explosive bullets of the Boer rearguard continued to crash into the fragile stonework of the farmhouse until the building itself seemed to shake and gaps appeared above the heads of the defenders. It had become impossible to fire back now and all that the men could do was to lie low, with hands covering their heads from the lethal stone splinters that flew everywhere.

'Where the hell are those twelve-pounders?' swore Simon. It was at least an hour since Jenkins had been sent on his mission and it had become clear that the white building and the kraal were protected from attack from everywhere but their front by a stone outbreak above and behind them. So it was not possible to surround the little fortress and direct enfilading fire onto the men within it. The Boers were not going to give up their guns without a desperate fight.

How desperate that fight was going to be became clear when, at last, Fonthill heard the crump of light artillery and the crack of shrapnel shells being directed above the heads of the Boer marksmen.

Simon ventured a quick and dangerous look through the open doorway and, as he watched, saw the little outlying pigsty, which had been sheltering three enemy snipers, suddenly dissolve into a cloud of red dust and stone as a shell landed directly onto it.

Even then, however, the Boers did not surrender. For at least another hour the duel continued, with shells being hurled at ridiculously short range at the men behind the walls and then into the white house behind, where they took shelter, and the Boers replying with their deadly soft-nosed bullets.

'You have to give it to them,' muttered Fonthill, lying spreadeagled on the floor, covered in red dust and stone fragments. 'They're brave men.'

'With all respect, sir,' growled the lieutenant, still holding the now inert form of his commanding officer, 'they're bastards.'

At last it was over. Simon sensed rather than saw or heard that Knox had arrived with his main body. He looked at his watch. It was eight a.m. and the fire on the compound had markedly increased. Was 352 out there? Then he heard a command and from his doorway saw men charging with fixed bayonets towards the Boers across the open ground. Within seconds, a white flag went up behind the kraal wall and what was left of the de Wet rearguard, filthy, bloodstained and half dressed, stood with their hands raised above their heads.

Suddenly a figure appeared in the doorway. 'Oh God,' cried Jenkins, 'are you still alive then, bach?'

'Almost, 352.' Fonthill painfully got to his feet. 'But there are those here who are not. See if you can get a doctor or some medics quickly, there's a good chap.'

Later, Fonthill met General Knox. He learnt that, while the battle at the kraal raged, de Wet had rallied some of his men and counter-attacked but had been beaten off by Knox's larger force. The meeting was not equable, at least from Simon's side, for, much to his disgust, Knox had given permission for the men to loot the Boer camp. There was no question of a pursuit being mounted for the escaped General de Wet, his president and the men who had fled.

'Surely, you must chase them quickly, General,' protested Simon.

'Oh, I don't think so, Fonthill. We'll never get the feller now. But by love, you did well finding him and attacking so well. This has been quite a victory, don't yer know. De Wet has lost his entire artillery. We've taken his four last Krupps field guns, a pom-pom and got back a fifteen-pounder and a twelve-pounder the bloody man took from us earlier this year. We've also captured all of his wagons. What's more, we've killed twenty-five of his rearguard, wounded thirty and captured the other one hundred and twenty. And others were wounded and killed when you first attacked. A good show, Fonthill.'

Simon shook his head sadly. Le Gallais had died of his wounds, as had many of his men. If only Knox had come up more quickly...!

Hammond returned later that afternoon. He had somehow missed de Wet's return but had picked up his trail on his second and final retreat, only to lose him again. So de Wet, President Steyn and the majority of the commando had got away once more. Was there no way of pinning

131

down this fighting Pimpernel?

Fonthill gave orders forbidding his own men from taking part in the looting and, that evening, he took count of the casualties to his small force. It had got away comparatively lightly, for it had been only peripherally involved in the fighting at the kraal. He had lost only one man killed and five wounded.

The next morning, just as Fonthill was contemplating the wearisome business of attempting to pick up de Wet's trail again, two telegrams arrived, brought up from Knox's base camp. The first, from Kitchener, congratulated Knox on 'his' victory – which, of course, disgusted Fonthill. The second, however, was addressed to Simon himself and was from General French. It congratulated him on finding de Wet and leading the attack but tersely requested that he should immediately bring his column to meet him at the little town of Machadodorp. No explanation was given for removing him from the hunt for de Wet in the Free State. Fonthill shook his head wearily. Was he being blamed for allowing the Boer leader to escape again?

## CHAPTER SEVEN

In fact, he was not. Nevertheless, the reality was worse. At a conference attended by Fonthill and the rest of French's senior officers, the general explained that he had been ordered to combine his cavalry and units of mounted infantry into one great column which would march one hundred and seventy miles north to the edge of Johannesburg to clear the countryside between the two railway lines from the south that converged there. This had become necessary, he explained, because the Transvaal had followed the Orange Free State into wholesale guerrilla war. The objective was to burn the farms, break the dams, take the cattle and so destroy the elements that fuelled the Boer resistance and enabled the raiding commandos to remain out in the field.

So began one of the most depressing passages in Fonthill's life.

He found himself and his little column subsumed into a giant force which, although mounted, bore little resemblance to the fast-moving units of cavalry with which French had founded his reputation. Burdened with guns and heavily laden wagons, this turgid line stretched for five miles and wound its way northwards at the speed of a pregnant ox. As it moved, it spread out and carried out its destructive work, harried all the way by marauding Boers, who picked at it like locusts in a cornfield, to the point where, on arrival at the outskirts of Johannesburg, French found that he had haemorrhaged a third of his wagons, twelve hundred oxen, more than three hundred horses and sustained a hundred casualties.

For Fonthill and his men, hand-picked to ride light and fast and fight the Boer commandos at their own game, the worst part of the trek was clearing the farms.

It would have been impossible to burn *every*

133

farm that dotted the veldt and the orders were to burn only those which showed open resistance, were known to have harboured commandos, or were close to the railway lines where damage had been done. Simon, ranging out from the body of the main column, deliberately spared most of the homesteads he encountered, unless he was fired upon. Nevertheless, he had his orders: farms were to be burnt to set an example to their neighbours.

The pattern, then, had often to be repeated. He would send a troop out ahead when a farm was sighted, to circle it and ensure that it harboured no antagonistic burghers. He always hoped that resistance would be met, for it made what followed easier to bear. Most of his fellow commanders, he knew, would ride up, order the family out and immediately set fire to the building and drive off whatever cattle remained, usually allowing their men to loot the homestead. Instead, Fonthill brought out the family and then ordered his troopers to help the wives and children to bring out the furniture and pile it on wagons before finding straw to set the buildings ablaze. He would then tell the family to ride to where the nearest railhead was situated so that they could be taken in care.

It was heartbreaking work. 'We didn't join for this, bach sir,' observed Jenkins, while helping a very old Dutch grandmother climb onto a rickety cart. 'I thought we was supposed to be fightin' the fierce Boer, not 'elpin' 'is family to move 'ouse, look you.'

Fonthill nodded, his mouth set in a grim line. He could not bring himself to hate the Boers,

134

despite their scant regard for observing the 'rules' of conventional warfare. In addition to their use of illegal exploding cartridges, stories were now common of the capture of armed burghers wearing British regimental clothing to add to others concerning their shooting, out-of-hand, captured unarmed Kaffirs working for the British. Nevertheless, he could not rid himself of the basic truth that they were fighting for their land, for their freedom.

He hated the scorched-earth policy that he was being forced to implement.

It was not a view, however, shared by many of his officer colleagues. Major Hammond, for instance, had immediately questioned the practice of troopers helping the families of the farmers to remove their furniture. 'Don't you think we're making it a bit too easy for them, Colonel?' he had drawled one evening as they sat at bivouac under the stars. 'Against orders, too, isn't it?'

'I didn't accept my commission to fight women and children,' replied Fonthill. 'This war is bad enough as it is, without us extending the boundaries of hate needlessly.'

He studied Hammond by the firelight. The man clearly retained his dislike of his commanding officer – and he was certainly not made to serve in an irregular unit such as Fonthill's Horse. His home was among the squadrons of the Household Cavalry, where wars were fought by gentlemen in ways that had been established years ago and had become enshrined in the annals of the regiments concerned. His questioning of the lack of sabre and lance when Fonthill had ordered a

135

charge with rifles was typical. It was clear that he could not think beyond certain well-ordered lines. Why did he not request a transfer, wondered Simon? Did he still have his orders to watch over his CO and report back to General French on his failings?

The young officers of the regular army who were serving in the more formal units in the great column were made of similar stuff, Fonthill noted. The difference between them and his own young subalterns were marked. These breezy young volunteers from the cities – not the well-endowed shires – of England and the wide-open spaces of Australia, New Zealand and the mines of Johannesburg were less contemptuous of the Boers. They were as courageous as the undoubtedly brave young regulars, but more independent in spirit and more open in mind.

Jenkins brought the subject up as he and Fonthill rode together one day in a rare moment of intimacy while on the trek.

'I 'ave to say it, bach sir,' he said, 'but yer average young British officer of the line is a bit stupid, ain't 'e?'

'And I have to agree with you, 352.'

'An' I suppose that's why yer average British general is a bit stupid, too, don't yer think?'

'Well, not all of them, of course. Certainly not Wolseley, nor Roberts or even Kitchener. But yes, I'm afraid that, in general, you are right.'

'Why is that, then, d'yer suppose?'

Simon sighed deeply. 'I suppose it goes back to the fact that, with the upper classes, the clever boys in the family did not go into the army; in

136

fact only a trifling percentage of sixth-form boys in our public schools choose the service for a profession. Boys with good income are generally jobbed into the crack regiments, like the Royal Horse Guards or the Life Guards, without any examination whatever. Now I ask you, 352, in what other profession would social position and money be allowed to override the claims of merit? Unless a boy has money of his own he cannot go into the smart regiments because the pay is too low and the standard of living is too high. And yet these regiments so often get the chance to lead in battle. All this, I think, helps to explain the tragedies we faced at Isandlwana in Zululand, at Majuba nineteen years ago and in the early days here in Natal and the Free State.'

'Yes. Right. I see all that.'

'But that's enough. I am beginning to sound like a socialist, which I certainly am not. Let's just leave it that I am very happy with the sort of young officer that we have in our own unit. Very happy.'

The purpose of the great sweep, however, was not only to destroy the farms but also to push before the advancing British lines those scattered members of the Boer commandos caught out on the veldt towards the new lines of forts that Roberts and Kitchener had set up like a great net across the plains. This was partially successful in that numbers of the burghers were caught like fish in the net and forced to surrender, but even more of them slipped through between the forts and rode out again across the veldt.

In the south, de Wet himself had seemingly not

been at all deterred by his narrow escape at Bothaville. Within days, he had regrouped, slipped between the newly built southern forts stretching between Bloemfontein and the Basutoland border and captured the little town of Dewetsdorp, named after his father. In the process, he defeated and captured the British garrison of five hundred Gloucesters and Highland Light Infantrymen. Within a twenty-five to fifty mile radius of Dewetsdorp there were five British forces, yet none of them were able to close in and prevent the town's capture. When relief did arrive, de Wet had slipped away again. How was he able to do it?

Simon learnt a little of the Boer leader's secret from a fellow officer in the Mounted Infantry, Captain Molyneux Steele, who had been captured by de Wet earlier in the year and been his unwelcome guest for several weeks before his release. The difference in military ability between the Boer leader and his own CO, Colonel Ridley, had been marked, he confided to Fonthill. Steele's capture had been completely due to the fact that Ridley had posted no scouts and was unaware that de Wet's laager was 'just over the hill'. As a result, he was easily captured as he rode, alone, across the veldt. In contrast, de Wet, the farmer, was a 'completely professional' soldier who was meticulous in methods of command.

'His hand was everywhere,' he told Simon. 'He rules his mob by the strength of his right arm and character. Superficially all was disorder in the laager, but there was order in the disorder.' There were no tent lines in the camp, no dressing by the right or by the left, but every wagon, cart and

138

tent was laid out in the same relative position, wherever they laagered. As a result, the Boers could strike camp with extraordinary speed. The whole laager could be on the move within ten minutes of the alarm or order being given.

This compared unfavourably with the British system whereby the black Africans were left to inspan the animals unassisted, harnessing twelve mules or sixteen great trek oxen to each wagon. In de Wet's laager, everyone lent a hand with the transport, as each man had been trained to do since boyhood. Discipline was also severe. Sentries who slept on duty were punished by being tied to ant heaps and shot if they moved. The general was rarely without his whip, which he employed liberally.

Steele had also been able to glimpse de Wet's method of employing his rearguard to such famed effect. 'He gets his wagons under way then places his fighting men in position,' he explained. 'Then he hands over to his second in command. After this, he gallops, usually alone, to the head of the wagons and drives back to the rearguard any skulker by fierce invective or his sjambok. Once there, he resumes command. He truly is a wonderful man, so full of energy.'

De Wet, Steele confided, hated having his commando impeded by the burghers' wagons, but, despite his orders and pleading, the Boers refused to give them up. This meant that the commando could only flee at the pace of an ox, which could barely do thirty miles a day. How, then, did the man consistently evade the thousands of British soldiers who pursued him? The secret seemed to lie in the corps of professional scouts that de Wet had recruited to serve him. The British had left this important part of field intelligence to conventional mounted troopers, but the Boer general had trained a special elite of horsemen who ranged invisibly far and wide and were acutely sensitive to the moves of the British pursuers and also to possible escape routes that might lie ahead. The combination of the speed of inspanning and early intelligence enabled the mercurial de Wet always, it seemed, to stay one move ahead of the pack baying at his heels.

Listening to all this, Fonthill was thankful that he had had the foresight to employ native trackers and also to eschew the use himself of cumbersome supply wagons. These two elements in his preparations surely had enabled him to find the elusive Boer general and to attack him. Even so, this forceful amateur warrior had escaped again and was even now, it seemed, about to cross into the Crown Colony.

It was at this point that Kitchener, now firmly in command after the return in triumph of Lord Roberts to London, hardened his policy of rounding up the Boer families left on the veldt by the commandos. Now, as he had intimated to Alice, he set in train the building of internment or 'concentration' camps specially to house not only the Afrikaner refugees, but their Kaffir servants as well. This imposed an extra burden on Kitchener's army, of course, already stretched as it was by the need to protect its long supply lines and pursue the guerrilla bands now raiding in the Transvaal as well as the Free State.

For Simon, it posed an additional moral problem. He had already decided that he would refuse to carry out any further farm burning and the prospect of his specially selected men being used now as escorts for this round-up of civilians caused him further heart-searching.

His problem was compounded by the hardened attitude of Alice, whom he had visited, of course, on his arrival at Johannesburg with the rest of French's great column. At first glad to see him, she had grown increasingly distant, it seemed, as his stay at their little hotel lengthened while Fonthill waited for further orders. She questioned him unrelentingly about his role in the farm clearances and also asked him to give an interview on the subject to a correspondent from the *Daily Mail*, which he refused to do. It was one thing to help his wife in her work, he reasoned, and quite another to extend that indulgence – at some risk to his position in the army – to a stranger. All in all, then, it was a huge relief when orders came through for him to mount up his column and ride south immediately. His old adversary, General Christiaan de Wet, it seemed, was on the loose again and was very close to crossing the border with the Cape Colony. Clearly, the Boer invasion of the Colony was now a very real threat.

Riding as hard as his care for his little Basuto ponies would allow, Simon's column reached Bethulie, close to the Orange River, the border with the Colony. General Knox had resumed his dogged pursuit and sensed that he was near to his prey. To his disappointment, Fonthill was placed under his command again. However, the general once again welcomed him wholeheartedly and immediately put him in the van of the hunt, giving him a free hand to roam out ahead of the main column.

Simon immediately sent out his black trackers to scour the area for news of the Boer. The net had already been thrown wide. Kitchener, taking strategic control of the hunt himself, had placed troops along the south, Cape-side of the Orange and drawn in other units in support of Knox, so placing a huge semi-circle around the river, enclosing most of the fords where de Wet could conceivably cross to enter the Colony. News had filtered through that the Boer leader had under his command two other daring commandants in former Cape rebels, P.H. Kritzinger and Gideon Scheepers. It threatened to be, then, a reasonably sized invasion of the Colony, rather than a daring pinprick.

It was hard riding for Fonthill's little command. Once again, he had eschewed the use of supply wagons and had confined his column to the backs of its horses in complete self-reliance, living off the country. The trouble was that the country was now wet, damned wet.

Heavy rain was marking the end of the old year 1900 when hard news came in at last. Simon, his officers and Jenkins were crouched under oilskins around a hissing fire, chewing biltong in the darkness, when a soaked Mzingeli threw himself off his horse and reported, 'Boers just the other side of Bethulie, Nkosi. Big commando.'

'Good.' Fonthill threw his remaining biltong onto the fire. 'How far away?'

'Two miles. Maybe three.'

'Saddle up, gentlemen. We will attack him at once.'

'Not on our own, surely, Colonel?' Hammond rose more slowly than the others.

'Certainly. We can stop him riding on, if not hold him completely. Sarn't Major, send a good galloper back to the general at the main camp. Tell him that de Wet is camped just to the east of Bethulie with his main commando and to come on quickly. Tell him that we are attacking him.'

Within minutes, the troopers were mounted, their heads down in the pouring rain, and setting off, following the lead set by Mzingeli and his tracker. Except for the weather, it was a repeat of Fonthill's attack at Bothaville, and as he rode, he planned his attack, remembering what Captain Steele had told him about de Wet. With his small force, he could not attempt to defeat the commando in a pitched battle. But there was, perhaps, a chance of capturing the Boer general and riding off with him. Steele had told him that the man usually slept in the middle of his commando. A strike, then, directly into the heart of the camp, crashing straight through the defences, and picking up de Wet and carrying him off in the confusion and darkness. No attempt to exchange musketry with that tough rearguard: a strike, straight to the centre and, if they could not carry off de Wet, then they must kill him. Surely, with the head severed, the snake would die.

He summoned his officers and Jenkins to gather around him as they rode and he explained his plan. There was a flash of teeth in the semi-

143

darkness from the younger men. Predictably, Hammond frowned.

'How will we know which one is de Wet?' he asked. 'These damned burghers all dress the same. How are we going to pick him out in the middle of the night?'

Fonthill nodded. 'It is not going to be easy. But Jenkins and I have met him and we know what he looks like. We all ride for the centre of the camp but the two of us will lead. Once we have identified de Wet we will capture him – knocking him on the head, if necessary, and slinging him over a horse. The rest of the column must protect us and then we all ride off, like blazes. Back the way we came. Understood?'

There was a mumble of agreement, although Hammond remained silent. The column rode on, the horses' hooves now sliding through mud.

Suddenly, without warning, there was a guttural cry from directly ahead and the night was temporarily lit by a score of gun flashes. Fonthill's horse reared as a bullet crashed into its breast, throwing him to the ground and, as he lay, winded, he was aware of men falling around him. He tried to struggle to his feet but his boots slipped on the wet earth and he felt Jenkins's arm thrusting him back onto the ground. As he lay, he realised that the attempt to capture de Wet had failed before it had been launched, for he and the Welshman were the only two who could recognise him.

Then he heard Jenkins shout: 'Dismount. Handlers, take the horses to the rear. The rest take cover. Squadrons select your targets and fire to the front. Fire at will!'

Hell! Why wasn't Hammond taking command?

Fonthill scrambled onto his hands and knees and felt a sharp thump on his shoulder which knocked him flat again and suffused him with pain. Bullets were hissing into the ground all around him and somehow he crawled to take cover behind the shape of his horse which lay inertly to his right. He lay there panting and looked around him to take his bearings. He could see very little, but enough to know that the men of the column were lying flat in the rain and robustly answering the fire that came from a slight ridge ahead of them. Except that, now, that fire had slackened and, as he watched, it flickered away and ceased altogether.

'Fix bayonets.' Jenkins's voice came from immediately to his right. 'Charge!'

Shadowy figures rose all around him and lumbered forward out of his vision. Simon dropped his cheek onto the mud and thought that he felt the thud of horsemen riding. Then he closed his eyes and allowed himself to drop into oblivion.

He came to what seemed like only seconds later and realised that Jenkins's arm was around him, gradually coaxing him to sit upright. The wounded shoulder jarred and he cursed with the pain.

'Ah, good. At least you're alive, bach.' The Welshman's voice expressed huge relief. 'Thought you'd gone for a minute, see. Nasty one on the top of the arm. Now, tuck your 'and inside your tunic, like that. Lovely. Now, we've got to try an' get you on this 'orse and get out of 'ere. Because when old

145

Wetpants sees 'ow few we are, 'e'll come back after us, as sure as God made little apples, particularly now that the bloody rain's stopped. Now. Foot up. That's right.'

Fonthill gasped. 'Where's Major Hammond?'

'Don't know. Not dead or wounded, as far as I can see. Captain Cartwright 'as taken charge. Now, make an effort. Up's a daisy. Loverly. Now 'ang on, 'cos I'm comin' up be'ind you, see.'

Somehow, through a mist of pain, Fonthill remained seated in the saddle until he felt Jenkins mount behind him, reach forward to grab the reins and then hold him steady with his other arm. In this fashion, the Welshman turned the horse and led them away, following other dim, mounted figures ahead of them.

One of them turned and came back. 'You've got the CO, Sarn't Major? Good. Well done.'

Simon recognised the nasal, Midlands twang of Captain Cartwright. 'Cecil,' he asked. 'What the hell happened?'

'Afraid we rode straight into their rearguard, which was well positioned. A Squadron out in the front caught it well and truly. My squadron and Forbes's were further back and, thanks to Sergeant Major Jenkins's initiative in taking charge at the front, we were able to deploy and return their fire. Then, when we charged, they'd gone – and from what we could see, so had the whole commando. Buggered off in a flash as soon as the firing started. But we had lost too many men to follow. I thought it best to fall back onto General Knox's main column in case the Boers turned round and came after us. If they do, we're

146

in no state to put up much of a show.'

Fonthill nodded his head. 'Quite right. Where is Hammond?'

'Don't know. As far as I know, he's missing. The only one, as far as I can see, for he's not among the dead or wounded.'

'How many men have we lost and what about the wounded?'

'A Squadron pretty well decimated, I fear, sir. They've taken all the casualties. Twenty-two killed and five wounded, not counting Major Hammond. Luckily, the wounded are all able to ride, although we've lost horses, of course. Afraid we couldn't stop to bury the dead. Just taken their name tags.'

Simon felt his head swim. Half of his lead squadron wiped out – including, by the look of it, their commander! He swayed in the saddle and felt Jenkins tighten his grip. He tried to concentrate. 'We should be able to come back and bury the dead when we meet up with the main column. Have you posted a rearguard?'

'Yes, sir. Although how anybody can find anybody in this bloody weather, I just don't know. It's come back raining harder than ever. Could be Birmingham.'

'Or bleedin' Rhyl, see.' Fonthill felt Jenkins's hot breath on his neck and forced a grin. 'I think, Cecil, that as soon as we can find a kopje or clump of rocks, we should halt and form a defensive ring. If de Wet does decide to counterattack, rearguard or no rearguard, we will be pretty vulnerable strung out like this.' A sudden stab of fear struck him. 'Did Mzingeli survive? Is

147

he still with us?'

'Oh yes, sir. I've posted him with the rearguard at the back.'

'Thank goodness for that. Fetch him back and send him ahead to find a decent place for us to stop and regroup.'

'Very good, sir.'

Fonthill and Jenkins rode in silence for a while. Eventually, the Welshman spoke in a growl from just behind Simon's left shoulder. 'Are you thinkin' what I'm thinkin', bach sir?'

'How would I know, until you tell me what you're thinking?'

'Where was bloody 'igh an' mighty Major 'Ammond, when the shit was flyin'?'

'Don't be disrespectful. Anything could have happened to him in this dark and rain.' But the same thought had been going round in his head. Hammond had been right behind him in the van as they approached the Boer lines. Could he have been hit in that first fusillade? If so, why wasn't his body found when the wounded and dead were assessed? He hoped to God that, somehow, he had not been overlooked and was not lying back there, wounded and in pain.

Within half an hour, Mzingeli had ridden back to suggest they deviate to the right where rocks had been strewn across the veldt, fringing a declivity which would offer protection for horses and men if they were attacked. It was an ideal defensive position and Simon dismounted with a sigh of relief. Immediately he was tended by the column's doctor, who had left his practice in Manchester to volunteer to serve in South Africa.

148

He bent his greying head and examined Fonthill with care in the growing light.

'You've been lucky, Colonel,' he said. 'The bullet has gone clean through the top of the arm without hitting the bone, although it's made a bit of a mess of your sinews there, hence the pain. As far as I can see, there is no need to operate. Just rest the arm in a sling and keep the wound clean. It should repair itself.'

'Good. What about the other wounded?'

'The only serious one has a shattered leg. I have bandaged the others and, in my opinion, they can stay and serve. With the Boers' shooting, it seemed it was either kill or slightly damage, with killing being the favourite. Luckily the light wasn't better.'

Shortly before dawn, the defensive ring heard a distant halloo and two horsemen approached. The first was one of the pickets posted far out to warn of surprise. The other was Major Philip Hammond.

The latter rode straight to where Fonthill was sitting, his arm strapped in a sling. He saluted and dismounted, with his usual air of sangfroid. His uniform showed no sign of wound or dishevelment, although his mount was mud-strewn.

'Terribly sorry about this, Colonel,' he said. 'Damned horse bolted as soon as the firing started and just couldn't control the beast. God knows where he took me but, in the wet and darkness, I had no idea where I was and I was soon out of distance of the firing and had nothing to direct me. I hear we've had a bit of a pasting, what?'

149

Fonthill examined him wryly. 'Very much so,' he said. 'I'm afraid that half of your squadron have been killed and five others wounded. De Wet got clean away again and, as you can see, we are waiting here until the general comes up. We've not exactly covered ourselves with glory, I fear.'

'Aw. Damned bad luck, sir. Bad luck.'

'Quite so. Now, Philip, go and find yourself something to eat. Once it's properly daylight we will move to meet Knox.'

Hammond flicked his helmet with a forefinger and strode away, leaving Fonthill to muse how a trained cavalry officer, who would surely have ridden all kinds of horses from boyhood, could find no way of controlling his mount once the firing had started.

Within the hour, Simon had ordered the command to saddle up and they were wending their way wearily across the veldt when they came up to Knox's advance guard. Fonthill could not resist looking at his watch. How far had the general advanced and at what pace? He shook his head wearily. Since reporting to Knox this second time, he had tended to give the man the benefit of the doubt about the speed of his movements. He had clung doggedly to de Wet's tail in the preceding months as the Boer had twisted and turned across the Free State, even catching up with him once or twice, despite his need to move heavy guns and supply wagons on the trail of the lightly equipped enemy. But, once again, he had failed to come up quickly enough to present de Wet with overpowering numbers in

150

open conflict. Would the regular army never learn, he wondered?

'You shouldn't have attempted to attack, Font-hill,' said Knox when the two met. 'Your job was to stay on the blighter's tail and send for me.'

'I was afraid he would move on before I could make contact, sir. And, to be honest, I didn't attack. In terrible weather conditions – wind, utter darkness and strong, driving rain – we blundered into his rearguard.'

The general nodded and twisted one end of his waxed moustache. 'Quite understand. We've done quite a bit of that these last few months. Sorry you've been wounded. Been seen to?'

'Yes, sir.'

'I hear you've lost quite a few of your chaps.'

'I'm afraid so, sir. Twenty-two dead and five wounded. We need to go back and bring back the bodies or bury them.'

'We'll move on and see what we can do. No hope of catching bloody de Wet, I presume?'

'I doubt it, sir. He moved very quickly, as usual, and with our casualties and in the darkness, I'm afraid I have no idea which direction he took. But, in this weather, he will have left spoor. Let me send my black chaps out and see if we can track him.'

Knox sighed. 'Very well. But I don't hold out much hope. Bloody man could be across the Orange by now. Never mind, send out your hounds, there's a good chap. And take a bit of rest. You look all in.'

In fact, Fonthill was immediately recalled to Johannesburg for medical treatment and for a meeting with French, who himself had been busy in the Transvaal, chasing the tails of Botha and a formidable new guerrilla leader who had emerged there, de la Rey. Major Hammond was left in command of the column and, before he boarded the train north, Simon had a heart-to-heart talk with Jenkins as they stood together on the station platform.

'Now, for goodness' sake,' he warned, 'don't give Hammond cause to criticise you. So, no drinking, and behave as the splendid senior warrant officer you are. Treat him with deference and respect...'

'Even if 'e is a stuffed shirt who gallops off when the firin' starts.'

Fonthill grimaced. 'Now, 352, that is most unfair. He may well be a stuffed shirt but he has reached a good rank in the service and French obviously rates him. We have no evidence at all that he is a shirker, so serve him well and look after the men. I hope to be away for only a couple of days or so and will catch you up wherever the column moves. Good luck, old chap.'

The two shook hands, but Jenkins looked decidedly glum as he waved his old comrade away.

Alice met Simon at the station in Johannesburg when he alighted. She was accompanied by a handsome young man with a slim moustache and a flashing grin.

'Darling,' said Alice, introducing them, 'this is James Fulton of the *Daily Mail*. We have ourselves now returned from being with French in the Transvaal and I have only just been handed your telegram at the station as we got back here.'

152

She looked a little flustered and seemed only to take in Simon's wounded arm in its sling as an afterthought. 'Oh, my goodness,' she said. 'Your telegram said it was only a scratch, but you are all strapped up. How bad was it?'

Fonthill reached out with his good arm and pulled her to him. 'As I said,' he murmured into her ear, 'it's only a scratch.' He kissed her and then released her and held out his hand to Fulton. 'How do you do,' he said. 'I hope you've been looking after Alice?'

'Certainly not, sir. She's far too independent to let anyone look after her. I have just been trying to learn from her.' He flashed his teeth in that confident grin. 'Here, let me take your bag.'

'That's very kind of you.' Simon turned back to his wife. 'I hadn't realised that you had been away. I haven't had a letter for well over two weeks.' He realised that this sounded like a rebuke and hastened to correct it. 'But, of course, we have been out on the veldt and we probably missed our post.'

Alice flushed again. 'I'm afraid I haven't written for two weeks, my dear. We ... I ... have been riding pretty hard, too, with French, you know. There has been quite a contingent of press people with him. But he never pinned down any of the Boer commandos, so we haven't had much to write about.'

'Ah, I see. Well, I'm glad that you were able to wait at the station for me. Not too long, I hope?'

'No. Just half an hour or so.'

Simon realised that their conversation was ridiculously stilted. They were addressing each other

153

with a studious politeness which was normally completely alien to them. This wooden formality, of course, was caused by the presence of Fulton. One couldn't exhibit one's normal loving exuberance while a complete stranger looked on. And yet ... he felt uncomfortable.

Fulton intervened. 'I hear that you had a lively brush with de Wet, Colonel,' he said. 'I would be most grateful to hear about it when you have a moment.'

'Yes, of course. But first I would like to have a cup of tea with my wife. It's been a long journey. I presume we still have our room at the hotel, Alice?'

'Yes, I have retained it, of course. Let us get a Hackney here at the station. Will you join us, James?'

For a moment, Fonthill thought that Fulton was going to accept. That would have been intolerable. But there was something in Simon's tone that even the brashest of men could not have ignored.

'That's very kind,' he said, 'but no thank you, Alice. I must get back to the compound and think what on earth I am going to cable about our gallivanting so uselessly over the veldt.' He seized Alice's hand and bowed low over it. 'Thank you for your company, Alice. I have enjoyed it immensely.' He turned to Simon and gave a half bow. 'Delighted to have met you, sir. I bid you both good day.'

He turned and walked away.

'Oh dear,' said Alice. 'You were a little peremptory with him, Simon. I hope he has not been offended.'

154

Fonthill looked at her quizzically. 'Surely not. Any chap with sensibility would know that, after a long absence, a man would want to be alone with his wife for a while.'

Alice coloured again – most unusually, for she was not coquettish, and certainly not with her husband. 'Yes, well... It's just that he's been very helpful to me out on the veldt when hunting with the pack.' She smiled at him, a great improvement he thought. 'Perhaps I'm getting a bit too old for this lark. Come on. Let's get back to the hotel and that cup of tea.'

There, she questioned him about the latest brush with de Wet. 'I am determined to get this fellow, you know, darling,' Simon confided. 'It's probably becoming a bit personal now, you know. Nearly had him twice, dammit, and he's always slipped away. Third time lucky, perhaps.'

Alice shook her head. 'It mustn't get personal, darling. It might affect your judgement. Remember Ahab and the great white whale.'

'Who?'

'Captain Ahab in that wonderful book from America, *Moby Dick*. He becomes obsessed with hunting down a great whale and it leads to his death. Don't let it happen to you.'

'Well, I don't know the book but I can't quite equate de Wet with a white whale, somehow. Anyway, what's your next great story?'

Alice put down her teacup. 'There's a woman out here, a Miss Emily Hobhouse. By all accounts she's a rather dumpy, middle-aged spinster who has appeared from nowhere, but she is tackling Kitchener hard on the subject of the concentration

155

camps that he is setting up to house the Boer refugees from his despicable farm-burning policy. This is close to my heart, so I want to meet her and find out what she is up to. If she stands up to scrutiny, then I want to help her. Give her as much publicity as I can.'

'Hmm. Well, my love. Do be careful.' He put down his own cup and moved towards her. 'In the meantime, I wonder whether...' He ran his fingers through her hair.

Alice pulled away from him slightly, her eyes failing to meet his and shook her head. 'If you don't mind, darling, I am so tired after all this travelling. And there's your arm ... I would like to sleep for a few minutes, if you would allow me.'

Simon stood stiffly. 'Of course. I have to see French tonight. I will curl up on the other side of the bed and ... er ... compose my thoughts.' But he was frowning and ill at ease as he removed his boots, undid his tunic buttons and lay down to rest, within touching distance of his wife yet, in fact, far, far away from her.

He met Major General French in the latter's tent that evening at the appointed hour. The general remained terse and not exactly welcoming, although he expressed conventional concern for Fonthill's wound.

'Are you getting attention for that?' he asked.

'Oh yes, thank you. I am seeing the doctor in the morning. It doesn't inconvenience me much. No bones broken and I can ride quite well with it. Frankly, General, I believe I could have stayed with my column and continued my duties and I hope that you will allow me to return to them as

156

soon as possible.'

French nodded. 'Good. Yes, well, I have read your report but I wanted to hear directly from you about this latest affray with de Wet. How the hell does he continue to get away from us?'

Fonthill took a deep breath and relayed the story, emphasising that it was the good work of his black tracker that led them to the elusive guerrilla leader. He repeated the commendation contained in his report of the good work of Jenkins in taking command of A Squadron in its reply to the fierce fire from the Boer rearguard but did not dwell on Hammond's absence. That could come out if it had to.

In fact, French did not ask the obvious question. Instead, he frowned and asked, 'How could you have blundered into the commando? I understand that you only had black scouts out in front?'

Simon sighed. 'Not quite, sir. We knew we were getting close to the Boers but we did not know how near. It was a question of following closely behind the black tracker who had discovered the Boer camp. So A Squadron led. It was pitch-black and the rain was driving down, hard in our faces. Our people out in front could hardly be blamed. In the poor visibility and conditions, the distance between them and the main column shortened. My responsibility, of course.'

'Yerse. Pity you couldn't have staked out and sent back for Knox.'

'Quite so, sir.' Fonthill's mind raced. He had emphasised the bad weather conditions in his report, yet French had seized on the fact that he did not have conventional outriders going ahead.

157

How did he know this? Hammond, of course. He decided that it was time to record the major's departure from the fight.

'It was also a pity, sir, that we lost Major Hammond in the fracas.'

'What? What happened to Hammond? He wasn't in your casualty report.'

'No sir. He is unhurt. But it seems that when the first shots were fired and I was hit, Hammond's horse bolted and he could not control it. It took him some way away from the action and in the miserable conditions, he lost his way. He rejoined our camp, after our retreat, just before dawn the next morning.'

French frowned. 'Good lord. Philip Hammond is one of the best horsemen I know. Used to hunt with him in Leicestershire. Strange business. Ah well, these things happen.'

'They do, indeed, sir. But it allowed Sergeant Major Jenkins to play a vital role in saving what was left of the squadron, for its officers were in the rear at the time. He also brought me round, as I lay unconscious under fire.'

Nodding slowly, the general made a note. Then he looked up. 'Fonthill, you are certainly showing initiative and good scouting work in at least finding this blasted Boer, if not pinning him down.' He leant forward. 'This chap is getting remarkable publicity back in Britain and on the Continent. They call him the "Phantom Raider", or some such nonsense. It is becoming even more important than before that we capture or kill him. He is making a laughing stock of us all. If he does get across the Orange – and it is clear that he is about to attempt this, of course – then he can cause all kinds of havoc in the Cape Colony, as we have discussed before.'

'Quite so, sir. I feel I have an almost personal grudge against him now. I would like to continue the pursuit.'

'Well, it's not just you, of course. Lord Kitchener has assembled a considerable army in trying to corner the bloody man.' He leant forward. 'But K feels that you might have just the right temperament and ability to lead us to him and make him either surrender or stand and fight.'

'Oh, he will never surrender. I am sure of that.'

'Very well. I want you to rejoin your column as soon as you are fit enough to do so. You will remain under General Knox's general command, although you will report to me overall. Kitchener has told Knox that you are to have as free a hand as possible and that your casualties are to be replaced and your command is to be increased in numbers. If de Wet crosses the Orange, then cross after him and pin him down in the mountains on the other side before he can penetrate further south. Those are your orders. Is that clear?'

'Perfectly clear, sir. Thank you for your confidence. I will travel south as soon as I can get clearance from the medics.'

French stood and held out his hand. 'Good hunting, Fonthill.'

# CHAPTER EIGHT

Alice saw her husband off two days later, waving him goodbye at the station with a heavy heart. She felt guilty, as guilty – if not more so – than when she had faced up to the fact that, married to Colonel Covington years before, she was in love with Simon Fonthill. She knew that she had hurt Simon and that he realised, although the matter remained unspoken, that someone or something had come between them. They had not made love during his brief stay in Pretoria for she had made much of her tiredness and her need to write her cables to London. They had failed to agree on the cruelty of Kitchener's concentration camp policy, although she knew that he had done his best to avoid farm burnings. He argued, she realised, as much to make debating points out of frustration from her coldness as from conviction.

Walking back from the station, Alice felt ashamed. She shook her head in self-dislike. It was, of course, James Fulton who had come between them. She had not been unfaithful in body to Simon but she knew that she had in her mind. On the veldt, as part of the correspondents' pack with French, she and Fulton had ridden side by side, laughing and joking – she even sharing with him journalistic titbits that she had gathered to spark up her own bulletins. This was something that she had never done before. Alice Griffith never, never worked with the opposition. She hunted alone, always. Except now she had revelled in the companionship, the animal attraction of this handsome man, so much younger than herself, who had flattered her with his attention and aroused within her emotions that she knew should play no part in the workaday life of a forty-five-year-old married woman.

They had kissed once, very briefly in the starlight under a ridiculously romantic Transvaal moon. Then, she had pushed him away, shook her head and walked back to the fireside. But, oh how she had enjoyed it! And the next morning they had resumed their playful, coquettish courtship, as though nothing had happened. But it had and they both knew it.

Alice paused for a moment as she now strode back from the station and let the memory of that moment flood through her. Then, she stamped her foot. This would not do! She must end this thing before it became dangerous.

She diverted on her route to the hotel and turned off to the journalists' enclave. But James was nowhere to be seen. She shrugged and walked on. She would face him the next time they met and explain that his pursuit of her must stop. Now, however, she must concentrate on her work.

A cable was awaiting her at the hotel from her editor, agreeing with enthusiasm her suggestion that she should concentrate on investigating the intriguing Miss Emily Hobhouse. The *Morning Post* had appointed another correspondent to lighten her load following Churchill's return

161

home and to replace the man killed at Lady-smith, so she was relieved of the task of hard news reporting which she had assumed over the last few weeks. Now she had the freedom to dig deeply for the colour stories that lay behind the campaigns. And, the editor wrote, the British public was growing uneasy about the camps. Alice now had a free hand to investigate and report on the doings of this little spinster in this militaristic environment. She rubbed her hands. Good. A story that she could get her teeth into – and one near to her feminist heart!

Alice had always followed the good corres-pondent's practice of developing and nurturing contacts in the most unlikely places. A close, confiding smile, a flutter of her eyelashes and even the placing of a one-pound note in receptive palms from time to time, where necessary, had always stood her in good stead. Now, she hurried to Kitchener's headquarters on some trivial pretence and was grateful to find a young subaltern she had cultivated busy at his desk. Did he, she wondered, know of this Miss Hobhouse who had been bothering the commander-in-chief and where she could be found? It was time, she confided, that the doings of this person were investigated.

The young man eagerly agreed. The woman, it seemed, had gained permission to visit one of the biggest of the new camps, at Bloemfontein, some one hundred and twenty-five miles to the south, and was there at that moment. The chief, it seemed, had been told by Whitehall that she should be allowed to go where she wanted, but he had curtailed her travelling only to Bloemfontein.

162

Alice flashed her best smile to her informant and turned away. No time to lose! She rushed back to the hotel, packed a bag and within the hour found a train that, blessedly, was about to steam south to Port Elizabeth on the coast, stopping at Bloemfontein on the way. Her press pass gained her admittance and, some two and a half hours later, she stepped down onto the platform in the capital city of the Orange Free State, now, of course, completely in British hands.

The pressure of reporting on the campaigns out in the field had prevented Alice from visiting any of these strange new camps before and she approached this one with interest, taken there by a young Kaffir driving a canopied Cape cart, hired at the station.

The development was, as she had expected, near the railway line. She well understood Kitchener's reasons for building the camps, or 'laagers' as he called them. Apart from denying succour to the Boers still fighting by preventing them from visiting their homes regularly, they were intended to provide secure camps to house those burghers who had surrendered to the British. They and their families were at risk from the Boer guerrilla leaders who had made it their policy to drive these men from their homes. They had to be housed somewhere.

Alice stepped down from the cart, dismissed the driver and told him to return for her within two hours. She stood for a moment looking at the camp. Her first impressions were favourable. Yes, Kitchener might be unfeeling but he was not a monster. This was a huge village of white bell tents, laid out neatly in militaristic lines, all pegged out on the brown veldt of the southern slopes of a kopje, rising directly from the railway lines. Yet, there were so *many* of them. The difficulties of feeding the occupants must be prodigious. And where, she wondered, was Emily Hobhouse? Looking from the lines of wire marking the boundaries of the camp, there was no sign of her.

At the guard tent, Alice showed her press pass to the sergeant and explained that she had arrived a little late to join the Hobhouse party. 'Where, pray, is it?' she enquired.

'There ain't no party, madam,' grunted the sergeant. 'Just that little lady on 'er own. She's somewhere in the camp. God knows where.'

It took Alice almost an hour of walking along the rows between the tents to find her. As she went, she realised that overcrowding was rife. Children were everywhere and, from what she could see, tents that were meant to house, say, six soldiers, were now sheltering double that number. There were no standpipes for water nor brick-built boilers and, indeed, cooking seemed to be a matter of assembling a few sticks in the open and attempting to light a fire under whatever pots were at hand. Alice attempted to talk to several Boer *huisvrouws*, but none admitted to speaking English. In doing so, however, she was able to look inside several of the tents. The floors were of beaten earth on which mattresses were lined, each touching the other. Of conventional beds there was no sign. This was midsummer and the stench under the canvas was nauseous. Alice coughed and covered her nostrils with her handkerchief. Disease was in the air, of that there was no doubt.

She found Emily Hobhouse squatting on a stool at the end of one of the tent rows, busily writing in a notebook. Alice had wired the *Morning Post* library in London and asked for background details on the little spinster and now she hung back, out of sight, and quickly re-scanned the details she had been sent. Miss Hobhouse, it seemed, was forty-one years old and had spent years in a little Cornish village near Liskeard as a companion to her father, an invalid archdeacon. Then, in a sudden and surprising burst of initiative, she had sailed for Minnesota and had embarked on a futile mission to convert Cornish miners to temperance, pausing only to be jilted by a fiancé in Mexico.

She had returned to England just as the war in South Africa was getting under way and had flung herself into supporting the pro-Boer Relief Fund for South African Women and Children. But she did have influential contacts, for her uncle was Lord Hobhouse, a distinguished Liberal peer, who had arranged for her to meet St John Brodrick, Undersecretary for War at Whitehall. The result was that, with official, if unenthusiastic approval, she had sailed for the Cape with the declared aim of distributing comforts to the interned Boer civilians but also with the intention of examining the conditions in the camps and reporting back to her Liberal sponsors back home.

Alice smiled as she examined this determined little woman. Miss Hobhouse was indeed as described: dumpy and spinster-like. Dressed as though for a cool, spring day in England's West

Country, under bonnet and several layers of stiff fabrics, she was busily scribbling, impervious to the heat or to the stares of the barefooted children who surrounded her.

Clearing her throat, Alice advanced. 'Miss Hobhouse?'

Without looking up, the woman held up her hand. 'Just a minute,' she said. 'I must just finish this.'

Alice waited dutifully. Then Hobhouse raised her head. If she was surprised to see an English woman coolly and unconventionally dressed in white shirt, jodhpurs and riding boots, she gave no sign. 'Yes, what is it?'

Alice held out her hand. 'Alice Griffith of the *Morning Post*.'

'Ah.' Emily Hobhouse rose awkwardly to her feet and shook Alice's hand. 'How do you do? I know of you. I have read your reports. Would it be presumptuous of me to think that we might perhaps have sympathies in common concerning this ridiculous war?'

'Well...' Alice smiled. 'Perhaps. But Miss Hobhouse, I am most interested in the purpose of your visit and what you are hoping to achieve. I have travelled from Pretoria to see you and I would be most grateful if you could spare a little time to talk to me about it – although I certainly don't wish to interrupt your work unduly now.'

'Good gracious, interrupt me all you like if you can help me tell the people back home about these disgraceful circumstances here.' Emily Hobhouse's cheeks glowed like apples under her bonnet. She swept her pencil round in an em-

166

bracing gesture. 'Do you know, madam, that there are eighteen hundred people here. *Eighteen hundred!* In tents designed to take perhaps eight hundred rough, hard-living soldiers. There are little children – here, you can see – who don't have shoes or proper clothes and I suspect are about to go down with the fever. I came out to disperse a few comforts from the Relief Fund but, good gracious me, these people don't need comforts, they need clean water, fuel for cooking, and proper food. These conditions are disgraceful and far, far worse than I suspected.'

Alice held up a hand to stop the flow. 'Miss Hobhouse, shall we find a little shade and perhaps you will allow me to take a note or two?'

The little woman nodded and they walked to where a solitary, sad-looking eucalyptus tree offered some shelter from the fierce sun. There, as Alice's pencil flew along the page – oh, how she wished again that she had learnt shorthand! – Emily Hobhouse told her of what she had learnt.

Here at Bloemfontein, it seemed, the city's military governor, Major General Pretyman, had been courteous and anxious to help. But he had revealed details of the most incriminating kind. The families had been cleared from their burning homesteads and put down under canvas without care or forethought. There was not enough water to go round; soap did not exist in the settlement; no meat was supplied to those families whose men were still fighting, only meagre vegetables; and even those who did have meat existed on rations that hovered at starvation rate.

'Some of the stories I have been told, madam,'

she continued, 'have been horrendous. For instance, our General Bruce Hamilton posted a notice, after he had burnt the town of Ventersburg, telling them to go to the commandos if they wanted food. Now, I am here and seeing for myself. The camp latrines are quite inadequate and the authorities can't cope. As you can see, the unemptied pails stand out in the sun, making the tents downwind of them unbearable to live in.

'The authorities are at their wits' end and they have no more idea how to cope with the difficulty of providing clothes for the people than the man in the moon. Crass male ignorance, stupidity, helplessness and muddling ... and they don't know how to face it.'

Alice took out a handkerchief and wiped her forehead. Miss Hobhouse, however, seemed impervious to the heat. 'What do you intend to do about it, may I ask?'

'Well, I am making a list now of the most vital deficiencies that I've seen here. That means soap, forage, more tents, brick boilers for drinking water, a tap water supply. I shall put these forward and see what the reaction is. Then I intend to visit other camps and report back to my sponsors back home – and, indeed, to the British public.'

Putting down her pencil, Alice leant forward. 'Miss Hobhouse, you asked earlier if I shared your opinions about ... what was it you called this war ... ridiculous?'

'Oh yes.'

'Well, let me tell you that I do, although my husband is a serving soldier out here and I don't approve so much of the Boers' attitude towards the Kaffirs and their idea of governance. Nevertheless, the farm clearances are, I believe, a barbaric act and I can see that this camp, at least, which I understand is the biggest, is a disgrace to a civilised nation. May I come with you and write in my newspaper about your activities and what you discover?'

Miss Hobhouse's eyebrows shot up. 'Travel with me? Well, my dear, let me warn you that I travel very light – although I have these comforts I intend to distribute – and also as quickly as I can.'

Alice smiled at the plump, overdressed figure before her. It would be hard to imagine any traveller looking less likely to move fast and untrammelled. 'Miss Hobhouse,' she said, 'in my work and with my husband, I have travelled in many rough and distant parts of the Empire over the last twenty years and I am very used to hardship. I shall not encumber you, I promise.'

The woman looked at her quizzically. 'Your newspaper is the *Morning Post*, I believe?'

'Yes.'

She tilted her head to one side as though in gentle disbelief. 'That seems to me to be an organ which often unthinkingly supports this Tory government. I fear, my dear, that, if the conditions here are typical, what you may have to report may be rather unacceptable fare to your employers and your readers.'

Alice nodded her head. 'Yes, I take your point. But my editor has already given me permission to write about you and your work, for, it seems, there is already some discontent back home about the camps and, indeed, the progress of the

169

war. It is true that the *Post* supports the war, but it is not jingoistic and I am used to treading carefully around the difficulty of reporting events that sometimes stick in the craw of our readers.' She sighed. 'The point is, however, that truth is sacred and...' she looked around her at the rows of tents '...I shall report not only what you say, but what I see. And being with you will allow me to see for myself.'

Emily Hobhouse gave a soft, gentle smile that lit up her homely countenance, replacing for a moment the frown that seemed to be her set expression. 'Well, you shall come with me, if you wish. You must pay your own way and I shall welcome whatever light you can shed back home on the circumstances of these poor people. But you must call me Emily and I shall call you ... what was it?'

'Alice.'

'Of course. Alice.'

'Thank you, Emily. Now tell me. What are your immediate plans, for I must think of cabling arrangements?'

'After seeing what I can do here, I intend to entrain to see about half of the camps here in the Free State – at Norvalspont, Aliwal North, Springfontein, Kimberley and Orange River. I have, of course, these basic comforts that I must distribute. Then I go to Mafeking in the Transvaal. That, I hope, will give me a fair sample of these places. Maybe I shall have time to revisit some of them before I return home in April.'

'To whom will you report?'

'To the committee of the Distress Fund, but I

intend to see that my report is also circulated to all members of parliament. If, as I expect, these conditions are widespread, then I hope to be able to put forward sensible suggestions for improving the system, if, that is, it cannot be removed completely.'

Alice nodded. 'I hope you will allow me to help you, Emily, as well as my journalistic duties will allow.'

'I shall be grateful. Let us start now, then, by seeing all the tents in this awful place that I have not been able to visit yet.'

'What? All of them?'

'Oh yes. We must be thorough.'

At the end of the day, the two women repaired to the simple hotel in the centre of the town where Alice was able to find herself a room next to that of Emily. In the morning, the two of them saw General Pretyman and submitted to him a list of essential requirements for the camp.

He accepted them without demur, although with a frown, and Emily explained that she would not be leaving Bloemfontein until she had visited the general again, in two days' time, to check on how well her suggestions had been met. Sitting silently at the meeting and watching how her companion handled the general, Alice realised that Emily Hobhouse was not only a determined woman but also a skilled and sensitive negotiator. There was no trace of bluster or the shrill insistence of the harridan. The case of the internees was put with reason and balance. Her admiration for the little woman grew. The next few months, she realised, could be very interesting.

171

The next two days were taken up with distributing round the camp some of the clothing and other comforts from the Distress Fund that had travelled with Emily and, in Alice's case, with carefully drafting and cabling back her first story. She was careful to write it in an unemotional, low-key style, keeping to the facts and stressing General Pretyman's seeming anxiety to help. She was anxious to avoid any editorial 'toning down'. She also wrote to Simon, stressing her thoughts of him and urging him to take care of his wound. Then she picked up her pen to tell James Fulton where she was, but thought better of it. He must be left to ponder her departure and her whereabouts. It would be good for him.

On the third day, Emily and Alice visited the general to enquire of the changes that had been made at the camp. As before, General Pretyman – what a strange name for one so stolidly, ordinary-looking! – was courteous and frank. It was agreed that soap could be provided, but only at one ounce per head per week, and also brick boilers. But fuel was 'too precious' to be spared and tap water impossible to provide because 'the price was prohibitive'. Emily warned that disease and deaths would follow but met with no bending of the official knee.

Alice spoke little but made copious notes. Nor did Miss Hobhouse continue to argue or make further demands. For the moment she would keep her powder dry. There were other camps to visit and, no doubt, other battles to be fought.

The two women now took to the crowded rail network. Their travels around the Free State and then, later, back into the Transvaal, coincided with a series of Kitchener's great 'drives' across the veldt, and everywhere the two women saw open trucks standing at sidings, full of women and children and the occasional man, exposed to the icy rains and hot sun of the high veldt. These sights, observed Emily, typified war 'in all its destructiveness, cruelty, stupidity and nakedness' and Alice could not remember seeing, in all her varied experiences of warfare, anything quite so heart-wrenching. The scenes, in fact, shook the two more than the sight of the camps, which at least presented a superficial picture of order and protection from the elements, with their rows of white bell tents, like medical dressings, thought Alice, covering suppurating sores.

The conditions in these camps varied, depending on various elements: the dedication and care of the superintendent in charge, the nearness of the supplies of water and fuel, the consciences of the local inhabitants and the care they showed and the dates when the camps were opened – for the earliest camps took first pick of the supplies.

Everywhere the two visited, Emily made pages of notes and then presented her recommendations for improvements, which were received with reactions ranging from wearied agreement and vague promises of remedial action to virtual indifference.

As they travelled, Alice continued to send her reports back to the *Post*. She struggled to keep indignation out of her stories, confining herself to factual accounts, leavened by descriptive quotes from Emily Hobhouse. She realised that not all of

173

her cables were published – 'too repetitively critical' was one editorial reaction. But she also knew that many were used, with, as far as she could tell, little subediting. She also gathered that opinion was hardening in Britain against the war and its effect on Afrikaner civilians and she was glad to be playing some part in creating this, although she realised that without having the determined Miss Hobhouse as a topical peg on which to hang her stories, she would have obtained far less space.

After six weeks of juddering, wearying rail travel, Emily and Alice returned to Bloemfontein to check to see what changes, if any, had been made since Emily's first visit there. They found that all the improvements that had been made – few as they were – had been swamped by new arrivals following the new anti-commando sweeps.

The camp itself, which remained the largest in South Africa, had doubled in size and more were expected. Since they had left six weeks before, there had been sixty-two deaths in the camp and the solitary doctor supplied for the settlement was himself laid low with enteric fever. Two of the Boer girls that Emily had trained as nurses had also died.

'I've seen enough,' declared Emily one evening as the two sat together in their little hotel in the city. Emily, temperate to the end, was sipping cocoa but, as the conditions in the camps had worsened the further they had travelled, Alice had taken to taking two nips of whisky before they retired every evening. It was, she said, 'the solace of despair'. She put down her glass now.

'Will you leave now?' she enquired.

'Yes. I will sail for England as soon as I can get a ship. This whole system has been a gigantic blunder. It is piling disaster upon disaster.' She leant forward. 'Do you know, Alice, I was thinking today of a parish I had known at home of two thousand people, where a funeral was an event – and usually of an old person. Here some twenty-five are being carried away every day. The full realisation of the position has dawned on me. It is a death rate not known except in the times of the Great Plagues. The whole talk is of death: who died yesterday, who lies dying today, who will be dead tomorrow.

'I do not have accurate figures, but I understand that there are now more than ninety thousand whites and more than twenty-four thousand blacks in these camps.'

She shook her head. 'I must return home as quickly as possible and present the facts to the British people. You have done wonders, my dear, but not everyone reads the *Morning Post*, you know.'

Alice took another sip of whisky, as though to anaesthetise herself against the scenes of death they had witnessed that day. 'What will you recommend in your report?'

'Well, of course, the huge deficiencies should be remedied immediately, with fuel, bedding, soap, clothing, diet and water supplies improved and the overcrowding and bad sanitation removed. Fundamentally, however, the whole system should be abolished. All those who have friends or relations who can take them should be allowed to leave the camps. No further refugees should be brought in.

175

What's more, seeing the growing impertinences of the Kaffirs, seeing the white women thus humiliated, every care should be taken to put them in places of authority.'

Alice hid a half smile. She had realised, of course, that Emily was a woman of her time with contemporary views about not mixing the races. But she was also a person of huge energy, great courage and simmering indignation with a moral backbone as rigid as the corset she habitually wore. 'Good luck, Emily,' she said, raising her glass. 'It has been a pleasure and an honour to be with you.'

The next morning, Emily Hobhouse was on her way home, pecking Alice lightly on the cheek and then bustling aboard a train for Cape Town, to where she had cabled to make a reservation on board a steamer leaving for Southampton in a week's time. As she watched her go, Alice felt a delicious shimmer of synthetic sympathy for those stiff-backed members of the Tory government – and of the right-wing members of the Liberal Party who supported them – who were not aware of what was awaiting them.

Back in the hotel, Alice completed her latest story on the camps: a summation of what she and Emily had seen over the previous six weeks and of what the doughty Miss Hobhouse intended to do on her return. She ploddingly then transposed this into cablese and took it to the cable office. Then, deep in thought, she returned to her room to write to Simon.

She had done so studiously once a week while

on trek with Emily and, in return, had received two letters from him. This was as much as she expected, because she knew that he was somewhere in the south, far away from post offices. In both letters, his tone was cheery, unsentimental, of course, but still lacking that warmth that she was accustomed to receiving from him on the rare moments when they had been separated in the past. He was clearly still uncomfortable with her and she sighed. The events of the last six weeks had taken her mind off both her husband and James Fulton to some extent. Fulton had written to her once, having somehow found where she was staying for three nights on her peregrinations, for she had not written to him.

Alice re-read his letter now, before attempting to write to her husband. It was full of the warmth that was absent from Simon's missive; cheerful, bouncing in style even, but saying how much he was missing her and that things were not the same without her by his side, with her smile, her soft skin... She threw down the letter and put her head in her hand. How she missed him, too, dammit! She realised that her self-imposed absence, her immersion in the doings of Emily Hobhouse had not removed him from her mind or her heart. Oh, what to do about it!

She closed her eyes for a while and then picked up her pen and wrote, 'My dear, dear Simon...'

# CHAPTER NINE

On descending from the train, Fonthill found that General Knox's camp had moved on and that his own column was said to be well in advance of the main force and was now 'somewhere across the Orange'. That meant that de Wet had, indeed, found a way of crossing into the Cape Colony and that Simon's reinforced column must be hot on his tail. God, things had moved fast in the few days that he had been away!

A sense of frustration descended upon him as he stamped around the remnants of Knox's army, demanding a sound horse and provisions so that he could ride on and catch up with his men. Not only was he out of the action but, it seemed, his much loved wife had somehow lost her senses and was obviously in some sort of relationship with a much younger man. Such a thing had never happened in their sixteen years of marriage and it shook the very foundations of his life. Oh, had it been a mistake to jettison all his principles and to rejoin the army as a regular soldier? It all seemed to stem from that. Well, there was nothing he could do about it, for he was too far away to fight this ridiculous affair at first hand. He must just rely on Alice, dear Alice, to realise how much he loved her and to understand where her duties lay – while he chased this slippery, wily, ruthless Boer...

A reluctant quartermaster captain eventually issued him with a horse and, even more reluctantly, a standard issue Lee Enfield and Webley revolver. 'If you're cavalry, you should have a carbine, sir,' he argued.

'But I'm not bloody cavalry, Captain. I'm mounted infantry. And I would like a bandolier with cartridges. Thank you.'

He set out following a compass bearing to where he had been told Knox could be found. And he found some relief in riding alone in the magnificent, rolling grassland and kopje-strewn country that swept down to the Orange River and the border with the Cape Province. His shoulder remained sore but he was able to extract much more movement from it now, even though he would be unable to use the heavy rifle he had demanded. Better not meet a Boer patrol, he reflected.

He soon came up with Knox's new camp and was relieved to find that the general was away. His ADC confirmed that Fonthill's Horse – now made up to some two hundred men and under the temporary command of Major Hammond – had ridden out two days before and had sent a message back to say that they had found traces of a Boer commando that had crossed the Orange at a place called Zanddrift. It seemed, however, that Knox had also received a strong report that de Wet was heading instead for the little town of Odendaalstroom, which he intended to take and to cross the river near there. As a result, the general had led a large force to head him off and had left that very morning.

179

Which way to go? It did not take Fonthill long to decide. His place was with his own column, so he hired a Kaffir to take him directly to Zanddrift. It was a risk, because he knew that two other Boer commandos, under General Kritzinger and Judge Hertzog, had previously penetrated the Colony and were now ranging deeply into the mountains that fringed the border. The trail that Hammond had followed at the crossing, therefore, could well be that of the two other commandos. Or would it? Mzingeli – if Hammond was trusting him to lead, that is – would never follow old spoors. The thought decided him. He would cross at Zanddrift.

There, he found the recent marks of many riders going down to the fast-flowing Orange but the water level was low and, dismissing his guide, he crossed with comparative ease, despite some initial apprehension about guiding his horse with only one hand in the swift-flowing water. On the other side, he realised that the terrain was now much more inhospitable, with barren hills rising to the south in a jumbled mass. How was he to track the column? He looked about him. What would Mzingeli do? Look for softer ground, of course.

He turned to the left and, sure enough, as the ground close to the river turned marshy, there he picked up again the traces of many horsemen. In addition, however, he noted the marks of several wagons and what could only be heavy guns. The Boers, of course!

His own column included no wagon or artillery piece, but there was no way of knowing if the hundreds of hoof marks included those of his own

180

men. He frowned. Better to follow the tracks of the commando, anyway. If Hammond was doing his job, then wherever were the Boers, Fonthill's Horse should be close in attendance.

He followed the clearly distinguishable signs of a commando on the march for a couple of hours until it began to rain again, so he resolved to camp for the night. He did not wish to blunder into de Wet's rearguard again – and this time on his own. Fonthill therefore tethered his horse, unpacked an oilskin, some cold biltong and dry biscuits – better not attempt to light a fire – and curled up miserably under a low tree. He eventually drifted off to sleep, lulled by rain dripping from the leaves and dreamt that Alice was walking hand in hand with Fulton and looking over her shoulder, laughing at him.

He awoke with a start to realise that someone *was* laughing at him. A rifle barrel was poked in his ribs and an Afrikaan voice jeered, 'Come on, Khaki. Time to stop dreaming and get on your feet.' Three Boers – dressed untidily in half-buttoned British army tunics, but Boers all the same, judging by their unkempt beards and slung bandoliers – were looking down at him and grinning.

Damn! Simon threw aside the oilskin and rose unsteadily to his feet, slipping his wounded arm back into its sling.

'Ah, wounded, eh?' The Boer with the rifle still at his ribs frowned. 'Where did you get that, then? And what are you doing out here, with a wounded arm?'

'I cut myself shaving,' said Fonthill coolly. 'And

181

I was just taking some exercise in your lovely sunshine.' He gestured upwards to where the rain now seemed to have increased in intensity.

'Don't joke with us, English.' The Boer leader was now scowling. Then he looked closer at the badges of rank on Simon's jacket and turned with a grin to his fellows. 'Ah, friends. We have captured a full colonel. What a catch. Come on. We take him to the general.'

Ah. The general! Fonthill's mind raced. Would that mean de Wet, or one of the other commando's leaders? If it was de Wet he must follow closely the direction in which he was taken so that, if he could escape, he could bring the column quickly up to the attack. But that must be his plan of action whatever the camp to which he was taken. His hopes were quickly ended, however, for one of the burghers produced a black handkerchief and tied it tightly across his eyes.

'You don't see where we take you, Colonel,' he said. 'And if you try to gallop off, we shoot you. Understand?'

Simon nodded. There was nowhere to gallop to, anyway.

They rode for little less than half an hour and Fonthill realised that he must have laid down to rest infuriatingly close to the enemy's camp. What now? He knew that the commandos rarely kept prisoners, for they were only an impediment to them in their fast-moving strikes. When retained, however, they did have a reputation for treating them well – or as well as their own stringent rations and living conditions allowed – before releasing them on the open veldt. Would they, how-

182

ever, keep a colonel? His capture could be a modest propaganda coup for them. He remembered how much the Boers had made of capturing Winston Churchill, that scion of English nobility, earlier in the war. But that was then and this was now. These commandos probably had no time for propaganda. They were just hard fighters, living from hand to mouth – and without proper clothing, judging by the uniforms these three were wearing. Or was this another example of the 'dirty warfare' tactics they were said to be practising, using captured uniforms as disguise to creep up to unsuspecting English outposts? Ah well. All would soon be revealed.

He could tell by the noise surrounding him that the little party had entered the Boer camp. He was helped down from his mount, although the cloth was kept tightly bound round his eyes, and then led to where he could smell woodsmoke and, deliciously, the smell of coffee.

After being kept waiting for perhaps five minutes he heard an interchange of conversation in Afrikaans before the blindfold was removed. He blinked and stared into a familiar face, with its high cheekbones, hard eyes and neatly cut beard. 'Good morning, General de Wet,' he said.

A slow smile crept across the Boer's weather-beaten face. 'Ah, Mr Fonthill. I see that you didn't stay a civilian long. A colonel now, then. And you have been chasing me. By golly, you have. Obviously annoyed because I took your horses. Though you got them back soon enough, eh? Come and sit down. Would you like some coffee?'

'Thank you. I certainly would.'

The general squatted on the ground next to the fire and beckoned to Fonthill to sit beside him. 'This coffee is foul,' he said, 'because, thanks to you, we can't get proper grains now. So we make it from old bedsocks and God knows what. Here, try it.'

Simon took a sip and wrinkled his face. 'General,' he said, 'if I had to fight on coffee like this I would have surrendered months ago.'

'Ach, man. It will take more than bad coffee to make us give in. Now, tell me, Colonel. Where is your column exactly? I know it is not far away looking for us. But I know you weren't leading it because I have scouts out behind us. What on earth were you doing out here, with your arm in a sling, all on your own?' Without waiting for a reply, de Wet shouted out a string of orders in Afrikaans, clearly giving instructions for the camp to break up and move on.

Fonthill decided that it would be pointless to dissemble. He told de Wet of his wound, his trip to Pretoria for medical treatment and his anxiety to join his column. 'So you see, General, like you, I was looking for my column.'

De Wet did not reply immediately and instead barked out a series of further instructions, clearly not happy with the pace of the inspanning. Simon took advantage of this to look around him carefully. This commando was huge, bigger by the look of it than those they had encountered already: perhaps sixteen hundred to two thousand horsemen. They were manoeuvring several large Krupps cannon into place behind oxen – ah, and he thought they had captured all de Wet's artillery

184

at Bothaville! – and the difficulty of doing so was the cause of the general's annoyance.

But it was the Boers themselves that most aroused Fonthill's interest. The few he had seen in his previous encounters with them were not as badly clothed, primitively shod nor as gaunt in appearance as these men now. Many wore only roughly cut hide sandals on their feet, or went barefoot. Their original farming clothes, where worn, hung in tatters and many, like the patrol that had captured him, wore badly fitting British army tunics and breeches. He also observed that many carried captured Lee Enfield rifles or British carbines to complement their Mausers. This was a rag-tailed army if ever there was one.

De Wet caught his eye. 'Not smart, eh, Colonel? But, by God, we can still fight. Because we fight for our country, you see. Now, will you give me your word as an English gentleman,' he allowed himself a steely smile at the phrase, 'that what you have just told me is the truth? As you can see, we are moving out anyway, so whatever you say, we will not be waiting here for your column or my old friend General Knox.'

'Yes, General. I give you my word that what I have just told you is the truth.'

'Good. I believe you. Now, we must take you with us while I decide what to do with you. We have taken recently to stripping our prisoners of their clothing – not because we wish to punish them, but because, as you can see, living on commando means hard riding and we need to wear what we capture.'

Fonthill nodded. 'The word is, General, that

you have broken the terms of the Hague Convention by wearing our uniforms to give you an advantage in attacking.'

De Wet shook his head vigorously. 'Not true. We wear your clothes to stop us getting ... what is the English word? Ah yes. Pneumonia.' He chuckled for a brief moment and then his face lapsed back into a seamed expression of fierce purpose. 'We don't care what you say. But speaking of this Hague thing. Is not your burning of farms and putting our women and children behind barbed wire breaking the terms of that? Eh?'

Fonthill frowned in return. 'I do not approve of that either–' He was interrupted by de Wet who spoke sharply to him in Afrikaans and then interpreted.

'I am sorry. I speak my language. I forget. I said that I had heard that you have burnt farms, too, but that you have been kind to the families. We appreciate that.'

Simon marvelled at the intelligence that carried these details across the veldt so quickly to the fighters at the front. 'Thank you,' he said. 'But I understand why Roberts and Kitchener were driven to do it. They had to cut off your supply of relief horses, food and drink – the supplies that kept you out on the veldt raiding our railway lines, lines of supply and townships. Your method of fighting, General, is a difficult one to combat. You know that. So more ... er ... unconventional methods had to be introduced to stop you.'

'Well. They do not stop us. But they make us angry. Very angry. We now invade the Cape Colony – and there are other commandos down here, on this side of the border, to raise rebellion here. It could end the war in our favour. We shall see.'

Fonthill shook his head sadly. 'No it won't, General. We just have too many men for you. You are vastly outnumbered and outgunned. You ought to stop the slaughter now and negotiate. Kitchener will listen. He is not Milner.'

De Wet stood, his face like thunder. 'On your feet, English,' he said. 'We move out. The war goes on.'

Fonthill stood. His horse, rifle, bandolier and revolver, of course, had all been taken from him but he was not bound in any way – probably because of his wounded arm – and no immediate guard was put on him. Everyone was busy around him and he remembered what Captain Steele had told him about the speed with which the Boers inspanned. Here, they were *running* between their tasks of dismantling their bivouac tents, untethering the horses, harnessing the oxen and man-handling the cannon into place.

He watched them with growing interest. These were the men who were leading the British such a merry dance, the men they were fighting; these were the hard core of the opposition, the 'bitter enders', as the burghers who had already surrendered called them. They looked like ruffians with their unshaven faces, blackened teeth, broken hat brims and tattered clothing. These fighters were the reason that British Tommies were burning farms, rounding up women and children and imprisoning them behind barbed wire on the open veldt. These were the enemy: farmers who could outshoot and outride professional soldiers, who prayed and sang hymns at every opportunity and who, not infrequently, flogged their Kaffir servants until their backs ran red with blood. These were the Boers.

Fonthill sighed and, now dismounted, trudged forward as the commando moved out.

He looked upwards to find the sun to give him an indication of the direction in which they were heading, but the sky hung down like a sagging, grey envelope and it was beginning to rain again, not heavily but in a soft curtain which added to everyone's misery. At least the ground was soft enough to leave plenty of traces for Hammond to follow – if, that is, he *was* following. Simon noticed that many of the burghers were without horses and others were walking and leading their tired beasts. It was clear that the strain of being constantly pursued was telling heavily now.

Sixteen oxen, he counted, were yoked to each of the wagons, which seemed to carry flour and ammunition, and eighteen to the Krupps guns. He thought that de Wet had given up such encumbrances. Evidently not.

Eventually, the commando came to what appeared to be a shallow lake that stretched before them. It was some thousand paces broad and long and offered no easy way around it. It was here, on hearing curses uttered ahead as the commando halted, that Fonthill realized that about ninety men who trudged in a guarded band before him were, in fact, British. It was clear that they had been captured by the commando and their horses commandeered. The pursuers were too close for the men to be released. Simon realised that he was lucky not to be guarded and decided not to join them. Better to stay loose, if he could.

The lake turned out to be only some three feet deep but the reality was that, in terms of its deterrence, it could have been thirty feet, for the bottom was glutinous mud. It was, in fact, a swamp. Horses and men could struggle through it with difficulty but the wagons and the cannon quickly became bogged down. Men were despatched to help the oxen by pushing the wheels until they too were caked in mud and looked like red-eyed creatures from some horror tableau. De Wet was ever present, screaming orders and laying about him with his whip.

Fonthill realised, from the desperation now written plainly on the general's blackened face, that he must know that British troops were not far behind him. If he was to escape, Simon realised, this was the time and place to do it.

Thirty oxen were now inspanned to each gun and, eventually, each was sucked through the mud and out the other side of the swamp. But the wagons resisted all efforts to move them and remained firmly embedded just a few yards from the beginning of the swamp. Eventually, de Wet gave up the struggle and ordered them to be pulled back on to firmer ground. He summoned a grey-bearded burgher whom Simon took to be a senior officer and spoke to him urgently, gesturing with his whip to the surrounding terrain.

De Wet splashed back through the churned-up water to the head of the column, most of which had now crossed the swamp. There he pointed with his whip and pulled away some three hun-

189

dred men, clearly choosing those with the fittest horses, and gestured for them to join the elderly burgher on the other side of the swamp. Immediately the men dismounted, and led their horses through the quagmire, where the leaders dispersed them among the undergrowth under the eye of greybeard. Ah! Simon realised that the famous rearguard was being mounted, with the aim of holding up the pursuers while the main commando escaped.

For the moment, all was confusion and he decided to seize the moment, idly moving towards where the wagons were still being pushed back, as though to help the men moving them.

Then he deliberately slipped in the brown glutinous water, quickly discarding his identifying arm sling as he did so, and emerged, dripping, covered in mud, looking brownly anonymous, just like the rest of the mud-covered Boers. Quietly, he began to move towards the edge of the swamp, where a thicket encroached into the water. Under its cover, Simon bent low and moved slowly away in a tangent, setting a course to take him around the edge of the rearguard.

Expecting at any moment to hear a shout and then a gunshot from behind, Fonthill moved on with his heart in his mouth, walking, half crouching, sometimes crawling, in a wide arc until he felt it was safe to turn back to pick up the spoor of the commando, which, hopefully, would lead him back to the pursuing British troops. It took him an hour before he came upon the beaten ground that showed where the Boers had passed, then, turning resolutely to the left, he tucked his aching arm into his unbuttoned shirt and marched towards freedom. It was not long before he heard the snort of a horse and the creaking of well-worn leather. He pulled back into the undergrowth.

It would be just his luck to be shot by a British outrider. In fact, it was the welcome sight of Mzingeli that met his gaze through the tangled leaves. The black man was bending low over his horse's neck and scanning the ground carefully.

'Mzingeli,' he called.

The black man's rifle appeared as if by magic and was presented to him. 'Who you?' he demanded, glaring at the mud-covered, scratched apparition before him.

'Simon Fonthill, old chap. And am I glad to see you.'

'Nkosi! Is it really you?'

'Yes it is. I've just been taking a mudbath. How close is the column?'

'Right behind me. Where you come from?'

'From de Wet's commando. Its rearguard is about half an hour ahead of you. I was captured but I escaped. Take me back to the column, there's a good chap. I don't want to be shot as some sort of mud monster.'

Mzingeli leant down and extended a hand to lift him onto the saddle behind, but Fonthill shook his head. 'I'll walk. I've hurt my arm. Lead on. Best be quick, I have urgent news for Major Hammond.'

Within minutes the two met the British advance guard, troopers riding cautiously, spread out across the trail. When they recognised Fonthill, they let out a cheer, which led to Hammond riding forward.

'Good God! It's Fo – the colonel.' He dismounted. 'Colonel, where the hell–'

'I'll tell you all about it in a moment, Hammond.' Fonthill kept his voice level. 'De Wet's commando is about half an hour ahead of you. He has been held up by a swamp that stretches for about a thousand yards either side of the trail and ahead of it. He has got about eleven hundred burghers through it, with three pieces of artillery, and they are moving on. But his wagons got stuck so he has left them at the edge of the swamp. They will look empty but, in fact, he has deployed his rearguard all around them, probably dug in by now and hidden by the undergrowth, so you could ride straight into a trap.'

'Ah, quite so, sir. Thank you. And you...?'

'I was riding to catch you up but somehow got ahead of you and was captured by the Boers. I escaped,' he grinned, 'as you can see, in the swamp. Have you been in action with them yet and where is General Knox?'

'No. No action. Couldn't catch 'em up because we started about two days behind them, as far as I can see. The general has followed a false trail – obviously laid by de Wet – and is about a day's march behind us, I would say.'

'Bloody hell! Now, where can I wash?'

Hammond turned and bellowed orders. A soldier appeared with a sponge, soap, leather fold-up bowl and a canteen of water.

'Thanks. Hold on for just a moment, while I clean up. Then I shall resume command.'

'Er ... very well, Colonel. I suppose that

rearguard won't go away.'

The mud had dried on Fonthill's tunic, shirt and riding breeches and he scraped it away with a knife. Then he gestured for the trooper to sponge his back while he soaped his face, breast, and hair and then threw the remains of the water over his head. Towelling himself down as best he could with one hand, he had a sudden thought.

'Where's the RSM?' he demanded of Hammond.

The major fixed his gaze somewhere over Fonthill's shoulder and replied in his distinctive drawl. 'I'm afraid he's under arrest, sir.'

Simon let the towel fall and, with his jaw dropped, regarded Hammond incredulously. 'What? Under arrest? On what charge, for God's sake?'

The drawl sounded even more languid in reply. 'Drunk in the face of the enemy, sir.'

Simon took a deep breath and forced himself to remain silent while he resumed slowly towelling his hair. 'Where is he now, then?' he demanded eventually.

'At the rear, under the care of one of the troop sergeants.'

'When was he arrested?'

'This very morning. There has been no time, of course, formally to bring charges.'

Fonthill fought to keep his emotions under control. This was the very thing he had dreaded. But he must not overreact. 'Very well,' he said, as coolly as he could manage. 'I will deal with the matter as soon as we have knocked off de Wet's bloody rearguard. Find me a horse and a rifle, will you? Then let us advance. Mzingeli!'

193

'Yes, Nkosi?'

'You heard all that. The Boer rearguard is ahead of us, quite near, but dispersed on the edge of a swamp near what appear to be empty wagons. Take two of your trackers and advance carefully on foot. Don't let the Boers see you. We need to find a way around them on both sides, so that we can attack them there as well as from the front. Find a way. Off you go. Take great care, now.'

'Yes, Nkosi.' For a brief moment the black man's imperturbable expression relaxed into a faint smile. 'I am glad you are back, Nkosi.'

Fonthill gave him an answering grin. 'So am I, old chap. So am I. Now off you go.' He turned to Hammond. 'Very well, Major. Send a rider back to Knox and tell him we've found the commando. Then put out an advance guard of twenty men, spread out and walking quietly on foot to prevent surprise. If the trackers can find a way for us to disperse to right and left – and the underbrush is not too thick near the swamp – order Cartwright to take his squadron to the left, Forbes his to the right and I will stay with you and A Squadron in the middle. We don't advance or fire until I give the order. Now pass this on and let us defeat this damned rearguard of de Wet's.'

'Very good, sir.'

Fonthill looked behind him and met answering grins from the subalterns and men of A Squadron. They all looked in good, fighting order. He nodded to them all, not recognising some of the faces. Then he remembered. The column had been reinforced and extended. As he watched, Cecil Cartwright and Colin Forbes forced their

194

way through the troopers and held out their hands, broad grins on their faces.

'Welcome back, sir.' Cartwright's Brummagem accent was like a breath of fresh air after Hammond's languor. Simon's heart warmed to him. 'Couldn't get a bath, then, where you've been?'

'No. The Ritz had run out of hot water. Now, Hammond has orders for you two. Report to him. We're going to be in action very soon.'

'Jolly good, sir. Good news.'

A horse, a rifle and a bandolier appeared and Simon busied himself with the saddle adjustment as an excuse while his mind raced. Drunk in the face of the enemy! It was a capital charge that could lead to a firing squad. He shook his head. Oh, 352, what had he done? Then a darker thought struck him. Despite his air of sangfroid, Hammond's features had carried an underlying but perceptible air of satisfaction when he reported the news. Jenkins's presence in the column in a position of such importance had always rankled with him. It had offended his very being as a cavalry officer brought up to see seniority rewarded only after years of conventional service. Could he have somehow contrived Jenkins's fall from grace? Fonthill frowned. The trouble was that the Welshman wouldn't need much encouragement to aid and abet such a conspiracy. Drink was Jenkins's abiding temptation. Well ... Simon mounted his horse. At least he had arrived in time. As the RSM's commanding officer, he would have to make the first judgement on the offence. There would be no summary hearing. But first, there was the little matter of de Wet's rearguard...

The column moved forward at a walking pace. At least this time, reflected Fonthill, there was no question of attempting to take the rearguard by surprise. It knew they were on their way. No surprise, then, but perhaps if they could outflank the waiting men and enfilade them, there would be the value of shock. For the rearguard was expecting to surprise and even ambush their pursuers. Unless, that was, Simon's escape had been detected and they would realise that he would have warned the advancing column. Ah well. They would just have to risk it.

After some twenty minutes, Fonthill held up his hand to halt the column, as Mzingeli, escorted by the sergeant in charge of the advance guard, trotted towards him.

'Wagons just up ahead, Nkosi,' the tracker reported. 'Boers there, all right, though not easy to see. But some signs of freshly dug earth. Means they have dug trenches, I think.'

'Thank you, Mzingeli. Are you sure you have not been seen?'

'Certain.'

'And can we disperse to left and right without crashing through thick undergrowth?'

'Yes. A few paces ahead, there is track that crosses this main path and curves round forward. If men go single file, it should be possible to curve round quietly. But I can smell swamp ahead.'

'Splendid. Well done, Mzingeli. Now,' Fonthill turned to Hammond. 'Major' – he could no longer bring himself to indulge in the familiarity of

196

calling him Philip – 'call all the officers forward, please.'

Surrounded by his officers, Fonthill issued his orders, elaborating on those given earlier to Hammond. The enemy was entrenched ahead on the edge of the swamp, he explained. The two flank squadrons were to spread in single file until they extended beyond the positions of the entrenched enemy. Trackers would go with them to indicate when this point was reached. It was unlikely that the Boers were spread widely because they would be expecting the column to advance unsuspectingly, four riders abreast and stretching back down the trail. Each squadron would be given fifteen minutes to deploy. Then, A Squadron would fire and this would give the signal to attack. Two volleys should be followed by a charge with fixed bayonets. The objective would be to eliminate the rearguard, destroy the wagons – which contained explosives – and then continue the pursuit of the main commando.

As he looked at the eager young faces around him, Fonthill involuntarily contrasted them with the mature, gaunt features of the burghers he had seen earlier in the Boer camp – all battle-hardened fighters, bedded down just ahead and waiting for them. He sighed. 'Good luck, gentlemen,' he said.

They quickly reached the point of deployment and Fonthill ordered the column to dismount and the handlers to take the horses to the rear. Where, he momentarily thought, was Jenkins now? And then he realised that this would be one of those rare moments in his life when he would

197

go into battle without his comrade at his side. He gulped. Well, there always had to be a first time.

The B and C Squadron troopers loped off to right and left, their rifles at the trail. Then, A Squadron spread out into the undergrowth on either side of the track and slowly, quietly began forcing its way towards the swamp. Soon, the tops of the wagons came into sight and Fonthill waved everyone to a standstill. He stood for several minutes, consulting his watch. As he did so, he shot several glances at Hammond, who was stationed in line, revolver in hand – no lower ranks' rifle for him! – some ten yards to his left. As far as Simon could see, his second in command looked perfectly composed – or was that a trace of perspiration glistening on his forehead? If it was, it was perfectly understandable, for the proximity of the swamp and the ever-present drizzle made the atmosphere uncomfortably humid. Then, as his watch showed that the quarter hour had passed, Fonthill slipped the bolt on his rifle to move around into the breach and waved for the line to move forward.

Very quickly now, the brush cleared and revealed the wagons drawn up on the edge of the swamp. They seemed empty but the Boers would not have posted men on them because of the ammunition stored there. Trenches, however, had undoubtedly been dug, for lines of earth disappeared into the bushes fringing the swamp and, now, rifles could be seen poking over the mounds, with the occasional Boer hat behind them.

Simon licked his lips. They were reaching the edge of the undergrowth and there were about thirty paces of open ground to cross before the enemy lines could be reached. Amazingly, it seemed that they had not been seen yet. He knelt and carefully rested his rifle on a low branch, for his injured arm prevented him from bringing it properly to his shoulder. Then, very slowly, he aligned foresight and backsight at a dim outline he could see at the end of the nearest Boer gun barrel. Oh, if only Jenkins, sure-shot Jenkins, were here to fire the first shot! That would certainly account for one of the enemy, at least. Then he squeezed the trigger and the sound echoed through the heavy air.

Suddenly, it seemed as though all hell had been let loose. A roar of gunfire rippled to right and left of him along the edge of the bushes, crashing in sequence and causing tiny fountains of soil and stone to spurt up from the earthworks ahead of him. Immediately, however, it was answered by a flicker of flame along the Boer trenches, sending bullets hissing through the undergrowth and causing gasps as they found billets in some of the troops facing them.

'Two volleys,' roared Fonthill, 'and then fix bayonets. Reload. Now. Volley one.' The sound was deafening in the moist air as seventy rifles boomed as one. Exultation seized Fonthill. 'Reload. Now, volley two.' Then, 'Fix bayonets. CHAAARGE!!!'

Thrusting aside his heavy rifle, Simon drew his revolver and scrambled to his feet and ran towards the Boer lines. He was dimly aware of rifle fire spluttering far to his left and right but more conscious of the cheering of the troopers of A Squadron all around him as they pounded towards the enemy. A mixture of perspiration and rain poured down his forehead, half blinding him, and he suddenly realised that he was mounting the Boer earthworks. He stood there for a second presenting his revolver, half expecting a bullet to crash into him, before he jumped down into the trench. An empty trench!

'What the hell?' He whirled round. On either side of him the troopers of his lead company were thundering down into the trench, presenting their bayonets – to no one. Somehow, in the few moments between the firing of the second volley and the arrival of the attackers, the Boers had fled. But to where?

He caught a glimpse of Hammond. 'Where the hell have they gone to?' he shouted. The major pointed with his revolver. On the southern side of the swamp, on a patch of higher, firmer ground, the Boers could be seen mounting horses and riding off, their heels digging into their horses' flanks as troopers from Captain Forbes's squadron broke cover and ran after them, firing impotently as they did so.

'Damn!' Fonthill slapped his thigh. 'They must have been ready all the time to cut and dash as soon as we appeared. They were off as soon as they heard me shout fix bayonets. And we've hardly got any of them, blast it!'

'Not quite, sir.' A moustached sergeant pointed with his bayonet. At least a dozen Boers were slumped against the trench wall, the backs of their heads shattered where the British bullets had exited. 'That's not bad shootin', sir, you know.'

Simon gave a faint smile. 'I suppose not, Sergeant.'

Hammond called across. 'Do you want to mount a pursuit, Colonel?'

Fonthill shook his head. 'No. By the time we get our horses up they will be miles away. I would rather blow up these wagons, so they can't come back for them, and then we must get after de Wet and his main body. Get some men to lay charges, will you, but take whatever flour they have left in the wagons, if any, for we can probably use it. Organise a burial party for the dead – on both sides – and check on casualties from the squadrons and give me a report. I will see that the horses are brought up.'

Wearily, Simon replaced his revolver in his holster and took a look around the open ground. No British soldiers lay there, but he knew that there would be some in the undergrowth, for there would have been little cover to protect them from the Boer fire. He recovered his rifle and walked along the edge of the bushes where the squadron had delivered their volleys. The medics were already kneeling by the wounded but, as usual, the Boer fire had been accurate and there were more dead with bullets to the head than wounded. He sighed and turned along the track by which they had entered the swamp clearing.

At the rear, where the handlers were still holding the reins of the horses, he saw a pathetic sight. Jenkins, his head bowed, was sitting on a log, his wrists handcuffed before him, and a corporal standing by his side with rifle and bayonet fixed. Simon's heart fell.

'Corporal,' he yelled. 'Take those damned handcuffs off the sergeant major this minute!'

'Wot?'

Fonthill realised that he must have presented a strange sight – bareheaded, his tunic covered in half-scraped mud and with his badges of rank quite obscured.

'It's all right, Corporal,' he reassured. 'It's Colonel Fonthill. Now unlock those cuffs, there's a good chap.'

Jenkins was regarding Simon open-mouthed and Fonthill realised that tears were beginning to course down the Welshman's face. 'Oh bloody 'ell, bach sir,' he said. 'It's you! Thank God for that... Oh, I'm sorry, so I am. So sorry, look you. I don't know what to say. But I'm glad you're all right.' He forced a wan smile. 'You look worse than I do. 'Ow's the shoulder, then? 'Urt you when you laugh, does it?'

Fonthill looked at the guard. 'Thank you, Corporal,' he said. 'Give me the keys. Tell the handlers to take the horses to the front. That will be all. The sergeant major will be in my care now.'

'Yes, sir. Very good, sir.' The NCO marched away, his face a picture of puzzlement.

Fonthill sat on the log beside Jenkins, under the puzzled gaze of the horse handlers, and spoke softly. 'Now, dear old 352,' he said. 'I think you'd better tell me everything that happened. Take your time and don't miss anything out – not *anything*, understand?'

Jenkins nodded, produced a filthy handkerchief from his breeches and blew his nose noisily.

Slowly, and then increasingly quickly, he told his story.

The column had camped two nights ago on the Free State side of the Orange, having ascertained where the commando had crossed but deciding it was unwise to make the crossing in the dim light of dusk. They had forded the river at dawn but then turned right along the riverbank instead of left, because de Wet had carefully laid a false trail that way. Jenkins had heard Hammond berating one of the black trackers. When Mzingeli had gently tried to intervene, Hammond had struck him across the cheek with his riding crop. Jenkins had then ridden up, and without a word to Hammond, led Mzingeli away to avoid him receiving further punishment.

'I 'ad a feelin' that the major didn't like that, see, 'cos he glared after me, look you. But I took no notice. But, equally, I gave 'im no cheek, see. I just rode away, with old Jelly in tow, so to speak.'

Fonthill felt his ire rise but merely said. 'Go on.'

Because the trackers had missed the main Boer spoor, the column had wasted more than half a day, so Hammond turned them round and began a forced march in the other direction – the true route taken by the commando. They had still no contact with the Boers, who seemed far ahead, so they camped that night in the rain, with little shelter for anyone. Then, said Jenkins, 'a most queer thing 'appened.'

'What was that?'

'In my sleepin' bag, when I crawled into it the previous night, was a full bottle of whisky. Now, I give you my word, bach sir, I 'ad never seen that bottle before in all me life, look you. In fact, I 'adn't touched a drop of the stuff at all on the march because I didn't 'ave any with me.'

Simon frowned and nodded.

'But, bless you, sleepin' out in that wet an' cold, with the damp penetratin' me poor old legs, I couldn't resist takin' a drop. An' then another one. I didn't stop to think too much about where the 'ell the bottle 'ad come from. If I thought about it at all, I thought it was a bleedin' miracle and I wasn't about to look that gift 'orse in the mouth, now was I? I woke up in the night feelin' miserable, the way you do when sleepin' rough, see, and took another drop. Before I knew where I was, I'd finished the bottle.'

'Were you drunk this morning?'

'No, not at all. Not staggerin' or shoutin' or anythin' like that. Just got a bad 'ead an' bad breath. Not late on parade, or anything. Lordy, it would take more than one bottle to knock me about, you know that.'

'So?'

'So, I'd 'ardly got out of me bedroll at reveille when the major rides up with the sergeant of the guard. "That warrant officer is staggerin'," he says. "Sergeant, smell 'is breath." Well, o'course, I smelt of drink, so I was arrested then and there and put on a charge for bein' drunk in the face of the enemy or somethin'. I can't understand it, bach sir. Honestly I can't. But I feel I've let you down and I'm right sorry, so I am.'

Fonthill was silent for a moment. Then: 'Where did you put your bedroll before turning in?'

Jenkins thought for a moment. 'With C Company. Their lines was the nearest, like.'

'Good. Now, I must think about all this. You will come up before me as your CO, of course – Major Hammond presumably believed that I wouldn't be back in time to hear the case and that he would do so as acting commanding officer. Now, 352, this is one of the most serious charges in the book and, if found guilty, it could mean the firing squad.'

'Oh bloody 'ell!'

'Quite. It's not going to come to that, if I can help it. But I must tread warily because our past association is known, of course. I must think. You will remain under arrest, of course, but no more bloody handcuffs. Now, stand up, put your helmet on straight and wipe your face. Goodness knows what Alice would say if she saw you like this. Stay here while I fetch the corporal. If you escape I will make sure you *are* shot.'

## CHAPTER TEN

The sound of the charges exploding on the wagons and the resultant boom as the ammunition within went up told Fonthill that the column should be moving. He instructed Jenkins to remain where he was and found the corporal who had been guarding him. 'The RSM remains temporarily under arrest,' he told him, 'so he remains under your care. But no handcuffs. March at the rear of the column.'

'Very good, sir.'

Walking back, Simon encountered Captain Cartwright and drew him to one side. 'Cecil,' he said, 'the RSM seems to have got himself into a bit of trouble while I have been away.'

Cartwright looked embarrassed. 'Yes, Colonel. I know.'

'He will come up before me, of course, but before he does so I would be most grateful if you could make some very discreet enquiries for me.'

'Of course, sir.'

'I understand that the RSM bedded down with or near the chaps of your squadron last night. Please get one of your NCOs – someone you can trust – to find out if any of your men saw Sarn't Major Jenkins with a bottle of whisky before he turned in. Secondly, ask if anyone saw *anybody else* with a bottle near Jenkins's bedroll last night. This could be important, Cecil, so I would be glad of your help – and your discretion.'

'You can rely on me, sir.'

Fonthill regained the head of the column and ordered the trackers out ahead to pick up the commando's trail, instructing Mzingeli to take great care to ensure that no false tracks should be followed. De Wet's cannon would surely slow him down and there was a chance that they could catch up with him before his rearguard could re-form and protect his back.

Rough graves had been dug in the marshy ground and the casualty list was handed to him. It made grisly reading. Twelve men had been killed and eight wounded, one of them seriously. The enemy dead numbered thirteen and no wounded had been captured. Presumably they had been taken off with the retreating rearguard.

Fonthill lifted his good arm and gestured ahead. Slowly, the column began picking its way through the slime and mud.

The pursuit continued for the rest of that day without any contact being made with the commando. It remained, it seemed, out of sight, out of range and frustratingly just out of grasp – somewhere ahead, moving fast. And Fonthill marvelled at the speed maintained by the Boers. True, they had no wagons now to restrain them, but they were still trundling the Krupps cannon and many of their men, he remembered, were without horses. They also had to keep their British prisoners moving with them, for to leave them behind would be to betray too much to the pursuers.

On the second day, they found real evidence of the plight of the commando. Their two cannon – the Krupps and a Maxim-Nordenfeldt – lay discarded by the side of the trail, hostages thrown to the pursuers, like supplies desperately tossed into the snow from a Russian sledge to distract the wolves close behind it. Fonthill gave orders that the guns should be ignored. General Knox could pick them up and carry them off as trophies – if he was following, that is. Simon scented that de Wet was now only just ahead, almost within reach.

The trail turned south, away from the river, and the going became harder, winding its way upward between a series of high ridges. Fonthill pushed his men hard. His practice now, when possible, was 'ride through the night, attack at dawn', his best hope of catching up with the Boer rearguard. This, however, had proved impossible. It became a cat and mouse game, with the Boer rearguard lying in wait and then opening fire, but then slipping away, leaving nothing but a few dug-out weapon pits and cartridge shells as Fonthill's men deployed to surround them.

So pursued and pursuers played their exhausting game through the broken ground and rivers of the northern Cape. Simon realised that de Wet could have no idea of the size of the column hard on his heels, otherwise he could have turned and crushed the chasing pack. As it was, the Boer slipped and slid in the corrugated terrain, turning and twisting like a trout caught on a fly. Sometimes, Knox's large and more slow-moving force caught up with Fonthill's men, only to fall behind again as the quarry took another evading turn. So the chase continued. At least the wily Boer was prevented from penetrating deeper into the Colony, for Fonthill heard that two other British columns were deploying along the passes to block the passage south.

It was exhausting work with so much night riding, and Simon had no time to convene a CO's hearing to try Jenkins, and the Welshman, now mounted again, was forced to plod along in the rear. Fonthill missed having his old comrade at his side, as much for his cheerfulness and constant support as for any advice he might have to offer. Views on tactics and strategy were never Jenkins's strong point. As it was, Hammond seemed to retreat into himself, a sullen and silent presence.

After ten days of gruelling riding, Fonthill felt he had his man, for the trail showed that de Wet was turning back north again, back to the borders with the Free State. Was he giving up his 'invasion'? That didn't matter either way, for Simon's scouts told him that the Orange was high and uncrossable. Surely, with his back to the river, the Boer would now have to turn and fight?

Fonthill turned in the saddle and shouted to the bedraggled band behind him: 'One more effort, men! I think we have them now.'

They passed Zanddrift, where two weeks before the raiders had crossed into the Crown Colony and it was clear that the Boers had stopped here and attempted to retrace their steps, but the river was running high and the spoor continued along the Colony bank, heading towards where Simon knew a large English force from the south were waiting for them.

And then, at an old, forgotten wagon drift, where the river suddenly appeared to be fordable, the tracks turned into the river and disappeared, only to reappear on the far bank. There, it could be seen clearly that they widened and dispersed, showing that the commando had regained the comparative safety of its homeland and been swallowed up again in the vastness of the Free State veldt.

Simon leant forward and bent his head over his saddle pommel. His wounded shoulder, now only roughly resting in a makeshift sling, throbbed as though the arm would break off and his whole body ached, protesting at the non-stop riding and the miseries of snatching only brief moments of sleep on the rain-sodden ground. He sighed and shook his head. Then, on impulse, he shouted across the muddy river, lifting his voice so that he felt it could be heard across the whole of the Orange Free State: 'You've got away again, de Wet. But this isn't the end. We'll catch you. I promise. We'll catch you!'

He straightened his back and looked around him in some embarrassment. Hammond glared stonily across the bouncing water but the men of A Squadron nearest to him caught his eye. A trooper in the lead raised his hat wearily and repeated the cry, 'We'll catch you! We'll catch you!' Immediately, the men behind broke into a ragged cheer, waving their hats and the cheer ran down the column.

Fonthill grinned back and suddenly felt better. He waved his hat in acknowledgement and stiffly dismounted. 'We will camp here tonight, Major,' he announced. 'Break out the tents.' He nodded to where a little clump of taibosch rough scrub mingled with patches of mimosa and crept down to the river. 'There should be kindling wood there. Once the horses are fed, let the men light fires and get a good night's sleep. Post only the lightest guard. We will be safe from attack here.'

Then he handed his horse to a trooper and walked back down the column, nodding to each man and murmuring, 'Well done, well ridden. At least we've stopped the bastards from invading the Cape. Well done. Couldn't have asked more of you all. Well done.'

At the rear, he found a weary Jenkins. He nodded to his guardian. 'Take a break, Corporal.

Thank you. Come back in ten minutes.'

Then he and his old comrade squatted companionably on the ground while Simon explained that they had now, at last, been forced to give up the pursuit. Jenkins nodded. "Ow long will they go on fightin', though, d'yer think?'

'God knows. De Wet, of course, isn't the only commando on the loose. There are several small ones still down here in the Cape, although from what I hear, they have not been able to rouse a rebellion. But in the Transvaal there are two sizeable forces under our old friend Botha and a general called de La Rey, and probably others too. It could go on for months yet.'

'And 'ave you 'eard from the missus?'

Simon frowned. 'Only one letter.' He cleared his throat. 'But I couldn't really have expected more. We've been on the move so much.'

A silence fell between them for a while. Then Jenkins spoke, deferentially bringing up what was on both of their minds. 'When ... er ... d'yer think you will ... er ...?'

'Hear the charges against you? Ah, any day soon. As soon as I can find a key piece of information. Maybe even tomorrow.' He turned towards the Welshman. 'When you come up before me,' he said, 'I want you to answer all my questions with clarity and tell your story just as you told it to me a few days ago. Deny explicitly that you were drunk and unfit to carry out your duties. And smarten up. Look like a sergeant major and all will be well.'

There was a discreet cough to announce the return of the corporal. Simon nodded to Jenkins

211

and strode away, walking along the line where the men were unsaddling, slowly erecting their bivouac tents and cutting wood for fires. Eventually, he found the man he was looking for. Captain Cartwright was deep in conversation with one of his sergeants.

Fonthill pulled him to one side. During the hunt for de Wet, Simon had not sought out Cartwright, not only because there had been little time for such an indulgence but also because he did not wish to put too much pressure on him. Now, however, was the time.

'Any news for me, Cecil, on the Jenkins matter?'

'Yes, sir. In fact, I was just going over the details with Sergeant Brewster there. I wanted to make sure I had the facts right.'

'Good. Let me know what you can.'

The two men stayed in quiet concourse for ten minutes, with Fonthill scribbling occasionally in his pocketbook. Then he nodded and walked away. He found Hammond painfully removing his riding boots.

'Ah, Major. Now that we have time, we will deal with the Jenkins matter in the morning, before we cross. Shall we say seven a.m.?'

Hammond allowed a flash of surprise to cross his features. 'Ah, very good, Colonel. Usual charge hearing?'

'No. Not quite. In view of Jenkins's seniority and of the seriousness of the charge against him, I will not hear the case alone. I would like the two other squadron commanders, Forbes and Cartwright, to sit with me.'

'And, presumably, with me?'

'No. As you are a principal witness that would be quite out of order. I shall need you to give evidence, with, of course, the sergeant of the guard with whom you arrested Jenkins.'

Hammond frowned. 'Sounds a bit ... ah ... irregular, if you don't mind me saying so, sir.'

'No, it is not. I have checked with army regulations.' In fact he had not, but he hurried on. 'I would be grateful if you would inform Forbes and Cartwright and the sergeant concerned accordingly. Seven a.m., then, outside my tent. I shall pitch it on the edge of the camp so that we shall have a degree of privacy, at least. Now get a good night's sleep, Hammond.'

'Ah, yes, indeed. Goodnight.'

Promptly at 6.45 a.m. the next morning, as the camp was awake, and bustling, Fonthill adjusted his hat and ducked outside his one-man tent and checked that his orderly had arranged three foldable chairs and an equally collapsible table behind the tent. He then sat and waited. It was not long before he was joined by Cartwright and Forbes, who sat on either side of him. Simon addressed them briefly on the form to be taken and nodded good morning to Hammond, who appeared with a slightly uncomfortable sergeant from his own squadron.

'Would you mind, Major, waiting with your sergeant until you are called, separately?' Fonthill spoke authoritatively. He was not at all sure that he was handling this hearing in accordance with army law but he was determined that he should remain in firm control at all times. 'Perhaps you would wait over there, beyond that tent, until you

213

are called to give evidence. I am sorry, but there are no further chairs. I hope, however, that this won't last too long.'

Hammond glared but touched the peak of his hat in salute and stalked away. Then the thud of boots on the sodden ground announced the arrival of Jenkins, dressed smartly, Fonthill noticed with relief, and marched between two sergeants, their pepper-and-salt moustaches showing their seniority in age at least.

'Sergeant Major, sir,' bawled one of the sergeants, 'quick march, leff right, leff right, leff right.' Then when the trio had reached the table. ''ALT! Cap orf.'

'Thank you, Sergeant,' said Fonthill, as urbanely as he could manage. 'At ease, the three of you, please. Now, Sergeant, would you please read out the charge against the sergeant major.'

The sergeant produced a piece of paper and read that at six a.m. on the morning of 24th of February 1901, Sergeant Major Jenkins had been found drunk and incapable while on active duty and facing the enemy.

'How do you plead to this charge, Sergeant Major?' enquired Fonthill.

'Not guilty, sir.'

'Very well. Let us hear the evidence. I believe that Major Hammond and Sergeant Wilkins are the main witnesses. Please call Major Hammond first.'

As though on the parade ground, Hammond marched into the small space in front of the table and stood at attention. 'At ease, Major,' said Fonthill. 'We don't appear to have a written deposition

214

of your evidence, so perhaps you would give it orally?'

'Very well, sir. On the morning in question I had cause to visit the lines where C Squadron were bivouacked and–'

'Cause? What cause, Major?'

Hammond frowned and blew out his cheeks. 'Well, I, that is, we were making the rounds just after reveille.'

'I see. And...?'

'I saw Sergeant Major Jenkins ... er ... staggering beside his bedroll.'

'Staggering?'

'Staggering, indeed.'

Fonthill put his pencil to his chin. 'Perhaps he could have lost his balance on just emerging from his bedroll. It often happens, I would think. Wouldn't you?'

'What? No. Oh no. The man was drunk.'

'What did you do then?'

'I ordered the sergeant of the guard, who was with me, to arrest the sergeant major for being drunk.'

'Yes, but how do you know he was drunk?'

'I could smell whisky on his breath.'

'But from what you have said, you ordered his arrest *before* you had smelt his breath. I repeat: how did you know he was drunk?'

'Ah, no, sir. My mistake. I recall now that I ordered the sergeant to smell his breath and when he confirmed the smell I ordered the arrest. We found an empty bottle of whisky in his bedroll.'

Simon made a note. 'Did the sergeant major resist arrest?'

'No, sir. He seemed ... ah ... unsteady and unsure about anything, in fact. He was, of course, quite drunk.'

'I see. Where were you when this occurred?'

'What? Oh, in camp.'

'Yes, I know that. But where?'

'Well, not far from here, actually. We had crossed the river at Zanddrift but followed the wrong tracks of the Boers and wasted much of the day before we turned back. We camped overnight at an unnamed place on the riverbank.'

'And the enemy was where?'

'Ahead of us, somewhere.'

'How far ahead?'

Hammond looked annoyed at the obvious irrelevance of these questions. 'Well, probably ten or fifteen miles or so. It took us quite some time to come up with their rearguard at the swamp.'

Fonthill made another ostentatious note and then looked up again at his second in command. 'So, when you arrested Sergeant Major Jenkins it was not exactly "in the face of the enemy", as you stated in the charge? The enemy was some fifteen miles away.'

'What? Oh, well, I suppose so. But we were very definitely on active service.'

'Quite so. But there is a difference, Major. The accused could go to a firing squad on that difference. All of us in South Africa are on active service, but not all are serving "in the face of the enemy". However, let us leave that for the moment. Now, is there any evidence that Sergeant Major Jenkins has been under the influence of drink at any other time during his service here?'

'Not as far as I know.'

'Very well.' Fonthill turned to his captains. 'Do you have any questions for the major, gentle-men?'

The two shook their heads negatively.

'Anything further to add on this charge, Major?'

'Er... No, sir. I think the evidence is clear-cut.'

'Very well, thank you, Major Hammond. We won't detain you from your duties further.'

His face set in a permanent scowl, Hammond saluted, turned smartly on his heel and strode away. Fonthill gestured to the senior sergeant. 'Call Sergeant Wilkins.'

Fonthill smiled at the new witness. 'Good morn-ing, Sergeant. At ease, please. Now,' he looked at his notes, 'I understand that, on the morning when you arrested Sergeant Major Jenkins, you were making your rounds as sergeant of the guard with Major Hammond?'

The sergeant looked puzzled. 'Yes, sir. Well, not exactly, sir.'

'What do you mean?'

'I had ordered reveille and I had made my rounds when the major rode up and asked me to come with him.'

'And where did you go?'

'Directly to where the sergeant major had just got out of his bedroll, sir.'

Fonthill shot a quick glance at his companions at the table. 'So the two of you were not making the rounds?'

'Well, no sir. I'd just done mine, anyway.'

'And when you arrived at where Mr Jenkins had been sleeping, what did you find?'

'Well, sir, the sergeant major was just getting up from his bedroll and he was a bit unsure on his feet, like.'

'Did he seem unfit?'

'Unfit? Well, I wouldn't say that exactly, but he was a bit wobbly.'

'How wobbly? Did he look as though he was about to fall over?'

The sergeant looked uneasy at the precision of the questioning. 'Well, sir, I wouldn't say that exactly. He was a bit unsteady, like.'

'And the major ordered you to smell his breath. How bad was it?'

The sergeant ventured a smile. 'I've known worse, sir. But I would say that he had definitely been drinking.'

'And the major ordered you to look in his bed-roll and you found an empty bottle of whisky inside it. Is that correct?'

'Yes, sir.'

'Very well. Now, while out on the veldt the rule is that only officers are allowed to carry alcoholic drink with them and that warrant officers, NCOs and other ranks will only drink such stuff when a general issue of rum is made. Is that not so?'

'Yes, sir.'

'Have you any idea, then, where the sergeant major obtained his whisky bottle?'

'No, sir. I suppose he brought it with him in his kit.'

Fonthill nodded and turned to the captains. 'Any further questions, gentlemen?'

Again the negative shakes of the head.

'Thank you, Sergeant. Return to your duties.'

Jenkins had been following the proceedings with an air of intense interest, occasionally opening his mouth to intervene but thinking better of it. Now his eyes widened with surprise as he heard Simon say, 'I understand, Captain Cartwright, that you have a witness whom you think could shed a little light on this case?'

Cartwright nodded. 'Yes, sir. As you know, Sergeant Major Jenkins bedded down with my C Squadron that night. I would like to call one of my troopers to give evidence.' He looked up. 'Sergeant, will you find Trooper Blackshaw at my squadron? He will be standing by, waiting for the call.'

Fonthill turned once again to his captains. 'Gentlemen, I don't wish to waste time, because we have a river crossing to make. So while we are waiting for this soldier, may I suggest that we hear Sergeant Major Jenkins's own evidence.'

'Of course, sir.'

'Very well. Now, Sergeant Major, you have heard the charge against you and the evidence. What is your reply?'

Jenkins stepped forward and took a deep breath. As he spoke, a small trickle of perspiration crept down the side of his face and disappeared into his great moustache. But, as instructed, he spoke clearly. He had, indeed, drunk the bottle of whisky while in his bedroll during the night. But he was used to strong drink and it had not affected him. On leaving his bedroll, he had stumbled a little because the ground was uneven but he was not drunk, he had not staggered and he was not unable to carry out his duties. He did not deny that

219

his breath probably smelt of strong liquor but he was definitely not drunk.

Fonthill regarded him steadily. 'Did you bring the whisky with you from Johannesburg?'

'No, sir. I had never seen it before when I found it tucked into my bedroll when I crept in at lights out.'

'Why, then, did you drink it?'

'Because, sir, I was freezin' cold, see, an' me legs was achin'. I didn't stop to wonder where it'd come from, except to think that maybe a kind friend – perhaps one of the officers' orderlies – 'ad slipped it into me bedroll. Anyway, I just drank it through the night when I woke up occasionally with the cold, look you ... er ... sir.'

'So you have no idea how the whisky came to be in your bedroll?'

'None at all, sir. On me mother's deathbed, I swear that.'

The escorting sergeant cleared his throat. 'Excuse me, sir, but Trooper Blackshaw is here.'

'Thank you, Sergeant. Bring him forward. Captain Cartwright, this is your witness, I believe. So please question him.'

Cartwright nodded and addressed the young trooper who now stood, a little apprehensively, before them. 'Blackshaw, you are in my C Squadron, are you not?' Fonthill had to disguise a half smile at the magisterial tone adopted by the young captain.

'Yes, sir.'

'Tell us what you saw on that night two weeks ago when we camped last on the banks of this river.'

'Well, sir, I was layin' out me bedroll when I saw the sergeant major doin' the same about a coupla yards away from me. Then he went off and said he was goin' for a pee.'

'What happened then?'

'I crawled into me own roll and tucked meself in well because it was a proper awful night, see, cold an' drizzling.'

'Was it dark?'

'Sort of, sir. Gettin' dark, anyway. Sort of very dusky.'

'Go on.'

'I was tucked in well an' truly but then I saw someone come back to the sarn't major's bedroll. I thought it was him at first, but then I see it was a trooper. I couldn't see his face but he had the flashes of A Squadron on his shoulder. He was carryin' a bottle of something, I could see that. Then he put it in the sarn't major's bedroll and sort of slunk away. I thought it a bit strange but I was dog-tired and went to sleep more or less straight away. I saw nothing more until I was awoken at reveille and saw the sarn't major bein' arrested.'

A silence descended on the little court. Suddenly, a *sakabula* or widow bird, with a long, undulating tail, swept low over them and caused a start of surprise. Then Fonthill intervened.

'Trooper, when Sergeant Major Jenkins was led away, was he staggering or in any way looking unstable?'

'No, sir. He looked a bit ... well ... fed up, but that was all.'

'Thank you. Get back to your duties.' He looked

221

at the senior escorting sergeant. 'Take Mr Jenkins away, Sergeant, and wait with him, both of you, behind that tent over there. We shall call you back in a moment or two.'

'Very good, sir. Sergeant Major, sir, cap on. Attenshun! Right wheel quick march, leff right, leff right, leff right.' Then they were gone.

Simon removed his wide-brimmed hat. 'Now, gentlemen,' he said. 'Let us review the evidence. But first I must not sail under false colours in this case. You all know that Jenkins and I served together as scouts with various elements of the British army intermittently over the last twenty years and, in that time, he became my comrade. He received the Distinguished Conduct Medal for his service with me in the Sudan some years ago, and I must tell you that I have recommended him for a bar to that medal for the initiative he displayed several weeks ago in our engagement with de Wet's commando at Bethulie, when he took over command of A Squadron after I was wounded and ... ahem ... after Major Hammond's departure. General Kitchener himself requested that I bring Jenkins with me when I accepted this commission. This all says something, of course, about Jenkins's character and ability as a soldier, but it also reveals my relationship with a man I call a friend. In fact, you could well say that I am not the most objective man to lead this tribunal.'

The two captains regarded him keenly but made no comment. So he continued.

'Nevertheless, this is my command and it is my duty to hear this charge. But I have asked you to help me in this task because there are unusual

222

elements to it and I am anxious to ensure that I could not be accused later of being less than impartial in judging Jenkins in this matter.'

Captain Forbes, the older of the two squadron commanders, frowned. 'I am not quite sure that I follow you, sir,' he said. 'Unusual features...?'

Fonthill nodded. 'I am afraid so. Firstly, the charge has been brought by someone of senior rank in this column, Major Hammond, my second in command. Normally, his word would carry overriding weight to that of the accused. But there are conflicting elements here.

'For instance, he said that he was making his rounds with the sergeant of the guard, but that was not true. The sergeant had already made his rounds. Major Hammond took the sergeant directly to where Jenkins was sleeping, as though he had some reason to do so.'

Forbes slowly nodded in agreement. 'Then,' Fonthill went on, 'he said that he smelt Jenkins's breath but he did not, he asked the sergeant to do so. These are details but details are important on such a serious charge. It goes on. He said that the sarn't major was staggering drunkenly, but we have two witnesses, Sergeant Wilkins and Trooper Blackshaw, who disagree.' He looked at his notes. '"Just a bit wobbly" were the sergeant's words and "a bit fed up" were those of the trooper. The charge of being drunk in the face of the enemy certainly does not stand, for to face the enemy Jenkins would have had to travel something between ten and fifteen miles.

'Now, Jenkins does not deny that he drank the whisky during the course of the night. The question arises, how did he get it? He denies carrying it with him and says that it was slipped into his sleeping roll. We now have Trooper Blackshaw's words that, indeed, he did see someone from A Squadron put the bottle into the sleeping bag.'

Forbes's frown deepened. 'Of course, sir, Jenkins could have bribed someone to steal a bottle – or indeed buy it – from one of the officers, and not necessarily from A Company.'

'That is true, Colin. However, there is also the possibility that someone – someone with a grudge against the regimental sergeant major, someone who had heard of Jenkins's occasional weakness for drink – could have arranged, or ordered, the bottle to be placed there.' He sighed. 'You see, gentlemen, what I meant when I said that there were unusual elements to this case.

'I must tell you frankly that I cannot convict this man on this evidence. Please remember that being drunk in the face of the enemy is a capital charge and could lead to the firing squad. Normally, in a case of this severity, one would bring a character witness for the defendant. Today, I must be that witness, for no one – probably on earth – knows him better. I assure you that in twenty years, I have never known him tell a lie. I have known him to be drunk, but only after a consumption of alcohol that would kill a mule, not merely one bottle, and never, never, when on duty. He is a splendid soldier whom this column would miss terribly if we found him guilty.

'Now, gentlemen, those are my concerns. What are your views?'

Cartwright spoke first, the earnestness of his

expression echoed in the fact that he did not try now to hide his flat, Midlands accent. 'I agree with you, sir,' he said. 'There are too many strange ... what is the word ... anomalies, I think it is, in the evidence to convict Jenkins. I also am impressed by your statement concerning his character. Although I think the putting of the bottle in his bedroll is strange, if you say that you have never known him to tell a lie, I don't see that we can suspect otherwise, given the other circumstances.'

Fonthill nodded. 'Thank you, Cecil. And you, Colin?'

Forbes, however, clearly remained perturbed. 'I am worried, sir, about your mention of someone having a grudge against Mr Jenkins and deliberately planting the bottle.' He raised his head and looked squarely at Fonthill. 'That could only be Major Hammond, by the sound of it. Are you accusing him, sir?'

'No, I am not.' Simon inwardly congratulated the man on his integrity and decided to speak frankly. 'I have no evidence and I must leave it at that. To bring such a charge would demand such an exercise in establishing evidence that it would break this column in two. We would, for instance, have to check the number of whisky bottles each officer took in his pack and attempt to establish if one was missing. I do not wish to embark on such a divisive undertaking while we are in the field.

'However, neither am I happy at such a senior warrant officer being convicted of a capital offence on such flimsy and conflicting evidence. At the moment, we are two in favour of acquittal – although, if we ultimately decide on that, it will be delivered to Jenkins with a severe warning about further drinking, I can promise you that. But, now, Colin, do you wish to make the acquittal unanimous or to submit a minority report recommending conviction. You must decide now.'

Fonthill clenched his buttocks in tension as Forbes frowned and considered his position. A two-to-one decision in favour of acquittal would seriously compromise the report he would have to make to French on the subject. A unanimous verdict would make his task so much easier.

Eventually, Forbes lifted his head. 'On reflection, sir,' he said gloomily, 'I must make it unanimous, in view of the unusual contradictions we have heard. But I would be much happier if you could assure us that no charges will be brought against Major Hammond in this matter, official or otherwise.'

Simon sighed. 'I will give you that assurance, Colin,' he said, 'unless, that is, further evidence emerges – *cast-iron* evidence, mind you – that would mean I had no alternative but to do so. Will you accept that?'

'Of course, sir.'

'Very well, gentlemen. Thank you for your time.' He raised his voice. 'Sergeant.'

'Sir.'

'Please bring Sarn't Major Jenkins here. Do not march him!'

'Very good, sir.'

Jenkins came to attention in front of the three, an expression of such anxiety on his face that Simon felt nothing but sorrow for his old friend. However, he adopted a stern expression and ordered the two escorting sergeants to fall out and to return to their duties. When they had departed, he addressed the Welshman curtly.

'Mr Jenkins,' he said, 'we have found you not guilty on the charge brought against you and that charge is now dropped. However, you did admit drinking a whole bottle of whisky while out in the field with the column and we all consider this to be symptomatic of what could become a serious problem, if you allow it. Any further transgression of this nature will be dealt with most severely. Now, dismiss.'

Jenkins's moustache began to twitch but the Welshman immediately smothered the embryonic grin. Instead, he looked sternly ahead and barked, 'Thank you, sir. I understand, sir. Thank you.' He saluted, turned smartly on his heel and was gone.

The three rose. 'Now, gentlemen,' said Fonthill. 'I will break the glad news to Major Hammond, and will you now get your squadrons across this bloody river as quickly as possible? We still have work to do.'

## CHAPTER ELEVEN

Alice was not at all surprised to find, on her return to Pretoria after waving Emma goodbye at Bloemfontein, a message at her hotel asking her to call on General Kitchener at 'her earliest convenience'.

Her round-up story of the camp visits had

pulled no punches this time and she had cabled a vivid picture of the fetid conditions there and of the growing death toll. Her hope was that, at the very least, the War Office in London would have asked questions of its commander-in-chief in South Africa. But she had no intention of meekly accepting a dressing-down from the formidable Kitchener of Khartoum. She had some questions to ask *him*!

She sent a quick message to his headquarters to enquire what time would be convenient and by return was told to come 'at once'. Ah, the battle lines were being drawn! A quick thought persuaded her to change into a floral dress with workmanlike but pretty pumps and she tied a well-worn but much loved apple-green scarf around her throat and brushed her hair. She applied a little face powder to soften the tan but nothing more outré by way of cosmetics. Alice wanted to appear feminine to the great commander – she hated the masculine pose adopted by some women journalists of her acquaintance – but she certainly was not going to flirt with him. From what she had heard, anyway, such tactics were a waste of time with the man.

At the door of the hotel, she was handed an envelope. Tearing it open, she read:

*I hear you are back. Why didn't you write to me? I have missed you so much. Can we meet tonight for dinner?*
*James*

Alice sighed and waved away the messenger.

'No reply,' she said. She tucked the envelope into her bag. He must have bribed someone at the hotel to let him know as soon as she returned. A little frisson ran through her. Dinner tonight! It was tempting. Then she tossed her head. She would think about that later. She had things to do first.

She hired a pony and trap to take her to Kitchener's HQ, for she didn't want to arrive looking dusty or less than her best. Alice realised that Kitchener had the power to order her removal from the corps of accredited correspondents in South Africa and that would never do. She was determined to fight her corner but she mustn't go too far. If just a touch of feminism might detract the great man from sending her home, then she wasn't above deploying it.

The guard at the gate of the unpretentious house gave her a big grin and a smart salute, which earned him a warm smile in return. Then she was ushered directly into the great room, with its *objet d'art* clutter and walls covered with pin-studded maps. Kitchener advanced to meet her with, to her surprise, a wide smile stretching his great moustache.

'Welcome back, Miss Griffith,' he said, gesturing her to a chair facing his desk. 'My, but you have been busy.'

Alice gulped. A charm offensive was not what she had been expecting. Then she remembered: Kitchener was renowned as a soldier, of course, but he was building a reputation also as a shrewd negotiator. She must be careful not to be sucked in.

'I have indeed, General,' she smiled. 'And I am so grateful to have the chance of discussing with you the question of the camps.'

'I am at your disposal, madam. Alas, we don't get the *Morning Post* out here, of course, but the War Office has sent me the gist of what you have been writing. This Miss Hobhouse seems to be a most formidable lady. I am sorry that I did not have the opportunity of meeting her. Now, let us have some tea.'

He reached out a large hand and tinkled a small bell. 'China or Indian?'

'China, please, with a little milk but no sugar.'

The request was conveyed to an orderly and Kitchener settled into his chair. 'Well, you have certainly given us a rough time, Miss Griffith – ah, I should have asked. Forgive me. How is your husband? I knew that he had been wounded and that he plunged back immediately into the fray in the south. Have you had news of him?'

Alice felt herself flushing. This would never do. She had not realised that the morose, allegedly misogynistic Lord Kitchener could turn on the charm so effortlessly. Perhaps this was the calm before the storm? 'Thank you. I am afraid I have not heard from him for some time. We both have been moving about the country rather a lot, but in different directions and in different degrees of comfort, I fear.'

Kitchener nodded. 'Well, from what I have heard, he is doing good work on the border. He has nearly pinned down the elusive de Wet – you will remember him, of course – several times. I am delighted that he decided to join us in this

230

miserable war.'

Ah! Alice realised that a door had been pushed slightly ajar. She jumped in.

'I suppose all wars are miserable, Lord Kitchener – you will know this better than anyone. But this one certainly seems to be particularly cruel, not only in conventional terms but in the way Boer civilians have suffered. These camps, you know, are a disgrace.'

Kitchener sat back in his chair and put his fingers together. 'So, it seems, you have written.' A pause ensued and Alice wondered whether he was waiting for her to build her attack, but then the general leant forward and continued.

'You and I, of course, have discussed before my reasons for clearing the farms and, although you may not agree with them, they were one of the few strategies I could adopt for ending this war, which is costing so many lives and, indeed, considerable expenditure by the British Treasury. In fact, I have to tell you that it is now beginning to work. More and more of the Boer fighters out there on the veldt are being caught in our net, as we corner them. You see, they no longer have their homes to fall back on to give them comforts and essentials. As a result, these commandos are hungry, riding broken-down horses and wearing threadbare clothes. It is gruelling work but we are wearing them down.'

'But you don't seem able to catch de Wet, Botha, de la Rey and the rest. The veldt may be burning, but they still ride it.'

'And they are splendid fighters, there is no doubt of that. They are fighting for their home-

231

land, they know the terrain far better than we do and they have courage and skill. But they cannot win. We outnumber them and are closing in on them all the time.'

Alice sighed. 'But the camps, sir, the camps. I understand that you now have ninety thousand white Boers behind the wire and some twenty-four thousand blacks. And the women and children are dying like flies.'

Kitchener nodded solemnly. 'Quite. Enteric fever. It's also causing more deaths among our troops than Boer bullets or shells. You would have thought that these sturdy Afrikaner families would have been more resistant to it, used, as they are, to outdoor living with crude sanitary conditions. But it seems they are not.'

They were interrupted by the arrival of tea and the general presided over its pouring with the fussy attention of a parson's wife. Then he resumed.

'Miss Griffith, I have to confess that I got this wrong. I believed that we – the army – could handle the camps without too much effort. Goodness, we move vast forces around the country and set them up in temporary accommodation all the time. We are good at it. But we seem to have got these internment camps all wrong. We have over-looked the detail involved in housing these families.'

He shook his head and the general looked suddenly weary. Alice had a brief insight into the weight of responsibility being carried by this famous man – 'K of K'. She remembered hearing that this master of detail and logistics (he was, of course, a Royal Engineer) found it difficult to delegate. He went on: 'We left too much to be decided locally and did not set up a proper administration to establish adequate rations, cooking equipment, water supplies and sanitary arrangements – all the things you have written about.'

Alice, her head buzzing, scrambled in her handbag for notebook and pencil. 'May I quote you on this, General?' she asked.

'Only if you report what I am doing to rectify the situation, madam.'

'But of course. Do tell me.'

'My masters in London have agreed that we should transfer the establishment and running of the camps – and we can't, of course, pull them down because, despite their faults, they are effective – I repeat, to transfer their complete administration to the civilian authorities. Lord Milner, therefore, is leaving Cape Town and moving up to Pretoria to take responsibility for the camps and, indeed, the civilian administration of the country. His talents in this area are well proven and immediate improvements in the camps, including the replacement of tents by wooden buildings to give greater protection to the families, will be undertaken. This will allow the army to get on with the prosecution of the war.'

Kitchener, his face now wearing a weary smile, leant forward. 'And I have another piece of news for you, Miss Griffith,' he said. 'General Botha, who now seems to have taken over the complete Boer leadership in the Transvaal, has agreed to talk to me about establishing an armistice.' He held up his hand. 'Now this certainly does not

233

mean the end of the war. Botha is probably the most amenable of the guerrilla leaders to an armistice, for his State, of course, contains more uitlanders than all the others put together and the Free State people in particular, who were the last to come into the war, seem now the most determined to continue it. So Botha will have his work cut out to get all the Boer leaders to the table. But, my goodness, it's a start.'

His smile widened. 'So there you are, madam. Two – what do you call 'em – scoops, isn't it, in one day.'

Alice did not immediately reply, for she remained scribbling, her head down. Then she looked up and gave him the most dazzling smile she could muster.

'Two pieces of good news, sir. You have made my day, in more ways than one. Now, please excuse me, for I must cable my people in London. I will, of course, pass my story through the censor here. I presume I will have no problems with him?'

'Certainly not. Fire away.' He stood and extended his hand. 'Perhaps you might find a way of implying that I am not quite...' hesitantly, almost bashfully, he searched for the right word '...the *monster* that I am sometimes painted. Now good day, madam. Oh, and do give my good wishes to your gallant husband when you next seen him.'

'I will, sir. I will. And thank you.'

Alice walked down the wooden steps from the veranda, astonished the sentry outside by patting his shoulder, and greeted the blue sky above with a great grin. Then she examined her fob watch. Good. She had time to get her story on the wire to catch tomorrow's edition. And what a story! If it was true that Kitchener had given her these two pieces of news exclusively then she did, indeed, have page lead copy here. She climbed back onto the trap, which she had kept waiting, and began scribbling straight away.

Halfway back to the hotel she looked up from her notepad. James! Well, she reckoned she would be able to write and cable her story and still have time to join him for dinner. She hugged herself with glee.

The two stories, which, of course, she put together as one, virtually wrote themselves and she had plenty of time to take them to the censor's office – where she met with a raised eyebrow but no difficulties – send a message to Fulton in the journalists' compound and then return to bathe and make herself ready for dinner. She felt no sense of betrayal at agreeing to see James over dinner. It presented itself as a civilised and, she confessed, pleasurable opportunity to tell him that whatever there had been between them was now over. They would continue to be friends, of course, but she was a happily married woman and that would be that.

Relieved at resolving a course of action to solve the problem that had been hanging over her for weeks, Alice dressed with care. She selected her only other dress, a well-cut apple-green, rather formal garment, made of the finest Egyptian cotton and cut low at the front to reveal a touch of décolletage. It was Simon's favourite and she felt a tremor of unease at wearing it, but, what the hell, tonight would be her last evening with James Fulton so she cast aside any insipient feeling of guilt. She slipped her only pair of high-heeled shoes on her feet and applied face powder and, this time, a touch of rouge. Alice had to admit that, looking at herself in the mirror, she felt deliciously naughty.

Fulton arrived at the hotel a little early and carrying a bouquet of veldt flowers: mimosa, ericas, maidenhair ferns, picked, he said, by himself that very afternoon. She accepted them with a light kiss to his cheek and inwardly marvelled at how handsome he looked, with his dark-tanned face and black wavy hair set off by white ducks and lightweight jacket. Despite the heat he had paid her the compliment of wearing a stiff white collar and brightly striped tie – old school or regiment? It didn't matter but she couldn't help speculating for a second or two on its provenance. After all, she knew nothing about his background.

'Dinner?' she asked. 'That sounds very grand for Pretoria. Surely there are only the stuffy old clubs and hotels. Where are we going?'

He flashed his teeth. 'Certainly no hotel or club. I have found a delightful little restaurant on the edge of town. Kept by two Chinese. Best food in the whole of South Africa. I promise you will like it. And they know their wines. Come on, I have hired a carriage.'

The carriage was open but he had provided a parasol, for the evening sun was still comparatively high. Pretoria was a pretty little town and as they drove through its leafy suburbs, with their

236

imported eucalyptus trees and bayonet-erect aloes hedging the gardens, Alice felt relaxed and replete, after the strain of virtual non-stop travelling and recording the miseries of the camps. As they drove, they began to leave the little wooden houses behind and headed towards the yellow veldt. Overhead larks and pipits sang and the regal pow bird sailed swiftly through the sunlight, a patch of colour against the blue.

Alice felt so elated that she had to share her good news about her interview with Kitchener. Fulton was impressed. 'Don't use it, though, James, will you?' she begged. 'Kitchener gave them to me exclusively. But I am telling you now so that you can have ample time to follow it all up tomorrow, if you wish.'

'Of course I won't use it.' He took one hand away from the reins and squeezed her fingers. 'Well done. You know, Alice Griffith, you are the prettiest woman in the whole of South Africa. And you're damned good at your job, too, blast it.'

Alice threw back her head and laughed. 'Stop flattering me, James Fulton. I am far too old for all that stuff.'

His grin disappeared and he leant towards her. 'Oh no you're not. And you know it.' He stole a kiss on her cheek and then quickly flicked the whip over the horse's neck. 'Won't be long now. It's just on the edge of town.'

The restaurant was little more than a hut on the edge of the veldt but it was comfortably furnished and two candles were glowing on the *stoep*, where a table had been set for two and covered in the crispest white cloth. Alice had developed a taste for oriental cooking in China and the two venerable Chinamen, who seemed to be the only staff, had prepared a meal of chicken, rice, pork and mixed vegetables that promised to be nothing short of delicious. The white wine, from the Cape, was crisp, cold and fruity on the palate.

They had just finished their first course, a noodle soup, when James put his napkin to his lips and rose from the table. 'Sorry, Alice,' he said, but I must ask you to excuse me for a moment. Mr Chang here has promised to order me some wine but I like this much better, so I am going to ask him to change the order. It may mean going through the catalogue for another choice out at the back. I won't be more than five minutes.' And he leant across and filled her glass.

Alice shrugged but put her nose into the wine glass and allowed the bouquet to rise through her nostrils. Then she settled back comfortably in her chair and raised the glass to her lips. Nothing much mattered tonight. She had sent her newspaper two good, exclusive stories that would undoubtedly make a page lead and she savoured the moment. Of course, she would tell James of her decision to break off their relationship but it could wait until the end of the meal – or perhaps even tomorrow? The warm, gentle evening, the wine, the company of a handsome, attentive man – it was all to be enjoyed for the moment. Goodness knows, she had been working hard enough over the last six weeks or so. Surely she could be allowed a little indulgence? Her thoughts turned to Simon, down there on the border with his injured shoulder, and she hoped that he was out of harm's way. She would write to him in the morning, a warm loving letter.

Fulton returned full of apologies and immediately refilled her glass as the main course arrived. Somewhere, a horse galloped away through the night and a bird screeched. He ordered chopsticks and she, still comparatively fresh from Peking, instructed him on how to use them. Their fingers touched as she did so and, once again, that frisson of excitement ran through her.

As they ate, they spoke about the camps and Alice recited her experiences of travelling with Emily Hobhouse. Fulton expressed his admiration for her initiative in finding the little woman and strongly supported her indignation at the internment of the Boer families and the conditions in which they were kept. While she had been touring the camps, he had remained with the press contingent who had spent most of its time with French chasing Botha and de la Rey in the Transvaal. Alice realised that she had so much in common with Fulton: their love of newspapers and the written word, their dislike of the war and, of course, Kitchener's farm clearance policy.

When the meal was finished, James leant across and said: 'There is a lovely garden at the back. Shall we take a cognac out there?'

Alice looked at her watch. 'Why not? It's such a beautiful evening.'

Fulton ordered the cognac – 'French, mind' – and they then strolled arm in arm round the corner of the little house to find what was, indeed, a charming little terrace and garden at the rear, shaded by shrubs and with magnolias in flower casting a strong enough perfume to combat the odour of cooking from the kitchen. Mr Chang himself brought out balloon glasses containing the delicious liquid and they settled on a swing couch perfectly placed under trees at the bottom of the garden.

There they sat, silently looking at the stars and sipping their brandy.

'You know I'm in love with you, don't you?' Fulton put his arm about her shoulders and pulled her towards him.

Alice did not resist but snuggled her cheek against his breast. 'No, you're not,' she said. 'It's the bloody wine, the brandy and the moonlight. So don't exaggerate. Journalists must be objective.' Then she ruined it all by hiccupping.

He laughed. 'Perhaps you're right.' Then he put down his glass and carefully took hers too and placed it on the ground. Then he kissed her, thrusting his tongue questioningly into her mouth. Alice froze for a moment – the moment of truth that she knew would be coming. Then she responded ardently, all the anxieties, the hardships and the self-questioning disappearing in a trice as she felt passion and, yes, lust swelling within her.

Fulton pushed her back and began unbuttoning her dress with practised fingers and then removing her undergarments. She lay back and let him undress her until he was caressing her and gently kissing her nipples. Alice closed her eyes and let the warmth of his embrace and the fumes of the alcohol sweep over her. She realised that she was being penetrated but she didn't care and she rose to meet his thrusts, all thoughts of morality and propriety dropping away from her as easily as her clothing.

At the finish, they both lay breathless and Alice realised that they were now lying on the grass. Suddenly, she felt cold. She looked up at him and saw that he was grinning at her, not smiling, but his face wreathed in a kind of animal grimace, showing satisfaction and, yes, mastery. She pulled away and reached for her clothing and began trying to dress with both haste and dignity. She achieved neither and Fulton burst out laughing.

'Here, let me help you,' he said.

'No, thank you. I can manage. Oh, James. I am not sure we should have done that. I am beginning to feel ashamed.'

'Ah, no, you mustn't, my love. It was all very satisfying, I would say, and we must do it again.'

Alice shook her head violently. 'No. No. I feel... I don't know what I feel. Yes I do. I feel ... like an animal. Oh God!'

His grin widened. 'Well, that's not a bad description, Mrs Fonthill. You were rather like a tigress, I would say.'

Alice felt a tear start and immediately produced a scrap of handkerchief and blew her nose. 'Please take me back to the hotel, James.'

He reached across and picked up her glass. 'Oh, come now. Finish your cognac. It's cost the earth.'

'Thank you, no. I have certainly had enough to drink for one night, thank you very much. Do please take me home.'

'Very well. Let me settle the bill.'

They drove back through the now much cooler evening without exchanging a word. At the hotel, Alice stepped down and looked up at him with tears in her eyes. 'I can't help thinking that you took advantage of me, James,' she said. 'But I do not blame you. I blame myself and I have to confess that I feel ashamed. I have never before committed adultery and...'

Fulton leant down and touched her cheek with his finger. 'That may be so, my dear, but you enjoyed it, now didn't you? Admit it.'

Alice looked at him and this time could not prevent the tears coursing down her cheeks. Without another word she turned on her heel and fled into the hotel. In her room, she flung herself on her bed and sobbed. It was a long time before she stirred herself to wash and undress, before crawling under the bedclothes, shuddering from the cold.

In the morning, as she breakfasted with a stony face, a cable was handed to her, delivered from the post office. It ran:

CONGRATS ON YOUR STORIES STOP SPLENDID WORK STOP NOT QUITE EXCLUSIVE AS YOU SUGGESTED FOR DAILY MAIL CARRIED MAIN THRUST OF THEM IN THEIR STOP PRESS BOXES LAST EDITIONS STOP BUT STILL GOOD WORK STOP KEEP IT UP STOP WOKINGHAM EDITOR

Alice's jaw dropped and she slowly put down

the cable. Then picked it up and read it again. How could he have...? Then she remembered the brief absence to change the wine order – and the sound of a horse galloping away in the night, the rider obviously carrying his scribbled stop press story, just in time to catch his last edition.

The bastard! She shook her head slowly and then lowered it into her hands. She had behaved like a young, stupid, impressionable girl!

She felt used and abused – and she had no one to blame but herself.

Then, slowly, a smile stretched across her face. What cheek! What audacity! And what charm! But never again.

Ah well. She had been taught a lesson that she would never forget. But could she now write that letter to Simon? To her husband, who now stood out in her mind as some brave, shining beacon of morality and courage. She gulped. No. Not to-day. She couldn't bring herself to write to him today, while she was so ... unclean. Tomorrow, though. Yes, she would write to him tomorrow. The warm, tender letter that he so deserved.

# CHAPTER TWELVE

Simon had the letter forwarded to him as his column camped on the Free State side of the Orange River, licking its wounds after the hard riding and often hard fighting involved in chasing de Wet. He opened the envelope with a frown,

243

expecting the worst, but his face softened as he read the letter. Alice gave no indication of what had happened to her with Fulton but she apologised for appearing 'perhaps a little distant' when last they had met and explained that her frustrations had mounted with the seeming endless nature of the war and the privations imposed on the Boer civilian families. She realised, however, that the strain was even greater on Simon and that her heart was with him all the time and she yearned for the time when next they would meet.

Immediately, Simon felt the ache in his shoulder virtually disappear and that in his heart melt completely away. He could face anything, as long as he knew he retained the love of his wife. He was even jovial, later that day, when he met Hammond. His second in command had taken the news of Jenkins's acquittal with a stony face, revealing no emotions at all. Fonthill had given him the reasons for the acquittal equally unemotionally, explaining that the decision had been unanimous and that, given Jenkins's seniority, his fine fighting record and the disturbing inconsistencies in the evidence against him, there could have been no other decision. Hammond had merely nodded and had not attempted to protest or argue.

However, Simon realised that the man had now declared himself as an enemy. For a moment, he had considered writing to John French, asking for Hammond to be transferred to another unit – preferably back to one in the regular army – that would suit him better.

Then he resolved to keep him in the column. Given the man's obvious closeness to French, it would be better to keep him where Simon could keep an eye on him, rather than leave him free to cause trouble from afar. Besides, Simon was intrigued to find out if the man really was a coward. There would surely be opportunities soon to test him further under fire.

In giving French his report on the two hectic weeks in the Cape, Simon had tacked on a brief summation of the charge against Jenkins and his dismissal of the charges – taking care to record that Forbes and Cartwright had joined him in considering them and that the verdict had been unanimous. Jenkins seemed to have slipped back into his duties with the column without discord and Fonthill ensured that their former, formal relationship was resumed without interruption, for his RSM was a vital link between officers and men in preparing the column for its future work. For now, they were resting, but General Knox was shortly to return to the Free State from the Cape Colony and Simon knew that they would be riding again shortly.

In fact, the orders came not from Knox but from French, out in the Transvaal. The general curtly congratulated Fonthill on chasing de Wet back across the Orange but ordered him to bring his column north, to Standerton in the Transvaal. Another big push was being prepared to net as many Boers as possible between the forts that were being built across the veldt. Fonthill's Horse would be needed to protect the flanks of the troops from attack from de la Rey as they plodded northwards. 'Some farm clearance will be involved,' he added and Simon's heart sank.

He checked the map and found that Standerton was too far south of Pretoria for him to visit Alice and he cursed. He welcomed the chance to grapple with de la Rey, who was proving to be as formidable a fighter in the Transvaal as de Wet was in the Free State but he relished not at all the miserable task of farm burning. 'Bloody 'ell,' said Jenkins when he heard the news. 'Can't they get the fire brigade to do that?'

Ten days later they were riding out on the right flank of a formidable force of regular infantry and mounted infantry as it plodded north across the undulating veldt. It seemed that comparatively little had been learnt from the last advance of this sort in which Fonthill and his men had been involved. A stream of supply wagons still slowed down the pace and Simon could not understand why this miniature army could not move without taking a contingent of heavy artillery with it. There were no sieges to be mounted. Why, then, trail these heavy guns with them?

Riding out on the open veldt, however, providing a screen for the right front flank of the main column, was pleasant enough work and Simon was hoping that this comparatively unpopulated corner of the Central and Eastern Transvaal would provide little opportunity for farm burning and that, if they did come across a homestead, it would be empty, or at least barren of any obvious source of supply for the Boers and therefore not eligible for torching. He had decided once again that he would eschew farm burning if he possibly could.

He put his men out in a screen, fan-shaped, to pick up quickly any traces of enemy activity. It was a dreamy afternoon, with patches of cotton wool balls of cloud gambolling lazily across the blue arch of the sky and, in truth, Simon had difficulty in not drifting off to sleep as he slouched in the saddle. His upper arm now seemed to have suffered no further injury from the reckless pace set by de Wet and his body and mind were at peace as his head nodded with the rhythm set by his pony's walk.

Then he was made instantly awake by a shout from Jenkins. 'Rider coming in, sir!'

One of the troop sergeants could be seen galloping towards him from far out on the right, alternately disappearing and then reappearing as he approached across the swelling downs of the veldt.

Then he slowed his horse to a canter and then a walk as he neared the column.

The sergeant approached. 'I'm with the lead troop in C Squadron, sir,' he said, removing his hat and wiping his forehead. 'Farmhouse about a thousand paces over to the right,' he said. 'Occupied, by the look of it, and there are Boer horsemen there. I saw their horses.'

'How many?'

'Couldn't be sure, sir. Maybe six or twelve, maybe twenty or more.'

'Did they see you?'

'Fairly certain not. Kept well down from the skyline.'

'Good. Have you told Captain Cartwright?'

'No, sir. He is about a quarter mile behind me, so I thought it best to report to you.'

'Quite right. Well done, Sergeant. Rejoin your troop and keep well out of sight of the enemy. Major Hammond.'

'Sir.'

'This may be a trick to lure us out so that a Boer commando can attack the main column. So deploy your squadron out thinly along the flank here and, when you meet Forbes's squadron, instruct him to do the same south of you. I say "thinly", but make sure that the flank is protected. I will take the rest of C Squadron and see if we can pull these Boers in. Sarn't Major!'

'Sir.'

'Ride out to where Captain Cartwright and the rest of his squadron are patrolling.' He paused, seeing that familiar expression of near panic appear in Jenkins's eyes at having to find his way alone anywhere. 'You'll find him out there.' And he pointed. 'Tell him to bring his squadron in to meet me at about five hundred paces that way.' He pointed to where the sergeant could be seen disappearing. 'Quickly, now.'

Jenkins galloped off.

'Hammond. You're in charge of protecting the column while I'm away. If you've not heard from me in an hour, alert the general that there could be an attack on his right flank. But I hope to be back by then.'

Fonthill half expected to hear a 'good luck, sir'. But Hammond merely nodded and turned his horse away to give his instructions for thinning out the protecting screen. Simon cantered away,

248

following the sergeant's path, until his own course met up with Cartwright and his squadron, plus a beaming Jenkins, so pleased that he had found his way there and back.

Fonthill briefly explained the situation to Cartwright and his two subalterns and ordered the squadron – about sixty men – to follow in column of fours behind him as he trotted forward, Jenkins at his side. After about five minutes, they were halted by the sergeant, who slid down a hill and then ran to meet them.

'The farm is just over the brow of that hill, sir,' he reported. 'Where are your chaps?'

'Spread out in a half circle, but they're well hidden.'

'Lead on, Sergeant. Come on, Cartwright and Jenkins. Let's take a look.'

They dismounted and crept to where, at the brow of the hill, there was a scattering of rocks, which offered cover to the troop keeping watch, and the three joined them, crouching low. Some three hundred yards below them, in a little hollow, sat a small mud-walled farmhouse with a familiar corrugated iron roof, a plain gable, a *stoep*, a cramped flower garden and, to the right, a low Kaffir kraal built of stone and now con-taining some twenty horses, all of which were being watered from a well-filled dam by a hand-ful of Boers.

Fonthill focused his field glasses on them. They were commando riders, all right; the wide-brimmed hats, the bandoliers, tattered waistcoats and, most revealing of all, a dozen or more rifles piled pyramid-style well within reach, all betrayed them. Further to the right was a bunch of willows clustered by another dam. More horses and men could be glimpsed among them. Switching his gaze to the farmhouse, Simon noticed, first, the pretty, green Venetian shutters covering the windows and then the door to the house, which was painted the same colour and was firmly shut. He swung the glasses round. He could see no sign of cattle or fruit trees. Nevertheless, it was clear that the farm was occupied and, judging by its neatness, owned by someone with a touch, at least, of taste and sophistication.

It was obvious that no British troops had passed this way.

Fonthill lowered his glasses and muttered to himself. 'Damn!' The rules were clear. If a farm was occupied, however temporarily, by Boer soldiers, it would have to be burnt. Yes, but first the Boers would have to be dealt with. He turned and spoke to the others.

'It could well be a trap but the only way of finding out is to attack. Now, trap or not, the Boers hate to be surrounded. They like to be able to ride off as quickly as possible if they lose a fight. So, Cecil,' the young man nodded, 'I want you to split your squadron and take half of it round to the right there, well beyond that clump of willows. Ride out wide and then spread out wide and, whatever, you do, don't let them see you. But particularly keep your eyes open to look for a larger commando, who might be lurking out there somewhere ready to attack us when we take the bait. If you see them, then fire three shots and ride back here.'

'Very good, sir. What are you going to do?'

'I shall give you ten minutes to take up your position and then take the other half of your squadron and lead a troop which will dash in and try and cut out those horses to prevent the Boers riding off. The other troop will line up here, dismounted and just below the ridge, and ready to open fire and support us. There may be other Boers in the farmhouse who could come out shooting. Now, don't fire until you hear our first shots. Make for those chaps in among the willows, dismount and see if you can encircle them and flush them out. I am particularly anxious to stop the buggers getting away this time, so make sure they can't mount and ride through you. Understood?'

'Absolutely, sir.'

'Good luck. Off you go.'

At the bottom of the hill, Fonthill gathered his two troops around him and explained what he wanted. The first dismounted troop would spread out wide, along the ridge surrounding the farmhouse, and direct fire on anyone firing from within the house. The other would ride in with him. He, Jenkins and two sergeants would leap the kraal walls and cut out the horses. The remainder would ring the kraal and fire on the men inside if they offered opposition. 'But for God's sake,' he added, 'let us go in first. Surprise is the main weapon here. They obviously have no knowledge that we are here. So we shall rush them. But no one is to fire unless they fire first or the four of us do. Understood?'

They all retired to get their horses and Jenkins

251

sidled up to Fonthill. 'Did you say, "jump the kraal wall", bach sir?'

'Yes. Don't worry. It's only about four feet high. I'll be alongside you in case you fall off.'

But Jenkins didn't smile. 'Just remember to grip with your knees,' he said, 'and lean forward as you take off and back when you land.'

'Very good, Sergeant Major. But I'm much better than you think these days.'

'Umph!'

Fonthill watched as Cartwright quietly trotted off with half of his squadron well below the crest of the hill and disappeared around a bend to his right. He waited for eight minutes then directed one of the remaining two troops to disperse as widely as possible around the hollow but on the reverse slope of the ridge. Then he ordered the remaining troop to mount, took a deep breath, drew his revolver and gestured for the troopers to follow him over the ridge.

Just before they reached the edge he looked around him. Jenkins was by his side, with a sergeant on either side of them. Behind them ranged the remainder of the troop, some fifteen in all. He licked his lips. Was it enough to charge the kraal? There was only one way to find out. He lifted his arm and gestured forward in the signal to gallop.

They crested the hill in a shower of stones and sped down the other side, their boots thumping their horses' flanks, their heads arched forward. Fonthill squinted ahead at the kraal. All of the Boers, it seemed, were concerned with their horses but then the drumming of the charge reached them and they looked up. With cries they

252

ran to where their rifles were stacked and Simon realised that it was a race against time. Would he and the others reach the stone wall before the Boers had time to claim their rifles, work the bolts, aim and fire? God! He realised it would be a close-run thing.

He levelled his revolver, pulled the trigger and shouted, 'Fire!'

There was little hope of him and his men finding their targets as they fired from the saddle at the gallop, but even so, Fonthill saw one of the Boers drop, clutching his breast. The man cannoned into the pyramid of rifles, scattering them. It gave Simon a few seconds' grace. Suddenly, the kraal wall was upon him and he desperately hauled back on the reins, leaning forward as he did so. The little Basuto pony took off like a bird and cleared the stones with ease. As he was thrown forward by the horse's momentum he pulled back – but just too late. He fell to the ground with a crash that momentarily winded him and sent a shaft of pain up through his shoulder from where his wounded arm hit the hard ground. But he retained his grip on his revolver and, squirming round, he fired at a burgher who was about to level his retrieved rifle at him. The bullet caught the man in the chest and he went down.

Suddenly, all was bedlam as firing began from all around the edge of the kraal.

'The horses, dammit!' shouted Simon. 'Get the horses!'

He was dimly aware that the Boer ponies in the kraal were rearing and screaming with fright and that Jenkins and the two sergeants were in their midst clutching at their bridles. Out of the dust and the gunsmoke – for it was clear that the remainder of the troop were now firing into the kraal and that the Boers inside it were firing back – a huge burgher lurched into sight. He raised his rifle butt and brought it down, aiming at Fonthill's head. Somehow, Simon, on one knee, lurched to the right, losing his grip on his revolver, which clattered away. The gun butt crashed into the ground near his foot, its stock shattering. The Boer kicked out blindly at Fonthill, catching him in the breast and sending him sprawling.

Flat on his back, his good hand clawing at the ground to give him purchase, Simon saw the giant burgher loom over him and reach down. Then, seemingly from nowhere, a figure leapt onto the man's back, a muscular forearm appeared around his throat, the butt of a hand under his chin and, with a terrible jerk, the Boer's head was snapped back and his neck broken. Slowly, the giant sank to the ground, Jenkins still fixed to his shoulders, as though welded there, and then the man lay still in the dust, his eyes wide and still glaring in anger.

'The horses!' shouted Fonthill. 'Have we got the horses?'

'Bugger the bloody horses,' Jenkins shouted in return. 'Yes, we've got 'em. Are you all right, though, bach?'

'Yes. Just winded.' Simon was suddenly aware that the crackle of gunshots all around had ceased, although there were others sounding much farther away up the hill. He crawled to his feet. Some fifteen Boers were standing sullenly by the kraal wall, their rifles cast aside, their hands in the air. Six other burghers lay dead or wounded at their feet. A ring of rifles threatened them from the other side of the kraal.

As he stood gasping for breath, Fonthill saw the ridge above him suddenly crackle into life as, to his right, the door of the farmhouse burst open and a handful of Boers ran out, firing their rifles as they did so. Within seconds they were all brought down.

Twisting his head to look higher up the slope to where the second dam was surrounded by willows, Simon saw the flashes of rifle fire and white smoke rising through the grey-green leaves. Was Cartwright holding his own? He gestured to the young subaltern commanding the troop surrounding the kraal.

'Carter. Get the surrendered men out of here and put them under guard. Have you lost any men?'

'Only one man with a flesh wound, sir. We were upon them before they could organise any defence.'

'Good. See if we can do anything for these Boers wounded here.' Then, to the two sergeants: 'Well done, you two. Make sure the horses are locked in the kraal. 352, come with me. Cartwright may need help.'

'What about the people in the farmhouse, bach sir?'

'I doubt if there are any Boers left in there, though there might be women and children.' Simon winced as a shaft of pain shot through his injured arm. He turned back to Lieutenant

255

Carter. 'Send six men into the farmhouse to make sure it's safe. Tell them to take care. I am going to see if Captain Cartwright needs help.'

'Very good, sir.'

Fonthill found his pony and, with difficulty, mounted it. As he and Jenkins turned to climb the slope, where the rest of the squadron still ringed it, he extended his hand to his old comrade. 'That must be the seven thousand, eight hundred and ninety-first time that you have saved my life, my dear old 352. I can't thank you enough. That chap was a bit big for me.'

Jenkins tugged at his moustache. 'As a matter o' fact, bach sir, 'e was a bit big for me, too. I'm gettin' a bit old for this game, I reckon.' Then he looked across shyly. 'Glad I was able to 'elp, though. Thank God I can still be a bit useful to you, instead of drinkin' meself silly during the night, like.'

Simon nodded in mock severity. 'So am I. So am I.'

Reaching the lip of the hollow he called the troopers down from where they still trained their rifles on the kraal and farmhouse below. He nodded to the subaltern in command. 'Good firing, Marlowe. Send an NCO down there with a couple of men to help Carter with the wounded and the prisoners. Then mount up with the rest and follow me to find Captain Cartwright. He may have bitten off more than he can chew.'

Indeed, the firing that could be heard from the clump of willows seemed now to be more intense and Fonthill dug his heels into his pony's side and urged him around in a wide sweep to seek

Cartwright. He found him with his troopers spread around three sides of the willow clump, the men spreadeagled behind the little cover they could find, and firing sporadically at the Boers seemingly well entrenched in the coppice.

'We've prevented 'em riding through us,' reported Cartwright. 'And they're in there with their horses. But I haven't enough men to charge 'em nor enough to encircle them completely. I am worried that they will burst out through there,' he gestured, 'where I can't quite complete the circle.'

'Any casualties yet?'

''Fraid so, sir. Two dead and three wounded. The Boers are shooting damned well.'

'Damn! Well, we may have to try a bit of bluff. Have you got a white handkerchief?'

'What? Oh, well. It's a bit grubby. Will this do?'

'That's fine. Now, give me a rifle.'

Fonthill tied the handkerchief to the end of the rifle and gestured to Marlowe who had now ridden up with his men. 'Spread out along to the left here with your men.' He indicated where the gap in the encirclement was evident. 'Then, when I give the order, I want all of the men to blast off with about three minutes of rapid fire. I want bullets to crash through that copse there. It doesn't matter particularly whether you hit any-body or not. It's the effect that matters. Right. Go and give the order and then report back to me.'

Puzzled, the two officers nodded and slipped away. They returned minutes later, their mission completed.

'Right.' Fonthill raised his voice. 'RAPID FIRE!'

257

he screamed. Suddenly it seemed as though the clump of willows had been hit by a hailstorm. As the rifles crashed out, pieces of bark were plucked from the trees and fronds of spidery willow leaves floated down. It seemed as though all hell had been let loose on that coppice for a thunderous three minutes or so.

Then: 'CEASE FIRING!' roared Simon. Slowly, he rose to his feet, waving the rifle with its flag. Then he began walking towards the willows.

'Gawd,' whispered Jenkins. 'The fall from the 'orse 'as affected 'is thinkin'.'

Fonthill halted about one hundred yards from the edge of the trees.

'I've come to parley,' he shouted. 'Who is in charge here?'

Slowly, the bushes parted and a tall, thin burgher stepped forward. His beard was black as night and cordite marks could be seen on his right cheek. He carried a British Lee Enfield and he was wearing what appeared to be a British army tunic. 'What do you want, Khaki?' he called.

'I am Colonel Simon Fonthill, commanding Fonthill's Horse,' shouted Simon. 'I have five hundred men with me and you are now completely surrounded, as that last burst of firing demonstrated. We have captured the farmhouse down below and the horses and the men in the kraal. If you don't believe me, send one of your men to look down into the hollow. You are completely outnumbered and, if you wish to stay and fight it out, then I am happy to accommodate you, but it would be a worthless waste of life. If you do not surrender, then I shall call up

258

artillery from our main column, which is only two miles away, and we shall have no alternative but to blast you to eternity. 'I am sorry, but you have fought well and it is pointless to continue. What do you say?'

The tall man stood in silence for a moment. 'Wait,' he called and turned back and disappeared into the trees. Simon remained standing out in the open. He hoped that the Boer had sent someone to confirm that the farmhouse had been captured. If they still resisted it would be hard work to overcome them. Genuinely a stupid waste of life.

It was five minutes before the burgher reappeared. 'We will surrender, English,' he said, 'on one condition.'

Fonthill's heart sank. 'What is that?'

'We hear that you have started to shoot Boers that you find wearing British army uniforms. We have little clothing of our own left and have had to wear your miserable tunics. Will you give me your word that we won't be shot for this, eh man?'

Fonthill nodded. 'Of course. We don't shoot defenceless men. Come out with your rifles held above your heads. Give me three minutes to tell my men.' He turned and walked back to the squadron.

'They're coming out,' he told Cartwright. 'Tell the men, no shooting.'

'Will do, sir. Bloody well done.'

Three minutes later, some thirty bedraggled Boers came reluctantly across the open ground, leading their horses and with their rifles held in the air. Fonthill, Cartwright and Jenkins walked to meet them. 'Do you have wounded?' asked Simon.

'Ja.' The Boer's eyes were tired. 'We have thirteen men in there who can't walk. More dead. Do you have food we can have? We were about to go down to the farm to find food.'

'Of course. Cartwright, see what you can do. Sarn't Major.'

'Sir.'

'Get back to the farmhouse. Send a rider to Major Hammond to say that we shall be bringing in prisoners. Oh, and see who is in the house. If there are women and children in there they will have been terrified by all the shooting. Then begin the business of bringing out the furniture etcetera. We shall have to burn the blasted place, I'm afraid.'

'Very good, sir.'

Fonthill's head was now spinning and his shoulder hurting like hell, although a quick inspection showed that the wound had not reopened. Leaving Cartwright to look after the Boers from the coppice, he slowly allowed his horse to wander down the slope back to the farmhouse, a scene of great activity, with the Boer horses being taken by handlers, the rifles gathered from the ground in the kraal and the prisoners being ushered away. Simon studied the little house as he rode. It was certainly a cut above the usual Boer dwelling, with its freshly painted shutters and the neat curtains hanging inside the windows, and he sighed at the prospect of burning it. But there was no question of riding away and leaving it. It had harboured Boer fighters and his orders were clear on this point. It could not be left standing.

Simon painfully swung down from the saddle and met Jenkins coming out of the farmhouse door. A strange-looking Jenkins, though, whose eyes were fiercely alive and his face agitated.

'I think you'd better come inside, bach sir,' he said. 'There's someone you should meet.'

'What? Who?'

'Come inside. You'll see.'

Frowning, Fonthill removed his hat and strode into the interior of the house. It was dark after the sunshine outside, but Simon could see that the room was well furnished, with dark mahogany chairs and a large table gleaming dimly and chintz fabrics lending a cosy look.

Crouching on a settee at the back of the room was a woman with her arms round two young girls, perhaps ten and twelve. The woman was attempting to comfort the girls who were sobbing and, as his eyes became accustomed to the light, Simon could see that she was strikingly beautiful. She was of mixed race for her skin was coffee-coloured and her hair, though streaked with grey, a glistening black. But her face was not Negroid: her nose was small and straight and not flared at the nostrils, her cheekbones were high and her lips not bulbous in the manner of Kaffir women, but sensuously curved. Under dark, curved eyebrows her eyes were black. It was clear that the shooting, particularly as the Boers had rushed outside, firing as they went, had terrified all three, but now the girls' sobbing had been reduced to snivelling as their mother comforted them. She looked up as Fonthill stood, gazing at them. Then she stood, urging her girls to do the same, and revealed a small, lissom figure with a full bosom.

'Hello, Simon,' she said, extending her hand.

Fonthill lowered his head and peered at her, still frowning. Instinctively he took her hand, then his face lit up. 'Nandi! Nandi, for goodness' sake!' And he pulled her to him and embraced her.

Jenkins, his face beaming, stepped forward and indicated the girls, almost proprietarily. 'An' these are 'er daughters,' he said. 'Er ... Simone and ... er ... Cyrilla, I think it is.'

The two girls were of lighter complexion than their mother but shared her dark eyes. Wonder had replaced fear in their faces now as they stood and gave Simon a brief curtsey each.

Solemnly, he reached out his hand and shook each of theirs. 'I am very pleased – yes, very pleased indeed to meet you.' Then he turned back to Nandi. 'But, it must be nineteen, twenty years, since last we met. What are you doing here? Is this your house?'

'Yes. I am sorry that you had to arrive here like this and cause all this killing and shooting.' Her hand trembled as she raised it to replace a stray strand of hair and she gave a rueful smile. Simon remembered well how white and small her teeth were, but there was a tear in the corner of her eye now. 'I would like to offer you food and drink, but those men took all I had. And there was precious little to start with.' The tear welled and then slid down her cheek. 'I wondered if I would ever see you and Mr Jenkins again. Now I have but I am sad that it is...' she waved a plaintive hand '...like this. I am sorry.'

'Oh, Nandi.' Simon put his arm around her shoulder. 'We don't need anything. Come on. Let's sit down. We must talk. Pull up a chair, 352.' They all sat. 'Now, I had not realised you had married. Where is your husband?'

Nandi put the corner of a white lace handkerchief to her eye. 'I married a Boer farmer. This is our home and, of course, these are our children.' She smiled through the tears. 'They are good girls.'

Simon did not like to ask, but Jenkins leant forward. 'An' where is 'e now, then, love?'

'He was killed at Ladysmith – what is it ... well over a year ago now. We have been struggling to manage and I heard that the British were burning all the farms and I have been dreading your troops arriving, but these Boer commando men came instead. And now you have come...' She burst into tears. 'It is all too much for me.'

Simon took her hand and his mind fled back twenty-three years, when he had first met this young, beautiful half-caste Zulu girl, the daughter of an Irishman named John Dunn and his second wife, herself the daughter of a Zulu induna, or chief, in the heart of Zululand, just before the outbreak of the Anglo-Zulu war. In attempting to gather intelligence for the British army about the warlike intentions of the Zulu king, Fonthill and Jenkins had been captured and imprisoned by King Cetshwayo. It was Nandi who had contrived their escape and, later, her evidence at a court martial after the battles of Isandlwana and Rorke's Drift that had led to his acquittal on a contrived charge of cowardice. Then, two years later, their paths had crossed again when he and Jenkins had answered her appeal for help when she had been abducted and held prisoner by Portuguese diamond smugglers in Kimberley. A couple of letters had been exchanged in the long years in between but the peripatetic lifestyles of Simon, Alice and Jenkins had ended any regular correspondence. For Simon, Nandi had become just a pleasant and rather erotic memory – for, although they had never been lovers, the half-caste girl had aroused the most tender emotions in him all those years ago.

Now, as he sat listening to her story in her comfortable little house and looking at her children, he remembered that it was his duty to burn down that house…

'And how is Alice?' asked Nandi, desperately trying to remember the niceties and struggling to sound as though they were taking tea in a country garden in Norfolk. 'I was so pleased that you had married her in the end.'

Simon cleared his throat and attempted to go along with the formalities. 'Thank you, Nandi. She is well and, indeed, she is here in South Africa, still writing for the *Morning Post* in London. She is now, I think, in Pretoria. You must meet her.'

'Oh yes, please. Perhaps she can come here and meet my children. That would be nice. But you never married, Mr Jenkins?'

'No, miss ... er ... missus. Call me 352. You always used to.'

As the niceties were exchanged, Simon's mind raced. How on earth could they throw out this beautiful woman, who years ago had done so much for him and Jenkins, and have her stand by as they set fire to her house? And she, still presumably grieving for her husband! He thought hard. There was no way round it. The prisoners were evidence of the fighting here and he would have to submit a report on it all, of course. If he refused to burn the house, there would be trouble and he would probably have to resign his commission. And after all that, the general would just send another patrol to torch it.

He cleared his throat again. 'Nandi, I hate to have to say this to you but I am afraid I must burn your house.'

'Oh, blimey!' said Jenkins.

Nandi put a stricken hand to her face. 'Oh no! Simon, not you. Not you, burning my house. Oh, how could you do that?'

The two girls were now regarding him with equal horror, their eyes wide.

Jenkins opened his mouth to speak but Fonthill held up his hand. 'There is no way round it, my dear, I'm afraid. Any house which has harboured Boer fighters must be burnt...'

'But I didn't invite them. They just rode in.'

'Yes, but those are my orders. If I do not obey them, then another British troop will just come and do the job. But listen. All is not lost. Do you have a good wagon with mules or oxen?'

'Yes. In the barn at the back. No oxen now, but I have two mules.'

'Good. Now, I want you to pack everything you can take with you and mark all the furniture that can go on the wagon. When you have done this, my men will load the wagon.'

'But where shall I go? We have no money, I have no husband and nowhere to stay. The Boers took all our cattle ten months ago and they gave me an IOU for them, but I think it is worthless.'

'Don't worry. I ... we – that is, Jenkins and I – intend to look after you.'

Jenkins nodded eagerly. 'Quite right, bach sir. Quite right. I 'ave some money saved up. I can–'

Simon shook his head. 'Thank you, 352, that won't be necessary. The one thing I don't lack is money. But you, my old friend, can help Nandi in a different way. You are hereby granted three weeks' leave. When the wagon is loaded, I want you to sort out three of the captured Boer ponies for the three ladies here.' He turned. 'Can the girls ride, Nandi?'

'Oh yes.'

'Good. Then, 352, get one of the troopers to drive the wagon and you accompany the party to Pretoria to look after them. Go straight to Alice at her hotel at this address.' He scribbled on a piece of paper from his notebook. 'I hope to God she is still there but I think she is. Book Nandi and the girls into the hotel and tell Alice that the cost will go on my private account. Then – are you remembering all this?'

'O'course.'

'Good. Then put the furniture in store and then you go house-hunting with Nandi. Because of the war, there should be plenty of properties going quite cheaply. Find a good house, and install them in it. Ask Alice to draw money on our joint account and pay for it.' He scribbled another note and gave it to Jenkins.

'Give this to Alice and explain the background. She will understand and want to help. She always loved Nandi. This note is asking her to set up an account at a bank in Pretoria on which Nandi can draw.'

Nandi had listened to all of this with an open mouth. 'No, Simon,' she said, her voice betraying bitterness. 'I do not understand why you must burn my home but I cannot accept all this from you.'

Fonthill shook his head. 'Nandi, no one hates the thought of destroying your house more than I, but I fear it must be done. Look, this war is not going to go on forever – in fact, I heard a rumour recently that Lord Kitchener and General Botha are getting together to talk of an armistice, although I will believe it only when it happens. I promise you that I will look after you and the girls until this stupid war is over. Then I will make sure that you come back here – I presume this is your land...?'

'Yes. We have about two hundred hectares.'

'Good. I promise that you will come back here and we will rebuild your house so that you can farm again. My dear, it is the least I can do. And don't worry about the girls. We will see that they go to a good school.'

267

Gradually, Nandi lowered her head and simply let the tears flow. Immediately Jenkins sprang up to sit beside her and take her hand, as Simon retained the other. And the three sat together for a while, the two children looking on with ashen faces. Then, eventually, Nandi straightened her back, extracted her hands and blew her nose.

'Thank you both very much. I am really most grateful. You must excuse the tears because, you see, this is our home and we were all happy here.' She sniffed hard. 'But if we have to go, then we have to go. Come along, girls. Pack your toys and then help me mark the things we have to take.'

The oldest girl looked anxious. 'Can we take Freddy?' she asked.

'Of course.' Nandi turned to Simon. 'He's our dog. We locked him in the outhouse when the commandos came.'

'Oh, you must 'ave a dog,' said Jenkins, his great moustache bending round in a grin. 'I always 'ad a dog, look you, back 'ome on the farm in Wales. You can't get by without a dog, now can you?'

She smiled at him, squeezed his hand and rose, shooing the girls before her.

Fonthill and Jenkins exchanged glances. 'What a bloody mess,' said Simon. 'What a bloody war! Come on. You'd better get that wagon hitched and organise a work party to take the furniture out. Oh, and I hope to God that Nandi can find the way to Pretoria because I don't suppose you can.'

A surprisingly confident Jenkins shook his head. 'Oh, we'll get there. Don't you worry, bach sir. We'll get there.'

Ninety minutes later, Fonthill sat on his horse and watched the specks that were the wagon and four riders disappear in the distance. Then he gave the order for a corporal to toss a stick of dynamite through the door. The house exploded and he caught a glimpse of the pretty blue shutters cartwheeling high into the air before the building collapsed into a roaring mass, sending sparks and flames high into the darkening sky.

Simon sat for a moment, his heart and head full of sadness, before pulling round his mount's head and urging it away.

His troopers were standing, mouths open, watching the conflagration and he rounded on them. 'What the hell are you gawping at?' he shouted. 'Mount up and move off. There's a bloody war still to fight. Mount up, d'you hear?'

## CHAPTER THIRTEEN

Before they could move off, however, there were graves to be dug and the prisoners to be set off under guard on the march to the main column. Fonthill knew that his haul of just under fifty captured Boers, plus some twenty who had been killed, would be regarded as 'a good bag', for Kitchener was now marking the progress of the war by how many of the enemy raiding across the veldt could be imprisoned or shot. His attempts at arranging a truce with Botha had ended in failure, mainly thanks to the intransigence of the

Free Staters. Reducing the number of men serving in the commandos was now the only way to end the conflict. Nevertheless, as Simon rode with his little convoy, he felt dispirited. Reaction from the few, intense minutes of hand-to-hand fighting and the ache from his injured upper arm and shoulder were not the only cause, he knew. Nandi re-entering his life brought back so many memories of his early days in Africa, capped then by the reality of having to burn her home – she of all people, who had so entranced him all those years ago and who had stepped in to help him when he needed it so – all of this sent a keen pang of disquiet through his tired body.

The sight of the tall figure of Major Hammond sitting astride his horse, ramrod straight, as they rejoined the march north did nothing to help his state of mind. Hammond, of course, was unwelcoming and equally not congratulatory on the success of the excursion. His moribund nature reminded Fonthill that, sooner or later, he would have to be dealt with. But not now. Not now, when his brain was in turmoil at the cruelty of this ugly war and his body aching for respite from the saddle and from combat.

So Fonthill and his men rejoined the turgid, military amoeba that plodded northwards, attempting to round up or crush the active bands of Boers riding the veldt in this part of the Transvaal. It was frustrating work now acting as a cavalry screen for the army, involving as it did many false alarms and excursions to follow tracks that might or might not be those of a commando. Luckily, there were few farms that needed to be destroyed and where they were met, Fonthill continued his practice of allowing the occupants to load their possessions and make their own way, either to one of Kitchener's camps or to join one of the guerrilla bands. If the former, he argued, then at least they would be looked after. If the latter, they would be a drag on the manoeuvrability of the commandos.

Alice wrote to him warmly, delighted, as she said, to be of help to Nandi and her girls and assuring him that she and Jenkins would find somewhere suitable for them to live. The Welshman, she confided, seemed to have become a new man, revealing a skill at crude conjuring tricks that delighted the girls and dancing attendance on their mother. In fact, Jenkins rather overstayed his leave and it was nearly a month after being sent on his mission that he rejoined the column, happily describing to Simon the little house they had found for Nandi that sat on the edge of Pretoria, near a church school which the girls were to attend.

'They're a lovely little family,' he confided. 'I started to teach the girls Welsh, but I could only remember a few words, see.'

Fonthill nodded. 'As long as you don't teach them barrack-room English, that should be fine.'

'Another thing.' What seemed dangerously like a blush lit up the Welshman's weathered features. 'Did you notice the girls' names?'

'What do you mean?'

'The names she 'ad given 'em.'

'Can't say that I did.'

'They're yours an' mine, see. Simone for you

271

an'...' he paused for a moment in embarrassment '...Cyrilla for me, although I don't think that's a proper name for a girl. She must 'ave made it up, look you.'

Fonthill grinned. 'Cyrilla, for Cyril! I thought you never told anyone your first name. Not anyone but me, that is. How did she find it out?'

Jenkins tugged at his moustache. 'Dunno. Must 'ave come out years ago...'

Before the big column had reached its destination, Fonthill was summoned to one of his rare meetings with General French, to whom he formally reported. This time the meeting was quite cordial – no adverse reports this time, then, thought Simon, from Hammond?

'Several bits of news for you, Fonthill.' French gestured for him to sit at a camp stool. 'Firstly, I have approved your recommendation for a second DCM for your man, Jenkins, a bar to his first. It's a bit irregular and I didn't like the sound of Hammond's charge – it certainly doesn't do for a 2IC to have concerns about the unit's senior warrant officer – but I have chosen to support you on this occasion.'

'Thank you, sir.'

'Secondly, Lord Kitchener has approved of the award to you of the DSO.'

Fonthill looked puzzled. 'DSO?'

'Yes. Distinguished Service Order. Came in in about 1886 for senior officers. Not been awarded much but it rewards exactly what it says, distinguished service in the field. In your case for the good work you did at Bothaville, your unrelenting pursuit of de Wet on the other side of the Orange

272

and, indeed, in this recent skirmish at that farm. Good work, Fonthill. Congratulations.'

The two men shook hands. 'Well, thank you, sir. I confess I hadn't heard of the decoration.'

A sly smile crept across French's features. 'I confess it got a bit of a bad reputation in the first half of this damned war, under Buller. It became known as "DSO – for Dukes' Sons Only". You're not the son of a blasted duke, are you, by any chance, Fonthill?'

'Good God no, sir. Just a humble major.'

'Good. All the better for that. Now, I know you will be glad to hear that I am taking you off this escort and farm-burning work.'

'I am indeed.'

'Thought you would be. Facts of the matter are that we think that we've stopped the Boers' attempts to cause revolt in the Cape Colony. The two commandos that did penetrate to the south have not been able to raise their compatriots to rebel and we've been able, as you well know, to throw de Wet out of the Colony. Trouble is that Botha and de la Rey are proving fiendishly effective at guerrilla warfare in the Eastern and Western Transvaal and the whole bloody country now seems aflame – and I don't just mean from our farm burnings.'

The general frowned. 'Kitchener is deploying all the troops he can but frankly, Fonthill, we could be in danger of losing this second phase of the war, despite our superiority in numbers, artillery and so forth. We are being stretched until our lines of communications and supply are twanging. Back home, after the recent death of our dear Queen, the government have been forced to raise income tax by tuppence and issue another, cheaper war loan. I tell you, this damned war with these farmers will bankrupt us if it keeps going and the public don't like it. But enough of all that.

'Now, to come back to you. Your friend de Wet has been lying low for a while after his attempts to invade the Colony. But our intelligence tells us that he has split his command into smaller sections. That means no more large confrontations but an increase in his harassment, because these smaller commandos will be more mobile. In fact, he has just caught a bit of a bloody nose at a place in the south with an unpronounceable name.' He jabbed his finger onto a map laid out on the trestle table. 'Here it is, look.' He took a deep breath. 'Verkijkersdorp.'

'Well done.'

French grinned. 'We think de Wet had linked up momentarily with de la Rey. A laager of women was being transported by us and the Boers attacked the escort. De Wet had to pull away without freeing the women and he received heavy losses. But he knocked over about fifty of our chaps and also got away with over a thousand head of cattle, enough to keep him going for many weeks, dammit. This feller remains a formidable fighter, there's no doubt about that.'

'Where is he now?'

'We are told that he has parted from de la Rey, who is back in the Transvaal, and he is headed – with his boss and great friend Steyn, the President of the Free State, plus members of the

State Cabinet – back to his old hunting ground here, in the middle of the Free State. I want you and your small column to get down there as fast as possible. It's a big area, of course, and ideal for cavalry. God knows where he is, exactly, so get down there and put out the black chaps that you think so highly of and see if you can find him. This is the home territory of de Wet and Steyn, of course, so the people will be against you. So don't start the fox until you're ready for him.'

Fonthill studied the map and nodded. 'Yes, it looks pretty wide open. But if he's there, we'll find him.'

The two men shook hands again. 'I don't need to tell you,' said French, 'what a great contribution it would be to the war effort if we could capture the Free State President, his Cabinet and his general in one fell swoop, so I do hope fortune favours you. Now, off you go... Oh, dammit, I forgot. Here, take the medals with you.' He handed Fonthill two small, flat boxes. 'This is yours and this is for your man. You'll probably have to hand 'em back when you get to England so that the King can present them to you formally. But we've got no time for that sort of thing down here. Now, get riding!'

On his return, Fonthill gathered together all his officers, plus Jenkins, and gave them the news. There was universal relief that they were to be spared further farm burning, although, as usual, Hammond expressed neither pleasure nor regret. Simon indicated on the map their destination.

'We'll make for just outside Reitz,' he said. 'It's obviously a small town, situated in what looks

275

like good grazing land. It's about a hundred and fifty miles to the south-east of here and maybe ninety miles or so from the border with Natal. But it's right in the middle of de Wet's homeland and somebody down there will have some idea of where he is, if, indeed, he is there.

'I want our black trackers to ride fast ahead of us, under Mzingeli, and then to spread out and pick up what they can about the whereabouts of this party. If they have Free State politicians with them then somebody should know. If we can define this, then we can ride in before dawn and catch the lot ... well, perhaps! These chaps are as slippery as eels. Now, Sarn't Major, please bring in Mzingeli so that I can brief him. Major Hammond, prepare the column to begin the ride south an hour before dawn. I don't want to waste a second.'

When Jenkins returned with Mzingeli the three hunched together companionably for a moment in Fonthill's tiny tent, as they had so many times years before when they had ridden with Jameson in the invasion of Matabeleland. Simon presented Jenkins's new medal to him and showed them both his own white cross. Then he produced a bottle of whisky and he and 352 each drank a congratulatory glass, with lemonade for Mzingeli.

'Give me your tunic,' said Jenkins, 'and I'll sew your new ribbon on it. Should it go above, alongside or under the CB?'

'I haven't the faintest idea. But you shouldn't be doing that. RSMs with two DCMs shouldn't be sewing like a bloody housemaid.'

'Give to me,' said Mzingeli. 'One of my boys do

276

it. Ready for morning. People should know you are both great warriors.'

They all laughed and raised their glasses to each other.

Mzingeli and the black trackers rode off in the darkness some two hours before the column itself struck camp. For Fonthill, it was a blessed relief to be up in the cold, crisp air, riding with no pain now from his wounded arm, with Jenkins at his side and a freshly delivered, brief but tender letter from Alice tucked into his pocket, to be reread when the column stopped for breakfast. The prospect of another encounter with the shrewd and determined de Wet filled him full of excitement. This was proper soldiering, not raising fires across the veldt! And would he be able this time to stop the Great Escaper escaping again? He gritted his teeth. He would give up his fancy new Order – and the CB, for that matter – to pin the man down at last.

Fonthill faced the old problem of pushing his column as fast as possible to catch the Boers before they moved on again, while not exhausting his horses. It was, then, nearly five days before they camped well outside Reitz, tucked in behind a kopje. There, they were found by Mzingeli and one of his trackers who had worked on a farm in the district.

The two men crouched in Fonthill's tent in the darkness before dawn to report to him as he rolled out of his sleeping bag.

'Steyn man is in a house in centre of town,' said Mzingeli. 'He stay there with his Cabinet people. About seven or eight.'

'Is General de Wet with them?'

Mzingeli shrugged. 'Don't know. Maybe. We kept watch but did not see him. But saw Steyn man. Old man with beard.'

'Where are the rest of your trackers? I hope you didn't alarm anyone by hanging around the place?'

'No. They out in country seeing if we find de Wet man. They come back here soon.'

'Good work. Thank you, Mzingeli. Now go and get some breakfast.'

Fonthill studied the scrap of paper that Mzingeli had thrust into his hand. In untutored scrawl it read: 'Corner of Uniefees Street and Kerk St, near church. Wooden house, one floor.' He presumed that meant that it was a bungalow. He thought hard as he pulled on his boots. Better to go and see for himself to plan the attack. Whether or not de Wet was there, there would be a presidential guard of some sort. But he didn't want a bloodbath. Surround the house and take them all quickly and quietly, preferably at dead of night. He peered out of his tent and saw that the darkness to the east was lightening. Better reconnoitre now and attack tonight.

Two hours later, three Boers and their Kaffir servant rode out of the camp towards the town of Reitz. Scruffily dressed, as farmers rather than fighters, Simon, Jenkins, Mzingeli and one trooper, a uitlander from Johannesburg who spoke good Afrikaans, made for the centre of the town, riding easily, as though they had come in for provisions.

'That the place, there,' said Mzingeli, as they

rode by a pleasant but unpretentious, cream-painted bungalow on the corner of two unmade roads, towards the edge of town. They rode straight past but Fonthill scanned the building from under his wide-brimmed hat. Three men lounged on the *stoep* and another could be glimpsed sitting outside at the back of the house. They all wore bandoliers and carried rifles. Half a dozen horses were hitched to the rail and, through a window, Simon could see what appeared to be a room full of people.

One of the men called out at them from the *stoep* and the trooper gave a desultory wave and grunted a reply.

'What did he say?' asked Simon as soon as they were out of sight.

'He wanted to know where we were from. I told him what we'd agreed, that we'd just ridden in from Bethlehem to get away from the Khakis.'

'Good. What d'you think, 352?'

Jenkins frowned, so that his lower lip completely disappeared under his moustache. 'Goin' to be a bit difficult to surround the place, it bein' on a corner, like, with two sides backin' on to other 'ouses. An' they'll be keepin' a good watch, look you.'

'Hmmm. I agree. Better not go back for another look. I don't want to give cause for alarm. But it certainly looks as though that little bungalow isn't the home of a lonely old lady. There's quite a bit going on in there. Right. Let's get back to camp. We'll ride out past the church to avoid them.'

That afternoon Fonthill called his officers together and explained their task. They would go into the town at about 1 a.m., when the moon was up. He would only take A Squadron but one troop would stay on the edge of the town, in case the raiding party came under attack, had to leave quickly and would need support to get away. The other troop, with Major Hammond, one sub-altern, Jenkins and himself would dismount near the church and walk in and then storm the house. Hopefully, they would be able to take the guards by surprise, call on them to surrender and then arrest everyone inside the house, without blood being shed. But if they had to shoot, they must shoot to kill.

'But remember,' he added, 'this town is sup-posed to be full of supporters of de Wet and Steyn, so we can't hang about. If there is shooting, all the neighbours could come out shooting as well and then we could be in a fine old mess. So we go in quickly and quietly. Any questions?'

Hammond brushed his moustache. Was there a glint of apprehension in his eyes? 'How many guards are there, d'yer think, Colonel?' he asked.

'Well, I only saw four but there will be more than that. Steyn will have his presidential guard with him. Could be up to twenty, I should imagine.'

'So don't you think we might need more men than just a troop, eh?'

'No. One troop, about thirty men now, with the other troop outside in reserve, should be enough. We can't take a bloody army in and wake the whole town.'

They set off shortly after midnight, their harnesses muffled and not a polished boot in sight, and reached the edge of the town with the moon racing between high clouds. Ideal for their purpose. Here the two troops divided and Mzingeli, Fonthill and Hammond led the first troop until they saw the spire of the wooden church ahead.

Then they dismounted and, taking their rifles from the saddle buckets, left their horses in the little churchyard, one man each looking after four horses. Treading softly, the remainder of the troop walked down Kerk Street in single file, Fonthill leading.

Just before the crossroads, he held up his hand and waved for his men to fall back into the little gardens that fronted the houses while he crept forward. From behind a stunted tree he scanned the house. He could only see two guards on the *stoep* and one of them seemed asleep – typical! However, there were probably more at the back.

He turned to Hammond and Jenkins who crouched behind him now. 'Right,' he whispered. 'We will go in on the run. Pass the word to fan out around the house. I can't see any horses but they might be at the back. I will approach from the front. Hammond, you take a section and double round the back. Ignore any firing. Just make for the back. I don't want anyone to escape. Now, pass the word and we will go in in exactly three minutes from now.'

Fonthill withdrew his revolver from its holster – his arm was still too sore to carry and use a rifle and bayonet – and took out his Hunter watch. After three minutes, he looked behind him. Hammond had fallen back and was waiting with a section he had selected some twenty yards or so towards the rear. But Jenkins and eager faces were waiting just behind him. He raised an arm, held it aloft for a moment and then pointed forwards, breaking into a run as he did so.

He was conscious that troopers were fanning out on either side of him and Jenkins and he were halfway across the crossroads when one of the guards on the *stoep* shouted, raised his rifle and fired. The bullet hit the ground at his feet and pinged away. Immediately, Jenkins fired his rifle from the hip, and suddenly a stuttering fire broke out from the veranda and from two other places in the little garden that fringed the *stoep*. But it was all too late. The lead troopers halted for a moment, knelt and let out a ragged volley which brought down the two men clearly visible on the veranda and brought moans from behind bushes in the garden.

Then Fonthill and Jenkins were on the *stoep* and crashing through the door which led into a lounge. The room seemed to be full of men in various stages of undress who were scrambling on the floor, some of them reaching for rifles and revolvers. Simon fired one shot above their heads.

'Don't think of firing!' he shouted. 'The house is surrounded and you will all be killed. Don't touch your weapons.' He was conscious of troopers crowding into the room behind him. 'Jenkins.'

'Sir!'

'Take five men and go through the other rooms quickly.'

The Welshman ran towards the nearest door and crashed it open with his rifle butt before running through it, followed by several men.

Fonthill was conscious of firing coming from the rear of the house and was immediately anxious for Jenkins until he realised that the shots were coming from outside the house. He pushed the muzzle of his revolver under the chin of the nearest Boer. 'Where is the president?' he demanded.

The man just shook his head, his eyes wide.

'General de Wet?'

That brought the same response. Then the man grinned, a most unexpected response, and nodded towards the window. Fonthill turned and saw an elderly man on horseback, *in his nightshirt* and with beard flowing behind him, galloping away down the street. A trooper ran after him, knelt and fired several times but the horseman disappeared into the darkness.

Simon swung back to the Boer. 'The president?' he asked.

The Boer nodded. 'Ja,' he said in a low growl. 'He always rides in his nightshirt.' Then he grinned again.

Fonthill shook his head and caught the man's eye. He couldn't help grinning in turn. 'Ah well,' he said. 'I just hope your president doesn't catch his death of cold.' Then he frowned when he realised that Steyn had escaped from the *back* of the house. What the hell was Hammond doing?

The question remained unanswered for Jenkins returned to the room, leading about a dozen men in various stages of undress. 'Don't know who

283

these blokes are, bach sir,' he said, 'but they don't belong to us. And look!' He held up three large saddlebags. 'I've copped the Crown jewels, look you.'

Simon became aware that more troopers had crammed now into the room and that all firing from outside had ceased. He scanned the faces of the men captured by Jenkins but de Wet was not among them. He felt his heart sink. Had the Boer escaped yet again?

He turned back to the Boer who had recognised the galloping horseman. 'Is General de Wet here? You will save yourself a lot of time and trouble if you tell the truth.'

'No, English. I tell you the truth. De Wet is not in this town. He is in the country staying on a farm not far from here. But you will not catch him. He will know by now you are here. But, I tell you...' the man nodded at the sheepish-looking men in Jenkins's care '...you have captured most of the Free State Cabinet and,' he gestured to the saddlebags, 'most of our exchequer, too, by the look of it.'

Fonthill nodded. 'Jenkins, take these men outside, keep them under guard and find horses for them. I don't want to hang about here. I am going to find Major Hammond.'

He moved onto the *stoep* and walked around to the back of the house. There, the horses of the Cabinet and the guards were tethered to a rail by a long rope, allowing them to graze in a long trough filled with feed. Four troopers, rifles in hand, were poking among the bushes.

'Where's Major Hammond?' he asked.

One of the troopers turned. 'Dunno, sir. He was behind us when we ran round here to the back.'

'*Behind* you?'

'Yessir. We were just in time to see that old chap leap onto a horse, cut the lead line and gallop off in his nightshirt.'

'Was Major Hammond with you, then?'

'No, sir.'

'Sorry, Colonel.' The languid voice of Hammond broke in from behind Fonthill. 'Just been round the other side and tried to chase that old chap. Afraid he got away. Was he Steyn, then?'

'He certainly was, the President of the Free State. We wanted him urgently. How the hell did he get away, Hammond, can you tell me? I told you and your men to cover the back of the house.'

Hammond remained cool, perfectly poised. 'Easier said than done, I'm afraid, Colonel. The firing from the garden was rather hot. We came in as soon as we could.'

Fonthill held his gaze steadily but Hammond did not look away. Simon nodded. 'Hmm. Very well. Get these chaps to move these horses out to the front. They will be needed for the prisoners. And give me a report quickly on casualties on both sides. We must move out quickly before the town rises against us.'

In fact, the neighbourhood remained remarkably quiet. It was as though this little suburb of Reitz was used to night disturbances, with rifles being fired on sleepy crossroads. Simon looked around. Not even a curtain was being twitched.

He walked to the front of the bungalow and called to Jenkins, who had herded the prisoners together. 'Send a man to get our horses. Major Hammond is bringing horses for these men out from the back. Mount them but keep them under close guard. I am going back inside to make sure we have missed nothing.'

'Very good, sir.'

In the second living room, Simon found papers spread across a table carrying writing that seemed to be in Afrikaans. He bundled them together and stuffed them into an empty envelope. Then he quickly completed a search of the rest of the house. Apart from a few personal possessions, he found nothing of interest.

Outside, Hammond was speaking to a sergeant. He turned as Fonthill approached. 'Casualties light, sir,' he reported. 'None on our side but five of the Boers have sustained flesh wounds.' He nodded to where five men were sitting, their backs to the *stoep* railing, while troopers applied field dressings to their wounds.

'Good. I don't want to take them with us. When they've been seen to, have someone take them across to that house over there and ask them to take care of them. I want to move out as soon as possible.'

While these orders were being carried out, Fonthill returned to the house and emptied the contents of the saddlebags onto a table. Inside were neatly tied bundles of ten, twenty and fifty English pound notes. He quickly counted. They totalled £11,500. Stuffing them back into their bags, Simon smiled. Not enough to defray the addition of two pennies onto income tax back home, he reflected, but also not a bad haul for the night's work. The Orange Free State would be considerably disadvantaged by the loss of the majority of their Cabinet and, by the look of it, a great deal of their operational funds. But he would have gladly paid it all to have captured Steyn and de Wet. He shook his head. These Boers seemed to have the fighting skills of Hannibal and the elusiveness of Houdini.

He gathered the bags together and within fifteen minutes he was leading his men, with its sorry group of prisoners, out of the town by the light of a pale, watery moon. On rejoining the backup troop he immediately sent it to scour the countryside and search any farms that might be harbouring General de Wet. He knew it savoured of shutting the stable door when the horse had bolted but it had to be done. Then, back with the main column, he ordered a middle-of-the-night breakfast to be provided for the prisoners and the returning troopers, before crawling into his sleeping bag, with one problem on his mind: was Hammond a coward or not?

He woke in the morning with no resolution to the problem. He could not closely question the men who had been in the section with the major at the house for fear of spreading the word that he suspected his 2IC. He sighed. The dilemma would have to remain unresolved for the moment. But he determined to find a way of putting the matter to the test in the not-too-distant future. Hammond was in too key a post for him to stay with such a suspicion hanging over him.

The matter would have to be resolved one way or another soon.

For the moment, however, he must take his prisoners to Pretoria and, he fervently hoped, see his wife again.

## CHAPTER FOURTEEN

The winter was now well established and a cold wind was blowing across the veldt as the column made its way to the north, taking a wide detour to avoid Reitz. The scouts had returned with no news of de Wet but Fonthill was uneasy. This was the Boer's heartland and Simon knew he would be stinging from the narrow escape of President Steyn, nominally in de Wet's care. Would there be an attempt to recapture the Free State's politicians? If so, it could be soon, here in these undulating grasslands, studded with flat-topped kopjes that rose from the verdant plains like ugly warts on the face of a beautiful woman. These rocky outcrops and occasional shallow valleys could provide ample cover for any number of horsemen.

By now, Fonthill had learnt that Kitchener had about 210,000 men under his command – the largest army that Britain and its Empire had ever sent overseas – but considerably more than 100,000 were needed for garrison duties and to protect the long British lines of communication. He guessed that, in the four States of South Africa, there were more than 60,000 British soldiers actively pursuing 20,000 members of the Boer commandos. These seemed overwhelming odds, but the sheer size of the country, the Afrikaners' knowledge of the terrain and the determination and ability of their leaders – the lawyer Jan Smuts and burgher Ben Viljoen from the Johannesburg area had emerged to join Botha, de Wet and de la Rey as gifted commando generals – all combined to reduce that British advantage in numbers.

Certainly, Fonthill felt no sense of superiority as he rode with his small force of one hundred and eighty men through countryside that took his breath away with its beauty and made him wince at his vulnerability. Accordingly, he took extra precautions. During the day, he sent his black trackers ranging far and wide for intelligence of enemy forces in the locality and ringed his little column with outriders to ensure that they were not taken by surprise. At night, he doubled the pickets, posting them some thousand yards from the camp.

Shortage of water and fodder was a complicating factor. Many of the dams and streams had run dry and, by this stage of the war, farms could no longer supply feed for the horses. Twice a day whenever possible the horses needed to be led to water, with one trooper riding bareback leading another horse, often only to a muddy dam. The conventional British cavalry horses ate twenty pounds of oats a day, Fonthill's little Basuto ponies considerably less. Even so, the daily ration provided by the army command was only eight pounds for each pony. It meant that the column's mounts needed to graze to supplement the rations. This need added to Simon's apprehensions about the vulnerability of his column.

Any mounted unit in the field is at its most unprotected just before dawn, when sleepy soldiers tumble from their bedrolls, pickets return to the fold and horses are rounded up and saddled. However disciplined the camp, it is a time of some confusion.

So it was that a little before daybreak de Wet struck.

Predictably, the Boers launched their first attack just before light, appearing from behind a small kopje, galloping down a gentle slope to where the horses grazed some two hundred and fifty yards from the camp, whooping and firing to stampede the beasts. The little herd, however, was well guarded and each animal was loosely tethered to a wooden stake driven into the ground so that it could graze. Although the noise frightened the ponies, so that they reared and plunged, virtually all of the stakes held fast. In addition, the guarding troopers dropped to their knees and opened a rapid fire on the attackers, who were forced to swerve away, their purpose foiled.

Fonthill was just pulling on his boots at the side of his bedroll – on the veldt he had ruled that no one should sleep under canvas – when he heard the firing. He got to his feet and grabbed his rifle. From where the horses were grazing he saw the flashes of gunfire. Of more direct concern, however, was the fusillade that was now directed down onto the camp from broken rocks much nearer, up at the top of the slope. Bullets hissed by his head but the fire in the dim light was badly directed and was too high. It was also returned, for the camp guard was now coolly directing its own fire back to where the Boer marksmen could just be seen.

All around Simon, half-dressed troopers were running to grab their rifles from where they leant in pyramids along the lines.

'A Squadron run to get the horses!' screamed Fonthill. 'At the double. NOW! Officers, direct your men to encircle the camp. Be prepared to repel a charge.'

He whirled round as he heard the thud of horses from behind him. He sighed with relief as he realised it was the pickets from the other three sides of the camp who were riding in now, their heads low along their ponies' necks. They rode into camp and flung themselves from their saddles. Then he swivelled back. That meant that the pickets stationed out wide from the side from which the Boers had appeared must have been overwhelmed. But without firing a shot! Surely not!

Fonthill caught a glimpse of Hammond running low with his squadron out to where the horses were under attack. Then Jenkins was at his side, shirt tucked into breeches, rifle and bayonet in hand.

'Will they rush us, d'yer think?' he asked.

'Yes. Probably try to ride us down, if there's enough of them. Get Forbes and Cartwright to come to me, quickly as you can. Then make sure the prisoners are guarded and are lying down. Tell them that they will be shot if they move.'

'Very good, bach sir.'

Jenkins doubled away and Fonthill was quickly joined by the two captains. 'Have you got your men out ringing the camp?'

'Spreading out now, sir,' said Forbes.

'Same with my lot, sir.'

'Good. I think they may try and charge us on horseback to try and cause panic. They will probably ride straight through the camp, dismount and then open fire at close range on us. It looks as though we are not surrounded so they'll come down that slope up there from behind those rocks. Who's in the rear here?'

'My squadron, sir,' responded Cartwright.

'Tell them to fix bayonets, hold their fire until the Boers are through and past them. Then give them rapid fire. I only hope that Hammond has been able to save the horses. Double away now.'

A bullet thudded into the ground at Simon's feet to show that the Boers were adjusting their aim and he ran, crouching, to join the thin line that faced the riflemen firing from behind the rocks. He looked along the line. There was precious little cover and each man was spread-eagled along the ground, so vulnerable to charging horsemen if he rose and fled. He bit his lip. He should have erected some kind of barrier round the camp, although there was precious little timber or stone to be found on this green grassland. At least it looked as though none of his men had been hit yet. Only a question of time, though...!

A grunt showed that, once again, Jenkins had reached his side, the first rays of the rising sun catching the beads of perspiration that ran down his cheeks. Fonthill gave him a welcoming grin.

'Good man. Now. It looks as though you could do with some more exercise. I want you to double along the line here and tell the men that horsemen could charge us. They should fire as they come in but they should not, repeat not, stand and run. They will be safe if they do not move, for horses will jump over them. Then they can turn and fire at the Boers' backs. But be careful. We have our own men behind us.'

'Bloody 'ell.' But Jenkins turned and loped away.

The firing seemed to die away and Fonthill directed his gaze to where the column's ponies were grazing. The light was not strong enough to see whether Hammond had been able to save them but it seemed as though the firing out there had stopped too. He hoped that the man would have sufficient sense not to try and bring the horses back into the compound now. They would be ripe targets for the Boers if he did so. Then a shout from the camp periphery made him turn.

'Here they come!'

He looked up the slope to see the edge suddenly grey with horsemen, stretching in a line behind the rocks so that they extended around the camp, about as far as one quartile of the men lying defending it. Then, as he watched, he heard a faint cry of 'Burghers, storm!' and the line trotted forward, broke into a canter and then a gallop so that it presented a magnificent sight, men bent low, their rifles presented as though they were lances at Agincourt, the ground now trembling beneath everyone's feet, attackers and defenders alike.

The Boers fired as they came, intended as much to instil fear as to kill, for few men can fire a rifle accurately from a galloping horse and, indeed, not one of the troopers were hit. More to the point, however, no one scrambled to his feet to run. Instead, a crackle of rifle fire ran along the thin line, bringing down perhaps ten of the horsemen as they thundered down the incline.

A panting Jenkins joined Simon and the pair threw themselves down a dozen paces or more behind the line. They just had time to fire a shot each from their rifles before the horsemen were upon them. Fonthill's mouth was dry as he glimpsed the terrifying wall of horseflesh rise as one unit above the line of spreadeagled troopers ahead of him before he closed his eyes, turned his head and buried his cheek in the grass. He felt the earth shake and clods of soil and grass fall all about him, then the noise and the storm had passed. He turned, wriggled upright and immediately felt a heavy blow in the middle of his back, which sent him sprawling down again, his rifle scattering away from him.

His head singing and the breath knocked out of him, he heard the crack of Jenkins's rifle and then, as though from far away, the familiar voice, 'Bach, are you all right? Come on. Sit up. They're turning back.'

'Yes. I'm all right. I think a hoof caught me in the back. Help me up.'

Jenkins's strong hands hauled him to his feet and thrust his rifle and bayonet into his hands.

Fonthill shook his head to clear it and spat soil from his mouth. The Boers had indeed ridden through the camp and were now dismounting beyond the far edge of the circle. But there was little cover for them there as they knelt to fire. Even so, the majority of the charging horsemen had survived the charge and now, after firing several shots, they rose and began to run towards the line of Cartwright's men, thinly spread along the ground before them.

'Look, bach!'

Jenkins's cry made Fonthill turn his head to the right and saw the welcome sight of A Squadron, now safely mounted, riding hard in from the grazing ground, Hammond at their head. As though on the parade ground, the squadron wheeled to the right, presenting its long flank to the enemy, and pulled up to the halt. Then the whole squadron hurled themselves from their saddles, handlers doubled away to the rear with the horses and the remainder of the troopers knelt on the grass and delivered a crashing volley into the Boers now running towards the ring. The range was too short for them to miss and twenty or more of the Boers crumpled and fell. The remainder paused for a moment, long enough for the squadron to work their bolts and deliver another volley, Hammond standing tall among them, aiming coolly with his revolver. Immediately, the attack crumpled and the remainder of the Boers ran back to their horses, mounted quickly and rode away, their heels drumming into their ponies' flanks.

'Bloody well done, Hammond!' Fonthill staggered towards the major. 'Now get after 'em. Don't let 'em get away, man.'

The major gave a cursory wave and shouted back for the horses. They were brought up on the run by their handlers and the squadron mounted, then, led by Hammond, it wheeled away and disappeared after the retreating Boers.

Fonthill stood unsteadily, Jenkins by his side, and watched them ride away. He turned and looked up at the hill. Rifles no longer ringed the rim.

'We've beaten 'em. They've gone!' He turned and shook Jenkins's hand. Then he wheeled round. 'On your feet, men,' he shouted. 'Captain Forbes. Captain Cartwright. Detail ten men under an NCO, each of you, from your squadrons and get them to double away to the grazing ground to bring in the remainder of the horses. We might still be able to get after the Boers. Quickly now!'

''Ere, bach.' Jenkins's hand gripped his arm. 'Sit down. You're staggerin' a bit. Goodness me. You've not been drinkin' now, 'ave you? In the face of the enemy, is it? Could be a capital charge. Dearie, dearie me.'

Fonthill grinned and slumped to the floor. 'Let me get my breath. God, that horse winded me! And I assured everybody that they would jump around us.'

'An' you was right. I don't think anybody 'as been struck who stayed down, see. 'Orses 'ave got sense. They don't want to land on somethin' uneven when they're gallopin'. They know they might turn an ankle or ruin a fetlock. Trouble was, you got up too quickly, look you, an' caught a late runner. Now, sit there a minnit, while I get this lot into shape.'

The Welshman turned and, with a voice like thunder, screamed: 'On yer feet all of you, you idle lot. Unfix bayonets. Rifles at the slope. Fall in by troop, NOW! Move yerselves!'

Sitting, drawing in great draughts of air, Simon could not resist smiling. Jenkins had undoubtedly turned into the very model of a modern sergeant major. What's more, the question mark over Major Hammond had been well and truly removed. The man had been as cool as a cucumber leading his men back into the fray. He was no coward. Fonthill felt relieved. To accuse a man falsely of cowardice was a dreadful thing. He knew, for it had happened to him many years before.

Leaning on his rifle, he hauled himself to his feet to see that the camp had regained some kind of order, with Jenkins bullying the men into ranks. The troopers had not returned with the horses and it was probably too late now to pursue the Boers who had been firing from the top. His thought now was for the wounded.

His small group of medics were tending six of the troopers who had been hit by the firing. In addition, two men lay dead. Behind him, he could hear moaning from the group of Boers who had been hit by Hammond's volleys. He walked slowly to the medics. 'Anyone hurt badly?' he asked.

'Don't think so, sir,' replied a corporal. 'More or less flesh wounds, though we've lost two men, I'm afraid.'

'So I see. Two of you carry on here and the others go over to the Boers and see what you can do for their wounded. Some of them have been badly hit, I think.'

Simon walked across to talk to one of the enemy wounded. He had had a bullet penetrate his thigh and was staunching the blood with a scrap of rag. Fonthill knelt beside him. He took a clean, folded handkerchief from his pocket and gave it to the Boer. 'Put that on the wound,' he said. 'It's a bit cleaner. One of our chaps will be with you in a minute.'

The man looked up. 'We meet again, then, Colonel,' he said with a pained smile. 'Remember me? I captured you in the wood, that morning in the Cape Colony.'

'Good Lord, so you did. So you are still with General de Wet?'

The Boer grinned ruefully. 'Well, I was. Until a few minutes ago.'

'So it was he who attacked us?'

'Oh yes. He has a score or two to settle with you, I think. But...' He winced as a shaft of pain ran through him. 'No hard feelings, I think.'

'I hope not. Lie still until our medics get here. We'll look after you.'

Hammond eventually returned to report that the Boers had had too long a lead on them and had got away. In pursuit, however, he had seen another party riding to the east. 'I think they must have been the fellers shooting down on us. Put the two together, mind you, and they would have probably outnumbered us still. Could have returned and had another go, don't yer know. Don't know why they didn't.'

Fonthill nodded. 'The Boers are strange

fighters. I suppose de Wet has now got so used to striking quickly and then riding off again, like mosquitoes biting, in fact, that he doesn't like to hang about. And he has become so accustomed to having a British force pursuing him just over the hill, so to speak, that he feels he must always be on the move.'

'Quite so, Colonel. In fact, I've heard Lord Kitchener call these guerrillas "the Mosquito Army". Damned appropriate, I suppose.'

Fonthill held out his hand. 'Thank you, Philip,' he said. 'You handled the retrieval of the horses and that counter-attack extremely well.'

For a moment, the tall man looked embarrassed. Then he shook hands, gave a brief nod and strode away.

The missing pickets rode in shortly afterwards, carrying the bodies of two of their number slung across their saddles. They had been surprised in the darkness and they had had no chance to fight back. They had been held back under guard while the Boers had launched their attack and then released as the attackers had streamed away.

Why had the camp guards not heard the firing on that still night? No one seemed to know. Fonthill presumed that the sound had not carried around the kopjes that studded the plain. He shrugged his shoulders. Another unexplained peculiarity of this strange landscape.

Once the dead had been buried – among the Boers they numbered nineteen, plus another ten wounded – and the hurt men tended to, Fonthill ordered a late breakfast to be prepared. Then, shortly after midday they set off again on their trek north.

The column called into the nearest large town to deposit the wounded and then continued on its way, with its prisoners, by train and arrived at Pretoria two days after de Wet's attack on them.

Fonthill found that Kitchener was away from his headquarters and that French was still out in the Eastern Transvaal on the trail of Botha. Hammond immediately applied for leave, which was granted, and, two days later, Simon was at last reunited with Alice, who had been out visiting the Boer civilian camps, checking on the improvements that had been made to them since the wide publication in Britain of Miss Hobhouse's report.

They embraced warmly in the confines of Simon's tent where the column had returned to its base just outside Johannesburg. This time there was no restraint between them and, after the initial embrace, Fonthill had no compunction about tying across his tent flaps to seal the entrance and leading his wife to his camp bed.

'For God's sake, Simon,' Alice hissed, 'we'll break it.'

'Doesn't matter.' He gently bit her ear. 'I'll pay barrack-room damages.'

They made companionable, middle-aged love, despite the constraints applied by the sturdy but narrow bed, and afterwards Alice felt whole and, somehow, clean again.

'By the way,' said Simon, gazing steadily at the canvas roof, 'how's your young friend, the good-looking one?'

Alice felt herself blushing and fumbled for her

handkerchief to blow her nose. 'Which one was that, then, dear?'

'You know, the feller from the *Daily Mail*?'

'Oh, I don't know. I haven't seen him for ages. I don't have to hunt with the journalistic pack any more. They've all been off out in the field in the Transvaal. I've been touring the camps.' She turned to look at him ingenuously. 'You know, that story I did about them caused a great rumpus but dear old K didn't seem to hold it against me. And the conditions in those camps have improved immensely. Milner has taken them over, and whatever you say about that scheming old devil, at least he has great administrative skills. Comes of being a lifelong bureaucrat, I suppose.'

'Good for you, darling.' He kissed her left nostril and Alice felt relieved that she had steered the conversation away from Fulton.

'Now,' she said, rolling away onto the grass. She stood and began adjusting her clothing. 'I want to hear all about this business at Reitz. I got your scribbled note but it didn't tell me much. It sounds like a story. Can you tell me about it?'

'I don't see why not. Phew! This tent is stifling. Goodness knows what's been going on in here. Let's go for a walk. I'm not on duty. Come on.'

So the pair of them, their love rekindled, walked hand in hand away from the camp onto the grassland and Simon told her of the night attack on the president's bungalow, Steyn's fleeing in his nightshirt – she nodded her head in delight at this detail – the capture of the State's exchequer and of the subsequent attack by de Wet. Alice scribbled furiously and then put down

301

her pencil.

'Sorry, my love,' she said, adjusting a pin in her hair, 'but this is a damned good story and I must get it on the cable. I shall get the train back to Pretoria right away. Have you told anyone else about this?'

'Of course not. Only in my report to French, with a copy to Kitchener, and neither of them will have seen it yet.'

'Good. Can you come with me to Pretoria?'

'No. I have one or two things I must do. I'll come tomorrow. Thank you for helping 352 in getting Nandi settled. I must see her and her children and make sure they are comfortable. Oh, and please ensure that stuff goes through the censor, or I'll be in trouble for talking to some Fleet Street scribbler – not to mention sleeping with her.'

'We didn't sleep. Goodbye, darling.'

The mention of the censor planted a thought in Alice's mind, which stayed with her through the brief journey to Pretoria. She had seen James Fulton only twice, briefly, since his seduction of her, and on both occasions she had forced herself to be quite civil, but nothing more. In retrospect, her act of unfaithfulness took on the aspect of a sordid aberration, robbed now of its excitement and glamour. She blamed herself for it, not Fulton. But what she could not forgive was the man's betrayal of her in stealing her story. It was an act of professional deceit that simmered in her mind. She realised that his pursuit of her was probably prompted by the thought that she could be used to further his career. Her lip curled. The

302

question of love, or attraction, probably never came into it. He should be taught a lesson...

Back in her hotel Alice concentrated on writing her story. She played down the fact that, once again, de Wet and Steyn had escaped – although she couldn't resist colourfully describing the elderly president's dash from the bungalow in his nightshirt, his beard flowing behind him – and emphasised the importance of the capture of his colleagues and of the money and the blow that this would be to the continuing resistance of the Free State. Dammit! She was a loving and supporting wife as well as an objective journalist. Simon should not be blamed for the escapes.

Alice duly delivered the cable to the young censor, who had no hesitation in accepting it, so laudatory was its tone. She returned to her hotel room and then drafted another story.

She wrote it out in pencil, occasionally crossing out a phrase or two to give it verisimilitude, and then read it with satisfaction. She scribbled on the top, as though it was an aide-memoire, 'MUST: put into cablese and send first thing tomorrow.'

It read:

*From our Special Correspondent in Pretoria.*

*Lord Kitchener of Khartoum, Commander-in-Chief of the British forces in South Africa, is to resign his post and return home. Britain's leading soldier has taken this decision because of what he perceives to be his failure to end the war against the Boers.*

*He told the* Morning Post *in Pretoria that the*

constant strain of building blockhouses across the veldt and of combating the guerrilla warfare tactics of Boer generals de Wet, Viljoen, Botha, Smuts and de la Rey was adversely affecting his health and he had decided to retire from the army. He would, he said, return home as soon as a successor could be found. He then intended to find a country house, possibly in Kent, and devote the rest of his life to gardening and local affairs.

The Morning Post *understands that Lieutenant General John French and Major General R.G. Broadwood are being considered by the Horse Guards as possible successors.*

*Lord Kitchener, who is 51, has always been considered to be in fine health. His constitution was never in doubt in leading a British and Egyptian expeditionary force across the Sudanese desert successfully to defeat the Mahdi's hordes at Omdurman in 1898. It is understood, however, that the psychological pressures imposed by the guerrilla war in South Africa have now proved to be too much for him.*

*His forced departure from the post of commander-in-chief will undoubtedly prove to be a propaganda coup for the Boers at a time when they are showing themselves to be doughty warriors, even when severely outnumbered.'*

Alice read it again and chuckled. What a damned good story! If only it were true and she had it exclusively! Never mind. It would fit neatly into the *Daily Mail's* predilection for sensational scoops. Now to see if the bait would be taken.

She looked at her watch. Four p.m. All the correspondents in Pretoria attached to Kitchener's HQ would have returned to the compound, writing their stories for tomorrow's editions – if they had a story, that is. She scribbled a simple message to Fulton: 'Would you have time to take tea with me in my room at my hotel today? I do hope so. I have something important to say to you. Please reply by bearer. Affectionately, Alice.'

Then she folded the message into an envelope, which she marked 'urgent', rang her bell and gave the message to the boy, slipped a ten-shilling note into his hand and instructed him to deliver it to James in the compound as quickly as possible. It was, she repeated to him, urgent and he was to repeat this to the recipient.

She sat back and pondered. Would it fetch him? Of course it would. If there were any doubt, the artful insertion of the word 'affectionately' would, she felt sure, tip the balance, stirring in him the thought that their relationship could, after all, be renewed passionately.

Alice retired to the bathroom that came attached as part of her little suite and carefully prepared herself for the encounter, brushing her hair and applying a faint touch of cosmetics. Then she arranged her 'story' on her writing desk, not too prominently but the pages left as though she had just finished writing, with her pencil across the leading page. Licking her finger, she plucked a hair from her head and, with infinite care, laid it on the top page, under the pencil so that a stray breeze would not blow it away. Then she drew up a chair by the window and waited.

The boy returned promptly and knocked on her door. The reply said: 'Will be with you at approx 4.45.' Good! She instructed him to tell the clerk at reception that Mr Fulton was to come straight to her room as soon as he arrived and then she resumed her seat, a little back from the window but near enough to see anyone who approached the hotel entrance.

Sharply at 4.43 she saw a hansom cab pull up and James Fulton step down. He was dressed casually but carefully, with a wide-brimmed white hat complementing his cream linen suit and white shirt, opened at the throat. He looked up at her window but Alice was carefully hidden behind the curtain. She saw him bound up the steps to the hotel and, three minutes later heard him taking the stairs to her room two at a time.

Quickly noting that the story was lying unobtrusively where she had placed it, Alice moved quickly into the bathroom, leaving the door slightly ajar. When he knocked she shouted, 'Do come in, James, the door is unlocked.' Then, when she heard him enter, she called out from the bathroom. 'Make yourself at home. I won't be a moment. Tea is on the table.'

Then she closed the bathroom door, turned on the tap of the washbasin and waited. She gave him three minutes and then entered, ensuring that she looked slightly flustered.

'I am so sorry,' she said, pushing back a stray lock of hair. 'A touch of the sun, I think.'

He stepped forward, full of concern. 'Ah, my dear. Have you seen a doctor? Can I do anything?'

'That's very kind but I am much better now, thank you. Oh, you haven't taken any tea?' Then, assuming some consternation, she rushed over to

306

the writing desk and thrust the story under the blotter, noting first that the strand of hair had disappeared. He had taken the bait. Now would he act on it?

He nodded towards the desk. 'Big story, eh?'

Alice pretended to look flustered. 'Good gracious, no. Just a potboiler to reassure the foreign editor that I am still alive. Nothing of interest, really. I'd forgotten I'd left it out. Now, please do have some tea.'

He frowned. 'I am sorry, Alice. You have caught me at a bad moment. I have a story to file.' He grinned. 'Just a filler really, not as interesting as yours, I bet. But I ought to get it on the wire tonight, so do excuse me if I don't stay. Although,' he took a step towards her and held out his arms, 'I must say you look ravishing. I have missed you, you know.'

Alice smiled and indicated a chair. 'And I you. But do take a chair for just a moment or two.'

'Yes, of course. You said you had something urgent to say to me.'

'Yes. Are you sure you won't have some tea? It's freshly made.'

'No, thank you. But perhaps I could come back when I have filed my story...?'

The implication was clear and she marvelled again at how warm were his eyes and how sparklingly white were his teeth. This time, though, there was no tightening of the buttocks or slight lurch of the stomach on her part. 'I fear not, James,' she said with a smile.

With a slight frown on his face, Fulton sat opposite her, leaning forward slightly. 'Very well.

307

Now what was so important?'

'Well,' Alice leant back in her chair. 'It's important to me, although perhaps not so important to you. You see, my dear, my husband has returned from the Orange Free State, where he has been wounded in the arm and kicked in the spine by a Boer's horse. He is, of course, right in the thick of the fighting and I have realised that I love him very much.'

She saw the muscles on Fulton's jaw tighten. She went on, 'I also realise that it was despicable of me to be unfaithful to him with you.'

'Oh, come on now, Alice.' Fulton's face was now set quite hard and she realised how malevolent he could appear when he was annoyed. 'You enjoyed the fucking even more than I did, I would say. Don't be such a hypocrite.' He flicked a non-existent piece of dust from one immaculate trouser leg.

Alice kept the faint smile fixed on her face. 'Well, I wouldn't know about that because I couldn't possibly compare our two feelings. But I have asked you here today to make it quite clear that our *affair*, whatever you call it, is over and I would be grateful if you would make no further approaches to me. I hope, though, that we can remain good friends.'

Fulton rose and made no reply but made for the door. There he turned for a moment and glared at her. 'I want you to know, Alice,' he said, 'that you weren't that good. I've had far better in the lanes behind Fleet Street.' Then he turned and slammed the door behind him.

Alice sat for a moment and then put her head

into her hands. How could she possibly ever have considered this man to have been better than her dear husband? His reaction and his language revealed him to be a complete cad. Then she smiled. I wonder what tomorrow will bring, she mused, for James Fulton?

In fact, tomorrow was quite uneventful for Alice and, as far as she knew, for the *Daily Mail*'s correspondent in Pretoria. The following day, however, provided a denouement.

In the street outside her hotel, she bumped into Bennet Burleigh of the *Daily Telegraph*. 'Alice,' he said, 'we've missed you recently. Where have you been? We all get the shivers when you disappear. Not another exclusive, please. We can't bear it.'

She smiled and glowed inwardly at the praise, for she respected him. 'No, Ben. Just a round-up of the concentration camps. They're better now, by the look of it. What's happening in the compound?'

'Ah.' He looked smug. 'Don't say you haven't heard the news?'

'What news?'

'That young pup, Fulton of the *Mail*, has been sent home.'

'Good gracious. Do tell me more.'

'It seems he either got hold of a bundle of false information or he fabricated a ridiculous story. He cabled that he had learnt that Kitchener was about to hand in his resignation and leave the army because he was said to be "under stress" at his failure to pin down the Boer commandos. Can you imagine K being under stress – or, if he was, admitting it?'

'Quite. What rubbish. So what happened?'

'Well the *Mail*, in its gutter press ignorance, published it and the roof immediately blew up. The War Office cabled K, of course, and he vehemently denied it and demanded an immediate retraction. Fulton couldn't substantiate his story, so the *Mail* had to climb down and publish an apology. Fulton has been sacked, of course, and has already set off for the Cape and London, tail between his legs, where, if rumour is to be believed, it will have company.'

Alice inwardly winced at the crude reference but also felt an inward shaft of sympathy for the young man, whose professional future was now ruined. It was accompanied by an equally sharp stab of guilt. Then both faded quickly as she recalled how, two days before, the concern in Fulton's face for her had been replaced in a flash by an expression of fierce malice as she had expressed her desire to end their affair.

'What a stupid young man,' she said. And meant it. Then she asked the question that had always concerned her. 'But how did he get such rubbish past the censor?'

'Well, the story is that he didn't. He bribed some young clerk to put the story on the official cable. Cheating to the end, you see.'

'Thank you, Ben. Whatever next? Now please forgive me. I am on my way to meet my husband.'

'Ah. Do give him my regards. I do wish he would give me the sort of exclusives that he gives to you.'

She pulled a face. 'Ah, you could never meet the price I have to pay. Good morning, Ben.'

# CHAPTER FIFTEEN

Alice, of course, told Simon nothing about the departure of Fulton. It was now an episode in her life that she was anxious to forget and certainly not one the details of which she wished to share with her husband. So she met him off the train from Johannesburg with a happy smile, particularly as she noted that his wounded arm seemed now to have completely recovered as he handed her into a cab for the journey to Nandi's house.

'Where's 352?' she asked. 'I thought he was coming with us.'

Simon shrugged. 'I don't know. Haven't seen much of him these last few days in camp, in fact. With the staff away, there's not much for us to do.'

They arrived in the tree-lined suburb on the edge of the town and Simon looked with approval at the little two-storied wooden building, fringed with eucalyptus trees. Nandi, in a pretty flowered dress and with her hair pulled back, thrusting her high cheekbones into relief, rushed out onto the *stoep* to meet them and kissed them both.

'Oh, Simon,' she said. 'I can't thank you enough for this house. But I don't know how I am ever going to repay you for it.'

He shook his head. 'For goodness' sake, Nandi.

You don't have to repay me. Alice and I have benefited extremely well from the deaths of our parents and we have invested wisely. We can well afford this. And I will keep to my promise to rebuild your farm, once this war is over. So stop worrying!'

Nandi looked down to avoid showing them the tears in her eyes, then kissed them both again.

'Where are the children?' asked Alice.

'They are in the garden at the back with 352.'

Fonthill threw back his head. 'So that's where he is! It seems he doesn't care about this war very much any more.'

Nandi looked embarrassed. 'Yes ... well. He is ... er ... very fond of the children, you know. I suppose it is because he doesn't have any of his own. And they love him.'

'Let's go through,' said Alice. 'I have to see this.'

They walked through the house and observed Jenkins and the children from a window looking out onto the garden. The Welshman was squatting on the grass with the two girls opposite to him, watching him intently, as he seemingly produced a penny from the mouth of the youngest, who squealed with delight.

'Ah,' said Simon with a smile. 'The disappearing penny trick. He once showed me how to do it – something to do with sleight of hand, of course, but I've forgotten how it's done.'

'No,' said Nandi, with a completely straight face, 'it's not a trick. It's magic. At least, that's what he told me.' Then they all burst into laughter.

Jenkins looked up in some consternation and they all joined the trio in the garden, where the two girls immediately became shy. The Welshman pulled at his moustache and looked sheepishly at Simon. 'Just popped over to make sure everythin' was all right, see,' he said, 'bein' as everythin' was quiet, like, at the camp.'

'Oh, don't worry about us. We can win this war without you, thank you very much.' Then Simon winced as he remembered that this was twice within the space of a couple of minutes that he had mentioned the war in Nandi's presence. For God's sake, it was only less than two years since her husband had been killed by the British and two months since he had burnt down her house!

He cleared his throat and went on quickly. 'Everything all right with you here, Nandi?' he asked. 'Do you need anything? Are the girls happy at their school?'

'Oh yes, thank you, Simon. Thanks to your generosity, we need nothing and the girls love their school.' Then her face clouded for a moment. 'Though I had a visit yesterday that worried me a little...'

'What?' Jenkins face immediately settled into a scowl. 'Who was that, then, eh?'

'Yes,' Alice joined in. 'Who was it Nandi?'

'Two British soldiers came to see me. One officer – I think he was a captain or something like that – and a sergeant. They wore red bands around their arms.'

'The military police,' exclaimed Jenkins. 'Bloody 'ell! What the devil would they want with you, then?'

'Come inside, Nandi,' said Simon. 'Sit down and tell us what they wanted.'

They left the children to play, trying to extract 352's penny from the most unlikely places, and sat in the little lounge, where Nandi had laid out coffee cups and small cakes. 'Would you like coffee now?' she asked.

'No,' said Jenkins, almost belligerently, 'tell us about these visitors, then.'

'Well, they were quite polite, but they asked me where I had come from and whether I owned the house.' Nandi looked across at Fonthill. 'I told them the truth, of course, and I hope I did right, Simon?'

'I am sure you did, my dear. But please go on. What else did they want to know?'

'I told them that I had come off the veldt south of Johannesburg and that you were an old friend from many years ago. I told them all about the Boer commandos being in the house when you arrived and all the shooting and that. And then I told them that you and your men had helped me take the furniture out and load it on the wagon and that dear 352 and the other soldier had ridden with us into Johannesburg and put us up at the hotel and that you had bought this house for us.' She finished breathlessly. 'It was all right to say all that, wasn't it, Simon? I just didn't know what else to say. You won't get into trouble, will you?'

Fonthill smiled. 'Good gracious, no, Nandi. But it's all rather strange. What else did they ask you?'

'Well, yes, there was something else. They asked about Jan, my husband...' she paused '...my late husband, that is.' She looked demurely into her lap for a moment before continuing. 'And whether he

314

had volunteered to join the Boer army. Which he had, of course, and I told them that. And then they asked me why me and the girls weren't in one of the camps. And that's when I told them about you and Jenkins coming, Simon.'

'Bloody cheek,' murmured Jenkins.

'Bloody cheek, indeed,' echoed Alice.

'Hmm.' Simon frowned. 'This is all very strange and I shall certainly make enquiries. Did they say where they were stationed?'

'No. I was becoming a little frightened at this stage.'

'I should bloody well think so,' grunted Jenkins. 'We shall 'ave to sort this out, bach sir, I'm thinkin'.'

'Well,' Fonthill waved his hand in dismissal. 'It's nothing to be worried about, Nandi. It's some sort of army bureaucracy, probably checking up to make sure that you are not some dastardly spy. Think nothing more about it. If you have another visit of this nature, though, be sure to tell me. In the meantime, I will make some enquiries. Now, tell me about these many years when we lost track of you. We must fill the gaps.'

And so the conversation settled into the recounting of Nandi's move back into Zululand to live with her father, John Dunn, after his app-ointment as one of the Zulu chiefs appointed by General Wolseley after the end of the Anglo-Zulu war, her meeting with Jan de Wath, the Boer farmer, their eventual marriage and her move to the Transvaal. Coffee was served and the cakes were consumed but, somehow, the conversation seemed stilted, with the shadow of the strange

315

visitors of the day before hanging over it.

Eventually, Simon and Alice made to leave. 'Are you coming back with us?' asked Simon of Jenkins.

'Er ... no, thank you, bach sir. I'll stay a bit longer, if that's all right with you, Nandi – an' if I'm not needed back at the camp, that is?'

'Oh, of course.' Nandi smiled at him indulgently. 'The girls would hate you to go just yet.'

'No,' added Simon. 'As long as you are covered back there.'

'Oh yes, bach sir. Sergeant Williams is standin' in. 'E's Welsh, so everything should be all right, look you.'

'Very well. But back tonight, please.'

'Very good, sir.'

In the cab riding back to the hotel, Alice smiled. 'Have you a feeling that we are going to lose Jenkins at last, darling? He seems to be getting alarmingly domesticated.'

'Never! Jenkins was always fond of Nandi. But he would never get married. It would be like taking a fox off the green Welsh hills and putting him in a cage. No, not Jenkins.' He grinned at his wife and then he frowned. 'I don't like the sound of Nandi's visitors, though. Interfering busybodies. I shall certainly make enquiries.'

In fact, the arrival of a small draft of new recruits and the need to bed them in occupied Fonthill's mind over the next two days and distracted him from following up the matter, that and a telegram from French saying that he was on his way back from the Eastern Transvaal and warning Simon that his column should prepare for a new assignment, the details of which he would explain on his return.

French arrived as Fonthill, now joined by Jenkins and Hammond, the latter having returned from his leave, was taking the column through training exercises out on the veldt and it was two days before he was summoned to a meeting with the general. Unusually, however, this was to be with Kitchener at his headquarters in Pretoria.

Simon had not met the commander-in-chief since his appointment nearly a year before and it was with some anticipation that he entered the familiar large room that was K's office. His new assignment, he presumed, must be important for him to be briefed about it by the C-in-C himself.

The two generals were sitting at Kitchener's desk and the victor of the Nile pointed unsmilingly to a vacant chair as Fonthill approached. The atmosphere seemed strangely oppressive, although the weather outside was cool.

'Fonthill,' said Kitchener, 'I'm afraid a rather serious charge has been levelled against you and we both felt that we should hear what you had to say about it before I allowed the matter to go any further.'

Simon blinked. 'A serious charge? Good Lord. What might that be, then, sir?'

The big man looked down at a paper on his desk. 'Do you know a Mrs Nandi de Wath?'

'Yes I do. She is a very old friend.' Fonthill shot a quick glance across at French, who looked vaguely embarrassed.

'I understand...' It was the turn of Kitchener to seem discomfited, for his words faded away.

317

Then he cleared his throat, adjusted his pince-nez and looked over the top at Simon as he continued. 'I understand that she is your mistress and that you are probably the father of her children. Is this so?'

Fonthill's jaw dropped and he gulped in indignation. 'Good God, no. This is absolutely untrue.'

Kitchener shifted in his chair and glanced across at French. 'I am glad to hear it. But I must ask you some more questions. You understand, of course, that our policy of farm clearances is, I suppose I must call it, controversial but I have given orders on what should be done when a farm has to be burnt?'

'Yes.'

'Well, I further understand that you have often contravened these orders in that you have often delayed at a farm, had your men take out the occupants' furniture and other belongings and allowed them to be driven off by the occupants before the house was burnt. So that they often, presumably, were not taken into care in one of our camps.'

'That is so, sir.'

'Ah! I see. However, in the case of this...' Kitchener looked down again at the paper on his desk '...Mrs de Wath, you went considerably further. Although when you arrived the farmhouse was occupied by Boer commandos and a lively action then ensued, which involved casualties, you delayed destroying the place for quite some time, although other enemy units might well have been in the area. Then you followed your usual practice of ordering your men to carry out furniture, but

318

you also deputed two men – including your regimental sergeant major – to accompany the family into Pretoria, where your RSM found them a house, which was bought with funds supplied by you. The inference seems quite clear: although you are a married man, there is clearly some sort of liaison between you and this lady.'

Fonthill opened his mouth to speak, but Kitchener held up his hand. 'Now, your private life, of course, is your own affair, Fonthill, and apart from disobeying the strict interpretation of my orders on this farm-burning business, you don't seem to have contravened any army regulations, although employing your RSM in this way while on active service sails pretty close to the damned wind, I would have thought. But I must say that your behaviour with this ... er ... Boer lady is bound to lead to gossip and, frankly, is not the sort of thing that I can condone from an officer of your seniority under my command. Now, let us both hear what you have to say on this matter.'

The C-in-C settled back in his chair and removed his pince-nez expectantly.

Fonthill drew in a deep breath and looked again at French, who was studiously gazing out of the window. Who had supplied this remarkably detailed information? A certain amount of digging had obviously been involved – and then the involvement with the regimental police. Where to start? He tried to concentrate.

'First of all, sir,' he began, 'I don't wish to give offence but it is ridiculous nonsense to accuse me of being the lover of Mrs de Wath and I am certainly not the father of her children. She is the

319

widow of a Boer burgher who lost his life at the siege of Ladysmith and they are his children. In fact, until we arrived at her farmhouse, I had not seen the lady for nearly twenty years.

'Both Sergeant Major Jenkins and my wife can confirm these facts because the three of us were all involved with Mrs de Wath, first during the Zulu war and then with General Wolseley's campaign against the bPedi nation shortly afterwards. In fact, we all visited her the day before yesterday at her house in Pretoria. But let me tell the background to that involvement years ago and why I still feel in her debt to this day.'

He then related how Nandi, as a young girl in her late teens and daughter of John Dunn, the trader who was an adviser to King Cetshwayo, had smuggled a revolver and knife into the hut where he and Jenkins had been kept prisoner by the King at his capital, Ulundi. This had enabled them to escape and so take part in the Battles of Isandlwana and, in his case, Rorke's Drift, for Jenkins had been wounded at Isandlwana and left for dead there. Fonthill's story had not been believed and, despite taking an heroic part in the defence of the hospital at Rorke's Drift, he had been accused of cowardice by his former commanding officer. At the court martial, it was only the evidence, given at the last minute by Nandi and confirming his story, that had convinced the court of his innocence.

'Jenkins was still in a coma in a hospital bed at that time,' he concluded, 'and could not give evidence. If Nandi had not heard of my plight and come forward, I might well have been shot for cowardice.

'Gentlemen, I promise you that that was not a happy prospect for a young subaltern. So I owe my life to this young woman and I am grateful that I was able to help her, back in 1880, when she ran into grave trouble with a party of Portuguese diamond smugglers near the Mozambique border, and now, when I was forced to burn her home.'

He held up his hand as French opened his mouth to interrupt. 'Forgive me, sir,' he said, 'but it is my turn now. The money for purchasing her house here came from the joint account of myself and my wife, which, of course, can easily be confirmed. So my wife was party to the purchase and was as anxious to help Mrs de Wath as I was – surely not the act of a woman who was being deceived.

'Now, concerning the charges concerning my RSM and the burnings. Well, I must plead guilty, I suppose. You said yourself, General, that this policy is controversial. I am afraid, sir, that to the men who have to do it, it is worse than that. It is hateful. We are used to fighting the enemy but not to evicting their wives and children from their homes and then burning them. We all understand why it has to be done but we hate being employed to do it.'

Fonthill was well aware that he was on dangerous ground here and he ploughed on before either of the generals could interrupt. 'You are quite right, sir, that I always have my men help the women and children bring out their belongings and I do not allow looting, as I believe is done in some regiments. It is also true that I

321

allow the families to ride off with their furniture. I reason that, if they make for the nearest town, then they will probably have people there who will help them, so that they won't be a further burden on the camps. If they join a commando, then that will restrict that unit's mobility and probably do us a good turn. So I saw no reasons to change my practice.'

Simon gulped in air and hurried on. 'The farm was burnt as soon as the family had left it. My scouts were out so I was fairly certain that there were no more Boer fighters in the area. As for Jenkins's role in all this. He was entitled to leave, having served non-stop for some six months, so I granted him three weeks to help take Mrs de Wath to Pretoria and I felt I could spare the trooper that went with them. Yes, we were on active duty at the time, but the absence of two men did not denude us.

'Finally, General, you were kind enough recently to approve General French's recent recommendation of the award of the DSO to me and a bar to Jenkins's DCM. I can only interpret this as the approval of both of you to my and his recent actions in the field – enough, I would have thought, to overcome any lingering doubts about these recent absurd accusations.'

A silence fell upon the room. Then, slowly, Kitchener replaced his spectacles, picked up the paper from his desk, briefly ran his eye over it once more and then, equally slowly, tore it into fragments and deposited it into his waste-paper basket. He stood, walked from behind his desk and held out his hand to Fonthill, who, puzzled,

322

grasped it.

'My apologies, Colonel,' Kitchener said. 'We both felt that this was nonsense, but we had to give you the opportunity of telling us so. Obviously, the matter will be taken no further and I would like you to apologise to Mrs de Wath for any pain or inconvenience that she has experienced. Now, I want you to put this completely from your mind and get back to the good work you are doing. Go into the room, a couple of doors along here, and French will tell you of your new assignment. Please give my compliments to your wife. Now, you must excuse me. I have much to do.'

'One moment, sir.' Fonthill released Kitchener's hand and frowned heavily. 'These charges have obviously been put forward by someone who seems to have been close to me in my column and has obviously been...' he sought for the right word '...spying on me. I would like to know who that was and have him removed.'

'He will be removed and French will see to that. You have our apologies for this matter and I don't want you to take it any further. We will certainly not. I won't have witch-hunts. Now, good day to you, Fonthill.'

Simon inclined his head. 'Good day, sir.'

French and he walked stiffly to the nearby room. The general closed the door behind them and gestured to two chairs placed at a small table.

He sat opposite Fonthill and eased his tunic. 'I extend my own apologies to you, my dear fellow,' he said. 'I fear that much of this is my own fault.

323

You see,' he leant forward, 'I have to confess I was not in favour of your appointment. I did not think it either wise or fair to appoint to your position someone with as little experience of regular army command as you had, and also your ... er ... forgive me, clear record of, what shall I say, disenchantment with the army and all its faults. I felt that was asking for trouble, but K overruled me.'

Fonthill sensed French's genuine embarrassment but couldn't quite let him off the hook that easily. 'So you appointed Hammond to spy on me? Forgive me, sir, but it was not exactly the action of a gentleman, if I may say so.'

French's florid countenance flushed an even darker shade of puce. 'You certainly may *not* say so, Fonthill. You will *not* use that language to me. I was merely doing my duty as I saw it. And, I suppose, Hammond was merely carrying out orders. Although,' the general's manner quickly ameliorated, 'I have to say that he carried them out with a zeal that showed he seemed to have very little respect for you.

'And,' French continued, 'I was a trifle worried when you reported that his horse had bolted at that sharp engagement when you nearly nabbed de Wet. Such a strange thing to happen to such a splendid horseman. But I couldn't bring myself to think of him as a coward, because I had seen him in action.'

Fonthill nodded. 'I was suspicious, but I agree now that he is not a coward. But how could he continue to give me deference and report on me to you?'

'Quite so. In fact, I told him some time ago that I did not need to receive these sort of reports in future because I was more than satisfied with your performance.' French jerked his head towards Kitchener's office. 'This stupid business came out of the blue and he obviously devoted his leave to find evidence to incriminate you. However, look here. You have received apologies from both of us now and there the matter must rest. As soon as I leave here I will order that Hammond be transferred immediately. So don't pick a fight with him – and that's an order.'

Fonthill inclined his head. 'Very well, sir.'

French stood and extended his hand. 'Let us shake hands, forget this matter and get on with the bloody war, eh?'

'Of course, sir.' Fonthill had an irreverent thought and could not but grin at it. It was like being forced to shake hands at school after an affray in the schoolyard. Childish, really. But, he reflected, the British army was rather like a public school in many ways: ivy-covered practices, stern morals, outmoded rules and regulations. He sat down again and composed himself to listen to French.

'Now,' French stroked his greying moustache and put a stubby forefinger behind his shirt collar to ease it. Simon noticed again that the man had a prodigious bull neck. 'You will know,' he said, 'that Kitchener's policy has to be one of attrition. We are building blockhouses across the veldt and linking them with barbed wire and literally driving the Boers into these vast compounds. It is hard and slow work but it is paying off.

'The Boers know this, of course, and they cannot afford to lose men and they are running out of time. So, once again, they are trying to ease the pressure on the two main States – the Transvaal and the Free State – by attacking elsewhere. You played a large part in chasing de Wet out of the Cape Colony. There are small bands of commandos down there still and some of them have penetrated to the coast. But they are being hounded and they are failing to raise rebels in the Colony to support them. But a new threat has emerged.'

Fonthill leant forward with interest. 'De Wet again, in the centre of the Free State?'

French shrugged. 'Well, he is certainly still there and we expect him to become active again at any moment. But there is only so much harm that he can do out in those great grasslands. He is not what I am talking about. It is Botha – I think you clashed with him early on, didn't you?'

'Yes. I think I had a slight advantage then, but there wasn't much in it.'

'Quite so. K has great respect for him and considers him probably the best strategic thinker of all the Boer generals. Well, we believe that he is planning to attack Natal, maybe through Zululand, maybe not. Our intelligence is very sketchy, but if he does get through, then he could do untold damage.'

Fonthill's interest was stimulated. Tackling Botha was far more challenging than farm burning. 'You want me to go down there with my column?'

'Yes. The border is pretty well defended on the

Natal side but he will certainly probe it and he will be looking to cross the Buffalo River. We think he will have about one thousand men with him, so, of course, he will completely outnumber you. What's your strength now?'

'About two hundred.'

'Yes. Now, remind me, Fonthill, of your approach to these Boer hunting trips of yours. I've read your reports, of course, but I have read dozens of others, too. Do you take artillery?'

'Good Lord, no. It would slow us down completely.'

'What about provisions? Wagons?'

'Certainly not, sir. If we are to do our job properly, then we have to move fast. If we get the chance, my motto is: ride by night and strike at dawn. The Boer is a fearsome fighter on horseback. Catch him before he gets into the saddle and he can be a very different proposition. He likes to be able to ride away from trouble if things get too hot.'

French smiled. 'My sentiments exactly. But come back to provisions. What and how do you take them?'

'If I reckon we shall be scouting away for, say, a couple of nights, then we can take the basics – water, tea, biltong, even a pouch of flour apiece – behind our saddles. If we're to be away longer, then we have mules. They are five times as fast as wagons with oxen, of course, and better than packhorses in that they can climb mountains, as we found in the Colony, trying to step on de Wet's shirt tail.'

'Excellent. Just what I wanted to hear. If we are

327

to pin down Botha it has to be by using a column like yours to catch up with him and bring him to the fight. If you can hold him for a time, we can get reinforcements to you. Now, there's a freight train that is leaving for the Natal border from Jo'burg the day after tomorrow. Get your men and horses, mules etcetera on it. I'm afraid it's open cattle trucks, but I know that you are used to hardship.'

'Where is Botha now?'

'I wish I knew. We know he slipped out of his hunting grounds on the remote eastern border of the Transvaal. We believe that he left behind what was left of his artillery and all of his wagons. Hence my point about moving fast. He is marching light and quickly with pack mules and pack-horses to support him. The open veldt of the south-east Transvaal has been relatively untouched by the war so far and Botha set up a pace that was too hot for the columns we thought we had on his trail – again – hence my questions to you. Our chaps seem to have just two paces: plod and slow plod. You, I know, are different. Hence my telegram to you.

'We think that Botha is heading for the British camp at Dundee, ten miles on the Natal side of the river. He would probably hope to get fresh food and horses there, and then cut the railway at Glencoe, on the main line between Durban and Pretoria and, of course, one of the two main arteries of the British army. But, apart from us, he will have problems with the weather. It has turned really sour down there: cold and wet and the rivers will probably be in spate. Not much fun for you, Fonthill, either, of course, but worse for him, because he will have had a hard ride from the north and fodder will be scarce.'

Fonthill looked thoughtful. 'When we find him, you want us to hold onto him until our heavy stuff comes up?'

'Exactly. You will be outnumbered, so don't tackle him head-on. Outbluff him if you can and delay him. Finding him is going to be difficult, so you may have to float a bait for him to rise to. Fisherman, Fonthill?'

'Used to do a bit, sir. On the Wye, Welsh Border country.'

'Good trout there. Experience should stand you in good stead. Now, remember, above all, you must not let Botha get into Natal. He knows the territory like the back of his hand so it won't be easy. But I think you're the man to do it. I shall be following you down. You will continue to report to me. You have the telegraph address.'

'Well, thank you for your confidence. We will do our best.'

The two shook hands again and Fonthill took his leave, walking out into the cold wind of the high veldt and wondering just how much colder and wetter it would be on the Natal border, which he remembered depressingly well from the Zulu war. He shook his head at the memory. At least not a bloody court martial this time, he hoped! Just clean, straightforward stuff, like finding a slippery Boer, ducking and weaving in his own territory and then fighting him with a force outnumbered by something like four to one. He groaned to himself. Easy!

# CHAPTER SIXTEEN

Fonthill took advantage of his presence in Pretoria to pay a brief visit to his wife before catching the train for the quick journey back to the camp south of Johannesburg. She was immediately interested in the news about Botha.

'Now for goodness' sake, Alice,' Simon interjected quickly. 'You can't use that. Word could get back so quickly to Botha and he would know we were on to him. And I would get sacked for telling you.'

She pouted. 'And is London so full of Boer spies that they would read my piece and cable it back to him so quickly?'

'Well, I think the answer to that is probably yes. So ... I repeat: don't use it.'

'Oh, very well. But,' her face lightened, 'let me come with you. There is absolutely nothing to write about here at the army's headquarters. The press corps is fed the odd scrap or two of so-called news from the general's table but we might as well be reporting on a vicar's tea party.'

Simon held up his hand. 'No, darling. I'm sorry, but you can't come with me. There are two good reasons. Firstly, army headquarters says where journalists can and can't go on active service and, secondly, it's too damned dangerous. I can't have my wife flitting about at my elbow when I'm trying to fight one of the best Boer generals in the whole of South Africa. It would distract me. Sorry, but no.'

Alice scowled. 'So I distracted you when the Pathans attacked us in the orange grove in Afghanistan, did I? I killed at least one of them myself. And what about when we had to laager and the Matabele surrounded us? Who manned – or rather, womanned – one of the wagons, with just a hunting rifle? And who shot that Boxer in the shoulder in China when he was about to butcher you, eh? And who killed the awful Gerald in Peking when he had taken a bead on you with his rifle? Who? Why me, of course. Your dear little frightened wife. That's who. Distract you, my foot. I wasn't in the way, then, now was I?'

Fonthill looked at his wife's flushed face and couldn't help but grin. He held up his hand again, in supplication this time. 'Darling, I'm sorry,' he said. 'I concede that you are twice the fighter I am and probably almost as good as Jenkins. I didn't mean to impugn your courage or your value in a fight when the chips are down.' His grin turned to a frown. 'But don't you see? If we are attacked I have much greater responsibilities now and you would add to them. I *would* be worried about you and you *would* be a distraction. I am sorry but I'm afraid you must stay here and report on K's tea parties. Now kiss me and let me go. I have much to do.'

Still scowling, Alice put her arms around him and kissed him soundly. 'Go then,' she murmured into his ear, 'but if you get yourself killed and I'm not there I shall never forgive you and I shall certainly never let you sleep with me again. So

331

there.' She poked her tongue out. 'Off you go and I hope you never find bloody Botha.'

Back in the camp, Fonthill found that Jenkins had arrived before him. The Welshman came bustling over. ''Ere,' he said in a loud whisper. 'Great news. 'Ammond 'as gone. Packed 'is gear and buggered off. Without so much as a goodbye kiss or farewell word to me. The word is that 'e's gone back to some fancy cavalry lot, see.'

Simon grinned and nodded. 'Yes, I know. Although I didn't think it would be as quick as that.' Then he recounted his conversations with Kitchener and French.

'So 'e was be'ind the police visit to Nandi.' Jenkins's eyes narrowed. 'The bastard. Telling all them lies, look you. An' frightenin' Nandi, as well.' He spat. 'I'll 'ave 'im for that. You'll see. 'E's a genuinely nasty piece of work. I'll see 'e pays for it.'

Fonthill put his hand on his old comrade's shoulder. 'You'll do nothing of the kind, 352,' he said. 'The commander-in-chief specifically ruled out any witch-hunts or reprisals. We are well rid of him. Now, go and ask Captain Forbes to see me. I shall promote him; he will command A Squadron and we can get on with the war.'

Shortly before dawn the next morning, the column paraded and loaded horses, mules and men into the open rail trucks and set off under a leaden sky towards the south-east. Rain was in the air and the atmosphere was cold, so Fonthill ordered the issue of rum to every man. Somehow, the issue seemed to have been exceeded in the case of C Squadron, under the command of the irrepressible Captain Cartwright, for there was loud singing from their wagons as the engine spluttered into life. Fonthill let it go. It was going to be a long and uncomfortable journey.

The journey from Johannesburg to Glencoe, where Fonthill had decided to detrain, was some two hundred miles. Uncomfortable, certainly, because the trucks, of course, were open and the weather cold and wet, but the line was clear and the little train rattled along at fifty miles an hour so that it was early afternoon when it wheezed to a halt at Glencoe. Fonthill had chosen the place as a central point near the Transvaal-Natal border from which he could ride quickly to confront Botha, once he had news of him. In consequence, Mzingeli and his trackers with their horses were the first to leave the train, with orders from Simon to spread out along the frontier immediately to bring back news of the Boer raider.

The rest of the column were descending in a confusion of noise from horses, mules and men when Jenkins, a wry grin on his face, found Fonthill.

'I think you'd better come with me, bach sir,' he said. 'Up to the steamer locomotive, like.'

'Oh, for God's sake, what's the problem now?'

'You'll see. Come on.'

They made their way through the throng of men and animals to the head of the train, where they were just in time to see the driver, his grin cutting a white swathe across his grimed face, handing down from the footplate a lady in riding boots, breeches and serviceable jacket, a familiar apple-green scarf at her throat but with a smudge of coal dust across her cheek.

'Thank you so much,' she said, bestowing on the man the most gracious smile. 'That really was a most enjoyable journey.'

'Alice!' screamed Fonthill. 'What the hell...? How dare you disobey my orders.'

'Oh hello, Colonel,' replied his wife sweetly. 'I do hope you and the men didn't get too wet. I had a lovely ride, I must say. I was allowed to pull the steam whistle at Newcastle. It was great fun.'

Simon refused to smile. 'Well,' he said, 'you can just turn around and get back up there on the footplate and ride back to Johannesburg. You are not staying here.'

Alice smiled at the driver who handed her a much battered leather valise. 'Ah, thank you.' She turned back to her husband. 'Oh, don't be such a grouch, Simon. You may be in the army, dear, but I am not and if you won't let me stay with your column, then I shall just buy a horse and ride out onto the veldt and find Botha for myself. From what I have read, he is a perfect gentleman and should make good copy. Apart from which,' she sniffed, 'I have to confess that that steam has ruined my hair, and much as I enjoyed the ride, I am damned if I am going to get back on that train just yet awhile, thank you very much.'

Jenkins coughed. 'I'll find 'er a tent an' bedroll, bach sir. Better I think.'

'What? Oh, very well, dammit. Oh, Alice. What on earth am I going to do with you?'

'Oh, it's quite simple, dear.' She took his arm companionably and walked him away from the hissing steam. 'Just let me camp by myself on the edge of the column – as I did, incidentally, when Chelmsford crossed the Buffalo and invaded Zululand not far from here. I shall stay out of your hair and look after myself – I have bought provisions – and all I would require is that you would let me know when something is about to happen, so that I can be there to report on it. Now, that's not a lot to ask, is it?'

'Alice, I hate it when you are arch. What is French going to say when he hears that I – seemingly – took my wife with me on this mission?'

'Well, darling, he need never know. Threaten to shoot any of your men who look as if they are going to tell him.'

Fonthill shook off her arm. 'Now you're being arch again.'

'No I am not. If the matter comes out I shall certainly explain that I hitched my own lift here – actually, it cost me twenty pounds but I shall not claim on the army for that. And, Simon, of course we will not live together out here. I shall keep my distance. I am not your wife, I am a journalist for the *Morning Post* accredited to Lord Kitchener's army out here. And I sense that there is going to be a good story here. So stop making a fuss, there's a good dear.'

'Very well. But I warn you, Alice, life can be – no, it will be – hard with a column like this. We ride roughly and we sleep in the open when we are out on the veldt. You will get no favours from me.'

Alice smiled beguilingly again. 'Accepted, Colonel. Well, just one little favour, please, when you ... er ... we ride out. I shall need a horse, dear, otherwise I doubt if my legs will allow me to keep up with you.'

'You shall have a horse, but don't call me "dear".'

'No, darling.'

'Alice!'

'Sorry, sir. Just joking.'

'Well, don't!'

'No, sir.'

Fonthill suddenly realised that their conversation had been observed by a ring of grinning troopers, some of whom were clearly assessing Alice admiringly. He frowned.

'Get about your duties,' he shouted. 'Do you have no orders?'

Sheepishly, they disbanded and Simon was relieved when Jenkins came back with a pony, already saddled and bridled. ''Ere we are, Miss Alice,' he said. ''E's a nice little beast. Your tent is bein' pitched for you on the edge of A Squadron over there,' he pointed. 'But not too near 'em,' he added hastily. 'The colonel is not too far away – and neither am I, if you want anythin', that is.'

'352, I would kiss you, if I was allowed to. Thank you very much. Au revoir, Simon. Oh, would you care to have dinner with me in my tent tonight, dear?'

'Alice!'

'Sorry, just joking.'

She picked up her valise and led the pony away, nodding and smiling at the troopers as she made her way to the lines of A Squadron. Simon and Jenkins exchanged glances.

The Welshman bent his huge moustache into a great smile. 'I've said it before,' he said, 'and I hope you don't mind me sayin' it again, bach sir, but she's a magnificent woman, your missus. A wonderful lass.'

Fonthill gave a rueful smile. 'That may be so, but she can be a bit of a handful when she wants to be. Like now! Come on, fetch Forbes and Cartwright and let's visit the resident military and see if there's news of Botha.'

There was, indeed. In the poky office of the artillery captain who was commander of the garrison at Glencoe they found a scene of great activity. A telegraph was chattering in one corner of the room and the captain was scribbling at a tiny desk, while subalterns and runners were toing and froing all about him.

He looked up with a frown as they entered. He stood and extended his hand. 'Welcome, Colonel, gentlemen,' he said. 'Sorry I was not at the siding to meet you but news has come in that Botha has struck just along the way, so to speak.'

'Really.' Fonthill stepped forward. 'Where? Do you have a map?'

'Yes, of course. Sorry I can't ask you to sit down. No seats.'

'That doesn't matter. Show me.'

The captain unrolled a large map and jabbed a grimy finger to an unmarked spot just north of the town of Vryheid, some fifty miles almost due east of Glencoe. 'Here,' he said. 'It's near the main crossing point of the Buffalo River on the border.'

Fonthill grunted. 'As you say, damned near to us. What happened?'

'Well, I don't have all the details but it seems

337

that Major Hubert Gough had been newly arrived with his battalion of mounted infantry to help guard the frontier at the crossing at de Jager's Drift. Botha caught him by surprise, in filthy weather, outflanked him and completely cut up his right-hand company. Gough had two field guns but the Boers captured them and Gough himself was captured, although he escaped during the night and made his way to the nearest British patrol.'

'So. What was the result?'

'It seems that Gough was completely beaten. One captain and nineteen men killed, five officers and nineteen men wounded, six other officers and two hundred and thirty-five men taken prisoner. But there's more: Botha captured one hundred and eighty Lee Metford rifles, thirty thousand rounds of ammunition, two hundred horses and the two field guns.'

'Blimey!' Jenkins whistled.

Fonthill frowned. 'It would be the horses that would be most precious to him. Did he keep them?'

'That seems to be the only good news. It seems he found the British horses useless because Gough had ridden them to death. And the field guns were too ponderous for him, so he sent them, the horses and the prisoners – stripped, of course – back to the British lines.'

'Yes, but where is he now? Did he cross the Buffalo?'

'No. It was in spate, so he couldn't. Nobody knows where he is now. He could be coming towards us or he could be just probing along the

338

Buffalo, looking for a crossing.'

'Hmmm. Are you reasonably strong here?'

'Yes, sir. We have enough men, although we have called up reinforcements.'

'Good. Let me look at that map again.'

Fonthill took it, swivelled it around and called Forbes, Cartwright and Jenkins to look over his shoulder. He traced the course of the river to the east and looked up at the captain. 'What are these two places?'

'Ah. Fort Prospect and Fort Itala. They are two British camps astride the Buffalo, virtually in Zululand.'

'Are they garrisoned?'

'Yes, sir. But I don't know at what strength.'

Simon looked up at his subordinates. 'I have a feeling in my water that that's where he will strike next. He will want to cross the border, of course, but he would love to do it with a flourish, not skulk across it in the middle of the night. And even if the river is too high here, he would love to follow up his success over Gough by knocking over these two camps, before he has to retreat back into the Transvaal. They seem to be comparatively remote, well away from the British forces here. They look vulnerable.' He thumped the table. 'I gamble that's where he will strike next. Gentlemen, let us give our chaps one fairly dry night under canvas, after their wet rail trip, and then we move out first thing in the morning. Even if Botha is not planning to hit this way, perhaps we can entice him. Thank you, Captain. Look to your defences, just in case I am wrong.'

'Very good, sir. Thank you – and good luck!'

Fonthill strode away, leaving the others to scamper after him, for there was a renewed spring in his step now. After all the recent months of chasing de Wet and burning farms, here seemed an opportunity at last of bringing a Boer general to battle. Oh, he would be vastly outnumbered by the sound of it, but if he could fight from a defended position, then that would even out the odds and there would be British garrisons already *in situ* at these forts to swell his numbers. He looked up at the sky. Should he move out now? No. The men would fight better after a decent night's sleep.

He turned his head. 'Come on, you three. Keep up. We might have a battle to fight.'

Just before dawn the column saddled up and moved out, Fonthill leaving orders for his trackers to meet at Itala. That night Simon had invited Alice to eat with him, his officers and Jenkins in a large army hut near the railway line. He explained Alice's presence among them by inferring that she had gained HQ's permission to join a column out in the field. Then he had outlined the risk he was taking in striking out to the east, but no one demurred. In fact, they all nodded in agreement at his analysis, Alice, of course, saying nothing but busily making notes. They moved now in all-pervading greyness, the drizzle soaking them to the skin. But they rode on. Fonthill was determined to reach the forts before Botha struck.

The distance to the nearest of the camps, Fort Itala, was some forty miles and the journey fringed the border into Zululand. It confirmed to Fonthill that he was right to think that Botha would select this route as his entry into Natal. Kitchener was relying to a large extent on the Zulus to defend their own border and Simon sensed that the tough, pragmatic Boer would choose these spear-wielding warriors – traditional enemies of the Afrikaners – rather than the British, with their modern weapons, as opponents if it came to a fight. He would bank on brushing aside the small army outposts at the two forts. The questions remained: could he get there before the Boer and was the Buffalo in spate?

They were forced to camp the night in the open under groundsheets that provided little shelter from the unrelenting rain that now thundered down like vertical stair rods. Head bowed, Fonthill trudged through the sodden ground to find where Alice lay shivering, her head just visible under her waterproof. He handed her a small flask.

'Here,' he said, 'whisky. It might warm you up. Sorry, darling. When we both said "for better or worse" I think this was what God had in mind for the worse bit.'

She reached out a grateful hand. 'I think you have deliberately engineered this to teach me a lesson. But thank you, Simon.' She unscrewed the cap and took a swig. 'Just what was needed. The good thing about this weather, I suppose, is that it should hold up Botha, do you think?'

Simon nodded, sending raindrops showering from the tip of his nose. 'Yes. But more importantly, it will deny him grazing fodder for his horses. He's been riding for days from the north in this sort of weather. His mounts will be

341

knackered and won't be able to feed in this mud. It will all deny him the chance to roam freely into Natal, even if he crosses the Buffalo or the Tugela further south. At least, I hope so. Can't stop, my love. Got to make my rounds. Sleep as well as you can and keep taking the medicine.'

He knelt down clumsily and kissed her before moving on.

The column was raised early and it pressed on through the day, Fonthill driving the pace so that they reached the first of the British encampments shortly after midday. The name of Fort Itala flattered it. Established only a month before, it was merely a collection of tents surrounded by shallow trenches, all huddled on a ridge at the foot of a small mountain. But Fonthill was relieved to find three hundred mounted infantry, under the command of a Dublin Fusilier, Major A.J. Chapman, well established and in good heart.

Chapman was delighted to have reinforcements and the two men shook hands. 'My Zulu scouts tell me that Botha is not far away,' he said, 'although it is not certain that he is intending to attack us. I have posted eighty men onto the top of the mountain which might just surprise him, if he tries to do so.'

'Hmm.' Fonthill frowned. 'We might have to entice him. How far away is the other fort and what sort of state is it in?'

'Prospect? Matter of fact, it's a far better defensive position than this one. It is a proper redoubt with rock walls impervious to rifle fire and barbed wire surrounding it. Fewer men than here but it should be all right.'

'Good. We can concentrate here, then. I will get my men to help you complete those trenches, but I would hate Botha to think that we would be a hard nut to crack so that he doesn't come on. Don't throw the earth high at the front. Flatten it out as though we haven't dug at all. That might lure him in and, between us, we can give him a bloody nose. Start now. We might not have much time. Thank God the rain has stopped.'

'Very good, sir.'

Later, as Fonthill's men were erecting their low bivouac tents, Mzingeli and three of his scouts rode in. They confirmed that the Boers were some ten miles away.

'They riding to the south-west, Nkosi,' reported Mzingeli. 'Don't know if they come this far. But it is a big commando. About thousand men. Some wagons but no big guns.'

Simon nodded. 'Good.' He smiled and put a hand on the tall man's shoulder. 'I hate to ask you this, Mzingeli,' he said, 'but I would like you and your men to go out again. Fan out and spread the word among whatever farms you can find that this fort is badly defended – just a few shallow trenches, that's all. Grab some hot food here before you go and come back when you have put out the rumour.'

'Ah. Understand. You want him to come to you?'

'Absolutely.'

'I spread the word.'

Fonthill then sent out two riders. The first to Fort Prospect to the east, informing the commanding officer there of the danger of an impending attack, and the other to the west, back to Glencoe, reporting the presence of Botha nearby and asking for reinforcements. Then he set his troopers to join Chapman's men in deepening the trenches and directed that a special, half-scooped-out, low rock-walled command post be dug out and erected behind the line, from which he could command the defence. Here, he could establish a small reserve and also ensure that Alice was safe. He looked high up to where Chapman's eighty men were on the mountain top. Should he bring them in to add to the main defences? He decided against it. If Botha tried to establish men up there or on the slopes to fire down on the camp, they would provide a deterrent. Then he waited.

The night passed peacefully, as did the next day, so enabling the trenches to be completed. The remainder of the black trackers came in and Mzingeli himself returned with his three men. They had all met Kaffirs to whom they had given the message that the white men at the forts were not expecting attack and were not ready for it. Fonthill and his men settled down to wait.

The attack came during the early hours of darkness, surprisingly, for the Boers usually liked to launch an assault just before dawn. A little before midnight the mountain peak became lit up by gun flashes and the crackle of musketry echoed down to the ridge below. The defenders ran to their positions in the trenches and Fonthill and Chapman stood in their redoubt, abortively focusing their field glasses in the darkness on the top of the peak.

'Damn,' murmured Chapman. 'I hope they've

not been overrun. Perhaps I shouldn't have left them up there on their own.'

'No,' said Fonthill. 'They've done their job. We just might have been caught with our pyjama bottoms down here, being attacked at this time of night. Let's hope they can hold out.'

But they could not. After about two hours of what was obviously fierce fighting, the firing on the mountain flickered and then died away completely. 'They'll come at us now,' said Simon, half to himself and half to Alice, who now stood at his side, Chapman having joined his men in the line. He squinted forward in the darkness. 'Damn. What we need is bright moonlight.'

As if on cue, the darkly purple clouds parted and a bright moon peeped through. It was just in time to illuminate a mass of Boers spilling out from the base of the mountain and running fast towards the line of trenches.

'Blimey,' muttered Jenkins. 'There's 'undreds of 'em.'

'Hold your fire,' shouted Fonthill, turning his head and repeating the order so that his voice echoed along the line. 'Wait until they pass the markers and wait for the command.' Parties of men had spent the day putting down white-painted markers around the camp, at three hundred and two hundred yards, so that their rifle sights could be adjusted accordingly. Now, as the dark figures swarmed past the furthest posts, an officer in the trench nearest the redoubt shouted 'At three hundred yards, FIRE!' The command echoed along the line and the trenches exploded in flame and smoke.

Simon heard Alice draw in her breath sharply as the leading line of attackers crumpled and fell. But the others – and there were plenty of them – came on running, jumping over the bodies of their fallen comrades, some kneeling to take aim and fire, but most of them propelling themselves forward as fast as they could run, their rifles swinging to and fro with the rhythm of their movement.

'Rapid fire!' screamed the order from the trenches. 'Fire at will!'

Again the volleys rang out, this time supplemented by more ragged fire as the defenders pumped their bolt mechanisms to thrust cartridges into the chambers of their rapidly heating rifles. All along the line, white smoke hung like a wraith above the defenders.

Fonthill ran his tongue along his dry lips and tasted again the sharp, sour, tang of cordite. He wasn't sure if he felt fear or just excitement. 'Now they'll fall back and start sniping,' he said.

But they did not. The Boers continued to run on into the fire, passing the two-hundred-yard posts so that their ragged clothing could now clearly be seen, some of them wearing British khaki tunics but with buttons now sadly tarnished. As the range shortened, more of them fell, throwing their rifles forward with the impetus of their charge as they collapsed.

'Good God!' murmured Simon. 'I've never seen Boers charge like this.'

'Aye, bach,' Jenkins echoed in awe. 'They're comin' on like stupid bloody Englishmen.'

'What brave men,' whispered Alice. 'What magnificent, silly, brave men. Don't they know they'll never win this stupid war?'

Simon shook his head. 'I'm beginning to believe they just might. I've never seen 'em fight like this. If they keep coming on like this, they could run through us. There are so many of 'em.' He turned to the men grouped around him in the redoubt. 'Fix bayonets,' he shouted. Then he turned back to Jenkins. 'Number the reserve, quickly,' he ordered. 'When I give the order, take the first fifty to the right, spread out thinly and support the line. I'll take the others to the left. Number now.' He looked down at his wife. 'If we have to go, Alice, you stay in here and stay low.'

She nodded, dumbly, her eyes wide, but Simon noted that she had filled three pages of scribbled notes.

In fact, there was no immediate need for the reserve, for it was impossible for the attackers to continue their rush forward in the face of such fierce firing and the Boers first paused, then crumbled, turned and retreated, spreading out quickly across the rough ground and seeking cover from where they could begin to return fire.

Jenkins, perspiration trickling down his face, nodded. 'I reckon, you gettin' the word out, bach sir, that we was poorly defended, 'as done the trick, see. They didn't make out the trenches in the poor light and they thought as 'ow they could just run straight through us. Now, I bet they just bugger off back to their 'orses, as usual.'

Fonthill was standing, his field glasses to his eyes, and he didn't respond for a moment. Then he said: 'Somehow I don't think so. They have

347

massed a second line back there at the base of the mountain. They will come on again when they've regrouped. I'm just going down to the line to check on our casualties. I won't be a minute. I'll be back before they charge again.'

'No, Simon.' Alice called. But he vaulted the low stone wall and was gone.

''E'll be all right, missus,' reassured Jenkins. ''E knows what 'e's doin', look you. 'E's a proper soldier now, see.' And his great grin lit up the redoubt.

Alice nodded back to him, her eyes sparkling with tears. Then she bent her head again and resumed scribbling.

Simon's head could be seen as he made his way along the trench, talking and clapping hands on shoulders. For a while he disappeared round the bend of the line and then he was back, half crouching now and skipping over the kneeling men, before he climbed up the reverse side of the trench and ran back to the redoubt with bullets plucking at the earth beneath his feet. He vaulted over the low wall.

'Just in time, bach sir,' said Jenkins. ''Ere they come again.'

The charge this time was presaged by a stuttering volley from the Boers sheltering behind rocks and declivities in the surface of the ground. But this was Boer gunfire, unerringly accurate, and men began toppling backwards from the wall of the trench, blood trickling from black holes in their foreheads, their helmets clattering away as they fell onto their backs. Then the rush began.

Simon turned to the men of the reserve. 'Right,'

348

he said. 'Supplement the fire. Fire over the heads of the men in the trenches. Set your sights at three hundred yards and then open up with rapid fire.'

Soon the redoubt, too, was overhung with clouds of white smoke as the reserve lent their support to the men in the trenches. And still the Boers came on, their white eyes bulging in their dirty, bearded faces, firing as they ran and as they neared the lines. This time they reached within one hundred yards of the trench before fading away, seemingly reluctantly, to retrace their steps, leaving dishevelled bodies all around them on the bloodstained ground.

Fonthill waved away the smoke and looked up at the indigo sky, now studded with stars. 'I hope to God the moon stays out,' he murmured. 'If they keep coming on and we can't see 'em until the last minute then we could be in trouble.'

'I think they're pullin' back, anyway.' Jenkins pointed. 'They're goin' back to the base of the 'ill.'

Simon focused his field glasses. 'So they are. Maybe they have had enough.'

But it was not so. After a few minutes it could be seen that the Boers were now crawling forward and reverting to their conventional tactics of making the most of whatever cover they could find and firing steadily and accurately. They were, of course, excellent bushmen and they seemed to disappear into the terrain, only the occasional rifle flash revealing their presence.

'Keep your heads down,' yelled Fonthill to the defenders ahead of him. 'Save your ammunition until they charge again.'

As the night wore on the situation lapsed into stalemate, with desultory rifle fire being exchanged between the two sides. It was dangerous now to leave the redoubt, but Fonthill slipped away again to go down to the line to check on the number of casualties and the state of the ammunition. He found that Major Chapman, now embedded in the line with some of his men from the Dorset Regiment, had been wounded in the leg, although not badly. The officer, however, refused to leave the trench for the comparative safety of the redoubt.

The two men briefly discussed the situation. 'I've never known Boers hang on like this,' confessed Fonthill. 'Have you?'

Chapman shook his head, grimacing with pain from his shoulder. 'It's most strange. But we know that Botha is a most determined chap and I guess this is his last chance of breaking through into Natal. Kitchener is pumping in men all the time to protect the frontier. What's the state of the ammunition, Colonel? We must be low now.'

'Not too bad but it all depends how long he keeps pounding us. We have an average of about thirty rounds per man. If–' He broke off as the first rays of the rising sun lit up the scene. 'Damn! Here they come again. I'd better get back. We may need our reserve this time.'

From the base of the mountain, men could now be seen running forward again and, from surprisingly near the trenches, Boers suddenly sprang from their sniping positions and joined in the rush forward. Once again, it was an act of great bravery, for the defenders now had their weapons perfectly adjusted to the range and their volleys swept along the leading ranks of the attackers, cutting them down like a giant scythe reaping a cornfield.

This time the tide surged up almost to the lip of the trench walls and Simon and Jenkins led out their reserve troops to kneel behind the trenches, bayonets presented, to add their close-range fire to that of the troopers before them. Even greater carnage would have ensued but for the fact that the British rifles were now over-heating and causing cartridges to explode in the breeches and to jam the guns. As it was, the Boers fell back again and resumed their sniping.

So it continued throughout the long, hot day, for the rain clouds had now completely receded. The courage of both attackers and defenders was undaunted, with the Boers creeping closer and closer between attacks and then rising to their feet with a shout and sprinting once again into the mouths of the British guns. It was clear that they were resolved to wipe away this opposition to their path to the south.

By late afternoon, Fonthill scrambled down again to the line and, in the confines of the trench, conferred with Chapman and the senior officers. Ammunition, they reported, was now down to about ten rounds per man.

Simon wiped his brow. 'Be sparing now, then,' he ordered. 'No reply to sniping. Just keep rounds back to be used only to fight off frontal attacks.' He had a sudden thought. 'Are your Zulus armed?' he demanded of Chapman.

'Yes. They've been firing from the line. But they

are awful shots.'

'That's not the point. If we have to surrender when the last rounds are fired, then the Boers will almost certainly kill them if they are found in possession of rifles. I think you should let them leave now, if they wish. They should be able to filter out round the back between attacks. I'll make the same offer to my blacks.'

'Very good, sir.'

Fonthill scrambled back to the redoubt and sought out Mzingeli and put the proposal to him. The tracker shook his head. 'I stay, Nkosi,' he said. 'Too old to run now. And I never run from Boers before. But I ask my boys.'

He came back shortly with the same answer. 'They stay,' he said. 'They don't think Boers win here. They want to keep jobs, anyway.'

'Well,' reflected Jenkins. 'I only 'ope they're right. It's true we can't 'ang on much longer.'

Within minutes, Chapman sent back a similar message. Alice, still crouching and writing, made a careful note.

'Wait a moment.' Simon raised his binoculars to his eyes, risking to stand up fully erect in the redoubt to get a better view of the base of the mountain. 'Yes, dammit! I think they're going. Look.' He handed the glasses to Mzingeli. 'My eyes are tired. What do you think?'

Gravely, the black man nodded. 'Yes, they go now. They are collecting wounded and mounting horses. Yes. They go.' He handed back the glasses. As he did so, a muffled cheer came from the trenches below them to confirm the fact, and Alice, her blouse stained with perspiration, put her arms around Simon's neck.

'Thank God, it's over,' she whispered. 'I don't think I could have stood much more of this carnage.'

Simon kissed her quickly and looked again through the field glasses. 'Botha must have taken a hell of a beating he couldn't afford,' he murmured. 'He had plenty of men when he arrived here but he must have expended so many lives and so much ammunition with these attacks that I can't see him still trying to get through to the south. He'll be on his way back to the Transvaal now, I reckon, if not with his tail between his legs, then at least with it tucked into his pocket.'

He lowered the glasses and turned back to Mzingeli. 'Get your trackers out to follow them to make sure that this is not a feint, but don't stray too near. They will be mean and looking for revenge.' He eased himself over the low stone wall. 'I must check our casualties and see to the wounded.'

It ensued that the defenders had lost about a quarter of their men but the Boers had inevitably suffered many more casualties. In fact, it was a double defeat for them, because later that day a rider came in from Fort Prospect ten miles away to report that it, too, had resisted a Boer attack and had lost only nine casualties to the Boers' forty. A party sent to the top of the mountain confirmed that the eighty men posted there had put up a stout defence but had been outnumbered by the Boers and been forced to surrender after two hours. They remained in post but bereft of most of their clothing, taken, as usual, by the enemy.

Fonthill pondered whether to form a pursuit party to harry the Boers' retreat, but the defenders were exhausted after their long night and day of fighting and he decided against it. Botha must be left to fight again another day.

## CHAPTER SEVENTEEN

As indeed he did. Fonthill's trackers reported that the Boer leader had turned back into the Transvaal with the remains of his commando, passing near the charred remains of his own farm, clearly having given up his attempts to invade Natal. But it was equally clear that he was far from finished as a fighting unit. As Fonthill was himself retracing his footsteps back into the Transvaal, news came through that a reinforced Botha had struck again, much further north. Near Bethal, he had surprised a British column led by Colonel Benson and wiped it out, with the loss of one hundred and sixty-one dead and the colonel himself.

Hearing of the defeat as he rode back with his own column, now depleted again – although Chapmen's men had borne the brunt of the casualties at the Fort – Fonthill shook his head with disbelief.

'It's like fighting the Hydra,' he told Alice. 'You cut off one head and another one grows. Will they never give up?'

It seemed not. As the spring wore on the better weather appeared, providing lusher grazing for cattle and horses and, it seemed, giving new heart to the scattered commandos. In the wild country of bush, hills and sunken rivers west and south-west of Magaliesberg in the Western Transvaal, de la Rey pushed the shrewd British General Keke-wich to a hard-fought draw and then, a few days later, at Kleinfontein, he decimated the rearguard of General Methuen, capturing supplies and wagons. Just outside Bloemfontein, in the Free State, two hundred British troopers clearing a farm were surprised and completely over-whelmed. In the far south, deep into the Crown Colony, small, independent Boer forces led by Smuts and Kritzinger were reported to be ranging far and wide, not raising active rebel support, to be sure, but winning skirmishes, looting, causing arson, pulling down fences and even flogging and murdering natives.

The one bright spot seemed to be the quietude of de la Wet in the Orange Free State – so much so that rumours spread that he had gone mad, was wounded or even dead. Then, he was stung into action by what appeared to be a letter to him from Botha – now himself said to be licking his wounds in the mountains of the far east above Vryheid – suggesting peace overtures again. The campaign that followed culminated in an attack that demonstrated once more that peace was the last thing on de Wet's mind.

On Christmas Day 1901, a line of blockhouses was being built by the British westward from the town of Harrismith, nestling at the foot of the Drakensberg mountains and near de Wet's old stamping ground of Reitz. Protecting the work was

355

a battalion of Kent and Sussex Yeomanry manning a hill called Groenkop, near the main road from Bethlehem. British intelligence had reported that there were only about seventy Boers in the vicinity. But de Wet was watching with a commando one thousand strong. Approaching the hill to reconnoitre, the Boer, completely ruthless as always where natives were concerned, shot a black herder near the British lines. Immediately, the garrison fired their guns, so revealing their positions. De Wet took note, crept away and waited until the garrison had settled down to sleep through Christmas Eve. Then, in stockinged feet, the burghers noiselessly climbed the hill, mounting on a side considered by the British to be too steep to warrant the posting of guards.

Many of the guards on duty, unforgivably, were asleep and, with a whoop, the Boers were among them, sweeping down through tents, horse lines and transport, firing and stampeding the animals. Some soldiers, fresh from their bedrolls, attempted resistance, but within the hour three hundred and forty-eight of the Yeomanry were killed or captured. The entire camp was looted, 'from plum puddings to clothes and ammunition', as one report later put it. Typically, de Wet killed twenty-five natives but rode off with his captured Tommies, later to set them free, shivering, on the plains below Reitz.

The news could not have been received at a worse time back in Britain. The constant, pin-pricking reverses out on the veldt, the news of farm burnings – the plains were referred to as 'the flaming veldt' in some of the public prints –

356

the scandalised reception accorded to Emily Hobhouse's report, the anti-war campaigning of Lloyd George and other Liberal politicians, all increased the pressure on the British government. Lord Kitchener himself, of course, was far from immune. The word was that he was continually locked head-to-head with the newly ennobled but still fiercely anti-Boer Lord Milner, the chief civilian administrator at his headquarters in Pretoria, and it was rumoured that he had offered to resign, only to be dissuaded by the prime minister.

Fonthill himself heard about de Wet's latest triumph as he led his men in an arid pursuit of the Boer General Piet Viljoen east of Pretoria. Viljoen, who had sprung, it seemed from nowhere, to be a threat of the de Wet-Botha-de la Rey stature the year before, now seemed happy to be in full retreat. Fonthill was leading a column, doubled in size, having been promoted to Brigadier by French, much to his amazement and apprehension, and Alice had remained with him. Tired of being a 'sweeper up of trifles' from the commander-in-chief's table at Pretoria, she had persuaded her editor to let her send a series of colour pieces back about life in the saddle pursuing the elusive commandos. Kitchener, perhaps impressed by her colourful and balanced account of the defence of Fort Itala, had raised no objections, so now Alice Griffith, whose readers of course had no idea that she was married to the intrepid Brigadier Fonthill she described so coolly, stayed with her husband. Predictably, it was not an arrangement that pleased Fonthill but his objec-

357

tions were swept aside by his wife, strongly support by RSM Jenkins, now a very busy sergeant major with some five hundred men under his eye.

Fonthill took his command on the heels of Viljoen to the foothills of the Drakensberg, where his scouts told him that the Boer had settled in comfortably at Pilgrim's Rest, high above, showing no inclination to come down to resume the fight. He reported accordingly back to French and it was with relief, then, that he was ordered to bring his column back to the Free State, where Kitchener was beginning his summer campaign against de Wet.

The commander-in-chief, determined to catch this will-o'-the-wisp once and for all, had allocated an additional fifteen thousand men to the project. They were divided into fourteen columns and posted around an area extending for one hundred and seventy-five miles south of the Vaal and a hundred miles east of the Central Railway. Simon's men took up post at a central point south of the town of Frankfort, where the rest of the army was to converge, having set out a net, moving inexorably towards the point in a series of meticulously planned marches, sweeping the Boers before them for five days, ending on the sixth – but with not a single Boer in sight.

Jenkins sniffed. 'The buggers 'ave watched us every inch of the way, bach sir,' he said. 'They will 'ave 'ad 'eliographs all the way along them 'ills, look you, passing the word on where we are an' probably where we were plannin' to go tomorrer.'

Fonthill nodded. 'You have to be right,' he said. 'They must have slipped between the columns at dead of night. Typical de Wet!'

And so it went on, in the Cape and all over the vast battlefield of the two Boer republics, with the individual Boer commandos sidestepping the ponderous British columns and striking swiftly, perilously maintaining their positions out in the field by feeding off their enemy's supplies. Truly, the veldt was now aflame.

Yet it was not all one-way traffic. Kitchener's long-term strategy of building blockhouses across the plains, linked with barbed wire, and then driving the marauding Boers before the British columns to corral them into the corners, forcing them to fight against overwhelming odds or to surrender, was very slowly beginning to pay off. It was true that the strategy was immensely expensive in terms of time, effort and manpower and it was not foolproof. Inevitably gaps opened up between the 'beaters' on the drive, and the Boers often slipped through at night. But what Kitchener called 'the bags' of prisoners taken gradually began to improve.

Fonthill and his enlarged column was involved in these drives and he and his men found them irksome, almost as bad as their farm-burning duties in the previous year. The military integrity of Fonthill's Horse, its *raison d'être* – to operate independently with slim resources, moving quickly and often at night to flush the commandos from their hiding places – was completely compromised by the need to move at the slow pace of the large forces herding the guerrillas before them.

'Blimey,' observed Jenkins to Fonthill. 'We might as well be bleedin' infantry. We're wasted, ploddin'' on like this.'

De Wet himself, once again, was nearly caught in these pincer movements. Hampered now by a large body of civilian refugees – for Kitchener had closed the concentration camps to further entries of women and children – plus thousands of cattle and horses, the Boer leader was driven before Kitchener's cordon of sixty thousand men who were closing in, implacably, all around him.

Eventually, de Wet and his unwelcome huge crowd of hangers-on, a total of some three thousand in all, were seemingly cornered in a remote valley, twenty miles south of Vrede, called Langeveld, Afrikaans for 'long expectation'. It was a lush, beautiful spot, a shallow basin, surrounded by flat hills and with a little stream, the Hotspruit, running along the bottom. The general would dearly liked to have stayed here for a while to allow the cattle to graze and his people to rest. But the British were all around him and he pushed on through the night, following the course of the stream along the valley bottom and lit by a mellow, full moon. His scouts had told him that a low cleft in the hills ahead to the south offered him an escape from the basin and he decided to lead his unwieldy caravanserai up the slope to take it.

Fonthill and his men were in the van of the British forces chasing the Boers and he, Jenkins and Alice were beginning the gentle descent into the valley when they saw, far away at its head, the Boer column begin to wind its way up the side of the hill to reach the exit.

'Now we have him, at last!' cried Simon. 'The

New Zealanders and Australians are dug in up there and he's caught in a trap.'

As he spoke, flashes of gunfire lit up the darkness ahead and it was just possible to see the burghers leading the column turn round and retreat down the hill. They met, however, the refugees at the bottom with their wagons and cattle and for minutes all was confusion as the wagons jammed, the oxen and cows impeded the fighting men and the refugees cried out in consternation.

Fonthill turned to his officers. 'Deploy your squadrons across the mouth of the valley,' he shouted. 'They might turn around and try and fight their way out this way. Quickly now.'

Alice looked up from her scribbling. 'Simon,' she cried, 'be careful of the women and children if they try and force their way through here. Surely better to let them through than cause civilian casualties.'

But neither of them needed to worry. As they watched, the tiny figures of the burghers at the head of the column suddenly broke away from the refugees and other fighting men behind them and surged up the hill towards the New Zealand and Australian lines. The noise of gunfire could clearly be heard above the lowing of the cattle and the shouts of the refugees and it was obvious that a fierce gunfight was in progress in the hill cleft. Fonthill stood in his stirrups and focused his field glasses.

'By God!' he cried. 'He's broken through. I can see them streaming over the pass and disappearing. The bloody man's got away again.'

Indeed he had. De Wet had stormed through

the Antipodean lines with six hundred burghers, President Steyn and his officials once again in their midst, and leaving behind all of the refugees, their wagons and their cattle and a minority of his fighting men. These were all captured by Fonthill and the other troops coming up fast behind him. In all, some eight hundred captives were taken – included de Wet's son – the biggest success of the guerrilla war to date. But, of course, the ruthless, ever-resourceful de Wet himself had slipped away again.

Yet could this game of hide-and-seek, of pursuit and pursued, attack and retreat continue for very much longer? Fonthill himself now sensed that, despite the defiance of de Wet, the most antagonistic of the Boer generals, there was a sense of exhaustion on both sides. Rumours were spreading that Botha once again was anxious to persuade his fellow guerrilla leaders to agree to negotiate for peace and the news that that great imperialist, Cecil Rhodes, had died seemed to indicate that an era was closing in South Africa.

The war, however, continued on its weary way. Even the confirmation that the Boer leaders were, in fact, gathering at Klerksdorp, under British safe passage, to begin the hugely difficult task of gaining agreement among themselves to sue for peace, did not end the fighting. And de Wet was not the only Boer commander eager to continue the hostilities.

Lieutenant General French had long been stationed in the Cape Colony attempting to pin down Smuts and the other scattered bands of guerrillas, and Fonthill received orders that he was to move his column to Lichtenburg, some sixty miles east of Mafeking in the Northern Transvaal, and report to General Ian Hamilton, whom Kitchener had appointed to coordinate a great effort to put down de la Rey. The two were both survivors of the Battle of Majuba Hill two decades before and knew each other slightly. On Fonthill's arrival they shook hands warmly.

'I'm no peace-at-any-price merchant,' said Simon, 'but should we still be fighting on, General, when the Boers are meeting under our auspices to discuss a possible armistice?'

A tall, thin, elegant man, Hamilton had earned laurels for his part in the defence of Ladysmith and Kitchener had promoted him from a desk job to bring de la Rey finally to heel. He now nodded his head firmly. 'Oh, yes. De la Rey is at this meeting at Klerksdorp but his deputy, Kemp, is a firebrand and we hear he is about to go very much on the warpath. There are about five thousand seasoned burghers hereabouts still wanting to fight. If they give us a knock now, it will give heart to the delegates in Klerksdorp who want to fight on and they could carry the day. If – as will happen – we give them a bloody nose, then that could seriously accelerate the peace talks.'

'Quite. What exactly is your plan, then, and what do you want my chaps to do?'

'I've got four groups about thirty-five miles south of Lichtenburg and I intend to start them on a great sweep through about a hundred and forty miles. First south-west, then south and finally south-east to the Vaal and Klerksdorp itself. That should give the Boers at the meeting a sharp reminder that we are very much still in the field. I want you to be in the van and find Kemp and lure him into us.'

'Have you any idea where he is?'

'Round about here.' He jabbed a long, beautifully manicured forefinger onto the map on his table. 'Near a tiny place called Boschbult, some sixty miles west of Klerksdorp. He had a go at one of our reconnaissance columns there the other day. We think he's still thereabouts. Get down there, Fonthill, and stand on his coat tails.'

'Very good, sir.'

Alice, suffering from a miserable cold, was left behind in Lichtenburg and, on the night of the 9th April 1902, Fonthill and his column were ranging along the banks of the River Brakspruit within about twelve miles of its junction with the Great Harts River. Simon knew that this was de la Rey's – and therefore Kemp's – territory. He and his men were riding, spread out in a screen, ahead of where the van of Hamilton's main force, under General Kekewich, were marching behind him, when one of Mzingeli's men galloped in.

'Many Boers ahead, baas,' he reported.

'How many?' demanded Fonthill. 'Is it a full commando?'

'Many, many, baas.'

Simon turned and summoned one of his sub-alterns. 'Ride back and find General Kekewich. He should be directly in our rear. Tell him we have found the main commando. Tell him I shall try and lure it in towards the farm ahead – what the hell is it called? – ah yes, Rooiwal. It's half a mile to the north. He should be prepared to meet the Boers there. Gallop now.'

Fonthill thought quickly. He did not wish to imperil his whole column which, although enlarged, would be no match for a full Boer commando in open ground. Yet he wanted to lure Kemp to attack. He called up Major Forbes and explained the situation.

'Let me have a troop of about forty men. Then take the column up ahead to the farm we scouted yesterday, Rooiwal, where General Kekewich should be concentrated. Sergeant Major Jenkins and I with the troop will try and draw the Boers into attack onto Kekewich's columns. Explain this to the general and merge our column with his force. Understood?'

Forbes's lined face seamed into a frown. 'Understood. But it sounds bloody dangerous to me, sir. Be careful. Let me ride with you and send Cartwright back.'

'No.' Fonthill grinned. 'I'm much fatter than you and will make better bait. Off you go.' The two shook hands and Forbes wheeled his horse round. Simon shouted: 'Jenkins, here please.' And then, 'Mzingeli. Go back with the column. Where's your tracker?'

The two men, white and black, joined him and then the three rode forward to meet the forty troopers singled out by Forbes. Then they sat their horses as the column turned and cantered away, watching until it had disappeared into the distance.

'Right,' said Fonthill. 'Gentlemen, we trot forward. I believe that there is a large Boer force about half a mile or so ahead of us. Our tracker

365

will show us where. When we see them, we will dismount and fire on them and then, when they attack, as I hope they will, we will remount and lure them onto the main British force to our rear. Now, good luck. In column of fours, to the front, trot.'

Jenkins pulled alongside Fonthill and the two rode in silence for a few minutes at the head of the little column and behind the tracker who cantered on some twenty paces ahead, continually rising in his stirrups nervously to look around him.

The Welshman leant across and extended his hand. 'I have a feelin', bach sir,' he said, 'that we won't be doin' much more of this sort of barmy stuff in the future, if at all. So p'raps, look you, we should just shake 'ands, like, an' remember all the times we've done it before.'

Simon took the hand of his old comrade and, for a brief moment, the two rode together, hands clenched, in silence. Then Fonthill nodded. 'Thank you for those times, 352. Stay close now.'

'Where else would I be, now?'

They had ridden for perhaps fifteen minutes when the scout suddenly halted and raised his hand. Fonthill and Jenkins cantered to his side. They found themselves looking down from a gentle rise on a quite amazing sight. Before them, some three hundred yards away, a vast gathering of horsemen, perhaps some seventeen hundred, were riding towards them in close order, a phalanx of bandoliered Boers, slouch-hatted, their ragged clothing clearly visible, stretching away far on either side of the little troop. Two men rode ahead of the commando, one wearing a bright-blue shirt.

On seeing the soldiers before them, the two turned in their saddles, gestured up the hill with their rifles to their followers and kicked their mounts into a gallop.

Fonthill's first thought was the fervent hope that Kekewich had had time to deploy behind him. His second was that there was no time to dismount and fire.

'Do not, repeat DO NOT dismount!' He shouted. 'Fire one volley from the saddle at the enemy ahead. Wait for the order. Steady the horses. Now. Select your target. Aim. FIRE! To the rear, gallop!'

The forty men, their rifles still in their hands, turned and spurred their horses into the gallop. They had a good start on the Boers, of course, and the advantage of being on top of the slope. Fonthill also fervently hoped, as he rode, Jenkins at his side, that the British ponies would be in better condition than those of the Boers, who had been starved of good grazing until recently by the rains. Then he was aware that bullets were whistling around him.

In the months of guerrilla warfare, the Boers, who had gained all their early victories in the war either from firing with amazing accuracy from fixed positions at the lines of British troops advancing towards them, or from slipping from rock to rock and taking their enemies by surprise, had now developed a twentieth-century version of the cavalry charge. They had used their superior horsemanship to attack, firing from the saddle while at full tilt – and often retaining their remarkable accuracy while doing so. Fonthill had noted this and now he sent up a fervent prayer that he and the rest of the troop would not have to play the hare to the Boer hounds for very much longer. Already, three of his men had been pitched from their saddles as bullets took their horses.

He looked ahead through wind-streamed eyes. Where the hell was Kekewich? They could not maintain this pace for much longer. Yet they couldn't slacken off for to do so would be either to risk a bullet in the back or be forced to surrender. They must continue to lead the Boers on, to commit them and not give them time to retreat once they saw Kekewich's three thousand men and his cannon ahead of them – if they *were* ahead, that was.

Then, at last, directly ahead, Fonthill caught a glimpse of sunlight reflected off a steel barrel, then another, until he could see figures deployed in a wide line in mealie fields. Kekewich *was* in place – but far enough ahead to be out of rifle range and to give the Boers time to halt, turn round and flee from a force that clearly outnumbered them.

Damn! Simon waved his hand to his little force indicating that they should slow down and he looked behind him. But Kemp and his men – the blue-shirted one, it later ensued, was the Boer General Potgieter – were not reining in. They galloped on.

Fonthill realised that his little force was screening the Boers from the British line, preventing Kekewich from firing, so he indicated that they should wheel to the right, even if it meant that the Boers would follow, for they, too, must surely have seen by now that they were galloping, in gallant Light Brigade style, directly towards well-placed artillery and infantry emplacements. He cast a desperate glance over his shoulder. The Boers were neither following nor pulling up. Ignoring Fonthill's manoeuvre, *they were galloping on, straight towards the British positions!*

Suddenly, free of the obstacle posed by Simon's troop, Kekewich's guns opened up. The Boers were riding, compactly, almost knee to knee, across a completely open and now level plain in broad daylight and providing a perfect target. The shells crumped among the densely packed horsemen and opened up a succession of gaps in the host. Still the Boers came on in a quite un-characteristically reckless fashion, as though seeking to add a glorious footnote to what had been a gruelling, hit-and-run two years. Now they were within rifle range and more gaps opened up in their line until, at last, at four hundred and then three hundred yards, they faltered and the main body turned and rode back. The distinctly blue-shirted Potgieter thundered on, however, with several companions, until they all fell only seventy paces from the British line.

Fonthill and his men, now pulled up well to the right of the charging Boers, watched the carnage open-mouthed.

'Bloody 'ell, bach sir,' panted Jenkins. 'What a stupid thing to do, eh? They was all committin' suicide, like. Not a bit like the canny devils we've been used to, look you.'

Fonthill blew out his cheeks and nodded. 'Amazing. Brave but idiotically stupid. De Wet,

369

de la Rey or Botha would never have done that. Kemp must have been mad to try a charge like that. I can't help thinking that this could have been the last formal battle of this sad and miserable war.' He took out his handkerchief and mopped his brow. 'Hamilton must get on horseback now, get in pursuit and finish the job.'

But there was little sign of this happening as Simon led his little troop in to join the main body. It was not until forty minutes later that Hamilton's cavalry came forward and set off in pursuit.

'I say,' said the ebullient Captain Cartwright to Simon as they sat watching the cavalry push through the maize and gallop off. 'See who's there, in the van. Philip Hammond, ain't it?'

Fonthill had noticed the Hussar sitting tall in the saddle and had shot an anxious glance at Jenkins, but the Welshman appeared not to have seen his old adversary. 'Hmm,' he answered. 'Well let's hope he catches old Kemp.'

In fact, the survivors of the Boer charge escaped and melted away into the vast countryside, as though they had never existed, but news reached Hamilton's command that the Boer leadership had agreed to open formal peace terms and had left Klerksdorp to move, under Kitchener's protection, to his headquarters at Pretoria to begin the talks. The next day, Fonthill, still listlessly combing the veldt as part of Hamilton's force, received a telegram from K himself. He was surprised but delighted by its contents:

CONGRATS YOUR RECENT GOOD WORK STOP PEACE TALKS BEGINNING HERE

PLEASE JOIN MY STAFF HERE IMME-
DIATELY YOU WILL MEET OLD FRIENDS
STOP BRING YOUR WIFE TO REPORT
WHAT I HOPE WILL BE JOYFUL NEWS
STOP REGARDS K

He showed the message to Hamilton, who extended his hand. 'Off you go, my dear feller,' he said. 'It looks as though K feels that the end is in sight at last. Thank you for all you've done. Leave Forbes in charge of your lot and take your fightin' Welshman with you. He deserves some leave, anyway. My regards to your wife.'

On the night before his departure, Simon, with Jenkins, was taking a farewell drink and saying goodbye to his officers with a mixture of relief that it seemed as though the war was winding down to a close at last and regret that Fonthill's Horse, his first and last command in the field, must surely soon be disbanded, when Captain Cartwright pushed through the throng, his round face bursting with news.

'I say, Colonel – sorry, Brigadier – have you heard the news about Hammond?'

'No. What?'

'A most remarkable thing, don't you know. The poor devil was seen this morning, just after dawn, making his way back to the Fifth Hussar's lines, absolutely stark naked.'

'Good Lord! What had happened?'

'Well, he said he had been lured out of the mess last night into the bush by some sort of strange message. Then, he said that he had been hit over the head by some unknown assailant and came to

371

this morning with a very sore napper and all his clothes gone.'

Fonthill shot a quick look at Jenkins, whose face was set in the same expression of surprise and puzzlement as the others. 'Gracious me. How strange.'

But Cartwright had not finished. 'Ah, but there's more. The feller's face, it seems, was covered in that stuff that women use – you know, lip rouge. He didn't know, of course, because he couldn't see himself. There's been a lot of talk and he has become the laughing stock of the cavalry. It just shows, doesn't it? You just don't know people, do yer?'

Simon nodded slowly. He emptied his glass and looked across at Jenkins. 'You certainly don't. Now, Sarn't Major, drink up. I think an early night is indicated. All things being considered, I think we ought to leave for Pretoria very early in the morning, for we must pick up Alice at Lichtenburg on the way.'

'Of course, sir. Quite right, sir.' Jenkins lifted his glass to Simon, although he avoided his eye, then he drained it in one gulp.

## CHAPTER EIGHTEEN

Simon had decided that it was time that Mzingeli returned to his farm in Rhodesia and so the tall tracker joined him and Jenkins as they set off, well before dawn the next morning, on their long ride to Lichtenburg. The three rode companionably together, with Mzingeli, as usual, remaining silent and Fonthill and Jenkins chatting only in mono-syllables, but all three enjoying the brightness of the morning and the crisp air of the veldt. Fonthill decided that nothing would be served by pressing his old comrade on the Hammond business. Sleeping dogs, he felt, should be left to lie.

They found an Alice cured of her cold but fretting at being left in the small town with only a brief telegram to say that her husband was on his way. She had heard vague rumours of a British victory at Rooiwal but nothing more and Simon's message had at least assured her that he was safe.

She read Kitchener's cable with delight. 'Good Lord,' she said. 'I wonder why he wants you on his staff at this late stage. Maybe he's offering you some sort of reward for your soldiering over the last two years. He wants you to be in at the kill, so to speak. And how kind of the old devil to call me in specifically to report on these talks, after all the trouble I gave him about the camps. He's got a heart after all. But what's this about "old friends"?'

Simon smiled. 'I've no idea. But I'll be damned glad to get out of the saddle for a while. I think, my love, that I've probably had just about enough of conventional soldiering now, thank you very much. It's uncomfortable, dangerous and gen-erally bad for the health. I never thought I would yearn for a bit of peace and quiet in Norfolk but, do you know, I think I do now.'

Alice looked at him, with just a trace of concern in her eyes. 'Yes, but do you think the Boers will

373

give in at last?'

'I honestly do think so, because I think that even the few diehards must concede that fighting on will just leave the country barren and exhausted. It depends, I suppose, upon how hard we press them. We must be ameliorative. After all, we virtually invaded their country, thanks, I believe, to that cold schemer, Milner. Let's hope that Kitchener can keep him under control in these negotiations.'

They handed in their horses to the military in the town and headed for the railway station, diverting only to the pharmacist so that Alice could replace her lip rouge that, she explained, she had somehow lost. On arrival in Pretoria, Alice found Jenkins and Mzingeli a shared room in her hotel but then Jenkins quickly made his apologies and slipped away, muttering that he had a little business to do.

Fonthill found the little town buzzing with excitement at the presence of the Boer leaders. Even Smuts had been summoned from the wilds of the empty plains of the north-west Cape Colony. As Kitchener made his way to the meeting room in his HQ, Simon bumped into him in the corridor and the great man shook his hand.

'Can't stop,' he apologised, 'but I did want to thank you for all you've done out on the veldt. I thought it only right, considering that I personally dragged you into this, to have you here at the end.'

'Will it be the end, then?'

'Oh, I am determined to make it so. I'm dashed if I'm going to let these chaps get away from the table without an agreement. Botha wants one, I know. I think Smuts can be persuaded. De le Wet is stoically still against it and de la Rey is uncommitted either way.'

Fonthill laid a hand quickly on the commander-in-chief's arm. 'I don't want to hold you up, sir. But what do you want me to do here? And who are the "old friends" you referred to?'

'Ah yes. De Wet and Botha. You've met both and you've had brushes with both. I think there is mutual respect between you. I will arrange for you to join the social meetings we're forced to have here. Just put a bit of gentle pressure on both as soldier to soldier. Explain there's no future now in fighting on but to keep negotiating, and explain that I will try and ease the way for them. Sorry, must go. Don't hang around the office. Consider yourself on leave.'

Fonthill thanked him and the big man stalked away. Simon, however, was not exactly pleased at the strangely amorphous task allocated to him. He complained to Alice: 'I'm no diplomat. If Milner and Kitchener can't do the job, how the hell can I, just over a glass of champagne?'

She pulled his ear gently. 'My husband can do anything he wants to,' she said. 'Just ask de Wet how the hell he kept getting away. That should please him.'

In fact, he found the glowering, surly Boer general happy to talk to him, when they met at an informal gathering before the chief negotiators were photographed for the records. 'Ah, Fonthill,' he said. 'A general now, eh – even if only a minor one. I should never have let you steal your horses back that day when first we met. I confess you gave me a fright or two after that. And you got away from me in the Cape.'

'Yes, I'm sorry about that. But I hated your coffee, so I left. But tell me, General, how did you keep slipping away from us all, when we were on your tail? You seemed to know what we were going to do before we did it.'

The dark eyes glowed. 'Ach. Intelligence, my boy. I had the populace on my side, don't forget – and I still do.'

'But you can't keep fighting now. There will only be ashes left. Keep talking to Kitchener. He desperately wants to end the killing. But you won't get complete independence. Find a middle way.'

They were interrupted by Botha, who pushed his way forward to shake Fonthill's hand. 'I heard that,' he said. 'It's good to meet you again. Brigadier now, I see. Well you earned it. The middle way is going to be damned difficult...' At this point, de Wet turned away to speak to another, long-bearded Boer. Botha drew closer to Simon. 'I want to find just that way,' he said, 'otherwise people like Christiaan here,' he indicated de Wet, 'are quite capable of going on until the very last bullet. But he can be turned. Get Kitchener to compromise and we will meet him. Good to see you, Fonthill. I hope we meet again – in peace.' He turned away to rejoin his colleagues.

Fonthill found these exchanges strangely comforting. He felt that if the bloodshed continued there would be nothing for the victors, whoever they were, to inherit: just a burnt-out country, studded with graves and left with a sullen

376

resentful people.

He shared his view with Alice, when they met at the hotel. She nodded emphatically. 'I have had my ear to the ground,' she said, 'and there will eventually be a meeting of minds, I am sure of that. Oh, a message from 352. He would like to see you. He is in the bar next door. Now, don't get him drunk.'

A strangely quiet and uncomfortable Jenkins was waiting for him in a corner of the half-empty barroom, a surprisingly small glass of beer before him. 'Let me get you another,' said Simon.

'Er... No thank you, bach sir. Not just now, see. I've ... er ... got something to tell you and I'd rather get if off my chest as soon as possible.'

'Good Lord! Sounds ominous. Very well. Fire away.'

'I won't be comin' back with you to Norfolk, look you, when this thing is over. Sorry about that, bach sir. But I'll be stayin' out 'ere, see.'

Simon sat back, frowning. Whatever he was expecting to hear, it was not this. 'Gracious me, 352. You're ending the partnership after all these years? Whatever are Alice and I going to do without you? Was it something we've done, or said?'

'Golly me, no. Not at all.' He looked down at the floor, then up again at his old comrade. 'Truth is...' and a great smile curved back his moustache '...Nandi and me are goin' to get married, see. An' we're goin' back to 'er farm to rebuild it and bring up 'er girls and, if we're lucky, 'ave a few of our own before I'm too old, look you. So will you be best man, like, an' Nandi 'as asked me to ask you if you think that Miss

Alice would be maid of honour?'

Simon sent back his chair with a crash and stood. 'This is magnificent news, old chap. The answer to both your questions is yes, of course. My God! Wait till I tell Alice.' He reached across and took Jenkins's hand. 'I will keep my promise to pay for the farm and–'

Jenkins shook his head. 'The word is, that if these peace talks end properly, like, the British government are goin' to compensate the Boers who lost their farms in the burnin', so we should be all right.'

'Very well. I've got a better idea. I'll get Mzingeli to send you down a breeding bull and half a dozen cows from the farm in Rhodesia to set you up with a herd.'

'Now that would be useful, I must say. Thank you very much, bach sir. Oh, just one last thing.'

'What's that?'

Jenkins smiled shyly. 'If, at any time, you do decide to go ... er ... adventurin' again, like, give me a call, will you?'

'Adventuring again? Well, I wouldn't go anywhere like that without you, old chap, rest assured. Now, let's go next door and join Alice and we'll take a bottle of champagne with us.'

'Very kind, sir, I'm sure. But, as you know, I don't drink...'

# AUTHOR'S NOTE

Fonthill, Jenkins, Alice, Hammond, the Captains
Forbes and Cartwright, James Fulton and many of
the bit players in this story are fictional, of course.
But Kitchener, Hamilton, Kekewich, Milner,
Methuen, Colonel Benson, Major Chapman, the
Boer leaders, their generals, the British politicians
and journalists I name very much existed. I have
described the battles and skirmishes as accurately
as a study of well-regarded sources allows, although, of course, I have thrust Fonthill, Jenkins
etc into the roles played by gallant British officers
of the time. By the same token, I have allowed a
little imagination to creep into the detail of such
descriptions, such as the night raid on President
Steyn's house in Reitz (which still stands and from
where, by the way, he *did* escape in his nightshirt,
riding bareback on his horse!).

Kitchener eventually had his way at the
Pretoria negotiations, revealing a surprising skill
as a diplomat, and giving the Boer leaders just
sufficient concessions (including the granting of
three million pounds for farm rebuilding) to
agree to surrender, although the word was
avoided. The British government were forced to
lean on Milner to get him to bend the knee, and
the much respected Boer Generals de Wet and de

la Rey held out almost to the end before conceding.

Botha, who had proved himself to be a skilled politician as well as a fine general, went on to become prime minister of a united South Africa, as, later, did Smuts. De Wet, alas, could never really bring himself to accept the Union's role as part of the British Empire and he led a Boer rebellion against Botha's government at the outbreak of the Second World War, serving a brief period in prison as a result. He eventually died in 1922, virtually forgotten. De la Rey was accidentally shot and killed during the uprising.

The war itself was the first serious wake-up call received by the British army, following the 'taps on the shoulder' delivered by such warriors as the Zulus during the last quarter of the nineteenth century. It revealed again the arrogance of the generals, who completely underestimated the Boer farmers. Even so, French, Haig and Hamilton went on to play major roles in the First World War. The Boer War, however, provided other fundamental lessons that were not learnt: mainly, that the power of the magazine rifle and machine gun firing from trenches had tipped the balance of warfare from attack to defence. The open spaces of the veldt also preserved the myth of the power of cavalry. These lessons had to be assimilated in the mud of Flanders.

# ACKNOWLEDGEMENTS

Two splendid professional guides and historians in South Africa helped me research this book. Anthony Coleman, of Dundee, Natal, took my wife and I through the gorgeous country of the Free State in the footsteps of General de Wet, and old friend David Sutcliffe, of nearby Newcastle, helped hugely by providing marked maps of the region. Any faults that have arisen in the storytelling, however, are mine and not theirs.

Once again I happily acknowledge other debts: to my agent, Jane Conway-Gordon for her unfailing support; Susie Dunlop and her staff at my publishers, Allison & Busby; the staff of London Library; and, of course, to my wife Betty for plodding with me round the battlefields, helping with the research and proofreading and for putting up with my bad temper.

Library bookshelves groan with the weight of Boer War books. I found the following to be particularly helpful:

*The Boer War* by Thomas Pakenham; George Weidenfeld and Nicolson, London, 1979

*Goodbye Dolly Gray* by Rayne Kruger; Cassel & Co., London, 1959

*Lord Kitchener and the War in South Africa*, edited

by André Wessels; Army Records Society,
London, 2006
*A Subaltern's Letter to His Wife* by J.R.L. Rankin;
  Green & Co., London, 1901
*Commando* by Deneys Reitz; Faber & Faber,
  London, 1929
*Three Years War* by Christiaan de Wet; Constable
  and Co, London, 1902